GOSPEL ZERO

ORDER OF THADDEUS
BOOK 8

J. A. BOUMA

EmmausWay
PRESS

Copyright © 2020 by J. A. Bouma

All rights reserved.

EmmausWay Press

An Imprint of EmmausWay Media Group

PO Box 1180 • Grand Rapids, MI 49501

www.emmauswaypress.com

No part of this book may be reproduced in any form or by any electronic or mechanical means, including information storage and retrieval systems, without written permission from the author, except for the use of brief quotations in a book review.

This book is a work of fiction. The characters, organizations, products, incidents, and dialogue are drawn from the author's imagination and experience, and are not to be construed as real. Any reference to historical events, real organizations, real people, or real places are used fictitiously. Any resemblance to actual products, organizations, events, or persons, living or dead, is entirely coincidental.

Scripture quotations are from New Revised Standard Version Bible, copyright © 1989 National Council of the Churches of Christ in the United States of America. Used by permission. All rights reserved.

PROLOGUE
ROME. AD 199.

Victor of Leptis Magna was a man who knew he was running out of time.

And quite possibly the Church of Jesus Christ along with him.

The controversies of late swirling back home across *Mare Nostrum* in North Africa—from the imperial territories of Numidia and Tripolitania to Cyrene and Egypt; from the cities of Hippo and Carthage to his hometown of Leptis Magna and Alexandria—all of them pressed in against the middle-aged man with worrying dread, rousing him from slumber earlier than he would have liked, yet later than he should have.

The man, limbs stiff from sleep and chest heavy with a suffocating, tarrying wheeze spawned from the loins of the Devil himself, sauntered across the vast room of his residence, high ceiling supported by thick columns of quarried stone and sparkling with an enchanted humid mist in the early morning light. The stone floor was cool and damp against his feet as he padded to columned, open-air windows draped by heavy indigo velvet curtains waving lazily in the early morning breeze. Ribbons of sunlight danced between the creases, beckoning him to taste and see the goodness of the Lord with the day's dawning, another day that promised both blessings and curses. Such was his life going on forty-five years now, ten of which shouldering the increasingly fraught, precarious position of God's people in Rome and beyond.

Victor parted the drapes and managed a smile, the burdens of his lot in life caretaking the Great Shepherd's flock lifting slightly in the warm kiss of the rising sun. He closed his eyes and breathed in deeply, his chest opening up with surprising invitation at the humid, salty sea air carrying along the scent of olives and juniper trees, sweet and cedary. The ends of his mouth curled upward now, the dual aroma reminding him of Tripolitania, of home. Of Heaven itself. Where life was simpler, straightforward, less threatened.

A world that seemed so far away, so long ago...

A pair of verses from the Hebrew Scriptures sprang to his mind, the Book of Lamentations. He quoted them from memory. In Latin, of course. After all, it was he who instituted the use of the language across the worshiping communities throughout the Roman Empire, in their liturgy and Scripture.

Misericordiae Domini quia non sumus consumpti quia non defecerunt miserationes eius. Novae diluculo multa est fides tua.

Victor mumbled aloud, *"The steadfast love of the Lord never ceases, His mercies never come to an end."* The man stood staring off across the Eternal City, brightening at the sight of fishing boats coasting lazily across the Tiber snaking past his perch, looking as though it were paved in gold. He went on, *"they are new every morning; great is your faithfulness."*

Great is His faithfulness, indeed.

Feeling surprisingly refreshed, the man strolled to a table piled high with scrolls, his bare feet cold against the stone floor reminding him of his ailments again. Reaching the desk, a cough suddenly overtook him. Wracking and hacking, doubling him over so that he braced himself against the desk's rough wood.

He thought he was going to die, then and there, leaving the one thing he needed to accomplish in his service as Vicar of Christ yet unfinished.

Then he recovered, the mercies of his Lord and Savior Jesus Christ returning to ameliorate his ailments, infusing his veins with enough vim and vigor to see through his final contribution to the Church before he gave up Saint Peter's chair and his very soul to Saint Peter's gate.

He just hoped it wasn't too late.

Victor took a crisp piece of papyrus off the top of a stash he used for Sunday homilies. The writing paper smelled of freshly pressed reeds and felt sturdy in his sweaty palms. Drawing the ornately carved wood chair beneath him and scooting to the desk, he sat down. He took one of the seven bronze pens cradled in the matching bronze ink pot between his fingers, its head gathering the rare, precious crimson liquid of red lead he favored for the holiest of affairs.

An urgency gripped him now. So he set about chronicling the list that would form the foundation to the Church's sacred Scriptures for centuries to come.

He withdrew the pen and started writing, carefully forming the Latin letters, making way for sentences leading to—

A heavy wood door on tired hinges at the back of his room thudded open against the stone wall.

The Bishop of Rome slid the pen across the papyrus, violating the letter he was crafting and nearly letting slip a Latin curse.

He glanced over at the door. His assistant Lucius was hustling across the stone floor, his footfalls clacking with urgency. He closed his eyes and inhaled a calming breath, then promptly replaced the pen drained of ink and stood.

"You know, there's a bell outside the door, don't you?" Victor complained.

"This can't wait, bishop," the man sputtered. "I bear urgent tidings of great import."

Victor stood and stretched his back, then sauntered back to the window. He threw open the curtains this time and grinned, chuckling to himself and shaking his head. His right-hand elder was ever the thespian, always bearing urgent tidings of great import, a performance that would surely top the greatest of dramas at the amphitheater.

He sighed, finding more fishing boats on the Tiber now, the river's early golden hue now a bright indigo under the cloudless sky.

"How many times do I have to tell you, dear Lucius. Never give a bishop bad news before his morning prayers."

"This can't wait."

Bishop Victor turned around and crossed his arms, wincing at the stiffness still present from the night. His assistant's face was an unusual shade of white that made the man look far sicklier than even himself. Perhaps it was that bad.

"Alright, what is it? What's happened?"

The man took a breath and swallowed.

Victor frowned. Ever the thespian!

"Just spit it out, Lucius!"

"Another gospel has been found in circulation."

"Oh, is that all..." The bishop began his journey back to his desk, his limbs stiffening once again and chest growing tight. "We have dealt with such pests before. Our dear Irenaeus, bishop of Lyons, called the dogs out for what they were. Heretics, the whole lot of them. Such men have been boasting they possess more gospels than there really are, aside from the four ecclesiastically recognized books. Matthew, Mark, Luke, and John."

He reached the chair and steadied himself, then sat, a growing dread churning in his belly. Though he betrayed none of it to his assistant.

Lucius said, "This is different. It seems to be gaining a head of steam now, since many have found it mirrors those the Church has recognized. Not only that, your very own parishes have been consulting the text, right here in Rome!"

"What?" Bishop Victor exclaimed, standing and instantly regretting it.

He sank back down, his assistant coming to his aid.

"I'm fine, Lucius. Stop fussing over me."

"Perhaps you should lie down. Not push yourself so. It will only make things—"

"I said, I'm fine!"

Lucius backed away; Victor dipped his head with regret.

"Forgive me for my outburst. If what you say is true, that the very churches I have been tasked to oversee have now succumbed to the teachings of those Gnostic sympathizers, then my task is made all the more urgent. Leave me, that I may affirm in writing what the Church has already confirmed in practice."

Lucius dipped his head and spun toward the door.

It thudded to a close, leaving Victor, caretaker of Saint Peter's Chair, to his business. The Lord Jesus Christ, Son of God, knew how urgent of an affair the Bishop of Rome was undertaking, how holy it was.

Especially now, given Lucius's news.

Victor resumed his position at the table, pinching a bronze pen between his fingers and readying himself for the task at hand.

Now, where was I...

"Ahh, yes!"

He withdrew the metal rod and returned it to the parchment, carefully scrawling the Latin letters to finish his record of holy writ: "*...those things at which he was present he placed thus.*"

Satisfied, he continued with the most important work he would ever devise in the waning months of his papacy—which was saying something, considering all that he had rendered in his decade stewarding the Church of Christ. He wrote:

> *The third book of the Gospel, that according to Luke, the well-known physician Luke wrote in his own name in order after the ascension of Christ, and when Paul had associated him with himself as one studious of right. Nor did he himself see the Lord in the flesh; and he, according as he was able to accomplish it, began his narrative with the nativity of John.*
>
> *The fourth Gospel is that of John, one of the disciples. When his fellow-disciples and bishops entreated him, he said, "Fast ye now with me for the space of three days, and let us recount to each other whatever may be revealed to each of us." On the same night it was revealed to Andrew, one of the apostles, that John should narrate all things in his own name as they called them to mind.*

He dipped the pen into the pot to retrieve more ink, then continued:

> *And hence, although different points are taught us in the several books of the Gospels, there is no difference as regards the faith of believers, inasmuch as in all of them all things are related under one imperial Spirit, which concern the Lord's nativity, His passion, His resurrection, His conversation with His disciples, and His twofold advent—the first in the humiliation of rejection, which is now past, and the second in the glory of royal power, which is yet in the future.*

Victor replaced the pen and chose another, reflecting on the news Lucius bore.

He had of course heard about the other so-called gospels coming out of North Africa, penned and propagated from the Nile region and spreading like an unholy, demonic locust across the seedbed of Christianity. Infiltrating, threatening, consuming churches around the Roman Sea, not to mention the very souls of his brothers and sisters in the faith.

But to think they had begun to reach his own shores, twisting the truths of God's good news in Jesus Christ, exchanging them for a lie built on pagan superstition? A shudder ratcheted up his spine as he considered all that it meant for his people.

A question rose to the surface that would surely be raised among the souls he caretaked: What if all they had ever known about God's Holy Word was a lie?

And then another, hot on the heels of that one and equally ominous: What if all the *Church* had ever told them about God's Holy Word was a lie?

Another shudder drove him to the stack of unused papyrus. He retrieved a fresh one and returned to his list, the matter all the more urgent:

What marvel is it, then, that John brings forward these several things so constantly in his epistles also, saying in his own person, 'What we have seen with our eyes, and heard with our ears, and our hands have handled, that have we written.' For thus he professes himself to be not only the eyewitness, but also the hearer; and besides that, the historian of all the wondrous facts concerning the Lord in their order.

Moreover, the Acts of all the Apostles are comprised by Luke in one book, and addressed to the most excellent Theophilus, because these different events took place when he

> *was present himself; and he shows this clearly—that the principle on which he wrote was, to give only what fell under his own notice...*

After finishing, the bishop replaced the pen in the ink bottle and sat back, reading through what he had written. These were the eyewitness accounts of Jesus from his very own apostles, orally transmitted before being written down and preserved by the Spirit of God himself.

Anger began rising deep within Victor's belly at the thought of another gospel rising to threaten this eyewitness. He crossed himself and said a prayer of forgiveness for his hatred of those who would seek to sully the memory of his Lord and Savior.

He took another pen dripping with red ink, a line of sweat beading now at his hairline. He ignored it, plunging back into his work preserving the Church's memory of what it recognized as the Word of God:

> *As to the epistles of Paul, again, to those who will understand the matter, they indicate of themselves what they are, and from what place or with what object they were directed. He wrote first of all, and at considerable length, to the Corinthians, to check the schism of heresy; and then to the Galatians, to forbid circumcision; and then to the Romans on the rule of the Old Testament Scriptures, and also to show them that Christ is the first object in these—which it is needful for us to discuss severally, as the blessed Apostle Paul, following the rule of his predecessor John, writes to no more than seven churches by name, in this order...*

Victor replaced his pen and retrieved another, continuing

his holy work with the list of the apostle Paul's holy epistles: the pair of letters to the Corinthians, the pair of letters to the Thessalonians, and the pair to Timothy; Ephesians, Philippians, Colossians, and Galatians; of course Paul's magnum opus, Romans; and then Philemon and Titus.

Another pen depleted, another pen in wait. He exchanged one for the other, his list of ecclesiastically recognized books gaining significance now as he confirmed all that the Spirit of God himself had affirmed in the heart of his Church. The bishop continued:

But yet these are hallowed in the esteem of the Catholic Church, and in the regulation of ecclesiastical discipline. There are also in circulation one to the Laodiceans, and another to the Alexandrians, forged under the name of Paul, and addressed against the heresy of Marcion; and there are also several others that cannot be received into the Catholic Church, for it is not suitable for gall to be mingled with honey.

The Epistle of Jude, indeed, and two belonging to the above-named John—or bearing the name of John—are reckoned among the Catholic epistles.

The Bishop of Rome paused, considering his words carefully before continuing. For what he would pen next was delicate in some circles. He wrote:

And the book of Wisdom, written by the friends of Solomon in his honor. We receive also the Apocalypse of John and that of Peter, though some amongst us will not have this latter read in the Church. The Pastor, moreover, did Hermas write very

> *recently in our times in the city of Rome, while his brother bishop Pius sat in the chair of the Church of Rome. And therefore it also ought to be read; but it cannot be made public in the Church to the people, nor placed among the prophets, as their number is complete, nor among the apostles to the end of time.*

Victor replaced the pen inside the bronze ink pot next to the others, shaking his cramping hand as he read through the last paragraph aloud.

"'And therefore it also ought to be read; but it cannot be made public in the Church to the people, nor placed among the prophets, as their number is complete, nor among the apostles to the end of time.'"

Yes, that is right. The Shepherd of Hermas, like the Apocalypse of Peter, was a worthy book of Christian reflection and discipleship. Just not to be read amongst the churches, for it was not part of the Holy Scriptures. It was not the Word of God itself.

If what he just wrote was delicate, his next few lines would be considered downright political! For it meant the drawing of a line in the sand. To some, a battle cry that would confirm what the Church proper had known deep in her bones for decades yet was too timid to voice aloud. To others, a challenge of legitimacy and power that would not go unanswered. Especially those heretics along the Nile threatening the memory of true, orthodox Scripture!

Then he thought of his parishioners, the ones he baptized as infants and buried at death in old age. They needed this list, as well as those generations proceeding from them. They needed to remember the revelation-witness God had gifted to the world.

Victor returned to the ink bottle and retrieved one of the bronze instruments. Consequences be damned. He wrote:

> *Of the writings of Arsinous, called also Valentinus, or of Miltiades, we receive nothing at all. Those are rejected too who wrote the new Book of Psalms for Marcion, together with Basilides and the founder of the Asian Cataphrygians.*

Drenched with sweat, hands cramping in on themselves, and bone-weary from the exercise, Victor leaned back in his chair and sighed. He read back through his letter, making a few changes here and there. Then he hoisted himself out of his chair and shuffled to his bed.

There, a rope connected to a bell below was affixed to a pulley system Lucius had devised as Victor's health started to deteriorate. He pulled it, and within a minute his assistant knocked at the door before throwing it open.

"Are you alright, sir?" the man said with a panicked rush.

Ever the thespian!

"Yes, I'm alright." Victor handed the man the stack of papyri. "See to it that my scribes copy this letter, word for word. Change not a dot, change not a tiddle. For it bears witness to the very revelation of God himself."

Lucius nodded, his face drawn with solemn recognition, then closed the door and hustled off.

Victor sauntered back to the window, the sun high in the sky now and early morning boats having moved on to other waters, other fish.

Such was life, moving on.

To other waters, other fish.

Other gospels, other texts.

The Bishop of Rome prayed he was not too late.

CHAPTER 1
WASHINGTON, DC. PRESENT DAY.

Silas Grey took another long, pleasurable pull from his second just-lit cigarette, then flipped close his lighter. Leaning against a lamppost on the corner of the street, he slowly exhaled the grey haze into the unseasonably frigid early morning spring air, hoping the street wouldn't become ground zero for another misadventure saving the Church from no uncertain doom.

Because after what happened four months ago, he was still pretty well fried from saving the Bride of Christ's backside.

Although he didn't really have a choice, considering the baton that had been passed to him after Rowen Radcliffe's death. Master of the Order of Thaddeus, ancient defender and guardian of the Christian faith stretching back nearly two millennia.

He took another pull from the cancer stick, as the lovely Celeste Bourne called them. A no-no that would for sure land him in the doghouse with the missus-to-be if she caught wind or whiff of his on-again-off-again habit. He'd picked it back up a year ago and swore to his fiancé and SEPIO partner that he would kick it back to the curb where it belonged. But something about stepping back into the driver's seat of a combustible mission staring down a house on a Monday morning shrouded in fog with temperatures hovering in the high 40s made him grab a pack of Camels at a convenience store when he surfaced from the DC Adams Morgan Metro stop.

Especially this mission. And especially this house.

Which had been all quiet on the Western front for the better part of an hour as he stood shivering against the lamppost.

Taking a final drag, then another, Silas flicked the butt into the road. He took off in a measured stroll toward a two-level row house of red brick pockmarked with age nestled at the end of a quintuplet row of them stretching the length of the cul-de-sac.

Stiff leather sole shoes clicked against the uneven cobblestone sidewalk with each step, a metronome counting off the seconds to his engagement. Hadn't worn them in over a year, along with the suit and the noose tied around his neck. But the mission required a certain costume for the certain neighborhood that held a certain house that had been phoned in by Matt Gapinski early that morning, his newly appointed assistant director of operations for SEPIO, the muscular arm of the Order. He was making a house call to confirm what one of their agents had spotted overnight.

Well, *house call* wasn't exactly right. *Infiltration* more like it. A good ol' fashioned B&E that would surely flood the street with reds and blues if he weren't careful.

So, hands in pockets and wool coat collar turned up with irritation at the springtime weather gone sour, he held his head high as if he owned one of the joints that were way beyond his pay grade.

Fake it till you make it, they taught him in Uncle Sam's Rangers outfit. Same with one shot, one kill. His personal favorite. At least for a time, until he handed in his Army-issued

Beretta and Humvee in exchange for a quiet life ruled by the pen and lectern at Princeton University filling the minds of America's finest specimens of well-bred and well-heeled young adults.

Silas chuckled at the thought. The last few years had been anything but quiet—what with getting sacked from the place he had poured his heart and soul into, a place that had become the core of his identity after fighting like hell in the Middle East, only to be nearly taken out by the archenemy of the Church stretching back two millennia. Not once, not twice, but seven times.

He sighed and shook his head as he walked underneath a Japanese cherry blossom tree, their buds of punch-colored petals still bunched in on themselves as if in a shivering huddle. Thankfully, the good Lord had seen fit to chart a new course for his life, one he wouldn't have imagined in a million lifetimes.

He chuckled again, still coming to grips with the turn of events from late last year. Silas Grey, Order Master of the Christian faith's chief guardian.

Not in a million lifetimes.

A bitter-sweet aroma, less fruity, more floral, wafted from more cherry trees above as he neared his target, surfacing a bitter-sweet memory from childhood when life was simpler, sweeter, less threatened. Without realizing it, one corner of his mouth turned upward in remembrance as he continued clacking along the cobblestone sidewalk.

On a warm, sunny, springtime day far different from that one, his father picked him and his twin brother Sebastian up from school early for some father-son bonding—a rarity, given Dad's high-level position at the Pentagon. They ran through the hundreds of cherry blossom trees gifted to America from Japan crowding the Tidal Basin surrounding the nation's monuments, their delicate boughs weighed down by bunches of those punch-pink petals waving with celebration at spring's arrival. Dad had taken the afternoon off to chase his sons through the forest smelling of honey, their giggles of delight still echoing through time three decades later.

Which was ironic considering what had happened the past year between the two brothers a decade after Dad died during the Pentagon attacks on 9/11.

Simpler, sweeter, less threatened. Indeed...

Silas took a breath and clenched his jaw. No time for silly, sentimental daydreaming. It was go time.

The target up ahead now, peeking from behind bushes slick with morning dew, sat a few blocks from the heart of a district in Washington that had seen a sizable revitalization in the past decade. Restaurants serving international fusion dishes from around the world had risen alongside flower shops and craft coffee houses, transforming the former sketchy neighborhood into one of the hottest on the DC market. And it showed.

Parked along the curb on both sides of the dead-end street sat gleaming Mercedes, BMWs, and Audis polished to perfection, testaments to the million-dollar price tags the homes fetched. Heavy curtains guarded the bay windows trimmed by white replicated up and down the street from gawkers seeking a glimpse of the politicos who held the strings of power across the alphabet soup of agencies that defined the nation's capital.

A wind gusted from behind as Silas reached a waist-high, wrought-iron gate painted black. He hesitated, glancing back up the street and behind, then pushed through, its hinges squawking in protest. A path of chipped red brick led through a patch of manicured, bright green grass and bunches of bushes impatient to bloom and on toward stairs leading up to a door painted a tasteful robin's egg blue.

He bypassed it for another path hidden through a hedge of thick bushes, but one he knew stretched alongside the house back toward the kitchen. Shamefully, the only reason he knew of it was because of what Gapinski had told him about the place after poking around during the middle of the night. He'd been to the house only once before. Which hadn't ended well.

Whatever. Again, no need for the silly sentiments. He had work to do.

Silas hustled along the pathway of stone pebbles toward the back, his coat brushing against a wall covered in green ivy and sending up a sharp, woody scent mixed with earthy notes and weeds. Reminiscent of the wild, untamed forests on bases across the South Pacific and Eastern Europe he and his brother would spend hours romping through while Dad kept America safe.

He cursed himself for allowing another memory of Sebastian to invade his mission-honed mind. Cursed himself for getting rusty after years in the Army Rangers had honed his mind and senses and muscles to act and react with battle-ready precision.

Cursed himself more for the weakness it evidenced, that his brother could still steal himself into his thoughts. Thought he'd gotten over all the backstabbing and lies and accusations, not to mention the biggest punch to the face of them all.

Putting Celeste's life at risk.

Guess he was wrong.

Soon he reached the back of the row house. A white wicker armchair and loveseat kept guard atop a patio of the same chipped red brick set in front of a stone fireplace anchoring the back of a privacy wall that mercifully enclosed the open-air space from nosy neighbors.

Silas eyed the door, confirming no sign of forced entry. He reached for the knob when a light suddenly bloomed across the wall, throwing exposing beams of yellow across Silas's face.

A door creaked open on tired hinges followed by a menacing, deep-throated bark from what sounded like an equally menacing dog, adding a double dose of terror that threatened to derail his early morning incursion.

Silas crouched low on his haunches then padded to the back corner of the wall that butted the adjoining row house property, cringing as his shoes clacked a little too loudly for comfort. He slipped into a narrow slice of darkness as the wretched animal continued its calls for investigation, praying to the good Lord above for a reprieve.

"Down, boy, down!" a nasally, high-pitched man with an Irish brogue scolded, seemingly disinterested in his pet's finger-pointing. "Get on with your business and be done with it, you old coot!"

The dog replied with a growl that made the hairs on Silas's neck stand at attention. After another scolding from his master, the animal sauntered off in exasperation at his calls being unheeded. He obliged his master, the sound of the dog doing his duty just on the other side of the wall joined by loud sniffs and another growl separated only by three inches of masonry.

A minute later, the furry sleuth was bounding back inside his abode. The light shut off with a flick after the door slammed shut, plunging the backyard back into early morning foggy darkness.

Silas sighed. He held his stance, back to the corner and arms raised for a fight, waiting a minute to ensure the coast was truly clear.

He stood then padded back across the brick patio. Reaching the secured back door, he stole a glance toward the front of the house and stood still. Listening, intuiting, discerning anything and anyone who may have caught a glimpse of some well-dressed bloke walking stiffly toward a house he had no relationship with.

Except he did...

Satisfied, he withdrew his keys, finding the one that had

been mailed to him at his office at Princeton those many years ago. Just in case.

This was one of those cases.

He just hoped the lock hadn't been changed. Wouldn't be surprised if it had, given all that had happened.

Finding the blue hardware store duplicate, he slid it into the lock and turned.

Click.

Silas took a relieved breath. He quickly turned the knob and slid inside his brother's house, closing the door softly behind him.

It was dark, the light of the cloudy morning barely finding purchase through closed lace curtains. It smelled of dust and must and mothballs. And also oddly of bleach and furniture polish.

His heart was hammering inside his head now that he had been cut off from the sound of the outside. He swallowed hard and took a breath, then stood still and quiet. The last thing he needed was Sebastian bounding down the stairs from above and finding his sodding brother sweating in his kitchen.

He waited a beat, then another, taking in the ostentatiousness of it all. With the granite countertops crowned by a Kitchenaid mixer he knew his brother never used and a Breville espresso maker he definitely did, along with Henckels knives and pots of herbs. There was a dark walnut wine rack filled with thirty or so bottles of reds. Brunello this and Chateau Margaux that, and then some off-label Malbecs and Meritages and Merlots that cost as much as his monthly rent. A gleaming black baby grand piano and leather furniture and crystal vases beckoned from beyond the kitchen's threshold through a well-appointed dining room and on inside a living room worth more than a year of his life.

Envy began worming its way through Silas as he continued taking in the house, one of his fatal flaws that still managed to get him every time he was faced with the success of others in the face of his many disappointments. Here was his brother, double doctorate who owned a home filled to the brim with the niceties of life he had always wanted but could rarely afford.

Whatever. At least he hadn't sold his soul to the Devil. Literally, as was the case of Sebastian, having become possessed by Satan himself and joined Nous, the chief architect of the Church's wished-for demise.

Better to lose tenure-tracked positions at godforsaken universities and houses filled with junk than one's soul, as Jesus said. Or would say if he were counseling Silas to climb down from his envious high.

He took a breath and shook his head, then literally turned his nose up at it all before taking a step forward.

Eliciting a creek from the floorboards that made him freeze.

He took another breath and let the seconds tick by, again waiting for his blond twin to come bursting through the living room beyond wearing a scowl that could kill.

Because he wouldn't put it past him to do so. Not after what he pulled at Mackinac Island.

But no brother came.

He resumed his pace, running a nervous hand across his close-cropped black hair as he strode across the walnut floor with determination toward the front of the house.

He walked into the dining room commanded by a circular cherry table, a crystal chandelier mocking him from above its center. Cabinets of fine English bone china, either Spode or Wedgewood, added insult to injury.

Swallowing another bout of envy, he continued on into the living room, passing an overstuffed tan leather chair anchoring the west side of the room atop a plush Persian rug embroidered with gold thread throughout the crimson and indigo fibers. A twin sat across from it flanked by a matching couch. He kept going past the baby grand piano toward the front door, confirming a second time that nothing looked amiss. No forced entry or obvious markings of intrusion. Same for the windows as he made his way around the perimeter of the modest floor, confirming they too were all tightly secured, even the bathroom sitting next to the stairs leading to the second floor.

He went to go upstairs when he stopped, the faint scent of souring boysenberry and oak notes catching his attention. He padded back toward the center of the living room to investigate.

There, perched on a shelf next to Sebastian's turntable, the one he lost in a dispute over Dad's estate when they squabbled over his possessions after his death.

He took careful steps toward the glass still cradling an ounce of purplish liquid. Reaching it, he squatted so that he went eye level with the wineglass, a lip mark still evident and shimmering in the dim morning light.

Silas frowned. That confirmed it. Sebastian had indeed been at his house last night.

He hung his head then stood.

But why? He hadn't heard word nor seen any sign of his brother since he scrambled out of that blasted cemetery on that blasted island those months ago. Had kept close tabs on his brother's house, waiting to see if the man would return. He hadn't, for months.

Until this past night...

Silas turned around to take in the room, catching glimpse of a record still resting underneath the turntable's glass.

The Sermon, by American organist Jimmy Smith.

Certainly had good taste in jazz music. Had to give his brother at least that much credit.

He stepped into the center of the room, planting his hands on his hips and scanning the room and wondering why the heck Sebastian had returned. Why he had risked returning home when he knew the Order and other interested law enforcement agencies—the FBI being one of them after his old girlfriend had been caught in the maelstrom of malevolent events—were hot on his backside.

Then he saw it.

Furrowing his brow, he padded across the polished hardwood floor to another set of shelves that held evidence of his brother's travel exploits. Sebastian styled himself as a hobbyist archaeologist, paying for trips to far-flung parts of the globe in search of arcane cultural experiences and objects, the evidence of which sat on several shelves flanking the baby grand piano. An African aboriginal mask, a Haitian voodoo stick, a reliquary holding a tooth from some Buddhist monk, even an ancient phallic idol from India. Though how or why he came into possession of that one he hadn't a clue.

None of them were what interested Silas. What did was an obvious void smack dab in the middle of the center shelf. As if something that had been there was now missing.

He leaned in for a closer look, then frowned.

While the rest of the shelf bore a sheen of dust, a circular spot was clear, the polished walnut wood shining through.

Silas ran a gloved finger across the surface to confirm what he saw.

Sure thing. Something was definitely missing. Maybe a round case or bowl.

He remembered the assortment of cultured artifacts from his last visit. It's what had led to the argument about faith and religion and spirituality that had tipped Sebastian over the edge after a series of proselytizing attempts by Silas.

But what was missing? And why had Sebastian returned for it?

A vibrating pulse against his left leg shook his attention.

Silas quickly reached into his pocket to silence his mobile device. Felt like the entire neighborhood must have heard the interruption. He spun around on instinct then glanced out a window next to the shelves, taking a deep breath to quiet his strumming heart at the turn.

All clear.

He retrieved his cellphone. An unknown number with a 609 area code was on its face.

Silas furrowed his brow with intrigue.

"Hello?"

He was met with silence.

He checked its face again. Still connected.

"Hello? Anyone there?"

"Yes, Professor?" a familiar man said.

He smiled at the sound of a voice he hadn't heard since he left Princeton University.

"Miles!"

CHAPTER 2

Silas ran a hand across his head and scratched the back of his neck at the surprise, mouth still open with disbelief. What a blast from the past!

The good-natured man on the other end of the line chuckled. "Yes, 'tis true. It's your old Princeton academic assistant."

Silas smiled widely with delight at hearing the familiar voice of the man who had faithfully served him for years while he taught Christian history and religious studies at Princeton, keeping him on track and on time. Always running late, he was, while Miles bellowed from the anteroom for him to get to it before Dean McIntyre sacked him for dereliction of duty. In the end, that's exactly what happened. Denied tenure and dismissed with cause for skipping out on his classes to save the Church.

His face fell at the memories. It fell at the pain that still lingered from getting denied the only thing he'd really ever been good at, teaching and academics, with such a promising future as a rising star within the hallowed halls of the Ivy League.

He'd forgotten how much he'd missed it all. The papers he'd presented on his latest research into the Church's relics of the past at the Society of Biblical Literature, as hostile as they often were to such notions. The books he had planned on writing to convince Christians of the authenticity of the Shroud of Turin, the purported burial linen of Jesus, his pet relic project that promised to provoke and nourish faith in these fraught times. The lectures and meetings with students, with all of their wide-eyed, eager questions and thoughts and theories about religion and faith and Christianity. Could do without the helicopter parents, didn't miss that for a second. But the rest...

Silas had held court at the office once held by the venerable Protestant Fundamentalist J. Gresham Machen. Which was ironic, because Silas was a former Catholic turned Protestant. Not because he had a problem with Catholicism, but because of the way he'd come back to Christianity through the on-base evangelical chaplain after drifting from his childhood faith. He relished the opportunity to not only build bridges between the two branches of the Church, but also to inspire a new generation to rediscover religious faith in the face of a modern world that rejected it as a delusion, the ravings of madmen, an opiate for the naïve masses. And he did it in a way that would make ol' Machen turn over in his grave but pleased the most pious of Popes: through relics.

His "History of Religious Relics" class was the most popular elective in Princeton's Department of Religion. Indiana Jones probably had something to do with that. As did Dan Brown, having popularized relics after wrapping them in the garb of religious conspiracies. Silas also guessed the experiential nature of religious objects of veneration also made the topic inviting. Gone were the days when any of the religious faiths could justify themselves purely on tradition alone. Personal experience, not dogmatic belief, ruled the day. And the relics from every religion offered interested students—from the committed Christian to the spiritual-but-not-religious type—

the chance to explore their spiritual questions through objects rooted in historical experience.

As an academic, Silas had spent the majority of his research probing these objects and plumbing the depths of their history. As a Christian, he was interested in connecting historic objects of Christianity to his faith in a way that enhanced and propelled it forward. Which was remarkable, considering Protestants dismissed such things as fanciful spiritualism at best and gross idolatry at worst. Perhaps it was the inner Catholic convert rearing its head. Or perhaps it was an extension of his own longing for more tangible ways to experience the God he had been seeking to understand his whole life. Perhaps still, it had come from his interest in helping his students find faith.

Yet there he was, rooting through his brother's home as Master of a barely known religious order. Far from those heady, headachy days of academia. And far, far from anything resembling a rising vocational star. With his old academic assistant on the phone, no less! A blast from the past, for sure.

But what the heck was Miles phoning for? Hadn't spoken to the man since he'd left over a year ago after clearing his office for good and leaving Princeton in his dust. Hoped it wasn't about Barnabas, the beautiful stray Persian cat he'd nursed back to health on a base at the end of Operation Iraqi Freedom, which he handed over to Miles to caretake after leaving the university.

Only one way to find out.

"Good to hear from you, Miles. But..." Silas cleared his throat. "Well, I must say, sort of out of the blue."

"I know, and there is a good reason for it, sir."

"Haven't talked since everything went down a year ago. Hope everything is alright. Nothing to do with Barnabas, I hope."

"No, nothing of the sort."

"Or Millie..." he said solemnly, referring to the petite elder who had served as his executive assistant for as long as Miles had served as his academic one.

"Dear Lord, no! All is well back home. Or, well, back at what used to be home..."

Silas frowned. Confused by the call as well as Miles's coyness, which was unlike him. Straight shooter all the way. So what was this about?

"Good to hear," Silas said. "Good to hear. So what's up, then? Why the early morning call? Need someone to substitute teach last minute?"

The two shared a chuckle. "No, nothing of that sort. It's..."

The man trailed off. Again, coy.

Now Silas was starting to worry. And growing impatient. The minutes were ticking by before the neighborhood would awaken. He needed to figure out what the heck was going on with his brother and that missing...whatever the heck it was! Not the time to play footsie with his former academic assistant.

"Come, Miles. Spit it out."

The man took a breath. "It's about your...well, replacement, sir."

"My replacement?"

"Yes. Dr. Hartwin Braun."

Silas had zero attention to the goings on at Princeton since he'd left. Hadn't had time to with the Church's well-being hanging in the balance. And didn't much want to, considering all that went down. Better to live and let live.

Truth be told, if he were honest with himself, his ego couldn't handle it. Couldn't handle the thought of someone else taking his place, lecturing those students—his students!—and shaping their minds with God only knows what postmodern, liberal religious revisionism nonsense.

More honestly: He couldn't handle the thought that he was *replaceable*.

Especially with the likes of Hartwin Braun.

Whatever. Water under the bridge.

He cleared his throat. "No offense and not to be rude, because I'd love a chit-chat catch up and all, but I'm sort of in the middle of something here."

"My apologies, sir," Miles stammered. "I was always one for ill-timed, intrusive phone calls."

"Miles, you're not intruding. Nice to hear your voice. Truly. But how about you get to...whatever it is you were wanting to get to."

"Right. Well, as you may or, as the case may be, may not know, Hartwin Braun, that up-and-comer German, was hired to fill your shoes last year."

Silas closed his eyes. Up-and-comer German. Nice.

"Although, let's be honest. No one from here to heaven could fill those shoes with any modicum of skill or grace."

He chuckled. "Thanks, Miles."

"Certainly, sir," Miles said proudly. "Anyway, Hartwin returned the day before from a recent trip, and he instructed me to contact a handful of names, men and women, for a consortium of the minds."

"Alright..."

"And, well, one of those names on his list was a one Silas Grey."

Silas was stunned. He had a hard time believing his name had seen the light of day on Hartwin's radar, given how *up-and-coming* the good German was.

The same age as Silas, nearly forty, Hartwin Braun was the great-grandson of the famous—or infamous, depending on one's point of view—Wernher Magnus Maximilian Freiherr von Braun, the German and later American aerospace engineer and space architect who was the leading figure in the development of rocket technology for the Nazis and later a pioneer of rocket and space technology for the U.S. As in, the V-2 rocket long-range guided ballistic missile employed by the Germans in WWII, and then Operation Paperclip as part of the coterie of captured German engineers and scientists who jumpstarted America's aerospace program.

Although Hartwin's grandfather was of more modest fame, eventually dropping the aristocratic participle "von" in favor of simply "Braun," the legend's great-grandson was a pioneer in comparative religious studies, with a special interest in both ancient völkisch spiritualities that fueled Nazi spiritualism as well as European Christianity, particularly early Medieval. But that wasn't all of it. Hartwin was a twin, the second of which further bolstered the von Braun lineage with similarly impressive accomplishments.

Markus Braun followed a different path, however, turning a million lines of code into a $16.2 billion tech start up called WeNet that rivaled the major social media networks—a constellation of platforms from video to publishing to newsfeeds, the most popular of which was WeShare. Brown hair, brown eyes, and built like a linebacker, the brother was a stark contrast to the wiry blue-eyed-blond Hartwin who had made a name for himself in the circles Silas used to frequent.

The professor's star rose particularly high when he turned his attention to archaeology, uncovering evidence that Christianity had come to Germany sooner than Saint Boniface, much to the chagrin of Rome and the Fulda Cathedral that holds the saint's remains. Yet despite this rise, he was shadowed by rumors that his brother was financing his exploits, and into shadier research and misadventures. And a less charitable one told at the up-and-coming German's expense to ding the man's golden-boy image implicated him in trading valuable cultural artifacts on the black market for profit and to increase his profile. Though no one could prove it, that didn't stop anyone from bandying it about at the Society of Biblical Literature cocktail hour. Including Silas.

But why the heck was the man calling on him? To some sort of *consortium of the minds*? With Hartwin at the helm? Wasn't adding up.

"Are you kidding me, Miles? Is this some sort of early April Fools' Day joke?"

"Nothing of the sort, professor!" the man protested.

"Just Silas. Not professor," Silas bit back.

He took a breath and sighed. Not necessary. He felt himself getting testy with Hartwin's overture. Miles was the last person who deserved his angsty sarcasm.

"Sorry," Miles said softly. "Silas, then."

"No, I'm sorry. Not called for. Not in the least. I should be so lucky to be called professor by my good friend Miles. After all, I suppose I do still hold a doctorate. Though I'm not sure what good it is anymore."

Miles laughed. "Yes, sir."

"Anyway, sorry but this just doesn't make any sense. Why me?"

"I'm not sure. Perhaps with your new role as Order of Thaddeus Master, the professor wanted an expert on the inside of the Church."

"Alright, but who else has Hartwin conned into joining his crew?"

"Another expert in New Testament studies, a Noland Rotberg from—"

"Harvard?"

"That would be the one."

Silas scoffed, mumbling under his breath: "New Testament expert my ass...."

"Now, profess—I mean, Silas."

"I know, I know. Consider me scolded. And the others?"

"Some blogger by the name of Trevor Bohls."

"Name rings a bell, though I don't know why."

"Apparently, he's something of a celebrity among progressive Evangelicals. A former pastor-turned-WeTuber in the Prosurgence Christianity movement. Whatever that means."

"Ahh, now I remember. Some slick flash-in-the-pan megachurch pastor from Grand Rapids, Michigan. Wrote some books and starred in some videos trying to make the Christian faith more palatable to culture. Made a real name for himself when he challenged the Church's teachings on Hell with his *Love Will Win* book. Universalism mumbo-jumbo nonsense, suggesting in the end everyone will win a participation trophy at the last judgment."

"Yes, well," Miles continued, "at any rate, he's on the list."

"Figures. Anyone else?"

"The last invitee is some ex-treasure hunter named Naomi Torres."

Silas coughed at the name, one of his own SEPIO agents. Which seemed off-the-charts strange, though perhaps coincidental. The Order was careful to protect the identity of its agents. No way Hartwin could know of his connection with Torres.

Or so he hoped.

"I'm sorry, but did you say Naomi Torres?" Silas said.

"Yes, why? You know her?"

He went to affirm when something in the back of his lizard brain told him to hold back. Not sure why, but if Miles was working with Hartwin, as unwittingly as he might be, probably best to hold the cards close. For now anyway, until he had a clearer sense of things.

"I've heard the name," Silas simply said.

"Yes, well, that's the list. Then of course there's you—"

"Miles…"

"Oh come on, professor."

"Silas," he corrected again, though regretted it.

Miles huffed. "Silas, then. You always were a bit of a pain in the you-know-what when it came to these sorts of things!"

"What sorts of things?"

"Sharing the limelight with others."

Silas chuckled. "Yeah, I guess so."

"From what I gather, and I don't know all the details, but what Professor Braun is planning aims to radically impact New Testament scholarship. And the Church."

Now Silas was intrigued. But then the empty spot on the shelf caught his attention. And he remembered what was what.

He was on a SEPIO mission that couldn't wait. And standing in the middle of his brother's living room in the rapidly waning dawn hours no less.

He raked a hand across his head again. "I don't know, Miles, I've got—"

He was cut off by flashing lights. Outside, at the front of the house.

"Hold on a second…"

He padded past the baby grand then past a front study to the front door. Parting a lace curtain with a finger that shielded a sidelight window to the left, he scanned the street.

There it was again. Two flashes. Then another.

And there was the perpetrator.

Gray plumber's van. The one the Order had used the night before to stake out the house.

Which meant trouble.

Not good.

"Miles, I gotta go."

"But, sir—"

Silas left the sidelight and padded back into the living room. "Where is this meeting of the minds Hartwin is putting together?"

"Consortium of the—"

"Whatever. Just text me the details."

"So you'll be there then?"

"Wouldn't miss it."

The two said goodbye and ended the phone call.

Before putting his phone away, he activated the camera and aimed for the blank spot at the center of the shelves bearing the cultural relics. He snapped a picture, then inched closer.

When a shadow passed behind the curtained window.

He slipped the phone into his pocket and shuffled against the wall to the right of the window.

Slipping a finger inside the curtain, he peeked behind it to find a figure shrouded in the dawn's shadows inching toward the back door. Big and bulky and dressed in black.

Not good.

CHAPTER 3

Silas's mouth filled with a coppery taste from the sudden burst of adrenaline, his heart picking up pace as he steadied himself with a stabilizing breath.

It was go time.

Again.

Although, perhaps he should just be grateful it took almost four months for some black-clad hostile to come calling. With him in his path.

Reaching behind his jacket, Silas retrieved his trusty Beretta. He made a quick check of the magazine, sliding it out then shoving it back in before switching off the safety.

Locked and loaded. Ready for duty.

Come what may.

He rounded one of the pretentious darkly stained wood pillars at the threshold between the dining room and living room and padded inside, sidestepping around the dining table in the round just as he imagined the hostile cresting around the corner of the house on toward the kitchen door.

Sidling up to the threshold of the kitchen, the right half of his body guarded by the crimson-colored dining room wall, the other half exposed with arm extended holding the Beretta, he waited for the inevitable.

One beat. Two beats. Three beats.

Nothing.

A ticking clock somewhere in the kitchen of marble and stone echoed back to him as he waited for the intruder to show himself. Or herself. He was certainly an egalitarian when it came to invading hostile forces.

Silas held his breath and held his stance.

Come on...

More nothing.

He eased his breath through his nose and stepped to the left, letting his arm drop slightly and letting down his guard.

Big mistake.

The door burst open, the wood trim splintering from the force of a sudden kick and the door smacking against the granite countertop before recoiling.

But not before *one-two-three-four-five* bullets buzzed inside.

All going high and wide, the hundred-year-old plaster walls exploding with injury above his head and behind his back.

Silas fell to his knees and offered a *one-two-three-four-five* reply of his own, the bullets burrowing into the door and jamb and casing.

Before it smacked open again and a masked, dark figure came barreling inside.

Straight for Silas.

Which he totally didn't see coming.

Forcing him to act fast.

Thankfully, Silas had been an All-State wrestler back in the day on the football off-season during winter at Falls Church High. Go Jaguars!

So he was ready.

He popped off a shot before the assault, the bullet slicing

through the intruder's shoulder before sailing through the door.

But it didn't stop the figure in black from smacking into his arm and sending the Beretta skittering backward.

It bounced on the floor before resting on the rug underneath the table.

Perhaps not as ready as he should have been.

Silas recovered and pushed back against the hostile with a Berserker grunt, sending him off-kilter and backward on his heels until he crashed into the countertop.

The man cried out as the Henckels knives spilled from their woodblock, scattering across the granite.

But the hostile was equally quick on his toes, pushing off with a bucking-bronco kick and smacking into Silas's chest, sending him back on his own heels but staying upright.

Like two Kodiak bears crashing into one another, erect and swinging and ready to battle it out to the death.

"Got what you came looking for, Silas?" the man said, voice deep and growly and very British.

Silas startled at the sound of his name, shoving off and throwing his hands up for the next phase.

How the heck does he know who I am?

"Who the hell are you? What are you after?" He took a swipe at the hostile, but his swing was easily batted away.

"Same thing as you I'd imagine." Again, that deep, growly British voice.

Not a cockney East Londoner, not Estuary English from Essex, and definitely not the modern incarnation of multicultural London English.

This was Queen's English. Oxford English. BBC English.

Whoever he was, he was quick on his toes.

The man came in with both arms swinging. First right, then an uppercut left.

But Silas was right there with him, bringing his arms up to bat away the punches.

"Impressive. For the brother of Sebastian Grey, that is." He added with a laugh, "Although you certainly fight like the man."

And now the mystery man knows my brother?

Time to fish for answers. Who knew how much longer they had before the neighborhood was crawling with DC's finest after the morning gunfire.

"So you know my brother then?" Silas huffed as the man repositioned. "What are you, Nous? Come to retrieve his toothbrush?"

The man grinned and came at Silas again.

But he was ready, smashing into the man, head down, and driving him into the granite countertop.

"Don't toy with me. You know bloody well that bowl bears the power of life and death for your beloved religion. Or so rumor has it. And you're dead if you don't hand it over, mate."

What bowl? Whatever it was, it didn't sound good. Not in the slightest.

Silas shook his head and replied, "I disagree," bringing his forearm across the man's neck and pressing like there was no tomorrow.

Because in many ways, there wasn't. If he didn't deliver the Army Rangers goods.

A choking sound erupted from the man as he struggled under Silas's weight and pressure.

Silas kept at it under the man's struggle, not letting up and fixing him with a determined glare.

Just a few more seconds...

But then something unexpected happened.

The man bit him. On his exposed wrist. Hard.

Drawing blood and sending lancing pain blooming from his wrist across his hand and arm.

Never had that before. First time for everything.

Silas cried out, as much from the unexpected turn as from the sharp pain.

He recoiled, letting the man go without thinking. But not for long.

Livid from the violation, Silas smashed his head into the man's face, then followed it up with a swiping hook straight into his bleeding shoulder.

That seemed to do the trick, sending the beast sprawling back across the counter again with a cry and sending knives clattering to the floor.

The man grunted but recovered, replying with a quick jab into Silas's solar plexus.

This time Silas was the one grunting. He stumbled back from the strike.

Giving the hostile the chance to let loose an uppercut of his own across Silas's face.

Which sent him flat on his back.

Silas winced as his head smacked against the stone floor, the world dimming and threatening to plunge him into total darkness. But he held onto consciousness. Barely.

He was getting too old for this. As in almost-forty old.

Before he knew it, the man was on top of him. And turning the tables.

He thrust both hands at Silas's neck, latching onto his throat and squeezing.

Silas grabbed at the hostile's hands then his arms, trying to wrench them away. It was no use. They were like solid steel pipes, clenching with unbreakable force.

He clawed desperately for the man's face and eyes and ears. Anything that might intervene.

Again, no use. The hostile leaned back out of reach with long arms holding fast. His only recourse was pressing against the man's bottom jaw to force him to ease off a bit.

The darkness dimmed as the man continued pressing, cutting off his air and threatening to end him then and there. He had to do something.

And fast.

Silas managed to twist his head sideways under the weight of the man's continued pressure to assess his final options. Which only seemed to give the hostile more purchase.

That's when he spotted it. A few inches away. But maybe, just maybe, within reach.

If only he could...

Silas wrenched his head back toward the figure in black, his lungs burning now from the last remaining oxygen being cut off by the hostile and his throat being crushed, the man's eyes bulging from behind the mask with a mixture of rage and self-preservation.

Now or never.

In one motion, Silas let go of the hostile's jaw with one hand, letting the man's full weight sink against his other one held stiff but losing steam.

With the other, he grabbed one of the Henckels he eyed resting near his right thigh. Hoping against hope it was in range.

Thank the good Lord...

It was.

Grasping the wood handle, he plunged the knife into the man's neck, sinking into flesh and muscle and cartilage, a sucking sound whispering as if slicing through a cantaloupe.

The man's grip instantly slackened, followed by a sickening gurgling sound before he staggered back off from Silas, hands reaching for his throat as blood burst from his mouth.

And then he slumped to the floor.

He twitched a few seconds before going still, the man's body relaxing as he met his Maker.

A racking cough seized Silas from the squeeze on his neck

as he sought desperate breaths. His head was dizzy from the lack of oxygen, and every muscle was taut from the fight. He let his limbs sink into the floor as he sought breath and sought answers.

Who the heck would want to bust into his brother's house? And why? What were they seeking? The same thing he was?

The missing artifact at the center of Sebastian's shelves leaving behind the print after a year's worth of dust?

The sound of boots crunching on the pebble rocks outside snapped him back to the moment.

It wasn't over.

Not by a long shot.

He scrambled across the dead body toward his weapon still resting under the dining room table as the sound of the footfalls neared. When they changed from crunching pebbles to the hard slap against brick, he knew his time was up.

Again.

Lunging for the table, Silas caught sight of his Beretta and grabbed for it. Finding purchase on the barrel, he snatched it out and twisted onto his back.

Slapping its grip into his other hand and aiming straight for the open door as a beast of a man with a bald head came into view.

Gapinski!

Silas instantly lowered his weapon and sighed with relief, letting his arm fall to his chest and body sink into the floor. Totally spent after the melee and darkening Death's door.

"Buddy!" Gapinski said, rushing inside before stopping short of the body and letting out a squeaking surprise. "What the hell happened here?"

"A hostile got into it with a Henckels," Silas said as he stood.

"I take it the knife won?"

He nodded, wincing and massaging his neck from the strain.

"Silas!" Celeste exclaimed, rushing inside behind Gapinski. "You alright, love?" She sidestepped the body, glancing at it before throwing her arms around his neck.

"Careful. The man nearly popped my head off."

"Sorry." She gave him a peck on the cheek before easing back.

"Thanks for the heads up, by the way," Silas said, throat raw and gravelly.

"No prob, Bob," Gapinski said. "We saw the bastard slip in through the front gate all cloak and dagger like. Figured you had seconds before he was hot on your hide to high heaven. Then when the shots started...well, we thought the worse."

"Who do you suppose we have here?" Celeste said, crouching beside the body and eyeing the knife before continuing on toward the man's face.

"Oh, come on. Like we need to check. Is there any doubt?" Gapinski asked.

Silas glanced at the man, hands on his hips as he sized up the hostile splayed on the floor, blood still pooling under the man out from the knife sticking out from his neck.

"We come looking for the 411 on mysterious goings on in Sebastian's pad," Gapinski continued, "and some dude shows up all Johnny-on-the-spot like? He's got Nous written all over him. Or her. Suppose the dude could be a dudette. Some kick-ass Amazonian chick sent to smoke our asses. Or Sebastian."

"Gapinski..." Celeste said. She peeled back the mask, revealing a white man with high, angular cheekbones and an equine nose, mouth open and dark eyes matching the vacancy.

"I guess that answers it."

She took out her phone and snapped a few pictures.

Silas crouched and reached for the hostile's wrist, even as the faint wail of sirens began floating through the open kitchen door.

Signaling major trouble if they didn't get to it.

He yanked back the cuff and prepared for the familiar intersecting lines bent at each of the four ends. Sort of like a swastika, but instead depicting a Neolithic image of a phoenix desert bird. Nous's tattoo calling card.

Nothing.

He eased the man facedown on the floor and did the same to the other sleeve.

Same result. Blank pale-white skin.

"I don't get it," Gapinski said. "If he's not the archenemy of the Church, then who is this guy?"

Silas patted down the hostile, searching him for anything that might—

And then he saw it. Peeking up above the man's collar.

He yanked it down, then further.

"What the…"

A small tattoo, but not the familiar intersecting bent lines.

This one looked more like a man. A cubist interpretation with a boxy body and triangular legs, arms poking out from the shoulder with a triangle neck and a circular head bisected by a horizontal line through the center.

Nothing Silas had ever seen before.

Gapinski whistled. "Now that there is some legit pagan ink. What does it mean?"

"What it means," Celeste said, crouching next to Silas, "is that it looks like Nous has itself some competition."

Gapinski shook his head. "Always something."

The sirens were growing in strength, shaking Silas loose from his trance taking in the tattoo.

Who the heck was this man and who the heck did he work for?

Had no clue. But plot had just thickened.

And with his brother's house at the center of it.

CHAPTER 4

Silas braced himself against the bare paneling from the back seat of the faux plumber's truck as it banked a hard right onto Cleveland Avenue NW, making a quick getaway from Sebastian's neighborhood and back to the Order's SEPIO command center.

"Hold on!" Gapinski said.

"Slow down, mate," Celeste complained, "before we get ourselves a cluster of bobbies on our tail."

"A what?"

"She means DC Metro," Silas said. "A Britishism for the police."

Gapinski threw him a confused look as he eased off the gas.

"Don't ask. I've had to acquaint myself with all manner of British slang the last few months."

Celeste frowned underneath a suppressed grin and swatted at him from the front seat.

"And gladly so, dear," he said with a wink.

She threw him a smile as Gapinski threw on the brakes, nearly careening into the right side of a maroon sedan backing out of a driveway.

"Gapinski!" she exclaimed.

"Sorry, my bad."

"How about we all take a breath and calm the heck down," Silas complained. "We made it out alive, and the bobbies are nowhere in sight."

Celeste flashed him another grin and pushed a lock of hair behind her ear. He loved it when she did that. He was just glad he lived to see her do it again. That was a close one.

Too close.

Not since that time a roving band of Iraqi mercenaries stumbled upon him and Colton on a stakeout had he been so close to Death's doorstep at the hands of another man.

He and his best friend from the Iraqi conflict were following up on a lead on the Ten of Diamonds from that ingenious most-wanted Iraqi playing cards deck good ol' Donny Rumsfeld's Defense Intelligence Agency put together—Taha Yassin Ramadan, one of three Iraqi vice presidents. He blamed Colton for choosing the spot, what he thought was an abandoned apartment a hop, skip, and a jump from a housing complex sheltering the Iraqi whack job.

Turned out to be not so much abandoned as temporarily vacated.

And when the owner returned, along with his band of roving Iraqi mercenaries, while Silas was taking a leak and his pal was catching a bit of shuteye after a particularly long stretch of observing—let's just say, he got a fresh take on the whole getting caught with your pants down cliché.

There were six of them. Three to one. Vegas odds. Which Silas vowed would never again see the light of day in a melee. Apparently, the good Lord had other plans since he'd been dealt at least three or four such hands the past two years since meeting the good folks at the Order of Thaddeus.

The Lord works in mysterious ways, as they say.

Colton managed to take out two of them before Silas could zip himself proper and help his buddy finish off the rest. By then it was too late. The shoot out and melee scared off the vice president and his entourage, scattering them into the four corners of the Iraqi countryside.

He and Colton, not to mention the U.S. government, were left high and dry. Fortunately for Uncle Sam, fighters of the Patriotic Union of Kurdistan captured the guy a few months later and handed him over to U.S. forces, God bless 'em.

Colton busted a gut afterwards when he pointed out a piece of toilet paper was stuck to Silas's Army-issued boots. Never let him live that one down.

Silas smiled at the memory. Always loved his laugh. The two vowed they'd make it through the war and marry and raise families in the same neighborhood. Since Colton was a Texan, the choice was pretty much made for Silas. Which he didn't mind so much except for the heat and 50-gallon hats.

Then Mosul happened, taking out his friend with a roadside bomb and blowing their post-duty plans to hell.

Silas frowned as Gapinski continued driving, holding the plumber truck at a steady pace now. Didn't know why that memory was surfacing then and there, but it annoyed him. Perhaps it was because Colton had been the closest thing he'd had to a brother since his own flesh and blood had peaced out of their relationship after Dad died. And now Sebastian was as dead to him as Colton was. Perhaps literally so, after what happened on Mackinac Island.

Gapinski hung a left and took a side street, snapping Silas back to the moment. He picked up the pace through a tree-lined neighborhood of red-brick and wood-painted houses stretching back to the 19th century, speeding past an elementary school with a weathered wooden swing set and a soccer field. Blowing through a stop sign, the van took a sharp left into a drive entrance near the base of the north transept of the Cathedral Church of Saint Peter and Saint Paul, the sacred structure looming large in the dead of night with stilled cranes and empty scaffolding standing watch. A sight for sore eyes, especially since it had been newly opened the past week.

A year ago, the face of America's church, the Washington National Cathedral and home to the Order of Thaddeus, had been completely ripped off in an act of terror replicated hundreds of times over around the world. Devilish flames had clawed up the spires at what little was left of the West facade of the cathedral after a suicide bomber exploded with persecuting terror. A deep crater in the patio before the grand entrance had smoldered with memory before the desecrated house of worship afterwards. Eventually, what remained of the cathedral's face drooped toward the ground in a slow-motion crumble of Indiana limestone, its spires and gargoyles and stained glass falling into an unholy heaping pile of rubble until much of the sacred structure lay in ruin.

For the past year, the cathedral had been undergoing extensive repairs and reconstruction to return it to its glory days. In the meantime, the Order of Thaddeus and its SEPIO special-ops arm had been using one of its original outposts at the Basilica of the National Shrine of the Immaculate Conception in Northeast DC. Finally, the Order had been allowed to return to its repaired headquarters. There was still more work to be done, but at least the crew could get their old space back.

The van disappeared through the black maw of a parking entrance and took a dip, moving swiftly underneath the national Christian architectural icon. The edge of the narrow drivable passage was lined with LED lighting, showing the way forward down under the massive building. Old stonework still standing from the terrorizing destruction shone in the faint light before curving into a spiral that revealed newer masonry. They turned ever downward beneath the stately structure before reaching the bottom, which was vastly different than either the stone-lined passageway or the stone-built building above it.

The light had noticeably brightened into a dim white, shining off the large car park of gray cement. Several cars, all black, were docked in parking spots and waiting to be used for similar covert operations. Gapinski parked next to one of them and the trio got out of the vehicle.

A memory flashed from the first time he had been brought down into the bowels of the Order's operation center.

He had just been rescued from the first in a series of renewed terrorist attacks perpetuated by Nous. Gapinski, Celeste, and Greer, another operative, had saved him from no uncertain death. When they arrived, the glass doors up ahead they were now nearing opened with a *whoosh*, and a tall, portly man with graying, thinning hair wearing a black cassock, neck ringed by a white clerical collar, stepped out into the underground garage to greet them.

Rowen Radcliffe, former Master of the Order of Thaddeus until he was killed protecting one of his own, Celeste.

Silas still remembered that tired, if not determined look he wore when he greeted them. As if the future of the Church rested on his shoulders. He could still hear his long cassock whispering and still see the carport light glinting off his golden buttons as the man rushed to meet the arriving party who had rescued Silas, apparently sent on a mission to rescue him by Radcliffe himself.

Man, he missed him. Silas wondered how on earth he would ever measure up to the example he set and the steady hand he offered the Order as his replacement. Wondered why on earth Radcliffe had ever tapped him to replace him as Order Master, something Radcliffe had apparently been planning for months before his untimely, dastardly end.

No reason to dwell on that now. They had a job to do. *He* had a job to do. Given what had just gone down.

The glass doors gently swooshed open, the scent of sanitized air flooding his senses. They shuffled into a familiar slate-gray hallway washed in the same dim, white light as the garage. Men and women swarmed about the halls ahead, doing their duty to protect and guard the Church.

"Let's gather the crew in my study," Silas said as he guided the party to the right and down another hallway to a T-juncture.

He almost stumbled over the words. *My* study. Felt crazy weird saying that. But Radcliffe's former office had passed to Silas when the former Master passed the baton along to him before his death.

"Who else do we need?" Celeste asked, glancing at Gapinski.

"Naomi, for one. Though with her in the field at that dig site in Libya, I'm hoping it's not too inconvenient."

"Torres?" Gapinski questioned as they weaved through a hall lined with windowless, nondescript doors, each armed with a keycard entry pad. "What's she got to do with things?"

"I want her experience in anthropology and to bring her up to speed in...well, whatever the heck this is. It would help to get Zoe on this as well, especially since she needs to open up a secure channel to Torres in the field."

They arrived at a set of double doors at the end of yet another hallway. This one was armed with a palm-reading entry pad. The Order's headquarters was as secure as any of the military installations Silas had worked at through his military career before joining Princeton. And below one of the most important religious buildings in America, no less.

Before placing his hand on the security measure, Silas said, "I'm going to head inside to take a breath. Meet back here when you've checked in at the ops center and brought back Zoe with Torres on the line."

The pair agreed and left as he placed his hand on the pad. It pulsed a light blue hue before turning a solid green. Then the doors opened, revealing a very different room from the rest of the Order headquarters.

Instead of the sanitized slate gray, the room was entirely clad in dark wood, fully restored to its former glory where Silas had first had his introduction to Project SEPIO, short for the Latin *Sepio, Erudio, Pugno, Inviglio, Observo.*

Protect, instruct, fight for, watch over, heed—the once-for-all faith entrusted to God's holy people. The Church of Jesus Christ.

Silas sauntered inside the room, exhaustion now setting in as the adrenaline high finally waned to nothing. All he wanted was his bed to sleep away the day. And a cigarette to smoke away the anxiety. He knew neither were an option. It was go time. And he was in charge.

Floor-to-ceiling bookcases lined the walls filled with modern and vintage tomes weighing down their shelves. Their heavenly, papery sweet-and-musky scent was a balm for the former professor. At one end was a large stone fireplace, the kind a person could walk into if they desired. A fire was crackling and popping away. At the other end was a large wooden desk, ornately designed with pillar legs and wooden sides. Reminded Silas of the time he stood before the Resolute Desk in the Oval Office when a buddy gave him a tour of the White House after hours. Behind it was a series of monitors, all dark and hiding their purpose. He didn't even want to think what was waiting for him when he brought them to life. The center of the room was commanded by a sizable Persian-style rug with two burgundy leather couches facing each other, complemented by two well-worn, overstuffed burgundy leather chairs at either end. Further on stood a mini bar nestled between two bookcases.

Silas headed there and prepared himself a scotch, neat. He flopped down in a chair with his drink and took a long swig, then another shorter one. The caramel liquid hit his stomach hard and instantly worked its magic, the alcohol filling his head with dizzying delight and the oakiness filling his senses with satisfaction.

He closed his eyes and sat still, cradling his drink with both hands. For a few minutes, before the gang returned, it was just him and the only sounds of the crackling fire and his breathing. He focused on the former while steadying the latter, drawing in measured breaths through his nose to calm his nerves, his throat still raw from the melee.

As he slipped into a quiet meditation, he recalled a question he asked Radcliffe the first time he sat in that very chair: *"Who are you people?"* To which the man replied, in perfectly polished British English, head tilted and smiling warmly, "Why, we're the good guys, Silas."

One end of his mouth curled upward. Good guys, indeed.

His R&R was interrupted by a knock at the door.

Silas opened his eyes and turned his head toward the entrance. A moment later, there was an unlocking *click* and it cracked open. A hand curled around the door and someone peeked inside. Neither Gapinski nor Celeste.

The man was rather tall and widely girthed, skin bronzed a lighter shade of ebony and face covered with a salt-and-pepper bushy beard—heavy on the salt. A wide smile stretched underneath, polished white teeth gleaming through a widening smile along with deep-set eyes into a look of delight.

"Master Grey?" the man asked, his voice warm and buttery and accented.

Silas sat straight and set the glass down on a marble top table resting next to him. Then he stood.

"Yes, I am he."

"Oh, blessed day! May I come in, sir?"

"Uhh, sure..."

Silas stepped forward as the man strode inside, the door thudding close behind him. He was shrouded in billowing light brown vestments, an interweaving pattern of green and black and blue running down the center. Resting on his bald head was a matching hat embroidered with the same pattern.

He took it off and extended his hand. "I am being so fortunate to make your acquaintance, Master Grey."

Silas furrowed his brow in confusion, but took it. "Likewise. But—I'm sorry, who are you?"

Withdrawing his hand, he said, "Why, Victor Zarruq. With the Board of Trustees for the Order of Thaddeus."

Silas offered a smile. "Yes, of course."

"You probably don't remember," the man went on, "but we met briefly last year at one of our annual gatherings."

He nodded again. "Yes, yes. Archbishop of Libya, isn't that right?"

"*Former* Archbishop of Libya, but yes."

"Good to see you again, Your Grace."

Zarruq chuckled, a deep belly laugh that shook his generous gut. "None of that 'Your Grace' business. Stuff and nonsense, that is. Victor will be fine."

Silas nodded. "Sure thing, Victor." He folded his arms and continued, "But to what do I owe the pleasure? I'm not missing a trustee meeting am I?"

"Oh, no. Nothing of the sort. The board asked me to pay a visit to…see how you are getting along in your new role."

To babysit me, you mean?

Silas held his grin and motioned for the seating at the center of the room.

"Please, sit."

The man bowed slightly and sauntered over, the whisper of his long brown robes reminding him of Radcliffe again.

Silas sat and reached for his drink. "So the Order trustees have sent you to spy on me, have they?"

Zarruq chuckled as Silas took a swig. "No, nothing of the sort. Merely paying a house call."

"For how long?" Silas said with a little too much accusation. He realized it and recovered, adding, "What I mean is, how long are you in town? I assume we've put you up in one of the dorm rooms beneath the nave. Although, I'm not sure we even have hot water yet with all the repairs still ongoing."

"I'll make do." The man paused and took a breath, settling into his seat across from Silas and propping his hands on his belly. He bit his lip before adding, "And it looks as though I may be sticking around for a bit."

"Really..."

"Not to spy, as you suggested. To *support*. Rowen had so many plates spinning in the air that I half imagined vestigial limbs had spontaneously sprung from the man to help him keep it all sorted!"

The two shared a knowing laugh.

Zarruq went on, "No one could possibly be expected to fill all of his shoes. The trustees recognize this. And so they've asked if I would...come alongside you in your important new role. Fully confident, might I add, that you are more than capable of taking the Order forward into the second decade of the twenty-first century."

Silas went to respond when he was interrupted by the door again unlocking with a *click*. It opened, and this time familiar faces appeared.

All drawn, eyes wide and wearing worried looks.

Silas leaned back in his chair and threw back the rest of his scotch.

What now...

CHAPTER 5

Celeste took the lead hustling into the study, Gapinski and Zoe bearing a laptop close behind. She stopped short when Victor Zarruq stood.

"Bishop Zarruq? What a pleasant surprise!" Celeste let slip a giggle and opened her arms for an embrace.

The man did the same, and it looked like some sort of reunion was taking place.

"I take it you two know each other?" Silas said.

"Of course," she said, pulling back, mouth still wide with delight. "It's Victor, Silas."

"So I hear…"

"Don't tell me you two haven't become fully acquainted yet, *Master* Grey."

"Been a little preoccupied getting my butt whooped at Sebastian's house."

"Put it here, my man," Gapinski said, clasping Zarruq's open palm with a smack and following through with the embrace. Even Zoe looked pleased.

Silas hung his head as the three chatted, his neck growing red at the thought the Order trustees sent the man to babysit his ass.

"For heaven's sake," Celeste said, "what are you doing here?"

"The trustees asked him to hang out with us a bit, lend a helping hand and what not." Silas added with a chuckle, "Although, if he's not careful, Zoe will have him running TPS reports every hour. But while I'd love to entertain a family reunion, it looked like you came with urgent news."

Celeste's grin quickly faded. She nodded. "That's right. We did."

Silas motioned for the seating area. He went to refill his drink while everyone else found their spots.

He uncorked a bottle of Macallan 18, thankful for the Order's resources, and poured two-fingers' worth.

He took a swig and closed his eyes, a level of anxiety returning that he hadn't felt since Iraq when he had commanded small platoons of men for Uncle Sam. And now four others were looking to his direction with the equivalent of the Joint Chiefs of Staff looking on. He sighed, wishing Radcliffe had chosen someone else.

Reaching to put the cork back into the bottle, a tremor overtook his hand. He clenched it tight into a fist then quickly plugged the cork back inside the bottle. He grabbed his drink with the other hand and quickly put his trembling hand inside a pocket.

What a day...

Strolling back to his chair, Silas said, "So what's going on?" Voice steady and steely, betraying no worry or dread.

"First off—" Zoe said, motioning toward the large-screen television mounted above the fireplace behind the group. "As you can see, we've got a very tired-looking Naomi on video now."

"Thanks, Zoe. How about you try sleeping on a cot in the middle of the North African desert under twenty pounds of bug netting and baking under the sun all day while rummaging through packed sand."

"Sorry..." she said, adjusting her trademark baby blue glasses up her face.

"Hey, Torres. How goes it?" Silas asked, sinking back into his chair.

"Hey yourself, chief. And hey to everyone else." She offered a quick wave. "Slow go, but loving life."

"I bet. What I wouldn't give to get back in the saddle of an archaeological dig. So you're making progress then?"

She nodded. "So far, the informant's information seems to be turning out."

Gapinski smirked. "Better be after all those clams we paid that guy. How much was it again?"

"Not important, Hoss, when the history of the Church is at stake," Torres retorted. "Anyway, we excavated a partial wall earlier in the day, and we're hoping for more this afternoon. If there's something significant in the sand, it'll show itself, one way or another."

"Great news. Sounds like clams well spent." Silas took a swig of scotch, then looked at Celeste. "So let's have it. What now?"

Celeste took a breath and nodded to Zoe. "Tell him what you discovered."

"More like what you all discovered."

"We've got another MI6 psychopath on our hands," Gapinski said.

Folding her arms, Celeste turned to the man. "Excuse me? *Another* MI6 psychopath? Who's the other, pray tell?"

"I mean..." His eyes widened; his mouth fell. "I, uhh. Crapola..." he muttered.

Silas laughed. "Probably best not to answer that if you know what's good for ya, pal."

Gapinski shifted in his seat and mouthed *'Sorry'* to Celeste, an MI6 veteran. She smirked and put on her best faux-ticked face before winking back. Much to the big man's relief.

"At any rate..." Silas went on, "What's the deal, Zoe? What'd we find?"

The petite Italian took a breath then opened up her laptop. "This is the deal."

She turned it to face Silas. He leaned in for a look.

At the top of the screen was a dark, grainy image. One of the photos Celeste had taken of the hostile whom Silas had fought off. Underneath was another image. Government issued, by the look of it. Next to it was a listing of stats. His name, known locations, and former place of employ.

MI6.

Silas leaned back and looked to Celeste. "This guy mean anything to you?"

"Haven't a clue who the bloke is. Must have joined after my time."

"But why would British intelligence be running ops on Sebastian's bachelor pad?" Gapinski asked.

Celeste scoffed. "No way that was an MI6 operation."

"Highly doubt Her Majesty's government is interested in my brother," Silas said. "No matter how off the deep end he's gone."

"Probably right. And the dude was sporting that creepy box man ink. Can't imagine the tat met government regulations. Even for the Brits."

Celeste frowned and smacked his arm.

"Ouch!"

"That was for both of your swipes at Her Majesty's former intelligence agents. Two for the price of one."

"I could only be so lucky..."

"Alright, let's focus, folks," Silas interjected. "Speaking of the tattoo. Any leads on that front?"

"Not yet," Zoe said. "I've cross-checked American government agency databases and also the Vatican's."

"No dice?"

"And no cigar. But I'm running it through INTERPOL now and should know something soon."

"Hope so, because I don't like another kid on the block at Sebastian's party."

"What tattoo?" Torres said, joining the conversation. "And sorry for my ignorance, but who's the new guy?" she added, nodding from the screen toward their Libyan visitor.

"Sorry," Celeste said. "Thought you two had been properly introduced before today. Victor Zarruq was the former Archbishop of Libya, Naomi, and a member of the Order's board of trustees. He was a close friend of Radcliffe's and worked toward revamping Project SEPIO, actually. Modernized it, gave it the sort of vintage Christian vision that has guided it these past days, isn't that right?"

The man chuckled and bowed his head, cheeks reddening as if embarrassed at the attention.

"That is partly correct," he said. "But you deserve the rest of the credit, my dear, nurturing it the rest of the way to its current incarnation."

"Too kind, Victor. At any rate, this here is Naomi Torres," she said, waving toward the screen.

"I am aware. Rowen was keen to bring you aboard, pulling out all the stops to make your adoption into the Order possible."

Torres stiffened, her head rising slightly with pride. "He was? He did?"

"Yes, my dear. Your superb archaeological fieldwork and academic acumen with indigenous people groups was an asset he couldn't pass up for his arsenal. Although, it didn't take any convincing to bring aboard the woman who discovered the *Urca de Lima*."

The man smiled knowingly. Torres giggled nervously from

the screen, pushing a stray lock of hair behind her ear as if exposed.

Silas eyed the pair. "Now that we're properly acquainted, as our resident Brit said earlier..." He threw Celeste a grin. "Maybe we can get back to figuring out what the bloody hell is going on here."

"That's my favorite Britishism," Gapinski said.

"I'm sorry," Torres said, cutting off any further reply, "but I asked about the tattoo earlier."

"Like I said. Creepy box man."

"Here..." Zoe said. "I'm sending you an image Celeste took from her phone of the dead operative. It'll pop up on your laptop."

"Dead operative?" Torres startled. "Sounds like I've been missing out on all the fun."

A soft *purr* came through the telescreen's speakers, indicating Torres received the image on her end.

"Alright, got it." She leaned toward the screen, brow furrowed with concentration. Then her eyes widened, and she settled back into her seat, bringing a hand to her chin and humming, as if with recognition.

"Tattoo ring a bell?" Celeste asked.

"Maybe...Or maybe it's nothing."

"But you've seen it before," Silas pressed.

"Not exactly. But it does match cubist representational figures of an obscure Gnostic sect called the Mandeans. Here, let me find an image to send your way." She clacked away on her laptop.

"Hmm..." Zarruq hummed, as if with recognition himself. He shifted in his seat and brought a hand up to his beard, stroking it and staring off into the ceiling.

"You know this Gnostic outfit?" Silas asked.

"Oh yes. Their origin probably goes back to before Christianity, drawing their name from the Aramaic word for *perception, knowledge, Gnosis.*"

"Manda."

Zarruq cocked his head and grinned. "Impressive. You know Aramaic?"

Silas reddened at the attention. "I know enough to get into trouble. But I'm not familiar with this group of Gnostics."

"Here we go," Torres announced. "Sending over the image now."

Another *purr* sounded from Zoe's computer. She turned it around for the others to view.

There it was. Same image of the hostile's tattoo in view. Several, in fact. Their bodies boxy, with the same triangle legs and neck, and stick-figure arms jutting out from their shoulders.

"Sure looks the same," Silas said.

"Except for the dudes' heads," Gapinski said. "Or dudettes, as the case may be."

"He's right," Celeste said. "The one on the bloke from Sebastian's home bore an oval bisected by a horizontal line."

"How so?" Torres asked. "The photo I got isn't the best quality."

"Like this..." she retrieved a notebook and pen from a pocket and drew the figure with the head in question. She stood and walked over to the screen above the fireplace, holding it up for her to view.

"Different enough, that's for sure. And importantly so."

"So this couldn't be the Mandean Gnostics?" Silas asked before taking a swig of scotch.

Torres shrugged. "Too early to tell what it means."

"May I take a look?" Zarruq asked, opening his hand for the notebook as Celeste returned to her seat.

She handed it over. "Be my guest."

He took it and eyed the image, turning his head this way and that.

"Hmm..." he hummed again with recognition, bringing his other hand to his beard and stroking it contemplatively.

"See something, Bishop?" Silas asked.

The man smiled. "Please, Victor is just fine. Perhaps, yes." The man scooted to the edge of his seat and brought a finger to the head Celeste had drawn. "While I no doubt believe this oval serves as a head for the markings, I believe it also functions as a secondary symbol."

"Such as?"

"Such as a Theta."

"A who?" Gapinski asked.

Zarruq turned to the man. "Not a who. A what."

Silas hummed with recognition and sat back in his chair. "The Greek letter. And first letter in the Greek word *theos*."

"The Greek word for God," Celeste said.

He nodded. "Or the gods, plural. The letter is also often used as a sort of shorthand symbol for God."

"It's all Greek to me..." Gapinski said.

"How original," Celeste mumbled.

"It has been known to symbolize man," Torres added from the screen, "with him squarely at the center of the world. Even on top of a mountain observing the world with understanding, the eye of intelligence that understands all. The Paleolithic Greek hunter herdsmen were viewed as those who ruled earth themselves as gods."

Gapinski sat forward. "So let me get this straight. The head of our box man tattoo is a symbol for God and some paleoman-god thingamabob?"

She nodded.

"And it's chilling on top a box man tattoo belonging to an obscure Gnostic sect serving as its head? Sound about right?"

"That's right."

"Always something," Gapinski growled, folding his arms.

Silas said nothing as he contemplated its meaning, taking a swig of scotch and feeling its effects dull his concentration.

"But what does it mean?" Celeste asked.

"God is the human mind, the seat of intelligence," Silas mumbled, "with the knowledge to be like the gods..."

"Knowing both good and evil," Celeste said, finishing the lines from Genesis chapter three.

Silas nodded. "Not only that: claiming the right to decide what is good and evil."

"Sounds like a bunch of Nous mumbo jumbo, if you ask me," Gapinski said.

"Except it's clearly not," Celeste said.

"No, it's not," Silas agreed. "At first, I thought the guy I fought off in Sebastian's house was there to retrieve something for him. Especially since he knew who I was."

"Knew who you were? That certainly adds another layer to it all."

Silas nodded. "But then he made a comment about my fighting skills that mocked Sebastian in the process."

"Like how you fight like a girl?" Gapinski snickered.

"Not appropriate in mixed company," Celeste whispered, patting the man's knee. "Go on."

Silas stifled a grin. "As I was saying..."

Gapinski folded his arms and hung his head.

"Thought the guy was there for Sebastian. To retrieve an overnight bag or at least something of value that he left behind. But he made a crack about him that seemed like he was a rival. An enemy, even. Now we know he's not from Nous, former MI6, and was probably there to steal something. Which Sebastian or one of his goons already swiped overnight."

"And what do you suppose that is, Master Grey?" Zarruq asked, arms folded on his belly.

Silas shrugged. "I wish I knew. I've been wracking my brain.

Visited the place only once. I remember the array of cultural artifacts he had on display. Shamefully, we got into an argument about it all. Especially the more religious types of artifacts."

"Religious types?"

He nodded.

"Such as?"

"Such as a Haitian voodoo stick, a reliquary holding a tooth from some Buddhist monk, and some phallic idol from India."

"Did you say phallic idol?" Gapinski asked, eyes going wide.

Silas nodded.

"As in an idol in the shape of a—"

"Gapinski..." Celeste moaned.

The man stood. "And that calls for a scotch of my own." He sauntered toward the minibar.

"Anything else?" she asked.

Silas shook his head. "Nothing out of the ordinary. Except for the missing one, which I assume the hostile was after."

"Did he say what it was?"

"Just something about a bowl. That it bore the power of life and death for our religion, for Christianity."

"Well that sounds sufficiently ominous."

"But I can't for the life of me recall what it was."

"Wait a minute," Torres said from the screen. "Did you say bowl?"

Silas looked toward the fireplace in surprise. "Yes...why? You know something?"

Torres bit her lip and narrowed her eyes. "Not sure. But the box man tattoo reminded me of something from grad school. In the late 19th century, a number of bowls were found in Iraq. Mandean magic bowls, they were called, something like thirty of them."

Silas sat straight and scooted to the edge of his seat. "And what were these...magic bowls?"

"Clay bowls inscribed with a special script derived from a Semitic East Aramaic dialect. The text ran the circumference of the bowl and spiraled down into the center."

"And what did they say?"

"Oh, you know, your run-of-the-mill incantations against all kinds of demons and disease and death. At least the one I remember reading about."

"And the others?"

Torres shrugged. "Perhaps you should ask your brother. Seems like he got his hands on one of them. If some dude with a Mandean-like tattoo was barnstorming his house in search of a bowl."

Silas sighed and sat back, head swimming from the revelation about the hostile and his tattoo and the possible object of his mission.

"Mandeans..." Bishop Zarruq said with the same air of contemplation. And with the same pose: head back, arms resting on his belly, hand stroking his beard.

A smile flashed across Silas's face at the scene. Reminded him of Radcliffe, the good-natured, grandfatherly sage with a steady hand guiding SEPIO and its exploits from the side.

Part of Silas was mighty thankful the Order trustees had seen fit to send the man along to help. Even though the prideful part of him resented it. But he was warming to the idea, as well as to the man.

Because the good Lord knew he sure could use a sagely, steady helping hand.

Maybe that was the point.

Alright, Lord. Hear you loud and clear down here...

"What do you have, Victor?" Celeste asked, all eyes turning toward the man and Silas refocusing his attention on him.

Zarruq offered a chuckle, those teeth gleaming brightly against his bronzed skin through that bushy salt-and-pepper beard of his. "'Tis true what the Hebrew Scriptures tell us. There really is nothing new under the sun."

"Do tell..."

The man shifted in his seat when the phone buzzed next to Silas with interruption.

He glanced at it, annoyance rising on par with what used to tweak Radcliffe when the blasted thing interrupted the flow of an operational briefing.

Must mean he was channeling the old Master after all.

It buzzed again, demanding a hearing. Silas huffed and punched the intercom button, echoing Radcliffe's role as the cranky Order head.

"Yes?"

"Master Grey?"

It was Abraham Patel, Zoe's right-hand man from operational support. Good agent who knew his stuff and could wield a laptop like Silas wielded his Beretta. They were lucky to have the young Indian man who could surely have risen fast at the best start-ups San Francisco had to offer.

Which meant taking a breath and not biting the poor kid's head off.

He did, then asked what was up.

"A live broadcast on CNN, that's what's up."

Silas shifted in his seat and sighed. "We're sort of in the middle of it here, Abraham. Can't it wait?"

"Nope. Your replacement is apparently readying to man a room with a bank of cameras at Princeton."

"Replacement?" Celeste asked, turning to Silas.

Silas's face fell. Imagined it went white, too, before flushing with envious irritation. Taking a breath, he said, "Hartwin Braun."

"*The* Hartwin Braun?" Celeste said. "Brother to that tech start-up, and the man who's made a name for himself parlaying fanciful religious artifacts and peddling alternative Christian voices?"

"That'd be the one. And my replacement at Princeton."

"Always something," Gapinski said.

Silas glanced his way, agreeing one hundred percent. And dreading what it meant.

With zero doubt Sebastian was somehow at the center of it.

CHAPTER 6
WEWELSBURG, GERMANY.

Sebastian Grey cradled the bowl in both palms, its heaviness adding to the weight of significance he bore.

Proof the Bible was a fake. That Christianity was a lie. Or so he hoped.

His breathing began to pick up pace at the thought, his hands sweating with anticipation and fingers tingling with delight at what it would mean.

And how fortunate he had discovered the first hint of what may lie at the end of the long dotted line leading to buried treasure. Some would even call it divinely providential. Whatever it was, the Universe had tossed him a big, fat, juicy bone those months ago while traipsing across the world seeking anything that would give him the answers to the questions he had been seeking his whole life outside the confines of the staid, stogy, stuffy, stale, and every other 'S' alliteration he could think to describe the faith he had once served.

The one he had devoted his pathetic childhood to that had beat him up, spit him out, and used him til he bled.

Literally.

Bile rose up his throat at the thought of what happened all those years ago at the hand of that priest. He swallowed hard before it crested his tongue, some of its sour fluid slipping past into his mouth. He let it, rolling the dark green liquid around his mouth to remind him of all he had endured for such a time as this.

Then a cold resolve flooded his veins as he held the basin belonging to the ancient spiritual sojourners who had guarded a secret for two millennia. A giddiness welled up inside at the thought of all that the Universe had kept secret.

For him to unveil.

But it was only one piece of the puzzle. A hint at what lay behind the veil of history's march just waiting for its revelation light to shine forth to enlighten mankind and wake them up to the fairy tale perpetuated by those dead, white men of old. To clue people into the powerful who suppressed the voices of the marginalized within the nascent upstart religion from the dawn of Christianity's marriage to the Roman Empire thanks to Constantine's conversion and his use of the Council of Nicaea to craft a religion and shape its book for his powerful political ends.

Yet there would be those who would stand in the way of his glory, in the way of his unveiling.

His brother Silas chief among them.

A fire crackled behind him and rain smacked the panes of glass that separated him from the herd milling about outside in worship. The sheeple still bowing down before that pitiful false prophet who died like a dog those many centuries ago.

He could still hear the peals of church bells clanging away through the weathery onslaught, their thunderous tones grating against his consciousness like nails on a chalkboard.

Until a crack of thunder overhead intervened.

That's more like it...

He set the bowl down carefully upon a red velvet pillow resting on the large wooden desk commanding the center of the room. He picked up a piece of paper with the beginnings of a translation of the inscription, the ancient Aramaic that proved troubling for his translator—and painfully slow. Could be days until he understood the full measure of its revelation.

But what little he could gather was all he needed to get him going.

...there is another, a Secret Book that stands above the Evangelists, a Truth above the truth claimed and a Story above the story told by the men and women of the Way, lost to the Way but known to the Knowers...

There is another. A secret book. A truth that stands above the one claimed by the Way. A story above the one told by the Church.

A new Gospel even...

From his childhood religious upbringing, Sebastian knew that *the Way* was an ancient term for those who would be known as Christians. And the *Evangelists* could only refer to that wretched foursome. Matthew, Mark, Luke, John. Which meant the relic bore the power of life and death for that wretched religion.

Just as the intel from that Nous operative had recently confirmed from rumblings elsewhere in the world...

And Sebastian Grey would search for it, discover it, expose it for all the world to see. Leaving the Church to burn in the furnace of its revelation-light.

A knock at the door shook him from his delight.

Sebastian cleared his throat. "Yes?"

The heavy walnut door swung open on tired hinges. His face brightened at the person who walked inside.

"My darling, Helen!"

He leaped from his chair as the tall woman strode inside,

her long straw hair braided and drawn up into a bun, her piercing blue eyes meeting his own before their mouths connected with passion.

They held that connection and held each other for minutes, the snapping of flames and smacking of rain keeping time.

They pulled back, letting out sighs of pleasure.

"I could take you right now," Sebastian groaned.

Helen giggled. "Later. Right now, you are being required in the Chamber of Enlightenment."

Oh, how he loved the way her words rolled off that German tongue of hers, in all their guttural glory, with her making each sentence into a participial phrase where none was needed.

Sebastian offered a feigned pout before kissing her gently on the cheek. "Until later, then."

"At which point you will be holding the title Nous Magnum Magister."

His mouth widened into a grin, his heart racing with the truth of the matter.

Grand Master of Nous, indeed...

Never saw that one coming. Not in a million years.

Dad would be proud. As would that dirty priest who raped him all those years ago.

After Rudolf Borg met his unexpected end at the hand of that bloody Brit Master late last year, the machinations of power within the storied nemesis of the Church began grinding away. With Sebastian at the helm.

Unlucky for Borg, fortunate for Sebastian.

It had been determined just a few days ago after several weeks of debate and even more weeks of those damn political gears grinding away behind the scenes. In the end, those who knew what was good for Nous—and them—quickly fell in line behind Sebastian. Those who hadn't...well, let's just say they either had a change of heart or it stopped beating altogether.

All that was left was to ratify the decision.

"Wish me luck," he said, giving her one final kiss before leaving.

The stone floor sent a frigid shock ratcheting up Sebastian as he slowly descended the stone stairway of his new home in Wewelsburg, Germany. It wasn't so much a home as it was a castle. And a famous one at that.

Built in the 17th century, it later became the central headquarters of the German SS and central command for Heinrich Himmler. Though it had become a sort of museum and youth hostel post-WWII, the former Grand Master of Nous, Rudolf Borg, had acquired the estate from his hometown and transformed it into his own needs: a fortress and nerve center of spiritual enlightenment and religious war.

Wind howled outside as a mixture of rain and now heavy wet snow beat against the thick interlocking stones of the ancient castle, a violent reflection of the nature of what was about to take place below.

He continued his descent, a red silk robe swishing with every step down the stairs. Reaching the bottom, he continued on toward the chamber but stopped short when he reached a statue commanding the center of the lower level.

Bird-Man Thoth, the ancient Egyptian god of wisdom. Of revelation. Of *gnostikos*, the divine knowledge.

It was a perfect replica of the colossal statue discovered near the mortuary temple of Amenhotep III in Luxor a decade ago. The statue towered over Sebastian, reminding him of his ancient calling and setting his face like flint against the unfolding plans that would finally hand his ancient sect the victory it had been waiting for two millennia.

He focused his attention on the ancient face, the ibis head peering down at him with a mask of pure gold and a black onyx beak, flanked by indigo ribbons, a crown of white and red feathers stretching upward. It was a true testimony to the enduring legacy of the ancient cult.

"You know all that is hidden under the heavenly vault," Sebastian whispered, quoting what Borg had taught him to pray, head bowed reverently before the stone effigy and surprising emotion rising at the memory of his dead mentor.

The man had become something of a brother to him, helping and honing his newfound purpose and spirituality. All that was gone. He was all that remained of their shared hatred, their shared mission.

He wiped his eyes. No matter. He clenched his jaw with resolve, then stood straight before Thoth and muttered, *"'Now that which has been hidden shall be revealed.'* And it shall be mine."

Lightning flashed behind him through the windows up the stairwell, illuminating the god of knowledge in flickering white light. A few seconds later, thunder rumbled in the distance, bringing Sebastian out of his trance.

He strode down the darkly lit hallway with purpose toward the gathering chamber of his new brothers, considering the sacred history of this sacred place that Borg had drilled into him.

Eighty years prior, Himmler signed a 100-year lease for Wewelsburg Castle. At the time, it was dilapidated and decaying, but he turned it into a training ground focused on occult, pagan rituals that would make it the center of the world. When the Nazis began losing the war, rather than let it fall into Allied hands, Himmler ordered the castle set ablaze and demolished. Although most of the interior was destroyed, the exterior walls were preserved and Wewelsburg was turned into a museum for reflecting on the horrors of the Nazi regime and Himmler's bizarre plan for world domination.

Until it was acquired by Borg and put to better use. Uses that would hopefully bring about a tangential end from those the Nazis themselves sought: The destruction of the Church and eradication of Christianity from the face of the planet.

A glowing light up ahead pulled Sebastian onward, orange and warm. Voices, low and incoherent, were chanting the ancient mantra he knew by heart now, having prepared for the ritual the past few days. A wicked bleating, high and heady and harried, sliced through the cacophony. He quickened his pace, pulse rising to match it with anticipation.

He reached the slightly ajar heavy golden door and pushed it open. The voices stopped as he entered. Facing him were seventeen Bird-Men, the Thirteen and four members of the Council of Five, all wearing the face of Thoth.

The god of knowledge.

"Brothers," Sebastian said.

The Bird-Men nodded in silent unison, welcoming the man who would become their new Grand Master.

Sebastian stepped into the circular cavern, emboldened by the sight of those he would soon command.

High and domed and made out of quarried stone, the room was illuminated by eight windows that flickered every so often with the storm's light. Thirteen torches displayed around the room offered a soft glow to provide the remaining light. They hung above thirteen small stone seats upon which bare-chested Bird-Men sat with ornamented shoulder drapes of gold and indigo beadwork, all wearing masks of pure gold, flanked by ribbons of indigo with beaks of black onyx.

Sebastian scanned the room like a man who owned the place. He lifted his head toward the high dome, smiling reverently at the symbol adorning its center: a swastika. Nazi in design but not in origin.

Far from a modern symbol of fascist oppression, it was an ancient religious one, taking the form of the familiar equilateral cross with its four legs bent at ninety degrees. Considered to be a sacred symbol of Eastern spiritualities, it dated back to before 2nd century BC. Small terracotta pots and ancient coins from Crete were found to have borne the symbol. And it had been used as a decorative element in various cultures stretching back to at least the Neolithic period.

Sebastian tingled every time he laid eyes upon the symbol. For it held all the divine promise of these pre-modern cultures for such a time as this.

Directly beneath the dome, in the middle of the room, was the crown jewel of the crypt: the ceremonial basin. It acted as a baptismal pool for the rite of passage into the upper echelon of the ancient order of divine knowledge and power. Tonight, it would be used for that very purpose.

His baptism into Nous as Grand Master.

Sebastian strolled further into the chamber, the dank, earthy scent and musty air making the hairs on the back of his neck stand upright in delight.

Seats were arrayed around the outer rim of the room for the Thirteen, the coterie of high-ranking associates representing the Wheel of the Year and the perfection of the earthly and heavenly alignment of seasons. Five more lined the front of the chamber, holding the Council of Five. The seats of the Pentacle, of Man.

Of God.

He took a deep, satisfying breath and strode toward a throne commanding the middle of the Pentacle seats. His chair.

He took his place among the Council at the center. To his right was the ceremonial ibis dress. It mirrored the statue of Thoth he had just passed, white and red plumes, gold mask and all.

He smiled and placed the headdress upon his head, then affixed the gold mask to his face. He removed his outer red silk robe and draped it over his chair, revealing a hardened muscular chest draped at the shoulders by an intricately beaded gold and indigo sash, his lower self wrapped in a loincloth of fine linen. As he sat down, a small muffled bleat arose from the center of the ceremonial basin.

He peered through his gold mask and over the onyx beak to the four-legged victim tied and muzzled in the center of the floor. It strained against its bindings, jaw trying to nibble at the muzzle keeping its mouth tightly closed.

Don't worry, darling. I'll make it quick...

"Brothers," Sebastian intoned, "I can safely report that we are on the cusp of greatness! Having successfully retrieved the artifact from my home, entrusted to me by the Universe, and verified the translation, I can confirm that it exists. A book from the original collection of religious texts the Church lost."

From around the room, several of the masked brethren nodded in approval.

One of the members spoke: "And what is this lost text, Sebastian?"

"It appears to be another Gospel."

A rushing of murmurs filled the chamber with echoing approval. Sebastian smiled underneath his mask at the affirmation.

"And yet," another man said from across the room, voice squeaky and grating and very Canadian, "the provenance of this bowl, as you describe it, remains a mystery. Doesn't it?"

Sebastian dipped his head absentmindedly before recognizing his weakness. He promptly stiffened and gritted his teeth before answering the senior member.

François Lefevre. A thoroughly Quebecan name if there ever was one.

And one of his chief rivals for the Grand Master crown.

Steadying himself, he said, "I understand your concerns, but they are unwarranted."

"And yet, it could be catastrophic if this is all some sort of sick joke. A ruse—"

"I said pay it no heed!" Sebastian roared.

The member leaned back against the stone backing of his pillar. The snapping of the torch flames provided the only sound in the chamber as Sebastian himself settled into his chair.

"I trust the provenance entirely," Sebastian said calmly. "Now, we must proceed with the evening ritual, ensuring our success and preparing for what is to come. We all know the sacred vow given to mankind from Thoth before he departed."

A rustling at the center of the room returned, along with a pitiful bleating.

The goat.

It was straining violently against its restraints, as if it anticipated what was impending.

Aumgn! the men chanted in unison, a prelude to their mantra.

Sebastian eased himself down from his stone seat, put his red silk robe back on, and walked slowly toward the center, his garment swishing in sync. He untied the animal and undid the muzzle.

A bleating, mournful cry instantly slipped past its lips.

Out from under his robe, Sebastian removed a jewel-encrusted athame knife passed down from Grand Master to Grand Master, from each successive generation all the way to Rudolf Borg and then to him for use in ceremonies such as this one.

In one sudden swipe, he sliced the blade across the goat's throat.

The bleating stopped as blood spilled from its neck onto the cold, hard stone floor. The animal twitched in his tight grip, then went limp, its life-force draining into the baptismal pool.

A rush of water began filling the basin, cool and clear. The blood mingled with it in crimson whorls.

François stood and made his way down next to Sebastian. "Let us christen our newest Grand Master with blood and water, declaring with one voice the Nousian Creed."

'*I believe in one secret and ineffable Lord,*' the men began to chant as one, *'and in one Star in the Company of Stars of whose fire we are created, and to which we shall return; and in one Father of Life, Mystery of Mystery, in his name Chaos, the sole vicegerent of the Sun upon the Earth; and in one Air the nourisher of all that breathes.'*

Sebastian knelt at the center of the pool, the water rising to his waist before shutting off.

'And I believe in one Earth, the Mother of us all, and in one Womb wherein all men are begotten, and wherein they shall rest, Mystery of Mystery, and in her name Babylon, Whore of Power.'

François waded into the water next to him, bringing a white linen cloth.

'And I believe in the Serpent and the Lion, Mystery of Mystery, in his name Baphomet.'

Sebastian closed his eyes, chanting along with his brothers the creed of his newfound spirituality.

'And I believe in one universal Gnostic Communion of Light and Life, Love and Liberty, the Word of whose Law is Nous that resides within.'

François brought the cloth up to Sebastian's nose, readying the baptism.

'And I believe in the communion of Nousati, the Divine Knowers of good and evil.'

François dipped him backward into the blood-stained waters as the men continued their recitation.

'And I confess one baptism of Gnostikos whereby we accomplish the miracle of incarnation and union with the Universe.'

Sebastian emerged from the water a Grand Master, marked by the blood of the sacrifice for the Universe's purposes.

'And I confess my life one, individual, and eternal that was, and is, and is to come.'

Aumgn! they chanted. Then again, deeper and deliberate with intonation.

Aumgn. And then again, capping the ceremony: *Aumgn!*

Sebastian stood and padded up from the pool along with François, taking a seat at the center of the chamber, face glistening with blood and newly christened the Grand Master of Nous. Ready to bear the mantle that was now his.

Whore of Babylon, come to devour the Church.

And he knew just how to do it.

There was a sudden knock at the door. An interrupting *thud* that violated every sacred rule that governed the chamber.

Especially during his baptism as Grand Master.

Heads turned toward one another in a whispering rush.

The thudding knock returned until one of the Thirteen nearest the door rose from his chair to unlock it.

When he did, a mousy man, hunched and visibly shaking with nervousness entered wringing his hands.

Something's happened...

"What is it?" François growled from his chair, rising back to his feet. "And it better be good. You're well aware of the rules governing—"

"It's the television, my liege," the man interrupted.

Another murmur at the breach of decorum.

The man seemed to realize his error, gasping and darting his eyes about. Those hands wringing themselves to death again.

"They've found it," he said with a rush.

"Found what?" Sebastian asked, rising as well.

"Gospel Zero."

CHAPTER 7
WASHINGTON, DC.

While Zoe fiddled with the television controls to bring up CNN, Silas sat waiting for the news at the edge of his seat. Literally.

He had scooted to the brim of the well-worn leather chair Radcliffe had commanded during several such occasions. When the Church was attacked by foes foreign and domestic. When belief in Christianity was challenged. When the survival of the faith itself hung in the balance.

And now he, Silas Grey, was the one responsible for filling those shoes to save the Church.

No pressure or anything.

He felt thrown back into the same inner panic that had gripped him in Iraq. When he wished he could go back to the way things were before he had raised his hand, stuck his neck out, and put it all on the line for a cause greater than himself. When the success or failure of a mission saving the world from no uncertain doom wasn't riding on his shoulders. When someone else was responsible for the survival of his men, or his nation, or his faith.

God, why did Radcliffe have to go and pick me for this?

In that moment, a voice surfaced in his consciousness. Clear as a bell, coming from the inside of his head.

It said: *'Before I formed you in the womb I knew you, and before you were born I consecrated you...'*

Silas took a breath, recognizing the words from the Book of Jeremiah, chapter one. He shook his head, disbelieving the words were meant for him as much as trying to chase away the voice. Probably just his subconscious doing its darndest to keep him from cycling down into a panic-filled void.

I'm not ready. I'm not able. I'm not—

Then it returned: *'My grace is sufficient for you, for my power is made perfect in weakness...'*

What the heck was going on? Were these words from God? Was he trying to send him some sort of signal, some sort of confirmation things would be alright?

But, Lord—

There it was again: *'You have come to royal dignity for just such a time as this.'*

Silas chuckled to himself at the final bit of encouragement from above. Chapter four from the Book of Esther, where Mordecai the Jew encouraged newly appointed Queen Esther that she had been strategically placed in the pagan king's court in order to help save their people. The designation of Order Master was the farthest thing from anything resembling *royal dignity*, but he understood.

Alright, Lord. Hear you loud and clear. Just please help me not to screw this up!

Whatever this is...

"Here we go..." Zoe said, snapping Silas out from his inner dialogue. "Naomi is still with us, viewing what we're seeing on the other end."

Torres dissolved away and CNN appeared, the familiar red chyron running below with the latest overseas fire, economic prediction, or presidential twitterstorm.

Along with a headline that screamed hyperbole, yet caused Silas to sink back into his seat with dread.

Purported 'Gospel Zero' Discovered, Promising to Rewrite Christianity.

"Gospel Zero?" Gapinski asked, his face twisting up with confusion. "What the—"

"Shhh..." Silas said, putting out a hand. "It's starting."

"If you're just joining us," a well-makuped anchor began, hair slicked back and glistening under too many klieg lights to count, a camera swooping in for a view, "this is a CNN breaking news report with Mara Mitchell standing by at Princeton University for what may amount to one of the greatest religious discoveries of our lifetime. Isn't that right, Mara?"

An equally well-makuped woman, hair blond and blown, lips glistening maroon, appeared on an 80-inch screen mounted next to the CNN anchor.

"That's right Kai," Mara said, smiling and nodding with enthusiasm. "We're coming to you live from Princeton where a university professor who specializes in comparative religious studies and sects of early Christianity has made a startling discovery."

Behind her stood an unmanned podium forty feet away in a large room of darkly stained wood-paneled walls, brass sconce lighting offering a warm, orange glow. The sound of camera shutters clacked away from off-camera, presumably from a phalanx of press summoned for the same discovery she was covering.

"In what some are already characterizing the discovery as Gospel Zero, the professor is said to have found evidence of another source used by the early Christian writers of the first four books found in the Christian Scriptures, known as the Gospels—apparently threatening to rewrite Christianity and our understanding of the Bible."

"That's some claim, Mara."

She chuckled. "I understand, and the professor is due anytime to explain it all."

"Can you tell us anything about the professor—a one Hartwin Braun, isn't that right?"

"Yes, that is right, Kai. Something of an up-and-comer in the fields of comparative religious and early Christian studies, the professor is the brother of another well-known Braun, Markus. Of course, that man is the enigmatic tech start-up genius known for launching the set of social media platforms on WeNet, and who has financed various humanitarian projects over the years, particularly cultural preservation. Hartwin began his tenure at Princeton over a year ago as professor of religious studies, making a name for himself with some significant finds in European antiquities and its relationship to Christianity."

Silas's ears were burning at the mention of the man who had taken his seat at the Princeton table. As much as he thought he was over getting sacked, and as much as he hated to admit it, he wasn't over it. He had a good life now in DC, with Celeste and with the Order. And considering he had free rein to research and write to his heart's content as Order Master, not to mention defending and protecting and expanding his faith...something inside of him still ached for what had been. Some wound still smarted, not having entirely healed after being passed over for tenure and then sacked.

A sudden flurry of camera shutters off-camera again and short bursts of white light brought him back to the moment.

A tall man with blond hair hanging to his shoulders in a wavy mass and high cheekbones strode across the screen to a glass podium emblazoned with Princeton's seal, a black and orange shield. The man was wearing a smart light blue suit with a bright red tie and all the airs of someone who was about to change history. He gripped the podium with both hands and eyed the audience in front of him and beyond the cameras, taking in the moment before launching his press conference.

"Here we go, Kai," Mara promptly said. "Stand by..."

Silas scooted to the edge of his seat again.

Here we go, indeed...

"Thank you for joining me on such short notice," the man started. "I apologize, for we Germans have a different view of time as you Americans." He smiled and chuckled, bright teeth gleaming as a few from the press pool echoed his laugh.

Silas wanted to puke.

"Before I unveil my little secret that is sure to rival the very best religious conspiracy thriller..."

There was that smile again, and laugh.

Silas rolled his eyes. *Get on with it, dude.*

"Beforehand, I want to tell you a story. It is about a community of spiritualists living in Galilee at the middle of the first century. For two decades or so, they had been followers of an upstart Jewish prophet who had been crucified by the Roman Empire. They had encountered him in various ways, catching glimpses of him through the few years of his ministry. From hearing his teachings unveiling knowledge about the deep truths and wisdom of life, to his rebuke of the religious elite of his day, to his ministry caring for the sick and the poor. Like many charismatic leaders, this man drew a large, devoted following, and this community in Galilee were as fervent with their devotion. A fervency that only grew after his death at the hands of the Roman Empire. For in his wise sayings and teachings they discovered one who taught them who had authority, and not as their scribes. The man had rivaled the very best Greek cynic philosophers of his day, offering sage sayings of wisdom that bested anyone else found within the Roman world."

The man paused to take a drink from a glass behind the podium. He set it back down and cleared his throat.

"Now, these followers of this Jewish Cynic sage," Hartwin went on, "were being meticulous in their oral transmission of these wise sayings and teachings. As was typical of such teachings in the first century. However, one day someone within that community recorded these sayings, putting pen to parchment to record this prophet's teachings. Sayings and teachings which found their way into two important early Christian documents."

He paused, that smile and those teeth returning as he scanned the room and panned the bank of cameras drinking up his performance.

"These early Christian documents have sat at the heart of the religion for centuries. In fact, they are found in every Christian Bible sold on Amazon. In every pew of every church throughout the world. These two documents containing the wisdom sayings recorded by this Galilean community are known as the Gospels of Matthew and Luke."

"What's he getting at, chief?" Gapinski asked.

"Not entirely sure," Silas mumbled while a dreadful suspicion began to grow.

No, it couldn't be...

"For centuries, scholars of the New Testament and origins of early Christianity have been knowing such a document exists. A Gospel Zero, as I am calling it. A ground-zero Gospel that sits at the heart of the others from which they drew their content. We scholarly types have a simple name for it. 'Q Gospel' or 'Q document,' coined from the German *Quelle* for 'source.' Although to date it hasn't been found, seemingly lost to history..."

The man paused again. But instead of taking a drink, he leaned closer, as if letting the cameras in on a secret.

"I'm here to tell you that I have discovered its existence. Q source is no longer lost to history. Gospel Zero is being a fact of history, a fact of *Christianity*. And I am expecting it will rewrite what we think about the faith, about the Church, about Jesus himself."

The room erupted with those flashing, clacking cameras again, along with a chorus of voices from the reporters gathered in the room.

Silas shook his head in disbelief. He was well aware of the theories surrounding the sources of the Gospels. The main theory being that Matthew and Luke used Mark as a basis for their historical record of Jesus' life, teachings, death, and resurrection, along with their own source material unique to each Gospel account plus another source called Q, like Hartwin said.

A Gospel Zero.

Had to give it to the man. Gospel Zero carried a nice ring to it that would surely play to the religious conspiracy thriller crowd. Not to mention the secular media who were all too quick to believe fanciful tales of alternative Gospels and Christian texts in the interest of undermining the faith. Especially during the Easter Season.

Reminded Silas of the Gospel of Jesus' Wife that had sent the media into a frenzied state of glee. Except that had turned out to be a forgery and this one, Gospel Zero, was a known entity to the scholarly community. At least in theory.

And Hartwin Braun had found it.

"Theory no more..." Silas mumbled as a voice rose above the din of the questioning shouts. Mara, the CNN anchor.

"Excuse me, professor! Professor Hartwin, where did this manuscript come from? Where did you find it? And who else has seen it, to verify its authenticity?"

The others quieted down, seemingly interested in the answers, the woman echoing their own questions.

Hartwin took a breath then went to say something but stopped, seemingly considering her question.

"Alright, I am willing to indulge. But just this one question, because it is being germane to my announcement. Alongside this discovery, there was another document. One that seems to verify the Evangelizers' use of Gospel Zero and goes even further..."

The man took another drink before continuing, then leaned forward and said, "This other document is being a missing piece to a list of approved New Testament books well known to scholars that has been at the heart of the Christian Bible canon for centuries, only this one is adding others that have been tossed aside in favor of the majority we carry in our Bibles today, as well as mentioning our Gospel Zero."

The room took a collective breath, as if breathing in the added revelation. Then it sighed with another round of cacophonous questioning.

"Alright, alright. Quiet please," Hartwin said, raising his hands and flashing his toothy grin again. Clearly relishing the attention and excitement surrounding the revelation of his discoveries.

When the room quieted, he continued, "Now, why this Gospel has been hidden or even suppressed by the Church, and whether its contents might be posing a threat to Christianity, it is being hard to say until it is fully analyzed. In one day's time, I aim to gather a handful of the best experts in such matters throughout the world to help us put together the pieces to verify Gospel Zero in the interest of better informing our religious dialogue and the Christian faith itself. Until then, stay tuned. That is all."

With that, the man strode from view.

And strode into a new chapter of the Church that had the potential to bring the house of cards down for good.

WEWELSBURG, GERMANY.

Sebastian stood statue still, arms folded and jaw locked

with a mixture of irritation and dread at the meaning of what he and his brothers had just witnessed.

Someone had beaten him to the punch. And just as he assumed the mantle of Grand Master.

His brothers would not be pleased. Would demand answers and a response. Would exact a pound of vengeance for the turn.

Even from him.

The news conference ended, and the BBC cut to a panel of anchor "experts" chattering on about the news from across the pond at Princeton, the ever-so-sensationally British slogan blazing hot across the bottom of the screen.

Is Christianity Done For? New Gospel Hints at Conspiracy of Suppression.

Leave it up to the British press to sensationalize a banal act of scholarship.

"Well, well, well, would you look at that. It appears we have ourselves a rival," François quipped, voice laced with a certain amount of glee and voicing what the others were probably themselves thinking. "And at the most inopportune time in Nous's history."

Sebastian took a breath and clenched his jaw tighter, continuing to stare at the television mounted in the command center of cut stone in the belly of Castle Wewelsburg, a BBC commentator continuing to chatter away after he muted the sound.

Indeed, it did appear they had a new rival. Though what that meant and who it was was anyone's guess.

He imagined his boorish brother wasn't far behind. Especially after that doozy of a revelation.

Which meant their work had just become far more complicated.

Of course, they had gotten a whiff of such a rival during the early morning hours on America's East Coast, news of the break-in at his home reaching him that afternoon. Thankfully, he had had the foresight to secret away his precious bowl artifact in the middle of the night and whisk it across the Atlantic to safe harbor.

The room remained quiet as workstation monitors arrayed around the room hummed and glowed with status reports on various Nous projects spanning the globe. He had cleared the room serving as the nerve center for Nous when the conclave from the chamber arrived for the breaking news out of America. Now it was silent.

Sebastian could feel all eyes looking at him from behind. Waiting for him to explain. Waiting for him to fix it.

Or else...

Suddenly, his veins flooded with the ice-cold realization that it was all riding on him. The future of Nous, the future of the collective human consciousness' century-long drive to wrench themselves out from underneath the suffocating confines of the Church's teachings and power.

His folded arms began to tremble at his breast. He clenched them tight, terrified someone had seen his show of weakness.

I am not ready for this...

Didn't matter. Not in the slightest.

So he turned around and faced his brothers, a sea of ancient ibis Bird-Men staring back at him from among the trappings of modern mission control.

He took a breath, then began to address them.

"Obviously, this complicates our plans. Although it also provides a modicum of confirmation for what had already revealed itself to us."

"Yes, Grand Master, obviously," François said, his voice laced with a well-duh tone that purged Sebastian of his cold dread and replaced it with a burning rage at his insolence. "The question is, what are we going to do about it?"

Tilting his head back and eyeing the room, Sebastian took a step forward. "Here's what we're going to do about it. Hartwin

Braun never said they discovered Gospel Zero itself, only proof of its existence. Which confirms what the ancient bowl from the ancestors of old themselves had hidden away in their sacred script."

"Meaning what?" François said with a challenging sneer.

He took another step toward him, puffing his chest out slightly as if ready to go to fists and drilling him with eyes of ice that surprisingly caused the arrogant nitwit to recoil slightly and dip his head.

"I meant no disrespect, Grand Master," the man said softly. "Only to inquire of the meaning of all of this in light of our own designs."

Good. Whimper. Recoil. Dip your head and beg for mercy.

Sebastian ignored him and swept the rest of the brothers with his gaze, his confidence growing after the minor victory.

"What this means, brothers, is that the hunt is on for Gospel Zero. And I know just what we are going to do about it. Beginning with that weasel, Hartwin Braun."

CHAPTER 8
WASHINGTON, DC.

I have no freaking clue what we're going to do about this.

Silas went to reach for the bottle of Macallan but thought against tapping into the Order's stash of scotch a second time that morning. Best to keep his wits about him for the road ahead. Even though his mouth watered for the heavy, astringent, oaky caramel liquid and his brain screamed for relief from the anxiety and stress and fear of what was waiting for him on that road.

Back turned to the people who were relying on him to lead the Order—to lead *them*—and figure out what the heck was going on, he popped a K-Cup into the Keurig mounted on the minibar for just such times and placed a mug under its spout. A minute later, he retrieved the hot brew, the scent of earthy spice hitting his nose on an updraft of steam. He took a swig, closed his eyes, and sighed.

I'm not ready for this...

Too bad. No choice. As the good Lord above suggested, he'd been chosen in the womb, empowered by his grace, for such a time as this.

Part of him believed it. Most of him didn't.

Regardless, he just wished the good Lord had seen fit to choose and empower some other sucker for such a time as this.

Silas returned to his chair and sat.

"So what's the plan, chief?" Gapinski asked, voicing what everyone else was collectively feeling. "And where d'you get the coffee? I'm running on fumes here."

Silas took a sip and nodded toward the minibar. "Help yourself."

Gapinski excused himself and Celeste told him to bring her back an Earl Grey tea.

"I'm sorry," Torres spoke up from the screen, having been brought back online after the CNN report ended, "but can I ask a basic, knuckleheaded question?"

Silas took another sip. "What's that?"

"What's the big deal? Why is this supposed finding, this Gospel Zero as it's been called—what's the big deal?"

"The big deal, Naomi," Victor Zarruq replied, "is that if proven to be true, that Q has been discovered, it would be one of the greatest findings in Christian archaeology since the Dead Sea Scrolls were discovered in the 1940s. But the bigger issue is how controversial it is to begin with."

"You're referring to the Synoptic Problem, isn't that right?" Silas said.

"Correct."

"The whatchamacallit?" Gapinski asked, bearing two hot Keurig drinks.

"The Synoptic Problem," Silas replied. "A problem that's not really a problem relating to the Gospels known as the Synoptic Gospels."

"Oh, yeah. Matthew, Mark, and Luke."

The bishop smiled. "Impressive."

Gapinski took a swig of his coffee and grinned. "What can I say. I paid attention during my Southern Baptist Sunday school hour. And my grandpappy was an SBC preacher." His face fell.

"That is, until he was blown to smithereens by terrorist whack jobs a year ago..."

Zarruq's own face fell, and he rested a hand on the man's knee. "I recall hearing about the unfortunate events last year. I am sorry for your loss."

Gapinski nodded and took another swig. "Sorry to be a downer. And sorry to detract from the mission at hand. So these Synoptic Gospels. What about 'em?"

Silas shifted in his chair. "These Gospels apart from John's Gospel all share parallels in many ways, and some differences."

"Such as?"

"Well, lots of passages appear in Matthew and Luke that are also shared with Mark. But then their order in the narratives often differ. And some of the teachings are worded differently or have a different emphasis. All of it has led many to claim some sort of problem with the Gospels. That they are unreliable and that there wasn't agreement in the Church about what Jesus taught or the history was wrong so all of it must be suspect."

"Which completely misses the entire point of the Gospels!" Bishop Zarruq exclaimed in a huff, folding his arms on his belly and shaking his head.

"What do you mean, Victor?" Celeste asked, sipping from her mug of Earl Grey and wincing. She groaned, "This is far from a proper cuppa..."

Zarruq took a breath and settled back into his chair, as if preparing for an extended lecture.

Silas couldn't help but smile. Reminded him of Radcliffe in more ways than one. The man was growing on him, especially considering the wealth of biblical and theological knowledge he seemed to possess. Perhaps him showing up wasn't such a bad thing after all.

The bishop said, "You must realize that the genre of the Gospels isn't like modern historiography or biography. The

Evangelists, Matthew, Mark, Luke, and John, were all taking actual events and teachings preserved in the oral tradition and memory of the believing community and shaping them into a narrative that told very specific aspects of the Jesus story in order to proclaim the good news of God's crazy love in Jesus' life, death, resurrection, and exaltation. Matthew, for instance, emphasizes Jesus' Jewishness, and his completion of the Jewish story and its anticipation of the Messiah. Which is why his account of the famous Sermon on the Mount differs slightly from Luke's, in not only content but location in the narrative. Matthew portrays Jesus as a sort of new Moses."

"Fascinating…" Celeste said.

"Scholars have pointed out that the literary style of the Gospels mirrors the first-century genre known as *bioi*."

"Sort of like biographies?" Gapinski asked.

"Something like that. It was an ancient method of narrating a person's deeds and words, particularly just after their death for the purpose of revealing the validity and true character of those deeds and words. Typically, there is only a bare chronological structure of their birth or their start to a public life. Then, between that start and their narrated death, the author fills in the gaps with anecdotal stories and sayings about the person, with a particular focus on their words and deeds. The climax of the *bioi* account is their death, and all that it signals for their life. It is understood the Gospels used the same sources to give their account about Jesus."

"If that don't scream the story of Jesus, I don't know what does!"

Zarruq chuckled. "Indeed, it does! The form was used by such ancients as Plutarch and Tacitus around the same time the Gospels were written. Us moderns are incredibly arrogant and not a wee bit ethnocentric to insist ancient Near East expressions of history conform to our modern Western ones."

"That's quite fascinating, Victor," Celeste said. "But what does this have to do with this Gospel Zero nonsense?"

The bishop clasped his hands together and scooted to the edge of his chair. "Right. Well, around 230 verses are shared between the Gospels of Matthew and Luke that aren't in Mark."

"So? What does that matter, that they aren't in Mark?"

"Because the scholarly consensus is that both Matthew and Luke used Mark's account of Jesus as a basis for their own accounts. Some of their material came from their own sources, the ones Matthew and Luke used for their accounts, whether oral or written. Then there was Mark, which scholars of all ranks and religious persuasions acknowledge as a sort of Markan priority. Where the Evangelist—from North Africa, mind you—where Mark's account formed a foundation for the others to build off from."

"Mind blown," Gapinski said. "And a little thrown off."

Zarruq chuckled. "No need to be thrown, Matthew. This idea isn't new, and this isn't a problem. It was common in the Greco-Roman world to collect utterances of revered sages for use elsewhere. Even Jewish wisdom literature of the day did this. Which means the fact that Matthew and Luke relied on others when they wrote their Gospel isn't unusual or an anomaly. It's not like the Gospel writers were divine transcribers."

"They weren't? I'd always thought it was like God took over their brains like some host from *Aliens*."

The bishop gave the man a quizzical look, then shook his head. "At any rate, don't misunderstand me," he said, shifting in his chair and wagging a finger. "God was absolutely, fundamentally part of the transmission process of Scripture. The Bible makes that clear. The apostle Paul tells us in 2 Timothy 3:16 that *'All Scripture is inspired by God and is useful for teaching, for reproof, for correction, and for training in righteousness so that everyone who belongs to God may be proficient, equipped for every good work.'*

Another way of putting *inspired* is that Scripture is *God-breathed*."

"Still sounds like *Aliens* to me."

"God himself has spoken to us through the Holy Scriptures," the bishop went on. "The Good Book is God's book, and we measure our story and our message against this collection of books. However, at some level, the canon of Scripture was formed by people. But we can also understand that the canon was formed by the Holy Spirit, by God himself. The authors of these books wrote exactly what God intended them to write, by the power of the Holy Spirit. Which means these words are *God's* words."

"But it was also the product of people, as you say," Torres said. "And a long line of the *men* sort of people, if I might add. Jesus, the Twelve Disciples, the apostles, the Church Fathers, the Popes."

"What are you getting at?" Silas asked.

"I'm just saying, plenty of Roman Europeans had quite the hand in forming what we've come to understand as Christianity—from our sacred text to our sacred dogma."

Zarruq leaned back and laughed, head thrown back and belly jiggling from the force of his response.

The others in the room looked at each other with confusion, and Torres folded her arms in an irritated, on-screen huff.

"That is being a good one, Naomi. Liberal stuff and nonsense that is," the bishop said with a dismissive hand-wave. "And I mean to be neither dismissive nor offensive, but the notion that Christianity is a Roman, European, and white male construct is a complete historical inaccuracy perpetuated by the very people you're accusing of forming some sort of Christian cabal! White European men, and not a small amount of white American men, too, might I add, have been perpetuating that lie for at least a century, if not longer."

The man chuckled to himself again, his bushy beard

extending into a widened smile and fluttering about as he shook his head.

"That conversation is for another time and day," he went on, "but let me be clear about this one we are having about the Holy Scriptures: We can be confident that what we have *is what God wanted us to have*. God through the Holy Spirit guided the formation of Scripture. Because, after all, he was part of authoring them! Regardless of the sources of the Gospels. Yet, while God primarily authored these books, he did so through the full participation of human authors under the guidance of their Jewish spiritual traditions, culture, and specific contexts."

"Divine inspiration," Silas added.

"Exactly!" Zarruq exclaimed, nearly jumping out from his chair. "This is exactly what the Church has meant by its teaching of divine inspiration. God influenced the authors of the Bible to communicate to humanity exactly what he wanted to communicate to us about himself, about us, about our story and God's Story. Divine inspiration means that God himself is saying something through the authors and through their writings, regardless of how the writers arranged their material and who they relied upon to account for it."

"You're speaking of Matthew, Mark, Luke, John, and this Q character?" Gapinski asked.

"And Paul," Silas added, "Peter, James, Jude, and the author of Hebrews. Not to mention each of the authors of the texts within the Jewish Scriptures, what we Christians call the Old Testament."

"Understand this," Zarruq said, scooting to the edge of his seat. "God himself is saying something in the Bible. Through the Bible God has spoken. Which means the Bible *itself* means something. This is crucial, because everything about our faith hinges on whether the Bible really is God's Word."

"That's brilliant, Victor," Celeste said, shifting in her seat and glancing at Silas. "Really, it is. However, I believe the topic of the hour is what to make of this Gospel Zero discovery."

"And what to do about it," Silas added.

Zarruq frowned and shook his head. "Forgive my tangent. Yes, the task at hand. What I meant to suggest with my monologue is that it isn't a problem if such a so-called Gospel Zero exists. A literary relationship between the Gospels of Matthew, Luke, and Mark makes total sense, with Mark serving as a foundational priority upon which Matthew and Luke constructed their narratives about Jesus, with another source added into the mix."

"But what is this so-called Gospel Zero business to begin with?" Celeste asked again.

Zarruq answered, "What it means is that something like a quarter of Matthew and a fifth of Luke share material with a secondary source outside of Mark."

"Gospel Zero?" Gapinski said.

"Or this Q source business?" Celeste added.

Silas nodded. "I wouldn't frame it as Gospel Zero, but I know it will sure sell well in the media."

"Already is," Gapinski said, face illuminated by the soft glow of his phone. "The hashtag #GospelZero is trending like a Kardashian."

"Are you on Twitter, Hoss?" Torres asked.

Gapinski scoffed. "Twitter? That's so, like, 2009. WeShare is where it's at with all the kiddos these days."

"For us uninformed ones, Victor, can you bring us up to speed on the specifics of Q, or Gospel Zero, or whatever we're supposed to be calling it?"

"Certainly, Naomi. The non-Markan resource in the so-called 'double tradition,' which suggests two sources informed Matthew and Luke, is regarded as this hypothetical Q document that's apparently now trending across social media."

"Coined from the German *Quella* for source, as Hartwin said?" Celeste asked.

"That's right. Only problem is, the exact wording, community, and stages of composition for such a document is completely unknown. Q has always been considered hypothetical by scholars without an actual document and with only reconstructions from existing material."

"Until now..." Silas said.

The truth of it seemed to wallop the room, quieting them with the force of it, the sound of the crackling, popping fire taking the place of conversation.

"The convocation of the minds..." Silas said, finally breaking the silence.

"What was that, love?" Celeste said.

He looked up, eyes widening slightly and blushing from her casual reference to their dating relationship. Recovering, he said, "Just before everything went down at Sebastian's house, I received a phone call from Miles."

"Your old academic assistant, from Princeton?"

"That's right."

"But what on earth for?"

"Phoned me on behalf of Hartwin."

"The Robert Langdon wannabe?" Gapinski quipped.

Silas smiled. "That would be the one. Totally forgot until now, but apparently he's gathering a few other scholars and Christian voices in the field for a meeting."

Celeste said, "A meeting? What kind of meeting?"

"Wouldn't say. But after what we just saw, I'd bet it's about Gospel Zero. Has to be."

"Who else did the man invite?"

"Me, some New Testament archaeological expert named Noland Rotberg."

"Noland Rotberg?" Torres interrupted. "The Harvard prof styling himself as the next Dr. Jones of the Bible, you sure?"

"Pretty positive. Why, you know him?"

"You could say that..."

"Do tell, Naomi," Celeste said.

She sat up straighter and took a breath. "We ran into each other a time or two in my former life. Good guy, if not a bit of a showboat. But he sure knows his stuff when it comes to ancient Christian background."

"Anyone else?"

Silas said. "Just some flunked-out evangelical megapastor-turned-WeTuber, Trevor Bohls."

"Oh, yeah. The guy who made a big stink about the afterlife a few years ago," Gapinski said.

"That'd be the one. But not the last."

"And who's that?" Celeste said.

Silas took a breath and glanced at the screen. "Me and Torres."

"Me?" Torres exclaimed, leaning toward her screen.

"Yep."

"But why?"

"Don't know. My guess is he's heard about your experience in the fields of archaeology and anthropology and wants your help verifying whatever it is he's found. But I'm not sure he's aware of your new place of employ with the Order. Or our relationship for that matter."

"Why do you suppose that's the case?" Celeste asked.

"Because Miles knew I worked for the Order as Master, which is why Hartwin wanted me. But he didn't ask me to bring Torres along for the ride. Just invited me at Hartwin's request, and then listed the other invitees, including Torres."

"As if we had no relation like the rest," Torres said.

Silas nodded. "Exactly."

"Something we can use to our advantage, then," Celeste said.

"What do you mean?"

She turned to Silas. "Have a think about it. If you both playact as though you don't know one another, then you two can work individually to tackle the mysterious Gospel Zero, while also coordinating your response should anything run amiss. And given the potential magnitude of the discovery, whatever it is at this point, two heads working behind the scenes to ascertain what the bloody hell is going on will tip the scales in our favor."

Silas flashed her a smile. He wouldn't have thought of that angle. Boy, was there a ton to learn in this new gig as Order Master. Knowing all the ins and outs of the Bible and Christian history and doctrine on top of the threats angling against the Church and all the possible contingencies and strategic responses SEPIO needed to plan—felt like too much to handle, and he felt totally unprepared for it. At least Celeste was at his side to help him navigate it all. About the only thing keeping him from lapsing back into the kinds of anxiety-fueled depressive bouts he'd had after his tours with the Rangers in the Middle East.

"Guess that settles it then," Silas said. "Torres and I will head to Princeton."

"You want me to abandon my work here in Libya?" Torres said, voice rising with a tinge of indignation. "But we're so close."

"I know how you must feel about this, but we're activating SEPIO on this mystery given the stakes. And Miles should be making contact with you soon anyway, if he hasn't already. I hardly think you can say no."

Torres folded her arms then nodded and sighed with resignation.

"And remember," Silas went on, "we don't know each other. Crucial we're free to go at this from two separate angles, but as a team."

"Understood."

Celeste added, "Silas is right. If Hartwin gets a whiff you two are coordinating to undermine whatever it is he has cooked up, I imagine he will call it all off and we'll be none the wiser. Which I don't quite fancy."

"What about us?" Gapinski said. "Can't just leave us twiddling our thumbs on the sidelines here."

"We'll follow up on the MI6-identified hostile and keep on the trail of the box man tattoo. Should keep us plenty busy."

Silas nodded and stood. So did the others.

It was go time. Again.

This time with Silas at the helm of the SEPIO mission and the Church's future.

He just prayed to the good Lord above he didn't screw things up.

CHAPTER 9
PRINCETON UNIVERSITY.

A bitter wind and biting rain slapped against Silas's face in assaulting sheets as he hustled past the Princeton University Chapel, its decorative and theatrical style of Gothic Revival architecture reminding him of the Washington National Cathedral back home. It also mocked him, a vivid reminder of the campus he once knew as home until he was forced to vacate it, rendering him homeless. Like a child orphaned without recourse, without a say in the matter. Thankfully, the good Lord had seen fit to adopt him into a new family, one not of his choosing but damn well the best he'd probably ever had, even apart from the military. And his own flesh and blood.

He glanced down at a faded fake gold-plated Seiko watch clinging to his wrist, a high school graduation gift from Dad pockmarked from three tours of duty with the Rangers across the Middle East. He picked up his pace, the rain having the same idea. He was going to be late for the rendezvous with Hartwin and the others. A constant theme when he was a professor at the university, so why stop now.

Yet the last thing he wanted was to start off on the wrong foot, given the potential stakes involved for the Church. The more he thought about it all the past evening after the news dropped about Gospel Zero, the more he was filled with a growing sense of dread about what it could mean for his faith. Because what do you do if all you've ever known about the Bible was a lie?

Which is why SEPIO wasn't taking any chances.

Early that morning, he had boarded an Order-issued jet and flown to Princeton Airport, a family-owned general aviation field that would suit them fine. They'd managed to hit every rough patch of air on their way over, reminding Silas how much he hated flying and causing a bit of delay coming in. Hence his hustle across campus in the pouring rain without an umbrella and his tardiness at arriving to his old office.

After they'd ended the call, Torres begrudgingly jumped on her own Order-issued jet for the flight back to the States after receiving her own invitation from Miles. Hadn't heard a peep from her since they'd ended the call. But from the plane logs he had access to as Order Master, he knew she'd complied. Wouldn't have blamed her if she'd continued her protest offline or just flat disobeyed his orders. He knew he would be spittin' vinegar if it were him, being in the throes of a promising dig and hot on the heels of an archaeological find that could impact how the Church understands her history. But she was a good troop, and with any luck she had already landed and was already waiting for Silas at Hartwin's office or wasn't far behind.

Celeste and Gapinski stayed behind to work on the case of the mysterious hostile with the equally mysterious box man tattoo, and how it all connected to his brother. They knew it had something to do with the missing artifact, the Mandean bowl that Torres had described, given what the downed hostile had revealed in the tussle. But what exactly was anyone's guess.

Silas didn't say anything about it before he left—mostly because he had no proof and he didn't want to look silly before the group—but some deep-down dread was flaring up a warning in his lizard brain that it was all connected to Hartwin and the Gospel Zero nonsense. Didn't know what in the slightest. But knowing Sebastian was in the upper echelons of Nous —probably as their Supreme Leader now that Borg was toast— and knowing the purported Gospel could seriously impact the Church and Christian faith, no doubt his apostatized twin was close by. Maybe even behind it all.

Silas continued on, enduring the continued onslaught, thunder rumbling in the near distance as cold rain water dripped down his face, a static sweetness falling on his tongue that both delighted and chilled. Boy did he hope Miles had a pot of coffee ready, because he could—

He stopped short when he saw it up ahead. Another mocking monument from his past emerging through the dawning darkness and sheeting rain.

A stone building of red brick wrapped in ivy looking like all the others strewn across campus.

His former lecture hall.

Silas slowed to a stop. Shivering in the spring rain, he stood underneath a well-endowed maple tree staring at the building, the rain soaking him under the orange glow of a sidewalk lamp, but he didn't care. Emotion suddenly, unexpectedly—and embarrassingly—rose in his throat at the sight. Thought he was over it all—the professional mortification, the personal shame.

Guess not...

The hundred-seat lecture hall was a time capsule of decades gone by containing the memories of fascinating lectures on Proust and Freud, logarithms and algorithms, thermodynamics and microeconomics that had shaped the minds of nearly three hundred graduating classes of America's brightest. It had also witnessed his lectures on religious relics and comparative religion. As did the hundreds of students over the years who had sat under his teaching.

He especially wondered how they were getting along.

Whether his favorites, like the moppy-haired Jordan Peeler, had explored more of the faith he had tried to let slip through his lectures and interactions with students. Whether they continued on the journey of seeking answers to life's deep questions. Whether they had met Jesus personally along the way.

Without him.

Silas swallowed hard and coughed, then wiped moisture from his eyes. Whether from the continued onslaught or the sudden rise in emotion he wasn't sure. Didn't want to know.

Whatever. Water under the bridge.

He swallowed hard and pulled the collar of his charcoal wool coat growing increasingly waterlogged tighter against his neck for relief, then continued hustling along. It was barely working. He kept his head down and angled into the wind as it whipped the rain something fierce.

Then slammed into someone tall and equally hunched in the onslaught.

The two startled before promptly apologizing.

Silas looked up. His face fell at the sight.

Mathias McIntyre. His department dean.

Former department dean.

Just great...

"Si—Silas Grey?" The man said with disbelief, the graying caterpillars chilling above his eyes turning inward with a mixture of disbelief and disgust.

It took everything within Silas to not shrink from the man who had sacked him. But he stood straight, quite satisfied to have run into his old dean, actually. And there was nothing McIntyre could do about it.

"The one and only," Silas said with a grin.

"But, but, but how?" McIntyre stammered.

"Well, I took a plane from DC to Princeton Airport and then an Uber—"

"No, I mean how are you here? *Why* are you here? You were fired!"

Silas's neck grew warm, his nostrils flared as he took in a stabilizing breath. "Why don't you ask your new Golden Boy, Professor Braun," he grunted before pushing past the man toward his old office.

"But, but, but..." Dean McIntyre continued stammering in the rain, the sound of his protests drowned by another clap of thunder.

"What a jack—"

Silas stopped himself, the voice of Miles chiding him. And Celeste.

No need to spoil his satisfaction with a foul mouth, she would have said.

Good point, darling.

Soon he reached the old building of stone and red brick that had held his old office. Surprisingly, McIntyre hadn't followed him. Probably calling Hartwin demanding an explanation, or Campus Security. Either way, it was go time.

He hefted open the heavy walnut door that led inside, its hinges protesting with an echoey groan. It smelled of a damp basement housing old books and vintage furniture and worn-out clothes still bearing their cheap cologne. He reached the stairs to the second floor and ambled toward his old office, his heart keeping pace with each step wanting to just get it over with.

Its door was cracked open, and the familiar red carpet gleaming under the soft orange glow of desk lamps, the scent of cinnamon stick wafting outside from one of Millie's candles.

Silas took a breath and pushed through.

The first thing he noticed was a tall perky blonde sitting where petite Millie had once sat, hair wrapped in a bun that meant business. Torres was seated in a visitor chair just outside his former office, chatting it up with Miles who was standing with his back to the door and wearing his typical starched white shirt and bow tie and cardigan sweater.

Torres glanced at him and stood, causing Miles to turn around.

His face instantly brightened, eyes seeming to mist over at the sight of his old boss and mouth growing wide with delight.

"Professor!" he exclaimed. "My goodness, you're soaked! Good to see you, old friend."

"Good to see you too, Miles," he said, embracing his former assistant who was more a friend. "And enough of this professor business."

Miles let go and scoffed. "Oh stop, yourself. You'll always be professor to me."

"Fair enough."

He removed his wool coat, which Miles promptly retrieved and hung on a wooden coat rack. He thanked the man and stepped toward Torres, hand extended. "And you are?"

Took her a second, but she promptly returned the favor. "Naomi Torres."

"Ahh, yes. From that rather renowned archaeological excavation unit out of Miami, isn't that right?"

She smiled. "That's right."

"Good to meet you." He smiled back then eyed the small anteroom, nodding to the unknown young lady. "Where's Millie?"

Miles's face fell. "Didn't you hear?"

"No, what happened?"

"She took a nasty fall several months ago."

"Oh, man..."

"Broke her hip, and she has been laid up ever since."

Silas frowned and shook his head. Guess it's true. The world really does move on without you.

"What a shame," he said.

"Indeed. But Angela here has been a godsend," Miles said, gesturing toward the blonde.

The woman waved a curt greeting before returning back to her keyboard.

"Professor Hartwin will be just a moment," he went on, "if you want to head inside his...well, your old office. Running a bit late with the other three invitees, but shouldn't be long."

"Three? I thought you only mentioned those Rotberg and Bohls characters."

"Hartwin brought in another fellow onboard. Not sure of his name, but I seem to remember him visiting a time or two." He stiffened and cocked his head. "Actually, when you were still teaching."

Silas furrowed his brow. "Really? Who?"

Miles frowned. "Oh, professor, you know I can't remember every Tom, Dick, or Harry you dragged in here. Why don't you make yourself at home and find out. He'll be back in a minute."

Silas nodded and pushed through the cracked door to his former office, Torres trailing. It was like stepping through Alice's looking glass: foreign yet all too familiar.

Same size and shape as he left it. A box painted cream with high ceilings and walls jammed pack with books. Although it still smelled of fresh paint, which irritated him. He'd been trying to get them to repaint the thing for years, worried that its flaking chips were a holdover from the days of lead-based paint. To no avail. Carpet had been replaced, too. By freshly stained honey oak floors, crowned by a tasteful crimson rug, patterned by indigo and gold whorls with cream fringing.

Silas smirked. *Probably got the thing at World Market. Or, more likely, while gallivanting around the world trying to disprove Christianity.*

He walked farther inside, his face falling at the rest of the changes that had scrubbed away his memory from the place.

No messy stacks of books piled around the room. No well-worn burgundy leather chair, one of the few things he took from his late father's estate. No chipped coffee mug stained from years of use with the crimson logo of his Harvard alma mater emblazoned on its face, the morning brew growing stale and cold.

And no football-sized feline furball bounding up onto his lap, nearly sending the remaining brew onto his checkered dress shirt. Eventually Barnabas would bound off Silas's lap and trot out of his office to leave him to his research. Sometimes he missed his old friend, but knew he was in good hands with Miles.

"Nice digs," Torres mumbled, eyeing the room before plopping down in an overstuffed cloth chair.

Silas ignored her, absentmindedly adjusting his tie and unbuttoning his blue blazer as he continued to scan the room. An envelope lying on the desk caught his attention, jumping his mind to that fateful day when he received the expensive-looking, cream-colored envelope. *'Dr. Silas Grey'* had been scrawled across its face in black ink, written by a fountain pen with the familiar gait of his former mentor, with a peculiar warning that didn't make sense until that fateful call that would forever change his life.

Then there was the middle-desk drawer, where a bottle of little blue pills had once nested. Their memory needled his consciousness, and his mouth began to salivate a Pavlovian response as the shame and weight and anxiety of the moment pressed in against him. Just one of his precious friends and a glass of water would make it go away.

'My grace is sufficient for you...' a still small voice spoke, the Holy Spirit bringing calm to his inner chaos.

Silas startled at the sound of more life entering the office. He glanced at Torres and stiffened.

And then the man himself stepped inside.

Hartwin Braun, wearing a brown tweed jacket that

screamed cliché and a grin that made Silas's skin crawl with irritation.

"Dr. Grey, I presume?" the man said, extending his hand with a greeting and standing taller than he would like.

Silas stood straighter to compensate and took it, squeezing the hand firmly and fixing the man with a grin of his own.

"That would be me."

Hartwin squeezed back, as if instantly dialing into the game of machoism, the two holding their grips a beat longer than was polite.

Then they let go, each withdrawing to their respective corners of the proverbial ring. For now.

Torres stood, extending her own hand and giving Silas a sideways glance.

"Ahh, and you must be the venerable Naomi Torres," Hartwin said, grasping her hand and offering it a peck. "I have been hearing all about your exploits. You come highly recommended."

She giggled at the show, her cheeks flushing and her free hand pushing a lock of hair behind an ear.

Silas wanted to puke. But he held it together. "We've just been getting to know each other ourselves. Haven't we, Naomi?"

"Uh, yeah, that's right," Torres said. "What an honor to finally meet the professor I've heard so much about. Especially those monumental discoveries about the Shroud of Turin!"

Laying it on a little thick, but it would do as a cover.

Hartwin grinned. "Yes, well, aren't we all pleased to finally meet the man, the myth, the legend known as Silas Grey. I especially fancied a rendezvous with the man I replaced."

Replaced?!

Silas said nothing, merely echoing the man's grin.

"So where are the others?" Torres said. "We appear to be a few shy."

Hartwin shuffled around to his desk and crouched next to it. "Waiting just down the hall…"

Silas peered over his shoulder.

The guy's got a safe?

He rolled his eyes with an equal amount of irritation and envy. He never had a safe. Though he never had use for one. But still…

"Just came to retrieve the final clue for our little adventure…" Hartwin went on. There was a *click*. "Ahh! Here we go."

He withdrew a large wooden box, polished and closed. On its face was a hydrometer, giving the impression the box was something like a humidor for holding cigars.

Hartwin stood and smiled, bearing the box with both hands. It was larger than it first appeared, the size of a massive tome. Reminded Silas of his old family Catholic Bible, an eight-pound brick wrapped in faded cream cloth passed down through the years.

What in the world?

The man smiled and shuffled back around the desk. "Right this way."

Silas glanced at Torres, who shrugged before following after the man. He followed her as Hartwin led them past Miles and the new gal, out of the office, and then down the narrow hallway flanked by the office doors of his former colleagues.

They reached a conference room. Hartwin opened the door, standing at its threshold.

"After you," he said, extending a hand inside and fixing Silas with those icy eyes again.

Silas nodded. Saying nothing, he let Torres enter first then strode past the man inside after her.

When they did, Torres let out a short gasp of surprise.

He gave a similar start at who was waiting for them.

The third guy.

CHAPTER 10

"Grant Chrysostom?" Silas said with dumbfounded surprise, pushing past Torres to mitigate any disastrous slips of the tongue as a cold dread washed over him.

He and Grant knew each other from their days at Harvard. Torres and Grant had known each other from a previous life as well, apparently even dating or something.

All before an operative with a vigilante special forces unit with the Mormon Church came barging in looking for something Grant stole at a dig he'd been freelancing his services for. Which sent Silas launching headlong into another operation with SEPIO for the Order of Thaddeus. And with a political conspiracy to boot during a presidential election.

One in a series of hair-brained mission that led him to his current lot in life.

So the three of them, along with Celeste and Gapinski, had worked closely together to solve the SEPIO case. Except no one in the room could know that bit of history if he and Torres were going to keep their cover.

Not good...

"Dude!" the man said, sounding like he had just stepped off

a California beach. Although, surprisingly not looking like it as he did the last time he'd seen the man. Dirty blond hair was trimmed close to the sides with bangs and top styled high, and he had shed the beachwear for something more corporate. White shirt and skinny black tie, charcoal blazer, dark denim. Never seen him so pruned and proper looking.

"I see you've traded in your long sleeve t-shirt, jeans, and Vans for corporate threads."

Grant walked toward his old pal with arms wide open. "Figured I should finally grow up and get a real job."

Silas smiled, and the two embraced in a bear hug. "Doing what exactly?"

"I take it you two know each other?" Hartwin interrupted.

"You could say that."

"Small world. I imagine you have met the others, Dr. Chrysostom, but our other newcomer is Naomi Torres."

Grant chuckled nervously and ran a hand through his styled hair. "Yeah, I'm aware."

Hartwin turned to him with shock. "You are?"

"Oh, yes. He's well aware," Torres said, folding her arms and widening her stance, flashing him a look that could kill twice over.

"Let's just say," Grant offered, "we've run in the same circles once or twice since post-grad school."

"Yes," Torres said, shifting her legs as she refolded her arms. "You could say that."

"Fancy that..." Hartwin said.

"That's crazy!" Silas said with dramatic shock. "You know me and you know her. And the three of us never met before. That's crazy!"

Grant scrunched up his face. "Uh, come again?"

Steady, Silas. Play it cool...

"I mean, we've known each other since Harvard and you've known each other since post-grad school," Silas said, trying to recover as he gestured toward Torres, his armpits growing wet from panic that he would screw it all up. "What are the odds?"

Grant said nothing, mouth open as if struggling with a handful of questions as he glanced from Silas to Torres and back again, knowing full well all that the three of them had gone through together.

"That's true, what are the odds?" Torres said. "Since Silas and I just met…"

She fixed Grant with another look, more forgiving this time but clearly communicating the man keep his yapper shut.

"Right," Hartwin said, "we can continue the reunion later and there will be plenty of time to get to know one another. However, why don't we take our seats."

Silas said to Grant, "By the way, how's your sister?"

"Mary?" the man said. "Why are you asking?"

He furrowed his brow. "No reason. Just wondering how she's been, that's all."

Grant chuckled and scratched the back of his neck. "Yeah, well, you know Mary. She's fine. But we should probably take a seat."

Silas frowned. "Yeah, right. Good to hear…" As the man took a seat, he mumbled to Torres, "What's up with him?"

She shrugged. "Who knows? It's Grant."

The pair introduced themselves to the other two men before taking their seats next to each other at a large oval executive table anchored at the center of the room.

Noland Rotberg, a solid man Silas's height with a handlebar mustache wearing an open collar green-and-blue plaid shirt and dark denim, seemed out of place at Harvard. But a showboat he was, as Torres had said. Looked the part and his loud, echoey laugh fit the bill, too.

Trevor Bohls looked like he walked off the set of Project Runway with his designer gray pants and pale-blue t-shirt and high-top white sneakers; those oversized, ironic black glasses that would make the 70s proud, even though he looked ridiculous; and that scent of grapefruit emanating from him in sickening waves. He barely looked up from his phone to acknowledge them. Probably hashtagging it up on Twitter or WeShare or whatever the heck WeTubers did, especially the flunked-out progressive megapastor types.

Silas slumped back in his chair. It was going to be a long day.

Grant slid next to him, then leaned over and whispered, "What's going on, buddy? With you and Torres?"

Silas glanced at him and smiled, fixing him with eyes that told the man all he needed to know: neither the time nor the place.

The man frowned but nodded his acknowledgment, then leaned back and folded his arms.

This was wild. And could complicate things.

He and Grant had studied together in separate doctoral programs at Harvard University's nonsectarian school of theology and religious studies. Silas under the direction of Henry Gregory, one of the foremost experts in Christian historical theology and comparative religion; Grant with Lucas Pryce, an expert in Semitic studies and a pioneering archaeologist whom Silas had taken down almost two years ago in yet another SEPIO operation. During their program, the two had been close friends but went very separate ways.

Silas's Christian convictions had drawn him into preserving the memory of the historic faith, and his Catholic background led him into relicology, researching mostly Church relics. Grant had been the spiritual-but-not-religious type, being drawn toward anthropology and the more adventurous field of archaeology. They had grown close on a dig at the fabled Tell es-Sultan with Pryce, the site of the biblical city of Jericho. Grant had even celebrated Silas's major win when he discovered a series of scrolls verifying the Ark of the Covenant and became enraged when Pryce took credit for it. They had tried to keep in touch over the years, but between his heavy class load and Grant's work as a globetrotting religious-cultural anthropologist with a bit of archaeology on the side, it had been difficult.

Judging by the suit, tie, and shiny shoes, apparently the man had moved into the big leagues.

"Alright, how about we begin the fun, shall we?" Hartwin took off his jacket and carefully folded it over a chair.

Just then, Silas's phone vibrated in his pocket with a message. He withdrew it and glanced at its face. It was Celeste. Apparently, they'd found a lead. Didn't go into it, but said she would report back once they knew more.

Hartwin huffed. "By the way, this is being a no mobile device zone. What we are about to be discussing and what I am about to be showing you is extremely sensitive in nature. I would hate for it to get into the wrong hands."

Silas scoffed as he slipped his phone back into his pocket. What was this, Langley? The J. Edgar Hoover Building?

"Right, let's get to it." The man sat at the head of the table and propped his elbows on its polished surface, bringing his hands together like a tent and eyeing the room with what Silas assumed was supposed to be some dramatic effect.

Get to it already...

"As I trust each of you have undoubtedly heard, yesterday I announced live to the world the discovery of the long-lost Q source document. What I am calling Gospel Zero."

"And might I be the first to say, bravo, Hartwin," Noland Rotberg said with a slight Western twang.

"Yes, yes. I got tingles when I saw the news!" Trevor Bohls added. "I imagine it will do wonders to inform the continued evolution of the Christian faith."

Silas rolled his eyes and folded his arms. *Suck ups.*

"Gotta hand it to you, prof." Grant said. "Nice marketing handle you got yourself there."

"And one that's apparently trending on social media," Silas added. "Whatever that means."

He turned toward Silas. "What, you're not down with the newfangled tech that's all the rage with the kiddos these days?"

"You sound like Gapinski," he mumbled. "And no. Not if it gets in the way of actual, legitimate research and historical inquiry."

"Which is why I am assembling today this consortium of the minds," Hartwin continued. "Because I'm afraid I left out a minor little detail from the news conference."

"Oh, yeah?" Torres said. "And what's that?"

Hartwin paused, as if preparing for some sort of fallout from his reveal.

"While I have discovered the mythical Q source, I haven't *found* the mythical document."

"What?" Silas said, a mixture of disbelief and relief colliding inside.

"Not yet, anyway," Hartwin quickly added. "The evidence of the document's existence is certainly there. But I am hoping that we can all put our heads together to uncover the greatest Christian archaeological find since the Dead Sea Scrolls."

"Hold on, partner," Grant said, sliding to the edge of his seat and raising a hand. "You went on national television and announced to the world you had discovered ground zero of the Christian Bible. Claiming to have the very thing that would rewrite Christianity itself."

Now Hartwin put up a hand. "That's not being accurate. I claimed no such thing. That was the bloodthirsty American media making such claims."

"Oh, come on, professor," Torres added. "You have to admit you left at least the impression you actually had the Q source document. From one archaeologist to another, you should have chosen your words more carefully."

Silas couldn't help but smile as he sat back and let Hartwin take the heat. Looked like a buffoon in front of his colleagues. Even Rotberg was starting to pile on. He imagined Hartwin expected pushback, but not this much finger-wagging.

"Then why the media conference? Why the dog and pony show if you didn't have the Q source document?" Grant asked.

"Yeah, I have to say," Bohls said, "you need to get yourself a new agent. Not ready for prime time, my friend."

Hartwin huffed, running a hand through his hair. "It was a bit premature, I admit. But for good reason."

"And what reason is that?" Silas asked, now joining in.

"I have reason to believe another party is on to me. Or rather, is on to the Q source. At least its existence, not its location."

"A bit conspiratorial, don't you think, partner?" Grant said. "Know where the CIA is stashing those downed UFOs from the 60s?"

Hartwin huffed again. He went to respond when Silas intervened.

"Alright, so it appears you fudged a bit on the numbers. Then what's the evidence you have for—I can't believe I'm calling it this," he muttered. "But for Gospel Zero's existence?"

Hartwin took a breath and put his elbows back on the table, putting his hands back into the tent. "How familiar are you with the Muratorian Fragment?"

"The who?" Grant asked.

"An ancient list of officially recognized and sanctioned books in the Christian Scriptures," Rotberg offered.

"Not so much a list of sanctioned books as an affirmation of what the Church had already considered to be part of the canon," Silas corrected. "Some have even called it an introduction to the New Testament, even a so-called reasoning list that offers pretty convincing proof of what the earliest Christians believed were divinely inspired texts."

"So what exactly is this fragment or canon list or whatever?"

Torres asked. "Because I'm certainly not down with the Church history lingo."

"The Muratorian Fragment consists of 85 lines of Greek text," Silas explained, "with the beginning and probably the end missing. It was discovered in the 18th century by Ludovico Antonio Muratori, an archivist and librarian at Modena, Italy, sitting in a manuscript in the Biblioteca Ambrosiana in Milan."

"Interesting."

"It also contained several theological treatises of the 4th and 5th centuries from Ambrose of Milan, Eucherius of Lyon, and John Chrysostom, concluding with five early Christian creeds."

"No relation, by the way," Grant added. "At least not that I'm aware of."

Silas ignored the man and continued. "Scholars generally agree that the Fragment was originally composed in Greek. On the basis of phonetic, graphic, morphological, and lexical features. The translation Muratori discovered is best dated to the late 5th or possibly the early 6th centuries. Fascinatingly, excerpts from the Muratorian Fragment were discovered in three manuscripts from the 11th century and in one manuscript from the 12th century, showing it was known as a valid list within the Church into the Middle Ages."

He took a breath and glanced at Hartwin, conscious he was basically hijacking his meeting. The man was leaning back in his chair and motioned for him to continue.

Silas nodded. "The missing beginning of the text probably contained a preamble and a comment on the Gospel of Matthew, and then it launches into a sort of listing of the books generally accepted to be part of the Church's canon. The Bible."

"Such as?" Grant asked.

"Such as Luke, John, and the Book of Acts. Paul's corpus, including Romans, the two letters to the Church of Corinth, Galatians and Ephesians, Philippians and Colossians, the two letters to the Thessalonians as well as both letters to Timothy, and then Titus and Philemon. He also mentions the Book of Jude and the letters from John in addition to his Apocalypse."

Hartwin offered a halfhearted set of claps from the other end. "Impressive, Dr. Grey. I was told you were the man for the job."

"Yes, impressive," Rotberg said with a slight sneer. "But you're forgetting a few more, aren't you? The Fragment lists other books that aren't part of the officially sanctioned canon of Scripture."

"You're right, it does."

"The Apocalypse of Peter, Shepherd of Hermas, and Wisdom of Solomon, isn't that right?"

"It is, however, the author of the original Fragment said that none of the three were to be publicly read to the people in church. He also excluded two alleged letters of Paul that were regarded as forgeries, a new book of the Psalms, and the writings of heretics."

Rotberg scoffed. "Heretics! Losers in the Church's struggle over power and control, more like it..."

"Hold up," Grant said. "So you're telling me that the Church decided which books were included in the Bible?"

Silas answered, "Sort of—"

"And why do you suppose that is?" Rotberg interrupted, playing with one end of his mustache.

Why don't you tell me, Rotberg?

The man was starting to seriously pluck Silas's nerves. He said, "What I suppose, *Noland*, is that early on there was a consensus forming within the believing community of Jesus Christ that some books were inspired by God and some weren't. Some were authoritative, some weren't. Some were genuine eyewitness accounts to Jesus' life, death, and resurrection—as was the case with the recognized Gospels. And some weren't. Which is remarkable if you think about it. That within a century and a half, the Church pretty well figured out its sacred texts. The same ones it has been using for two millennia. Not all religions can claim such a consensus, that's for sure."

The man continued playing with his mustache. "Touché, *Silas*. But don't forget about the missing books."

"Missing?" Grant asked.

Silas was feeling a little uncomfortable speaking about added books and missing ones to the Bible with his old friend who had issues with faith and religion.

He nodded. "That's right. The Muratorian Canon doesn't include the Book of Hebrews, the Book of James, and neither of the two epistles from Peter. But it doesn't matter."

"Why's that?"

"Because by the end of the 4th century, the list was complete and the canon closed."

"Ahh, yes," Rotberg said, "Athanasius' Festal Letter number thirty-nine."

"Festal what?" Torres said.

Silas shook a dismissive hand. "Doesn't matter right now. What matters is that before there was an official list of books, the Gospels and Paul's letters were widely used early on. Already at the beginning of the 2nd century, they were being copied and sent around to the various churches, as well as recited orally. So by the time the Church finally said, 'Yes, these are the ones,' there was already a group of books that were viewed as authoritative. The Church had already viewed some letters as special vessels that communicated what God wanted to communicate to us."

"Now this is important," Silas continued before Rotberg or anyone else could jump in. If he was going to be part of—whatever it was he was part of, he was going to set the stage at the beginning. "Because certain people who would like to deny the historicity of the Christian faith would want us to believe a bunch of dead white guys chose only certain books and threw away other ones—that early Christian leaders conspired with the Roman emperor Constantine to create the Bible, in order to suppress minority voices that didn't help their version of Christian events. Two words: not true!"

"Oh, come off of it!" Rotberg said.

"It isn't! And any Church historian and New Testament scholar worth his salt knows it."

Silas probably just offended half the room. He didn't care. In fact, he liked being back in the academic saddle. Reminded him how much he missed going toe to toe with the beasts of the academy who would want to shred the faith apart.

"Not only is this just not historically accurate," Silas continued, "it also displays a level of ignorance about how ancient cultures transmitted events and information. The Gospels were initially transmitted orally before being written down in what we have as the Gospels. This was a common practice and resulted in reliable records in those days. Then there were the letters in the New Testament, like Paul's and John's letters, which were written but then transmitted orally and copied and passed around among the churches. By the mid-2nd century, there were already lists of books widely used throughout the Church."

"Yes, which I identified as the Muratorian Fragment at the start," Hartwin interjected. "But we have gotten ourselves far, far from the beaten path, methinks."

Silas took a breath; so did Rotberg. The two men offered passing glares across the room as Hartwin continued. Silas had a feeling it was going to get interesting between them two.

"Now, Dr. Grey, I want to circle back to something you said earlier, about the missing part to the Fragment."

"At the beginning, making reference to the Gospel of Matthew. What of it?"

"Well, that's what I've assembled you all here for today. And what led me to assemble the conference on Gospel Zero."

Silas leaned forward; so did Rotberg.

"What are you saying, partner?" Grant asked.

Hartwin stifled a grin, clearly relishing the moment. "What I am saying is that I can confidently tell you the original Fragment is not missing the beginning section and that—"

"Wait a minute," Silas said, raising a hand of interruption. "You're telling us you've seen this original version?"

"That is being correct—well, sort of," Hartwin corrected himself. "A version of it, anyway." And then he let himself grin. "What is being even better is that you can be seeing it for yourselves."

He hoisted a polished wood box onto the table with a thud, saying nothing but holding his grin and eyeing the table. The one he had retrieved earlier from the safe in his study.

The table collectively stood and leaned forward, eyeing the box and drawing the same conclusion Hartwin soon voiced.

"I am having this other version of the Fragment here in this box." He tapped its cover. "For your translating and reading pleasure. Which you will be quickly seeing makes reference to our long-lost Q source document."

"Gospel Zero..." Silas whispered.

"Precisely."

CHAPTER 11

Silas's heart was hammering in his chest, his breath keeping pace as Hartwin withdrew a stack of parchment folios that looked similar to what he had glimpsed countless times throughout his career as an academic.

Old, brittle papyri stained brown with time, Greek characters in dark brownish ink from ancient hands scrawled across its face in neat lines, their revelations whispering an invitation to come hither and listen to their tales from old.

No...wait.

He stepped toward the table for a closer look, examining the characters more closely.

Not Greek, Coptic—a dead language that was essentially Egyptian but based on the Greek alphabet.

Which was strange, because experts had assumed the original Muratorian Canon containing the introduction to Christian texts had been written in Greek and then translated into the Latin that marked the one remaining sample, dated somewhere around the 6th century. A most curious characteristic indeed.

More importantly, no one had suggested another version existed, much less in Coptic.

Until now...

Silas wondered what else lay undiscovered.

He closed his eyes, taking in a whiff of the surrounding air, filling his head with the dizzying scent of damp earth and incense and old paper. He stood back, continuing to lean toward Hartwin but trying not to appear too eager as the man carefully placed each manuscript page on the table in front of him.

The folios reminded him of the Dead Sea Scrolls, the ancient Jewish scrolls of Hebrew Scriptures discovered in the desert caves in Israel on the northern shore of the Dead Sea. Scholars had dated the scrolls from the last three centuries BC to the first century AD. His stomach fluttered with the same delight as when he cast his eyes on those ancient Jewish scrolls during a special doctoral seminar with Henry Gregory, his mentor who had been murdered by Nous. But these were different.

This was a version of an original Church document, which were rarely found nowadays. Or at least purported to be. What Gregory wouldn't have given to be standing in his shoes right then. Legit or not.

Silas folded his arms as Hartwin finished his display, casting a skeptical eye on what the man had suggested. A Coptic version of the Muratorian Fragment listing the originally acknowledged books of the Christian Bible? Hardly seemed possible. Unlike with stone or clay tablets, saying it's rare to find ancient manuscripts in any archaeological context is an understatement, given they usually disintegrate over time due to bad climate. And it's next to impossible for a near-perfect one to survive millennia, even small scraps.

Not to mention twelve folios resting on a table in the middle of a conference room in Princeton!

But possibility wasn't what mattered. *Provenance* did.

As a trained expert in religious relics and manuscripts, especially the Church kind, he knew the proof was in the provenance, the chain of custody from a secure archeological context having been excavated, uncovered, and documented by the professionals. Where the folios had been found, who had found them, how they had been excavated and preserved, and how they had made their way to Hartwin were all questions burning their way through Silas as he took in the view. All the who-what-where-how questions of any good detective sat at the heart of the kind of work he was forced to leave in these hallowed halls of Princeton.

And he was giddy with delight at picking them back up, itching for an archaeological mystery to solve.

Rotberg was the first to move, sidling up to Hartwin's right. Soon the others followed, with Grant moving in for the kill on Hartwin's left and Torres joining him. Trevor Bohls joined Rotberg, mobile device in hand, filming it all.

Silas didn't know what to make of it. All he knew was that he needed a cigarette. Not only to deal with the envy rising up the back of his neck, but also to quash the dread churning in his belly. After Iraq, it had been little blue pills to deal with mild PTSD from what he had experienced. The residual effect still lingered, especially during pressure-cooker times like staring down the barrel of a monumental discovery that could rock the Church.

With him responsible for mitigating the fallout.

If this was indeed another version of the original list of recognized New Testament books from the 2nd century, and it somehow listed Gospel Zero or Q or whatever the heck it was, along with others *not* officially recognized by the Church. Some would wonder what was in Gospel Zero that Matthew and Luke didn't use—and why it wasn't included as a separate Gospel book, like Mark was. Others would want to point to it as proof the Church suppressed books that didn't toe the dogmatic line. Either way, the Order of Thaddeus, not to mention Christianity, could be dealing with a serious threat on their hands.

With him in the middle of it.

Grant whistled. "Not bad, prof."

"I must say, Hartwin," Rotberg said, "when I heard about this Gospel Zero business, I busted a gut the size of Texas."

Bohls laughed. "Yeah, a real LOL moment in the faith, that's for sure."

"But now..."

Silas rolled his eyes at the display. It was all too much. As far as he was concerned, all they had were a bunch of old papers stained with ink. Now the work began.

It's go time, SEPIO...

"Interesting find you got there, Hartwin," he said, stepping closer to the others with arms crossed. "But you have to admit, it all seems a bit sketchy."

Hartwin grinned. "I've anticipated your skepticism and—"

"I mean, come on. A stack of papyri folios just falls into your lap purporting to be another version of the original list of New Testament books?"

"Again, I understand your skepticism, and I am assuring you all will be—"

"And said folios just happen to make mention of one of the greatest unresolved mysteries in New Testament scholarship and Church history, the lost Q source?"

Hartwin huffed, his face growing red at the rapid-fire questions.

"I don't know..." Silas said next to Torres, rubbing his chin. "Seems too good to be true. You sure you're not being played? That it's not some elaborate punking scheme to—"

"It's not!" Hartwin interrupted flatly, with force. He huffed again, then went on, "As you can imagine, I was certainly skeptical myself. Which is why I arranged a full battery of tests—from microscopic imaging, ink testing, radiocarbon analysis, multispectral imaging, infrared microspectroscopy, and then another round of radiocarbon dating just for good measure. The work has taken several months."

"And the verdict, prof?" Grant said.

"Passed with flying colors! Dating to the turn of the 6th century. Both the paper and the ink. Which makes this the oldest version we have of the original listing of New Testament books."

"That's not entirely true," Silas corrected. "Many date the Latin Muratorian Fragment from the 5th century."

"*Some*," Hartwin corrected. "Some are dating it as being from the 5th century. Plenty of others suggest it is being 6th century, even into the 7th."

Silas rolled his eyes. "Regardless, most early Church scholars place the original sometime in the 2nd century. That's the value of the Muratorian Fragment to begin with."

"And what is your point, good sir?" Rotberg asked, leaning back and stroking one end of his curled mustache.

"I sense a lecture coming on," Grant moaned to Torres. Who stifled a snicker.

"The point, *Noland*," Silas went on, ignoring his friend, "is that what's important to realize is that the original list dates to the end of the second century. Which means that the majority of the books we've come to know as the New Testament were already being widely acknowledged as authoritative for faith and life in the Church—within one hundred years of being written."

Rotberg snorted a laugh. "Widely acknowledged as authoritative for faith and life. That's a good one, Dr. Grey. If not a bit disingenuous."

"What the heck do you mean by that?"

"You know as well as I do that there were plenty of other Christian texts and even Christian *Gospels* being circulated throughout the early movement. Nag Hammadi proves that!"

Silas huffed. He went to respond when Torres turned to him and said, "Nag Hammadi?"

Grant said, "The cache of Coptic Christian texts found in the Upper Egyptian town in the mid-40s. Quite the find, too. And totally by accident. A pair of brothers came across them stuffed in clay jars while digging in a field."

"Impressive," Silas said. "But let's get it right. *Gnostic* texts, not Christian."

Rotberg snorted another laugh and shook his head. "You would..."

He turned to the man, neck reddening with irritation. "Would what?"

"Write them off as merely *Gnostic*, because that allows you to dismiss the minority, but very real voices within the Church shaping the early faith and life of the community you're so concerned about!"

"Minority voices," Silas sneered. "And you would! Long before such minority, *heretical* voices—"

Another snort of laughter interrupted, but Silas didn't let the man gain a foothold.

"And, yes, for the record I just dropped the H-bomb. Because my point is that books mentioned in the Muratorian Fragment were the books that were eventually inducted into what we call the canon of Scripture by the Council of Carthage at the end of the 4th century, which really only affirmed that those were the ones that were *already* being widely used as authoritative books for centuries. So I don't really care what a stack of unknown, untested, unscrutinized pieces of paper says!"

Silas took a breath, regret beginning to churn in his belly.

He'd always been a bit of a hothead when it came to defending the faith. To his brother, which created the rift that led to their current lot, and to others. Now was not the time to spout off, not when he was heading a SEPIO mission to get to the bottom of it all. Kid gloves were needed, not a jackhammer.

He sighed. "Sorry for getting a bit agitated with the notion of some two-bit mystery list of New Testament books that suddenly surface, referencing a mythical primitive Gospel."

Hartwin laughed. "But, Dr. Grey, that's not all there was."

Confused, Silas turned to the professor. "Excuse me?"

"Our two-bit mystery list of New Testament books, as you put it, was bearing a cousin."

"A cousin?" Torres said. "As in, another fragment?"

"Precisely, my dear."

"Not bad twice over," Grant said.

Silas threw him a look.

"What? It is pretty impressive."

"What's the other fragment?" Silas asked.

"Several lines from John's Gospel."

Hartwin removed a piece of separating wood from the box's bottom, covering a secondary compartment. He withdrew another parchment and set it below the other twelve.

Rotberg craned toward a piece of parchment the size of a small greeting card and whistled. "Now that there is legit manuscript contraband."

Silas pushed past Torres and Grant toward the newcomer. He leaned over it for a better look. To his surprise, it was written in the same Coptic. It was highly unusual to find an original Gospel fragment written in the dead language.

Heart picking up pace, Silas licked his lips and began to translate the small fragment, his brain reaching back into his memory of language studies. Instantly recognizing the translation:

In the beginning was the Word, and the Word was with God, and the Word was God. He was in the beginning with God. All things came into being through him, and without him not one thing came into being. What has come into being in him was life, and the life was the light of all people...

The Gospel of John, chapter one.

"As you can see, it is a fragment of John's Gospel, the first chapter," Hartwin said. "One of the most recognized portions of the New Testament."

Silas folded his arms. "You're right. Speaking about Jesus Christ and his divinity."

"You'll be pleased to know that the fragment was run through the same battery of tests and arrived at the same dating result as the version of the Muratorian Fragment. Which, by the way, was discovered alongside the folios you see there in front of you."

"All that proves is that they were cut from the same parchment, not that they are legit."

"Such a skeptic, bro," Grant said, elbowing him in the side.

Silas ignored him. "All I am interested in at this point is the provenance of the folios. And I guess now this new fragment of John's Gospel."

"A worthy starting point," Rotberg acknowledged, leaning in to inspect the parchments.

"I was anticipating your skepticism," Hartwin said, "and was figuring such questions would be top of mind. But all in due time. I have a proposal first."

"Oh, yeah?" Torres said, "And what's that?"

"That Silas and Noland, here, set about translating the folios first. I have already spent some time with their translations myself, but I want you to see what I am talking about. Then we can be talking about provenance."

Silas scoffed. "Why would I waste my time on something that hasn't yet checked out?"

"He has a point," Torres said. "Issues of where, why, and how are usually the first questions to clear the deck in my line of work before we take any archaeological find seriously. Especially with all the quacks out there peddling this and that artifact."

"Oh, I don't know," Rotberg said, leaning back from the table. "I would fancy getting a crack at translating the folios as soon as possible. I should think a man of your caliber and character would want to as well, Dr. Grey. I say we get to it and worry about provenance after the fact."

"And I'll record it all for the watching world!" Bohls said. "But what should we hashtag it? That's the question…"

Silas scoffed again.

"So what do you say, Grey?" Rotberg went on. "Care to join me? Or perhaps your translating chops aren't what they used to be after leaving the academy."

I'd put my translating chops against yours anytime, pal!

Instead of saying what he wanted to say, and more, Silas took a breath and ran a hand across his head to the back of his neck, rubbing it as it reddened with irritation.

"Fine. Have it your way. But let's get to it. I've got a plane to catch if this nonsense isn't cleared up by the afternoon."

Hartwin brought over two comfortable leather chairs for the pair at the end of the long conference room table in front of the folios. Grant and Torres stepped behind Silas. Bohls, cell phone in hand to film it all, stood behind Rotberg. Then the pair set about translating the folios.

Took a few hours and a few more pots of coffee, but by late morning Silas and Rotberg finished their translating and sat back with satisfaction. They looked at each other and shook hands, both pleased with their results.

And equally shocked at what it said.

CHAPTER 12

Silas sank into his chair with dread after he and Rotberg finished translating the Coptic folios. Stunned and shaken.

What do you do when all you've ever known about the Bible turns out to be a lie?

Rotberg scooted back with a spring in his step that communicated clear approval. If not giddy, drunken glee at what the supposed Coptic Muratorian Fragment said.

Hartwin did the honors reading aloud what Silas and Rotberg had translated for the rest of the group. And no doubt for the eyes of Facebook and WeShare on the other side of Bohls's social media accounts.

He stood and cleared his throat:

> *We declare to the catholic Church that what she has received from the Spirit of God and the pen of men, being widely accepted by the councils of Christ's shepherds and useful for teaching, for reproof, for correction, and for training in righteousness, so that everyone who belongs to God may be proficient, equipped for every good work.*

Along with Luke, using their sources, including Mark and the one from Galilee prepared by the man from our Savior's homestead, Matthew recorded those things at which he was present he placed thus.

The third book of the Gospel, that according to Luke, the well-known physician Luke wrote in his own name in order after the ascension of Christ, and when Paul had associated him with himself as one studious of right. Nor did he himself see the Lord in the flesh; and he, according as he was able to accomplish it, began his narrative with the nativity of John.

The fourth Gospel is that of John, one of the disciples. When his fellow-disciples and bishops entreated him, he said, "Fast ye now with me for the space of three days, and let us recount to each other whatever may be revealed to each of us." On the same night it was revealed to Andrew, one of the apostles, that John should narrate all things in his own name as they called them to mind.

And hence, although different points are taught us in the several books of the Gospels, there is no difference as regards the faith of believers, inasmuch as in all of them all things are related under one imperial Spirit, which concern the Lord's nativity, His passion, His resurrection, His conversation with His disciples, and His twofold advent—the first in the humiliation of rejection, which is now past, and the second in the glory of royal power, which is yet in the future.

What marvel is it, then, that John brings forward these several things so constantly in his epistles also, saying in his own person, "What we have seen with our eyes, and heard with our ears, and our hands have handled, that have we written." For thus he professes himself to be not only the eyewitness, but also the hearer; and besides that, the historian of all the wondrous facts concerning the Lord in their order.

Moreover, the Acts of all the Apostles are comprised by Luke in one book, and addressed to the most excellent Theophilus, because these different events took place when he was present himself; and he shows this clearly—that the principle on which he wrote was, to give only what fell under his own notice—by the omission of the passion of Peter, and also of the journey of Paul, when he went from the city of Rome to Spain.

As to the epistles of Paul, again, to those who will understand the matter, they indicate of themselves what they are, and from what place or with what object they were directed. He wrote first of all, and at considerable length, to the Corinthians, to check the schism of heresy; and then to the Galatians, to forbid circumcision; and then to the Romans on the rule of the Old Testament Scriptures, and also to show them that Christ is the first object in these—which it is needful for us to discuss severally, as the blessed Apostle Paul, following the rule of his predecessor John, writes to no more than seven churches by name, in this order: the first to the Corinthians, the second to the Ephesians, the third to the Philippians, the fourth to the Colossians, the fifth to the Galatians, the sixth to the Thessalonians, the seventh to the Romans. Moreover, though he writes twice to the Corinthians and Thessalonians for their correction, it is yet shown—by this sevenfold writing—that there is one Church spread abroad through the whole world. And John too, indeed, in the Apocalypse, although he writes only to seven churches, yet addresses all. He wrote, besides these, one to Philemon, and one to Titus, and two to Timothy, in simple personal affection and love indeed; but yet these are hallowed in the esteem of the Catholic Church, and in the regulation of ecclesiastical discipline. There are also in circulation one to the Laodiceans, and another to the Alexandrians, forged under the name of Paul, and addressed against the heresy of Marcion; and there are also several others which cannot be received into the

Catholic Church, for it is not suitable for gall to be mingled with honey.

The Epistle of Jude, indeed, and two belonging to the above-named John—or bearing the name of John—are reckoned among the Catholic epistles. And the book of Wisdom, written by the friends of Solomon in his honor.

We receive also the Apocalypse of John and that of Peter, though some amongst us will not have this latter read in the Church. The Pastor, moreover, did Hermas write very recently in our times in the city of Rome, while his brother bishop Pius sat in the chair of the Church of Rome. And therefore it also ought to be read; but it cannot be made public in the Church to the people, nor placed among the prophets, as their number is complete, nor among the apostles to the end of time.

Of the writings of Arsinous, called also Valentinus, or of Miltiades, we receive them. Those too who wrote the new Book of Psalms for Marcion, together with Basilides and the founder of the Asian Cataphrygians.

But the others recognized as Holy Writ are included: The Wisdom of Solomon, and the Wisdom of Sirach, and Esther, and Judith, and Tobit, and that which is called the Teaching of the Apostles, and the Shepherd. And those falsely accused of treasonous heresy, the Gnostics as they are known, we also approve the following: The Gospel according to the Egyptians, The Gospel according to the Twelve Apostles, the Gospel according to Thomas, The Gospel according to Judas, and The Secret Book of John. Though they are not canonical but even disputed, yet are recognized by many churchmen. We do not in any way want to be considered ignorant because of those who imagine they posses some knowledge if they are acquainted with these.

I write this in my own hand, Victor of Leptis Magna.

Hartwin ended his reading. The room stood and sat still and silent, contemplating all that the man had read.

Grant was the first to speak: "Who the hell is Victor of Leptis Magna?"

"A pope..." Silas muttered.

"What was that, partner?"

He sat up and cleared his throat. "Pope Victor I. The first, and only, African Bishop of Rome. He was from Tripolitania, also known within the Roman Empire as Leptis Magna."

"And he authored this...this Muratorian Fragment thingy?"

"No one is certain who authored the *original* Muratorian Fragment. Some believe it originated in Rome, and it would make sense for someone of his caliber and importance to have overseen the making of such a listing of Christian texts."

"And as you can see, he makes mention of Gospel Zero." Hartwin grinned with intoxication. Silas thought the man would topple over from the revelation.

"Not only that, look what the good Bishop cops to!" Rotberg said with a gleeful chuckle. "The Bishop of Rome, a Vicar of Christ, acknowledging the suppressed texts of early Christian communities were recognized as legitimate Christian texts. Even originally recognized by many in the faith itself! I knew it, I just knew it! This will change the entire course of early Christian studies."

Silas scoffed. "What a load of crock..."

"Excuse me?"

He stood, getting animated now. "I said, it's a load of crock!"

Grant tugged at his sleeve. "Silas...bro—"

"No, this is important—"

"Oh, for Pete's sake don't be so dramatic," Rotberg scolded.

"I'm not being dramatic!" He sighed and ran a hand across his head. OK, maybe just a little. He sat and took a breath.

"You translated it yourself! You cannot deny what it says."

"I don't care what it says," Silas bit back. "It makes sense of neither Church history nor Church teaching. And this gets at the heart of what this whole damn thing is about in the first place!"

"Oh, boy," Grant said, folding his arms and grinning. "You know it's about to get real when Silas begins to cuss."

Silas ignored him, pressing forward. "There were three reasons given by the early Church for a book to be included in the canon."

Rotberg sighed. "Orthodoxy, apostolicity, and catholicity. Yes, I've heard this before. Your shtick."

My shtick?!

His neck grew even more red.

Silas chuckled. "I know, Noland. Big, complicated words. So let's break them down. First, orthodoxy. A book like the Gospel of John, or Paul's Romans, or James's letter conformed to the Rule of Faith. It reflected right beliefs in the Christian faith. Early on there was already a standard for right beliefs. And a book had to conform and affirm those right beliefs."

"And second?" Rotberg said, one end of his mouth curling upward.

"Second, the early fathers considered apostolicity as a benchmark for inclusion in the canon. Meaning, the book was written by an apostle or under the direction of an apostle. Someone who was part of Jesus' ministry or directly sent by him, like Paul or John."

"So orthodoxy and apostolicity," Grant said.

Silas nodded.

"And?"

"And finally, a book had to be *catholic*—small 'c' not big 'C.'"

"As in, universal?" Torres said.

"Exactly! The book in question was widely used throughout the Church. It also meant that this book had *authority* throughout all the churches of the time."

Rotberg stood. "And what is the point of all this?" he asked, sauntering off to a beverage cart of tea and coffee. Hartwin joined him.

"The *point*," Silas said, "Is that early on in the life of the Church, Christians and Christian leaders used these three strict measurements—orthodoxy, apostolicity, and catholicity—to judge whether a book should be included in the Bible. The Bible, the canon of Scripture, was formed through a deliberate process, that involved both God and people. The books we have had to meet certain criteria, and they were already being widely used and thought of as authoritative for faith and life by the time they were included in the canon."

"Yes, yes, yes," Rotberg said, returning to his seat with a cup of tea. "We understand this faith and life business."

Hartwin returned with his own cup. "We do, Silas. And we're not sure we understand the point of your soliloquy."

Silas sighed. This was getting exhausting. He looked to Torres and Grant for support. They gave none.

He frowned, raking a hand across his head and ending his...*soliloquy*, as Hartwin put it.

"Look, let's not dance around the fact that among the six of us, I'm the one who cares most about historic Christian orthodoxy."

"Oh, yeah?" Torres said, crossing her arms. "Speak for yourself!"

He held up a hand. "Sorry, I don't mean to speak for everyone. But I have staked my professional life on defending the vintage Christian faith. When I was a professor, here at Princeton. And now in a more direct role as Master of the Order of Thaddeus. So that's my reason for being here. And this, this, whatever it is—it completely flies in the face of Church history!"

"What do you mean, partner?" Grant asked, giving Silas a window to regain control over the conversation.

"Take Irenaeus," he said, "one of the most important early

Church fathers. He regarded the twenty books that later appeared in the Church historian Eusebius' list as canonical books. He defied the false teachings raging throughout the Church by quoting from most of what we understand to be New Testament books, including the four Gospels, Acts, Paul's letters, Hebrews, James, 1 Peter, 1 and 2 John, and Revelation. But the most widely recognized canon list, if you want to call it that, comes from Athanasius. As you mentioned Noland, his *Festal Letter 39*. In it, he named all the books of the Old Testament, those of the Hebrew Scriptures, and then the books in the New Testament. Here, let me..."

Silas fished out his phone to bring up the letter.

When he saw three missed calls from Celeste and a text message waiting for him to read.

No time for that now.

He swiped it to life and brought up an ebook app, searching for a collection of early Church resources. Finding the letter, he read a portion:

Again it is not tedious to speak of the books of the New Testament. These are, the four Gospels, according to Matthew, Mark, Luke, and John. Afterwards, the Acts of the Apostles and seven Epistles called Catholic—of James, one; of Peter, two; of John, three; after these, one of Jude. In addition, there are fourteen Epistles of Paul, written in this order. The first, to the Romans; then two to the Corinthians; after these, to the Galatians; next, to the Ephesians; then to the Philippians; then to the Colossians; after these, two to the Thessalonians, and that to the Hebrews; and again, two to Timothy; one to Titus; and lastly, that to Philemon. And besides, the Revelation of John. These are fountains of salvation, that they who thirst may be satisfied with the living words they contain. In these alone is proclaimed the doctrine of godliness. Let no man add

> to these, neither let him take ought from these. For concerning these the Lord put to shame the Sadducees, and said, Ye do err, not knowing the Scriptures.' And He reproved the Jews, saying, Search the Scriptures, for these are they that testify of Me.'

Silas slipped his phone back into his pocket. "What's key here is that for Athanasius, as well as the other Church leaders of the time, these recognized books were considered the *'fountains of salvation,'* for in them and them alone did they contain *'the living words'* that *'they who thirst may be satisfied.'* He insisted that these twenty-seven books alone proclaimed the doctrine of godliness and contained right teaching for salvation."

"Now, now, Silas," Rotberg said, pulling out his own cell phone. "If you are going to parlay my arguments using early Church sources, why don't you be honest about the fact good brother Athanasius continues."

He cleared his throat and read:

> But for greater exactness I add this also, writing of necessity; that there are other books besides these not indeed included in the Canon, but appointed by the Fathers to be read by those who newly join us, and who wish for instruction in the word of godliness. The Wisdom of Solomon, and the Wisdom of Sirach, and Esther, and Judith, and Tobit, and that which is called the Teaching of the Apostles, and the Shepherd.

Silas smiled and chuckled. "Oh, come now. If you are going to parlay *my* arguments using early Church sources, *Noland*, why don't you be honest about the fact that Athanasius continues his letter by explaining: 'But the former, my brethren, are included in the Canon, the latter being merely read; nor is there in any place a mention of apocryphal writings. But they are an invention of heretics, who write them when they choose, bestowing upon them their approbation, and assigning to them a date, that so, using them as ancient writings, they may find occasion to lead astray the simple.'"

A sudden alarm cut off the argument, blaring with an echoey menace from the hallway.

Silas shot out from his chair on instinct. Torres was close behind. The others remained seated.

Hartwin laughed and held up a calming hand. "Nothing to be worrying about. Just the blasted fire alarm. We have been having trouble lately with that thing."

Silas ignored the man, walking to the door and opening it. Sure enough, the annoying, grating clang of a fire alarm, complete with pulsing white lights announcing danger.

His trusty Beretta seemed to throb at his back with the scene of people, confused and concerned, popping their heads out before heading down the hallway, bathed in strobing white light.

Grant stood, then he motioned toward the door. "Should we…"

"Nonsense!" Hartwin said. "Like I said, it has been happening all this week."

Silas closed the door, unsure but resigning back to his chair.

They waited for the noise to abate. It didn't.

The professor shook his head and mumbled something to himself in German. "At any rate, as I was saying—"

He was interrupted by the jiggling of the door handle, catching the table's attention.

Then it opened.

And in walked three people none of them expected.

Especially the lead. Who Silas recognized but couldn't put a finger on it.

CHAPTER 13

A woman trailed by two more men rushed inside. One of the large goons, neck looking like another extension of his head, closed the door with purpose. The other, same head-neck combo and an apparent twin of the other by a long mile, pulled out a semi-automatic rifle that ruffled the feathers of Hartwin and Rotberg and Bohls. Goon One followed suit. Dented Heckler & Koch weapons that looked like they had seen their fair share of business. Both men, very Bavarian or Prussian looking, were all attitude, all muscle, all shoulders and arms and legs wrapped together in a menacing package that towered above the woman.

She was her own kind of package. Same Germanic stock, with long blond hair tied up above her head into a mean bun, face pale and drawn tight but also smooth, wearing a trench coat and stiletto boots that meant as much business as the pair of H&Ks.

And looking vaguely familiar.

"What is the meaning of this?" Hartwin exclaimed, standing with surprising courage in the face of a clear and present danger.

Silas had to hand it to the man. He joined him, that Beretta screaming now for attention at the middle of his back, as did Grant and Torres who threw him two looks that told him all he needed to know for the moment.

They were with him. And they were ready.

Except so was the mystery woman.

Who opened up her trench coat to retrieve her own piece.

An odd-looking thing that was all black with a futuristic design. Sort of like a stormtrooper rifle from that pop-culture space opera, bearing only half a nose and a standard pistol grip. He knew his weapons, and if he didn't know better, it was another H&K. But this was a prototype of an automatic rifle the West German government abandoned after German reunification. Only a thousand or so were made, carrying a three-shot burst feature that slung 2,000 rounds per minute toward its target. A G11 it was called.

Not good.

Silas glanced at the two goons again before settling on the one hostile who appeared to be in charge.

Then it hit him.

"Helen..." he muttered.

Sebastian's plaything or girlfriend or whoever she was.

He had first seen the two together over a year ago in southern France on the hunt for the Holy Grail. SEPIO had apprehended her and Rudolf Borg at a pagan worship site in Germany, but she'd weaseled her way out from the authorities. And then she had turned up again last Halloween in a pagan ceremony that almost cost Celeste her life. The same one Sebastian had helped preside over before turning rabid and possessed and scampering off into the forest before the authorities came calling.

Apparently she'd avoided them a second time.

He hoped this cat had only a few lives left. But something told him she was a sly one. Just like his brother. A deadly duo, to be sure.

"You know this woman, Grey?" Noland asked Silas with disbelief.

He took a breath. "She knows my brother, Sebastian."

Which makes Nous an official player in all this drama.

"Small world," Hartwin said, matching Rotberg's disbelief.

"Nice guns, lady," Grant said.

Helen smirked, then said with a wink, "Mine or theirs?"

He furrowed his brow then blushed, muttering, "Cheeky..."

"I'll say it again," Hartwin said. "What is the meaning of this?"

An end of Helen's mouth curled upward. She carefully placed one foot in front of the other, taking her time to walk the length of the conference room, her stilettos clicking off a sort of metronome until the inevitable. All the while keeping that stormtrooper-lookalike at her side, finger primed at the trigger.

She reached Silas, who was fixing her with narrowed eyes and reddening from rage at the thought that Sebastian was once again at the helm of some wicked plan.

One that seemed to have the Bible dead-center aim.

"How is my brother?" he growled.

Helen leaned in and whispered, "Tasty." Then she leaned back with a smile and said, accent thick and guttural and husky, "I will be telling him you are saying hello. I am sure he will be finding it a surprise that his brother is at the center of this."

"And what is *this*, exactly?" Silas said.

She smiled, then motioned with her G11 toward the folios still splayed across the table.

Silas's stomach lurched with dread. But not with surprise.

Gospel Zero...

"Pack it up, Professor Braun," Helen said.

Hartwin protested, "But how can you—"

"Not on your life," Silas said, whipping out his Beretta and pointing it right between Fraulein's eyes.

"I say, Dr. Grey..." Rotberg exclaimed.

The two Bavarian goons had a different sort of reply.

As one, they whipped their own weapons toward the group, stepping a foot forward and shaking the room with their stance. Literally and figuratively.

Hartwin and Rotberg and Bohls recoiled as one.

Lucky for Silas, Grant and Torres did not. Although they didn't reply with their own weapons. Which was probably good. For now.

Helen giggled. Something throaty, something smoky. "And what is it you are thinking you are doing, Silas? Hmm?"

Silas said nothing.

What am I doing?

"The alarm has cleared the building of all students and faculty," she continued. "So there is no one that will be hearing the boom, boom, boom that will be going down here."

Had to hand it to her. Not a bad move for a rookie. Or was she?

He eyed the woman, then glanced at the other two men aiming for the group with far more spraying power than his Beretta. They'd brought firehoses to a spitting match. And he was on the losing side of that competition.

He flexed his fingers around his weapon's grip, but retreated with resignation, lowering it and taking a step back but keeping it at his side.

Locked and loaded.

She offered a weak smile and lowered her weapon. The two stooges did not.

"There we are," she said, all at once husky and silky and smooth. "Sebastian said you were always a pushover."

Heat instantly sprang to Silas's neck. He nearly popped her then and there for his brother's insult. But he held firm.

"Now, Professor Braun, if you would." She motioned toward the folios with her weapon again. When the man didn't comply, the goons took a shaking step forward. Which sent him into motion.

Hartwin carefully gathered the pages of the purported Coptic Muratorian Fragment giving credence to the crazy claim that Gospel Zero existed. Although what the mystery text said was anyone's guess.

Which was probably the point.

Sebastian and Nous and whoever had seen something that made them think the Q source document was genuine. That it existed somewhere, in some form.

And they wanted it for themselves.

To do Lord only knew what.

After gathering the pages, the professor gently placed them inside the wooden box.

Helen reached out a hand, the other firmly gripping her weapon.

Hartwin glanced at Rotberg, then reluctantly handed it over.

"*Danke.*" She placed the box under her arm and backed away, weapon extended.

She called out, "Nice doing business with you, Silas Grey."

One of the goons opened the door, and the other strode through followed by Helen. The remaining goon raised his weapon and backed into the hallway, closing the door with a finalizing, echoing thud.

Hartwin slumped into his chair and started cursing in German, the still-clanging fire alarm seeming to agree with his anger.

Silas ignored the man. Let Rotberg and Bohls comfort the good professor. He had other things to worry about.

He readied his Beretta again and padded to the door. He went to call after Torres when she padded up to his side.

"You ready?" he said, reaching for the handle.

He heard her slide a magazine into the bottom of a pistol. He caught sight of a SIG Sauer P320. SEPIO's weapon of choice.

He flashed her a grin and nodded. Grant joined the group and showed him his own piece.

"Guess we're all three locked and loaded then," Silas said.

"Never leave home without one after what happened last time I visited you here," Grant said. "Which makes me think you and this place have some sort of ongoing cursed relationship."

Suddenly the fire alarm stopped. Which probably meant help had arrived. Which also meant they didn't have long to act.

Silas frowned, then nodded to the pair. It was go time.

Torres yanked back the door for Silas to engage. He did, stepping into the hallway, sweeping it with his Beretta.

As he expected. Barren.

"Where do you think you are going to be going?" Hartwin shouted from inside.

Silas popped back in and drilled him with a stare. "To get you back your friggin' fragment."

"But—"

He ignored the man and stepped back in the hall, weapon extended and ready for anything. Torres and Grant quickly followed.

The raging sound of warning had stopped, but the strobing had not, casting eerie white light and darkened shadows across the corridor. Nothing and no one stirred. Just office doors left open in the rush to exit.

Silas wanted to take his time padding down the hallway, but Nous had a head start on them so he ignored the open doors. Normally a major operational no-no, and he knew better. But he doubted any hostiles would pop out at them. And if they did, he had Torres and Grant to back him up.

He knew the only way out of the office building was back

down to the lobby and out the front door. He made quick work of the corridor and was nearing the stairwell—

When a man staring at a piece of paper stepped out of an open door.

Silas trained his weapon on him but held steady.

The man threw his hands up in the air and screamed bloody murder.

Miles.

"Miles, it's me!" Silas shouted, placing a hand on the man's shoulder.

Which sent him back into a screaming fit.

He cursed silently to himself. The last thing he needed when Nous was escaping was a frantic civilian getting in his way. Especially Miles.

"Professor Grey?! What on earth are you—"

"Don't have time to explain. Go get Hartwin and the others. They're back at the conference room. They'll explain it all." Silas nodded at Torres and Grant, then pointed at the stairwell with his Beretta. "Let's move out!"

They did, shoving through the door leading back downstairs and leaving Miles in their wake.

Training their weapons down the stairwell, they shuffled to the main floor and burst out into the lobby.

Nothing but flickering white light.

It's what was lying beyond that made Silas's heart sink.

A sea of people milling about. Professors and students and other office personnel, with a smattering of firefighters and campus police officers now making their way toward the entrance. It was like a bad episode of Where's Waldo, with Nous somewhere in the mix.

Not good.

Silas quickly stuffed his weapon at his back. Torres and Grant did the same.

He glanced at the pair and started walking toward the door as the rescue and security personnel entered inside.

"Sorry, got caught up in a meeting," he said to a guy waddling inside wearing a blue rain jacket, Princeton University security badge, and a scowl. The fuss probably took him away from his late-morning Starbucks run. Poor guy.

He paid them no mind, and the trio quickly ran outside. Thankfully, the rain had stopped.

But that didn't matter when Nous was on the lam. And the mystery fragment with evidence of Gospel Zero.

"What do we do?" Torres asked, hands on her hips and scanning the students and faculty waiting for their day to be put back in order.

Panic was ringing in Silas's ears now as he joined her in sweeping the crowd.

Where indeed...

He waded through the people milling about. Nowhere in particular, and not at all expecting to see Helen and her goons. Just taking it in and giving his mind room to breathe so that—

There it was. Three blocks to the north.

Nassau Street.

"Guys!" He called out before heading toward the main road through town.

"Hold up!" Torres shouted after him.

He didn't, taking off for the most obvious line of escape. Within a minute he reached it, stopping short at the front end of a low-ride indigo BMW with chrome wheels leading a line of parked cars. Surely a Princeton student's ride.

"Where's the fire, chief?" Grant said, running up out of breath.

"It's the main drag in an out of town," Silas said, huffing himself as he scanned up and down the street. "Most obvious escape hatch. Look for anything that might scream getaway vehicle."

"You really think we're just gonna come up on our baddies like a 50s-style Western?"

Squealing tires a block up the road caught their attention.

Silas spun around to catch a black panel delivery van peeling out onto Nassau.

"Well I'll be." Grant said. "Did that just happen?"

"The Lord works in mysterious ways," Torres said.

"I guess so..."

"Now what the heck are we gonna do about it?"

Silas stepped into the road, staring after the car as it sped away.

The chirp of a car alarm disengaging drew him back to the line of cars.

The blue Beemer.

A young man was walking up, head down, jamming out to his AirPods without a care in the world.

Oh, to be a twenty-year-old college student again.

The man reached for his driver's side door, keys in hand.

Giving Silas an idea.

"Sorry, pal," he said, drawing his weapon and aiming it at the twenty-something. "Today ain't your lucky day."

The guy startled and threw his hands in the air, backing up and stumbling over the curb, an AirPod falling out of an ear as he sprawled backward on the sidewalk.

Silas rushed to his side and snatched the keys. He unlocked the doors and yelled, "Get in!"

"Are you insane, prof?" Grant said but obeyed.

Torres said something in Spanish Silas took as resigned agreement, but clearly not happy.

Neither was he.

He shoved the key in the ignition and brought the car to life, then leveraged all the German-engineering bits of the BMW to chase after Nous tearing down Nassau toward freedom.

Oh, to be a twenty-year-old college student again....

"Did we seriously just carjack a college kid?" Grant asked.

"Looks that way," Silas said, dodging a student who was trying to cross the road.

"Not very Christian of you, that's for sure," he mumbled.

"Agree. But now's not the time to stand on principle when the rugs been ripped from under—"

"Watch out!" Torres exclaimed.

Silas slammed on the brakes as a white Honda pulled out in front of him from a road on his right.

Red light. His side.

He laid on the horn. The Honda responded in kind.

"I don't have time for this," Silas mumbled.

He spun the wheel and floored it past the offending obstruction as a chorus of equally miffed vehicles sounded their disapproval.

"You do realize you're just racking up the offenses each block we go, right?" Grant said. "Let's see, there's theft, speeding, running a red light, oh and general jackassery."

"Dude, would you—"

And then he saw it. The next block.

Black panel delivery van.

And the light just turned red.

He grinned. "Gotcha..."

Then he didn't.

Thanks to a massive black Suburban barreling from the south after it played a card from Silas's own deck. And at a good clip, too.

The beast smashed into Nous's top-heavy van in a full broadside, somehow toppling it to its side with the force of it all.

Brake lights flared up everywhere as the traffic braced itself from every direction. Then doors opened, and people fled.

Putting up roadblocks straight out of some disaster movie that mucked up Silas's next move.

Which was made for him at the sound of rapid *rat-a-tat-tat* gunfire.

Two tones, two timbres.

Now three and four and five.

Then six and seven and eight.

Not good.

Silas shoved open the door and leapt outside, Torres and Grant close behind.

He crouched low with extended weapon, weaving past freaked-out civilians and using the abandoned cars as cover on his way up Nassau and straight into the maw of action.

Then it all ceased.

All eight gunfire tones. All eight gunfire timbres.

It was quickly replaced by slamming car doors.

One. Two. Three.

Then squealing tires chased by wailing sirens in the distance.

Not good twice over...

CHAPTER 14

What is that noise?

The world suddenly grew hollow, all sound drawing to a muffled tone yet punctuated by a tuning-fork ting.

But it wasn't just the sound that was jacked up to high heaven.

The world was dimming at the edges, all light and life blurring into a matte-finished landscape of fleeing people and abandoned cars and side-line gawkers.

But that wasn't the worst of it.

Silas's chest started growing tight. His breathing grew dense, like sucking through a coffee stir stick. The pain of a thousand sledge hammers began banging away inside his head and his mouth filled with the taste of pennies from an oversaturation of adrenaline.

Not now, dammit...

The familiar repercussions still rippling across the expanse of his timeline out from those blasted deserts in the Middle East.

It's what those little blue pills were for that he'd chucked in the trash cold-turkey style a year ago. It's why he sucked on those cancer sticks a few times a week and downed the glasses of scotch a few times a day on top of the myriad of other ways he'd tried to keep the overwhelm at bay.

Get it together, Grey!

He dropped to a knee and dipped his head. Then he started the countdown.

999, 998, 997, 996…

A mental ritual he'd developed to pull himself out of the stress disorder that still clung to him, crawling at his head and heart every chance it got.

990, 989, 988, 987…

When the panic and the anxiety and the—

"You alright, partner?" Grant said, coming up to his side.

"Are you hurt?" Torres asked.

Silas shoved off from the pavement, heaving a breath and bracing himself from toppling over.

"I'm fine," he growled.

"Are you sure? A bullet didn't catch—"

"I said, I'm fine!" he snapped. Then he took a breath and ran off.

No time for apologizing or explaining. That would come later.

Silas dodged a frantic coed as he raced toward the overturned van, rear glass blown from the impact and revealing a hollow shell inside.

No movement. No sound. No one inside.

The other vehicle had sped away, leaving in its wake a trail of debris and a few cars turned all catawampus from its sudden arrival.

He slowed as he approached the overturned van, extending his weapon on taut arms. Ready to shoot on sight and ask questions after the fact.

Goon One and Goon Two were sprawled on the pavement. One at the bumper and one behind the toppled beast. Blood gushing from bullet wounds they definitely weren't recovering from.

But no Helen.

Silas crunched across shattered blue glass, steadying his weapon for action as he padded toward the passenger door open to the sky.

He trained his weapon toward it then reached inside for a quick peek.

No one, no nothing.

"She gone?" Grant asked, coming to his side.

Silas said nothing, shuffling around the vehicle to search the area.

When a man came around the other side.

His heart seized in his chest, and a shot of fight-or-flight fuel pinged his brain to raise his weapon and take option one.

Except the dude was thin with long hair stuffed under a stocking cap, wearing ripped jeans and a Goodwill-looking flannel with arms raised, exposing an Apple Watch. Some sort of Princeton grunge chic.

Definitely not your run-of-the-mill hostile.

Luckily for Thin Dude, years of military training and boots-on-the-sand know-how stayed Silas's hand.

Poor guy nearly crapped himself, recoiling and shouting an expletive before backing up.

Silas took a breath and lowered his weapon, then Thin Dude scampered off.

"That was a close one," Torres said.

"For him or me?" Silas said.

"Both. Don't think you want a mistake like that on your conscience. Or record."

No, he didn't.

"Lucky for him, you're a pro at this."

"Something like that. But we've got a bigger problem than a scared civilian."

"Yeah, like our claim to fame disappearing," Grant huffed after checking out the inside a second time. "She must have run off with the damn thing."

"Or was taken by whoever it was who pulled up all Johnny-on-the-spot," Torres added.

"Or that."

Silas cursed himself as he spun back toward the vehicle, sirens blaring closer now and coming in fast. His first big mission since losing Radcliffe and he can't even keep Nous in his sights long enough to—

"Hold on..." Torres said.

He glanced up to find her running to a white Ford something-or-other. Car seemed out of place, front passenger wheel jacked up on the curb and bumper kissing a toppled blue postal box. And Grant said he had committed criminal offenses a mile long with his car-jacking stunt. The feds don't mess around with toppled mail—

Then he saw it. An arm slung across the pavement from behind the Ford's rear end. Still gripping an assault rifle that clearly hadn't gotten the entire job finished.

Torres padded toward the hostile with weapon at the ready. Silas quickly followed with Grant close behind.

The assault rifle looked Russian made. One of the AK lines, if he had to place it. Not his choice of firepower but it got the job done as far as it was concerned.

The hostile was an oaf dressed in black—aren't they all?—face masked with the same nylon material he encountered at Sebastian's place. Tall and muscular and very much dead in a pool of blood seeping beneath him.

"That ain't Helen, is it?" Grant asked, moving in for a closer look.

"Don't think so," Silas said. "Not the right kind of weapon."

"Or body," Torres added. "Clearly a musclehead, probably left behind by the other party that rolled up on them."

And I'll give you one wild guess who it is...

Ignoring the sirens that were sounding too close for comfort now, he walked over to the man, face kissing the pavement. He crouched next to him then yanked back his mask and collar.

Torres sighed. "There it is..."

"There what is?" Grant asked.

Box man tattoo. With the head of a Theta.

The man-god.

Silas stood. "Sure is."

"Wait, you've seen that ink before?" Grant exclaimed as Silas walked away.

"We better jet," Torres said.

"First things first..." Silas jogged back to the BMW that had serviced their chase. He threw the keys inside and closed the door.

Crossing himself and confessing his theft to the good Lord above, he rejoined the pair to make sense of whatever the heck had just gone down.

Took some doing, weaving down side streets and taking a wideberth approach to the university campus to avoid the authorities who soon swarmed Nassau Street, but they made it back to Silas's former office. Rescue personnel had mostly cleared the area after giving the all-clear to return inside. They slipped into the stream of people entering, then made their way back to the conference room.

"Don't you think we should check in with Celeste and Gapinski?" Torres said.

"We will. But first things first..." Silas said as they reached the second floor. He paused, saying, "I want to know why the heck Nous just showed up and then was taken out by the same mystery group that showed up at Sebastian's place."

"You think the prof is in on it?" Grant asked.

"Seems like a stretch," Torres agreed.

"Don't know what to think," Silas said, reaching the conference room door. "But time for some answers. And let me do all the talking, alright? Because none of this is adding up, and I'd like to play this close to the chest until we figure out what's what."

"Whatever you say, pal," Grant said.

Torres nodded.

Silas shoved through the door, finding Hartwin and Rotberg each nursing a cup of tea while Bohls was typing away on his phone.

Hartwin stood. "Thank God you're alright!" He set his cup down, then took a hesitant, if not greedy, step forward. "Did you recover...I mean, did you find—"

"Sorry, prof," Torres said. "The folios are lost to history again."

The man's face fell, and he slumped in his seat.

Rotberg stood and put a hand on the man's shoulder. "Who were those men and that woman?"

Silas took a sideways glance at Torres then took a breath. "Part of what you might call a terrorist outfit called Nous."

The man flinched at the name then took a seat. "Terrorist outfit? Nous, you say?"

"As in, the Gnostic divine reason?" Hartwin added.

"Something like that," Silas said, not knowing how much to reveal given the fluid nature of it all. "The organization I'm now with has been tracking them for some time, trying to stave off their attempts to undermine the Christian faith. And, well...it appears they've struck again."

Hartwin let out a slight gasp and hung his head, shaking it and saying something in German.

Silas took a step toward the man. "What aren't you telling us?"

Hartwin muttered something to himself but said nothing.

"Answer me!" Silas shouted, startling the man. "What the heck is going on here?"

"I am not knowing what is going on here!" he shouted back. The professor sighed. "Forgive my outburst. I was warned something like this could happen, but was not paying it any heed."

"What do you mean, warned?"

"Just that I should be careful and keep a close eye on the folios. Because there was no telling who could be after them."

"By whom, partner?" Grant asked.

"He didn't give any specifics."

"Who didn't?" Silas asked.

"My brother."

Torres asked, "But why would your brother suspect someone might be after them?"

Hartwin shrugged. "Antiquities have always been a love affair of his. He was having to spend his billions on something." The man offered a chuckle before continuing, "Something the two of us have been sharing. One of the few things, actually…"

Silas knew of the brothers' dealings and exploits on the antiquities market. Sounded like something they had bonded around. Understood the feeling, one that had long past with his own flesh and blood.

"At any rate," the professor went on, "I was telling him about what I had discovered, and he said there might be plenty of people who would want to steal such valuable artifacts."

Grant stepped toward the man. "Did he mention any specifics? Name any names?"

He shook his head. "He didn't say. But I guess he was being correct."

Silas raked a hand across his head. This wasn't going anywhere. He asked, "Well who did you get the folios from? Perhaps there's a connection there between what happened here."

Hartwin replied, "An antiquities dealer out of Miami."

"Miami?" Torres startled, glancing at Silas.

Silas knew she had ties down in those parts from when she worked for her uncle. So that was promising. With any luck, she had a connection with the outfit that could move this thing along.

"Do you recall which one?" Silas said.

Hartwin shook his head. "No, sorry. A graduate assistant, on loan from Free University in Berlin, he dealt with the provenance of it all. Although, I suppose this doesn't change much of anything, does it?"

"What do you mean, prof?" Grant asked.

"Given we have the translation and all."

"But what doesn't it change?" Torres said.

"Why, the existence of Gospel Zero. And the quest to go fetch it!"

Silas twisted up his face with confusion. "Fetch it? You mean, go after this Gospel Zero?"

"Precisely! It's what we were discussing over tea when you arrived."

"It's going to make a righteously sick episode on my WeTube channel," Trevor Bohls said, head still glued to his device.

Silas shook his head. What a blowhard. "And what was it you were discussing?"

Rotberg said, "It's why the good professor, here, brought us all together in the first place."

Torres folded her arms. "Which is?"

"A treasure hunt," Bohls said, coming up from his device.

"Excuse me?"

"*Ja*, Trevor is being correct," Hartwin said. "I was intending to send you all along after Gospel Zero after we were verifying the new Muratorian Fragment version, two-by-two."

Silas rolled his eyes. "How biblical..."

"Thieves may have stolen our base text, but we have another." Hartwin held up the translation from Silas and Rotberg. "It's in here, I just know it!"

"I don't know. All I recall of interest with regards to Q is something about the man from Galilee and a reference to the home of our Savior."

"Which is?" Grant said.

"Come on, Grant," Torres said. "I know you were raised a proper Catholic."

"K through Twelve, but it didn't stick."

"I can see..."

"Hey!"

"It's Nazareth, brainiac. The home of our Savior."

Grant whistled. "Impressive. Didn't know you were all Johnny-on-the-spot with Bible trivia, sweetheart."

She stepped back and drilled him with a look to back off. He put his hands up and did.

Silas went to respond when his phone vibrated, drawing his attention to his pocket.

He pulled it out. Celeste.

He frowned. That's right! He had forgotten she called three times before.

"Hold on a second," he said. "I've gotta take this."

He walked away from the group and answered the call. "Hey, Celeste. I was meaning to—"

"Are you alright?" she interrupted. "You haven't answered a bloomin' one of my calls! And there are reports that Princeton was under some sort of attack? Is that right? And why haven't you been answering my bloomin' calls?"

"Hold on, slow down."

"You slow down! You've been giving us quite the fright over here without answering your bloomin' phone!"

Three bloomin's in a row. This was serious.

"Celeste, hold on, let me explain. We've been in the middle

of it with Hartwin and then, yes, what you could say were terrorists."

"Like the jihadi whack jobs we spanked last year?" Gapinski said over the phone.

"Let him finish!" Celeste said. "I've got you on speaker over here with Gapinski and Zoe."

"So, yeah," Silas went on, "we've been having it out over here. But we're alright."

"What happened?"

Silas took a breath, still disbelieving the past day's events—all of them, from the Gospel Zero revelation to the Muratorian Fragment version, from Nous storming in led by Sebastian's lover to another apparent rival taking them out.

He said, "It was Nous, with Helen in the lead."

"What?" Celeste said. "Nous, there at Princeton?"

"That's right."

"And who is Helen?"

"Isn't that Sebastian's chickadee?" Gapinski said.

"That would be the one. Which is how I knew it was them. But there's more. She stole a version of the Muratorian Fragment—story on that in a second. When we managed to catch up to her and her goons, someone else took them out."

"Took them out? Who?" Celeste asked.

"Box man tat guys?" Gapinski said.

"That's right. And it looks like they may have kidnapped Helen on top of getting away with the fragment."

"Which is?"

"What looks like a 2nd century list of New Testament books approved by the Church. With Gospel Zero referenced at the top."

"Dang..."

"That's one way of putting it," Celeste said. "Especially since the Order's chief rival has just been apprehended by an upstart organization we know nothing about. And that's not even touching on the fact verification of an apparent new Gospel has proven to have been unearthed."

"*Alleged*," Silas emphasized. "But yes, all true. Only it's been stolen. We managed to make a translation of the original, but we weren't able to verify anything more. Nothing about its origins and provenance, how Hartwin came to possess it. All we got from him was some story about getting it from some outfit in Miami."

There was static silence on the other end.

Silas looked at the face of his phone. Still connected.

"You guys still—"

"Did you say Miami?" Celeste said.

"Yeah...Is there something I should know about?"

"You could say that. We've been having it out over here, too. Though clearly not like you. In following up on a lead on the mystery man you took out at your brother's house, we discovered a bit more about the bloke."

"And what was that?"

"He did indeed work for MI6. A one, Andrew Sterling. And a sterling record, at that. No negative reports, no black marks. Apparently, one day a few years ago he just quit and vanished."

"Is that unusual?"

"Somewhat, though not uncommon. However, he had recently popped back up on Her Majesty's radar while trafficking in stolen artifacts out of the Middle East."

"What kind of artifacts?"

"Religious."

"Sounds like our guy. But what's the Miami connection?"

"In a coordinated effort with INTERPOL and the FBI, MI6 tracked Sterling to an outfit out of Miami."

"Really?"

"Yes, but you're not going to like it. And neither is Torres."

Silas looked toward his partner, who was engaged in a discussion with Grant and Hartwin about something.

"Why is that?" he asked.

"Because the outfit is San Jose New World Salvage and Exploration."

"I don't under—"

"It's her uncle's company."

"The one who passed last year, who she worked for before the Order?"

"Right. And it's the link between the hostile you killed at your brother's house and now your adventure at Princeton."

And also the link in Gospel Zero's provenance...

CHAPTER 15
MIAMI, FLORIDA.

Silas held the plush creamy leather armrest of his chair in the Order-issued Gulfstream with a white-knuckle grip as it touched down on the tarmac at Miami International Airport. The plane bounced once, then again before the buzz saw rushing sound signaled its halt.

He hated flying. Always had. One of the reasons he had joined the Army instead of the Air Force. Dad probably had something to do with that too. Always complaining about the fact that the good Lord above didn't see fit to equip us with either wings or gills. So there was damn near no reason mankind should be globetrotting on air or sea. Of course that didn't stop Dad from dragging his sons from base to base as a colonel in the Army.

Silas wanted to follow in his footsteps when he died that fateful day on 9/11 after Flight 77 slammed into the Pentagon wing that housed Dad's office. Didn't know flying was part of the gig when he was tapped for the 75th Ranger Regiment, the lethal force where agility and flexibility of operation in all types of terrain and weather using a variety of insertion methods was the name of the game. Including flying. He'd eventually gotten over his fears enough to stay in and lead his men to victory, many times over.

And there he was again, flying into Lord only knew what. This time leading another SEPIO mission for the sake of the Church.

He opened the shade as the plane taxied to their reserved private terminal. Mid-70s, no rain, and not a cloud in the sky. The western horizon was beginning to show signs of what was sure to be a blazing sunset, a palette of ripened-peach colors streaking across the sky. A stark contrast to the day they left behind at Princeton.

After Silas got the startling news from Celeste, he pulled Grant and Torres aside to debrief, giving Hartwin some lame story about the authorities needing some answers to continue their cover. To say that Torres was shocked was an understatement. Flat out denied the possibility that her uncle's outfit was working with the terrorists to undermine the Christian faith. Was even more adamant that he himself wasn't personally involved, given the timeline Hartwin described when the set of folios would have passed through his hands a year ago if he arranged it all.

Silas understood the protests. Torres probably couldn't stomach the idea that her deceased uncle was somehow embroiled in the mess, wanting to preserve what little memory she still had of the man after he passed from liver cancer last fall. Which included preserving the dignity of the place he'd poured his blood, sweat, and tears into. And since she herself had worked with him and helped build the place, she had skin in the game.

Silas reassured her that nobody was saying any of it was her uncle's fault. Only that there was a connection somehow between the Coptic Muratorian Fragment and her uncle's Miami outfit.

Torres would have called up her cousin Lucas who had

taken over running the joint then and there had Silas not intervened. Gave her a direct order when she protested and began dialing anyway. Couldn't risk the mission by jumping the gun. The plan instead was for her and Grant and him to rendezvous with Gapinski and Celeste in Miami. It was a quick three-hour flight. So they'd have more than enough time to pay a visit and get some answers.

Because the good Lord above knew they needed them. And the trail of questions seemed to start with Torres's family. Took some convincing, but Torres relented and agreed.

When they returned to Hartwin, he proposed they fly at once to Nazareth, where the Coptic fragment had made mention of Gospel Zero originating. Promised his brother would pay their entire way, sparing no expense on their treasure hunt. Silas proposed instead they split up into two groups of threes, arguing it made the most sense for Hartwin, Rotberg, and Bohls to work together given their connections, and him and Torres and Grant to go off together since Grant knew him and Torres. Of course he still didn't mention the three were about to take a side trip to Miami. Hartwin relented and the two groups went their separate ways.

Silas glanced over at Torres as the plane continued taxing. She looked dejected, distant, disheartened. Understood why. Couldn't imagine a family member presenting as one thing only to learn they were an entirely different person, collaborating and cavorting with an enemy bent on destroying her faith.

Actually, he could...

He looked out the window, the peach-colored sky growing more bruised, wondering where Sebastian was, what he was doing and planning and plotting next. Especially considering his lover was somewhere out there. Probably still missing, possibly captured by a new enemy. Even dead at their hands.

A shadow passed over the window as the plane slid into a private hangar, soon stopping on squeaky brake pads.

Silas unbuckled his belt. Torres was still staring out into the darkened hangar void. He reached over and squeezed her knee. She startled, turning her gaze to Silas.

"Sorry to hear about your uncle, that he got caught up in this mess," he said. "I know how you might feel betrayed or that his involvement and his company's involvement seems unbelievable, or any number of things. Just remember that we don't know anything. Not yet, anyway. So let's go get some answers, alright?"

Torres took a breath and offered a weak smile of thanks, then nodded and unbuckled.

Silas crouched through the narrow entrance then descended a similarly narrow set of stairs, followed closely by Torres and Grant. Waiting for them was an oversized black Mercedes SUV, the Order's apparent vehicle of choice for all things SEPIO.

The doors opened and out stepped Gapinski from the driver's side and then Celeste from the passenger's.

"Look what the cat dragged in," Gapinski said.

"Hey to you too," Silas said. He gestured behind him and added, "You remember Grant Chrysostom."

"Yeah, I remember. Shoots well enough, though a bit limp-wristed if you ask me. But I guess he can join in the fun." The man offered a wink and a chuckle.

Grant smirked. "Gee, thanks, partner. But next time your ass is being overrun by special-ops Mormons in a South American jungle, don't come calling on me."

Celeste approached Torres. They embraced. "How are you getting along, mate?"

Torres shrugged. "Well enough. But like Silas said, we don't know anything yet. So why don't we get to it?"

Silas liked Torres's no-nonsense approach. And she was

right. They didn't know anything. About any of it. He hoped to change that starting now.

Gapinski manned the SUV's helm. Celeste rode shotgun. Grant squeezed into the very back row and Silas slid next to Torres in the middle seat.

"Little excessive, don't you think?" Silas mumbled as Gapinski brought the beast to life.

"Nothing but the very best for the Church's knights in shining armor."

"We're gonna have to have a chat about our vehicle expense account one of these days."

Gapinski weaved his way out of the airport under an evening sky now blazing purple and pink and dimming fast to indigo. Soon, they were driving down U.S. Route 1 through a dense corridor of hotels and offices and restaurants under the orange glow of streetlights, the night crowd beginning to trickle out onto the sidewalks.

"So what's the plan, chief?" Gapinski said from the front.

Before Silas could answer, a white stretch limo passed them filled with screaming cougars spilling out from the open panoramic moonroof, drinks in hand and bright red and pink lipstick set stark against pale, wrinkly, aged skin.

"I vote we go where the Golden Girls are headed," Grant said. "Sounds like a much better proposition given what we've been through the past twelve hours."

"While I don't disagree," Silas said, "I think we'll begin to gain some clarity after our visit with Torres's former crew. At least, that's my hope."

Celeste turned around and looked at Torres. "I'm sure there's a perfectly fine explanation for all of this."

"I know you're right," Torres said, shifting in her seat. "I'm just worried more than anything, knowing what's already happened and what *tío* might have gotten his company wrapped up in and Lucas wrapped up in before he—"

Emotion caught in her throat, and she turned away toward the window.

Celeste frowned, rubbing her knee and glancing at Silas for help.

"He's the reason I am who I am, you know?" she said.

"No, I don't know, actually." Silas turned in his seat toward her.

Everything in him wanted to use their drive to put their heads together to strategize and push Gapinski to get moving faster to get the answers he'd been wanting all day. But he sensed he needed to do more than just assemble the troops and move 'em on out.

He said instead, "Tell me about it."

She seemed to brighten at the suggestion, turning in her seat toward him. Grant leaned forward from the back for a listen.

Torres pushed a lock of dark curls behind an ear and offered, "My parents were killed by a drunk driver when I was a teenager, and, well, my rich Venezuelan uncle took me in. Raised me like one of his own sons. The daughter he never had."

She laughed and wiped her eyes. "And by rich, I don't mean drug-money rich. Like all the cliché *gringo* novels like to stereotype all *latinos y latinas*. As if we're all just living in a perpetual episode of *Narcos*. No, his was oil money. Which might be the next best cliché, now that I think of it." She wiped her nose, then went on, "Anyway, he funded my graduate program at UCLA studying Mesoamerican and pre-Columbian cultures. He took me into his salvage and excavation business after graduation and set me loose to do my thing."

"San Jose New World Salvage and Exploration, isn't that right?" Silas said.

Torres nodded. "And then when I royally screwed up by breaking international law and getting greedy, hawking stolen artifacts on the black market and he nearly lost his business—" she paused, emotion catching in her throat again. She cleared it and continued, "After all I put him through, he forgave me and came through when the Order needed him."

"I'll second that," Gapinski said from the front. "The man and his crew are studs."

Silas remembered what Torres's uncle had done over a year ago, lending a helping hand to take down a presidential candidate conspiring to destroy authentic Christianity.

He said, "Sounds like a great uncle." He took a breath, but pressed, "And I don't want to sound insensitive, but do you know what any of this could be about?"

Torres shook her head. "No, not at all. I'm surprised he was even in the artifact business to begin with."

"I thought that was exactly his type of business."

"San Jose New World Salvage and Exploration deals in sunken treasure ships in the Caribbean and archaeological digs in South America. Not trinkets and papyri from the Middle East."

She paused, staring outside as they continued driving through downtown Miami. "I don't know what *tío* got himself into, or Lucas and the rest. Which is what has me worried. I don't want his memory to be tainted by some religious conspiracy that brings down the Church!"

They rode in silence, heading south to an industrial district on the outskirts of Miami. Gapinski followed the address Torres gave him, driving to a large warehouse near an inlet where a sizable expedition-style boat was docked.

"Do you miss it?" Silas said, nodding toward the docked whale.

"Sometimes. Certainly beats getting shot at and blown up by religious terrorists." She smirked and pointed to the boat. "When I was out on that boat and in that warehouse uncovering the mysteries of ancient cultures, the only thing I had to worry about was sunburn and the occasional shark."

Gapinski pulled through an open entrance, fence topped with barbed wire, then slid into a parking spot and turned off the car. "Luckily for us the sun has set, and I don't plan on dipping my fat hinny into the ocean, so no worries on the shark front."

"And let's just hope Nous has other things to worry about," Silas said, getting out of the SUV.

"Like the other bully on the block?" Celeste said, doing the same.

"Exactly. It'd sure be nice to follow a clue without the drama."

Gapinski smirked, slamming his door shut. "Fat chance."

Silas frowned. Unfortunately, he knew how right he was.

Sound from the emerging downtown nightlife filtered across the water combined with the gentle hum of boats and crashing waves. Other than that, it was dead. Which suited Silas just fine.

The smell of fish and taste of salt on a gentle wind breezing off the water reminded him of a life far, far away from the frenetic, do-or-die vocation he signed up for. Twice over now. Part of him longed for the simplicity that such a life offered, like salvaging treasures under the sea or carefully peeling back layers of dirt to unearth forgotten civilizations. Or even simply manning a taco cart up the beach. Even better, scrubbing boats clean of barnacles and repairing torn sails.

Now there was honest, simple work. Why not skip town and open up a sailboat repair shop? Kick back at the end of the day at the edge of a weather-worn dock with a bucket of ice-cold Coronas, lime wedges stuffed down their necks until gouts of foam spilled over. Maybe a hot dog in hand or a bag of chips and the feel of the setting sun at the back of the neck. Celeste on one side, a Golden Retriever on the other. Now there was honest, simple work.

This? Crunching across a gravel parking lot overgrown with weeds and an annoying tree frog croaking in the shadows, approaching a three-story warehouse of rusting corrugated metal siding, roof sagging under the weight of decades of neglect and seagull droppings, waiting for the next black SUV to come riding up with a load of anti-Christian terrorists?

Silas wondered how many years of this he really had in him. And he was barely four months into his gig as Order Master! How the heck did Radcliffe do it all those years?

'My grace is sufficient for you....'

There was that still small voice again. Which he appreciated. He just wished God's crazy love would show up with a job offer at a sailboat repair shop. Bucket of Coronas at the ready.

Grant opened the door to the warehouse. Torres led the way inside a darkened, quiet hallway lit by a solitary fluorescent light down the middle, the smell of damp wood and must and old things strong.

"You sure somebody's home, Torres?" Gapinski whispered.

"My uncle was a workhorse, so were his sons, and he trained his people well. They're here. Somewhere."

Voices echoed toward them. Torres glanced back and nodded forward.

She led them farther inside, past what looked like a break room, dark and smelling like burnt coffee, and an office with a large picture window, a 70s-era steel executive desk with a lamp shining brightly on top and a well-worn leather chair turned away, a tear opening up on the seat back.

She said, "They've gotta be down this way. *Hola, alguien aqui? Lucas, es Naomi...*"

Soon they made their way to a large room with a low ceiling, cheap wood paneling covering the walls and more fluorescent lighting. A large table commanded the center, maps and documents strewn about, and a grouping of leather chairs and a couch sat at the other end. Looked like where they conducted their research and cataloged their finds.

"I don't get it?" Gapinski said, hands planted on his hips. "Where's the party?"

"Only place left is the back garage," Torres said. She turned toward a side door at the corner of the room. "It's this—"

She was interrupted by the cocking of a shotgun.

"Don't move, *amigos*," a man growled, voice low and buttery. "Not a single step if you know what's good for you."

No one moved. Except Torres.

She turned around and walked between Silas and Celeste, then smiled and offered a small wave. "*Hola, Lucas.*"

There was a gasp. "*Naomi?*" her cousin exclaimed, a fit man their age wearing a black t-shirt with a clean baby face.

He set the weapon on a table before rushing over to embrace her. He pulled back and laughed, mouth wide with delight and hands grasping her shoulders as if he couldn't believe his eyes.

The pair talked in rushed Spanish while the other four looked on. She gestured toward them, seeming to explain their unexpected visit.

Then Lucas's face fell. Thick eyebrows above dark eyes dipped inward as he listened. He retrieved the shotgun again, sending all the signals he needed, and whispered his reply.

He was nervous.

Which made Silas nervous.

He glanced at Celeste, who wore the same look of concern.

What did the man know?

"Come, please. Let us sit," Lucas finally said, gesturing toward the grouping of chairs and couch. He set the shotgun back down and walked over to the side door, disappearing through it while the others took a seat.

"What did he say?" Silas asked Torres.

She took a breath. "He'll explain it all. Just...hear him out, alright?"

"Sure. But now you're making me nervous."

Lucas returned with a hardscrabble woman, hair long and silver, he introduced as Maggie and his father's partner. They were accompanied by a brawny, middle-aged man named Burt, who Torres explained was the captain of the docked fish and director of operations. The two looked pleased to see Torres, but a bit shaken.

"Could I get you anything?" Lucas asked. "Water or soda?"

Silas could use a stiff one, and a cigarette, but welcomed the caffeine. The others asked for the same.

"Let me have a first crack at him, would you?" Celeste asked. "I have some experience in these types of matters."

Yes, she did. As former MI6 and as director of operations for SEPIO, she certainly knew her way around an interrogation.

Silas nodded as the man returned, arms full of soda cans. Lucas handed them out then retrieved his shotgun and flopped into one of the chairs. Then Celeste got to work.

She moved to the edge of her chair across from Lucas. "Right. I assume Naomi explained why we are here."

Lucas sat up and glanced at Torres. "*Sí.* She did."

"Then why don't we take it from the top, shall we?"

The man nodded and sighed.

"You were the originator of the newly discovered Muratorian Fragment folios in possession of a one Hartwin Braun, is that right?"

"Not originator. The middleman."

"But the professor bought them from you?"

He nodded.

"How was it that they came to be in your possession?"

"Someone approached me and my father last year looking to unload a cache of papyri."

"Who?"

The man ran a hand through thick, wavy black hair. "I do not recall the exact name, but they are in my files. I can pull them for you. But I remember he was German. Something like Strauss or maybe Stern something."

Celeste looked to Silas. He said, "Could it be Sterling?"

Lucas tilted his head. "*Si*. I believe that was his name, yes. Something Sterling."

Celeste retrieved her phone and brought up the image of the dead guy from Sebastian's home.

"Was it this man?" she asked, turning the phone toward him.

His face fell. He brought a hand to his mouth and nodded. "Who is he?"

"Not a German antiquities dealer, we can tell you that much," Silas said.

"I don't understand how you got into this mess in the first place," Torres said, shaking her head. "This was never *tío's* ambition, to deal in artifacts."

Lucas shrugged. "We had no choice, Naomi. *Papi* was running huge debts and bordering on bankruptcy. The money was good, and we thought it was a way out of the hole."

"Debts? Why didn't I know any of this?"

"You never asked, *mi prima*."

"I don't mean to interject into what I understand to be a delicate family situation," Celeste said, "but time is a bit of the essence at the moment. Now, when you say that Sterling approached you, and that you mediated the sale to Hartwin, how did that happen?"

"It's like I said. The German, or whoever he was, showed up proposing to hire us as a middleman who would transact the transfer of papyri discovered in Egypt."

"Egypt?" Silas asked. "Where?"

"Luxor. The paperwork for provenance seemed to check

out. He had receipts of purchase, a trail that documented their origin."

"Do you have this paperwork?" Celeste asked.

Lucas nodded. "I can get it for you."

"Brilliant. But what of Hartwin? How was that connection made?"

"By Sterling himself. He suggested we approach the Princeton professor."

"So he approached you and your father wanting to hire you to mediate a transaction for a sale, and he already had a seller in mind?"

"That's right."

"Did Hartwin know about this deal?"

Something seemed to click inside Lucas's eyes. They narrowed and then darted toward Torres before opening again. He shook his head, saying nothing.

"I think we'll see that paperwork now," Silas said.

He stood and left down the hall toward the office they had passed earlier. A few minutes later, he returned bearing a large manila envelope.

"It's all here. Copies of the bills of sale. Both for the original buyer as well as to Hartwin. Certificates of provenance. Even copies of the folios themselves."

Silas startled. "Copies of the folios?"

Lucas nodded. "*Si*. We like to document everything we receive with pictures and photocopies. And we did here as well. Both sides of each folio."

"Wait a minute, partner, " Grant said, putting up a hand. "Did you say both sides?"

"*Si*."

"But why? The goods were only on the one side."

"Not that I remember. It looked like notations had been made on the backsides of some folios."

Silas sat straight, brightening. "Hand it over."

"What is it?" Celeste asked.

"We only saw what was written on one side of each folio," Grant offered as Silas undid the metal clasps holding the flap closed.

Silas slid out a stack of papers and started ruffling through them. "Which means we only translated one side of each parchment."

He found the photocopies of the folios. Black and white but good quality. He started with the first page, turning it over.

Finding Coptic scribbling on the underside.

His mouth went dry with excitement. He turned it back over and translated the original in his head, recalling it mentioned *'the one from Galilee prepared by the man from our Savior's homestead.'*

The reference to Gospel Zero.

Hopeful, Silas turned the photocopy back over and translated the note.

His mouth widened into a grin.

Bingo.

"Find something, partner?" Grant asked.

Before he could answer, the lights cut out.

Plunging the entire warehouse into utter darkness.

CHAPTER 16

Startled cries echoed throughout the space as dark as pitch.

Now Silas understood what people meant by *'pitch black'*—the idiom originating from the sticky, resinous, black or dark brown substance obtained as a residue from the distillation of wood tar or turpentine.

About summed it up.

With the doors closed, the sun having slipped beneath the horizon an hour ago, and the room smack dab in the middle of the warehouse, light was hard to come by.

"Always something," Gapinski said.

Silas couldn't agree more.

A beat later, something outside coughed and rumbled to life, as if rudely awakened from a deep slumber it didn't ever expect to climb out from.

Yellow emergency lights snapped on at the corner of the room. A sense of relief seemed to wash over the space.

But just barely.

Because they were far from out of the woods.

Gapinski was the first to stand. He whipped out his trusty

SIG Sauer. "Twinkle, twinkle little star, how I wonder what you are..."

Silas followed suit with his Beretta. "Thank the Lord for generators."

Celeste stood and armed herself as well.

So did Torres. "I don't know how many times I told *tío* how cuckoo in the head he was for installing that propane hunk of junk out back. Glad he didn't listen to me."

"No offense, love," Celeste said, "I'm jolly well glad he ignored you as well."

"Yeah, thank God for paranoid uncles," Gapinski said.

"Alright, folks, this ain't a drill," Silas said, focusing the troops to the moment at hand. He released his magazine for a quick double check before slamming it back inside. "It's go time."

Yet again...

"I knew when you cats walked through the door at Princeton that trouble was close behind," Grant complained, fishing out his own weapon.

Gapinski smirked. "Glock? Figures..."

"Hey, don't mock, pal. I'm liable to have to save your ass with that—"

"Shh!" Silas hissed, holding out an arm. "Listen..."

They did. Everyone held still until the whining warble of something in the distance came into range, and growing in strength.

"What do you reckon it is?" Celeste whispered.

"A helicopter?" Silas asked.

"Aliens?" Gapinski whispered.

"Speedboat," Torres said. "Or some other rig." She walked to the side door leading to the back dock and cracked it open.

The sound grew louder. More of a buzz-saw growl now, an angry tone and timbre that meant business.

It also meant trouble.

And it was fast approaching.

"Who are they?" Lucas said gripping his shotgun, voice quivering and shadows creased across his brow in the yellow light that betrayed fear.

Silas eyed the man. Clearly no match for trained, hardened special-ops hostiles. Whoever they were.

"My guess is the same group behind Sterling. Come to, well, clean up. And since they cut off the power outside and are now arriving by boat—"

"There's a good chance we're monkies in the middle?" Grant asked with interruption.

"Something like that." Silas pointed to Lucas. "You stay here with Maggie and Burt. And keep that shotgun handy."

"But—"

"No buts. We've got this. You don't."

The man took a breath and nodded.

Silas turned to Celeste. "You and Torres go out back to meet our new arrivals. Gapinski and I will go out front to check things out. And I know SEPIO's policy about violence in the field and all."

"Right. Aim to incapacitate, not kill," she said.

Gapinski snorted. "Doubt our box-man tattooed yahoos out there got that memo. And if they did, we're toast."

"Anyway," Silas went on, "just do what you need to do and watch your six."

"Is that an order?" Celeste asked, grinning wryly.

"You bet it is."

"What about me?" Grant said.

"Stay here and don't break anything. And that's an order, too, pal," Silas added before the man could protest.

He frowned but nodded.

Silas padded to the door that led them into the conference room, Gapinski close behind. Celeste and Torres quickly assumed their own positions at the side door, while the other four remained huddled in the center.

Here we go. Back into the fray.

ON THREE, GAPINSKI OPENED THE DOOR TO THE HALLWAY THAT led through the heart of the warehouse and back outside.

One. Two. Three.

The door was thrown open.

Silas took a step inside the darkened corridor, pivoting with back at the wall to his right and Beretta swinging on taut arms down the hall. Ready for anything.

Empty, but for yellowy illumination.

With the main electricity off, the hallway felt warm, the air stale and staid.

The generator must be keeping the minimal running. Which included the yellow lighting straight out of a 70s dive motel and probably security and computer network infrastructure. But not the air conditioning.

Silas wiped away a bead of sweat that started snaking down the front of his forehead. Waiting, intuiting, discerning what might come next through the door anchored at the end of the long hallway running the length of the warehouse.

Nothing. It stood calm, cool, and collected.

For now.

He glanced to his left at Gapinski, who was still waiting just inside the conference room. Celeste and Torres had already headed out into the back of the warehouse toward the sound of that buzz-saw growl.

He smiled. His kind of lady. Always running toward danger.

Movement at the corner of his eye pulled him back down the hallway.

A change in lighting. A shadow, then a shadowy figure.

At the door.

Silas didn't wait.

Shoot first, ask questions later had been something of an unsaid rule back in Iraq. Had to be with what he and his boys had faced. Not official Army policy, and not proud of it. Just the way things were fighting those cowboys' war built on those phantom WMD weapons and false nation-building promises.

Still lived and died by that rule. Which totally flew in the face of what he had just reminded Celeste of.

He pinched off several shots. But nothing major. Just a *one-two-three-four* hi-de-ho introduction to let them know who was in charge. All high and wide. Not aiming for center mass.

Whatever it was that was massing at the end of the hallway.

He didn't wait to find out.

Silas took off toward the target, Gapinski hot on his heels.

He slipped into the break room still smelling of burnt coffee, the sweet smell of his old Princeton office. Always kept a Mr. Coffee running throughout the day. What he wouldn't give for a cup of—

A *one-two-three-four-five-six* rejoinder came splintering through the door, followed by a six-shot echo from another weapon. Different tone, different timbre.

A little overkill. But it did the job of sending Gapinski scurrying past Silas for cover.

"Jeeze Lousie, brother," Gapinski complained. "What was all that talk about not shooting to kill and then blowing past your own orders?"

"Change of plans," Silas said, reaching around to offer a *one-two-three-four* reply. "Thought we should introduce ourselves all proper like to the new kids on the block."

A *one-two-three-four-five* follow up from their new friends sent both scurrying deeper inside for cover.

"Yeah, well, consider us introduced," Gapinski said. "And what are we gonna do about it? We're sitting ducks here."

Silas stepped back to the plate, leaning around the threshold of the break room entrance for a peek.

Nothing. Door stood calm, cool, and collected, if not a bit shredded.

But not for long.

"Got some sound advice back in my days with the Rangers," Silas said, gripping his Beretta and readying for round two.

"And what was that?" Gapinski asked.

"Always run away from a man with a knife, run toward a man with a gun."

"That's crazy talk! Uncle Sam taught you that?"

"No, Jimmy Hoffa."

"And look how that turned out for him."

"Either they're busting through or we are. And I'd prefer we had the element of surprise, not them. You got my six?"

Gapinski slid a hand across his bald head and nodded.

Silas nodded back. "Door opens out, and then our SUV is sitting to the right, so make for that. Should shield us from the hostiles and take the brunt of their gunfire."

His partner groaned. "Not another Mercedes down the tube..."

"Either it or us."

"Next time we're driving a BMW. Don't mind them getting trashed by religious whack job terrorists handing out bullets like it's Halloween."

A creaking door on tired hinges echoed faintly.

From the left. Down the hall.

"Now or never, partner," Silas whispered, raising his weapon.

"Do or die," Gapinski replied.

Silas stepped out and opened fire.

Sending *one-two-three-four* bullets sailing toward the door and running along with them.

Two sunk into someone double his weight before he could get off a shot, dropping him like a used bathrobe.

Another fell back as Silas raised his weapon. He pulled for the fight.

It popped off a single shot before clicking empty.

"Sonofa—"

"Don't worry, I got your six," Gapinski said, pushing past him and laying down fire as the hostile staggered back on uncertain feet before dipping out of sight stage right.

His partner kept going, followed closely by Silas. He slid out the empty magazine and shoved a backup in just as they reached the first downed hostile.

Gapinski leaped first, then Silas. His partner popped off a few shots before they emerged into the night.

To find an empty parking lot, except for their Mercedes.

Silas swung his Beretta left, sweeping it with anticipation. Lapping waves and a white security light hung on a pole leaning at the corner of the lot was all that greeted them.

Until he heard the soft crunch of gravel from his right.

He swung to meet the challenge.

When Gapinski put up a hand and gestured for their SUV.

"Come out, come out, wherever you are," Gapinski taunted, aiming for their Mercedes as he crept sideways toward its rear.

The hostile had hijacked their bunker!

Silas followed his lead, but went for the front. "You're outmanned and outgunned. Give up now or forever hold your peace."

No reply but the waves and that annoying tree frog from earlier.

Reaching the passenger's door, he squinted for a look through the tinted windows. No use.

Gapinski glanced back from the rear and Silas nodded back.

Time to end this.

Silas eased around toward the front end.

When a flash of black from below caught his eye.

Just in time for him to take a knee before the corrugated metal siding sparked with violence.

Not the pistol kind from earlier, but the AK kind from Princeton.

He sent his own reply over the hood. Which wasn't needed.

Because a few beats later, Gapinski put the hostile down cold. Four to the back, no questions asked.

"Thanks," Silas said, standing and out of breath. "I owe you one."

"Buy me a brewski when this is all over."

"There's a six-pack with your name on it."

Silas bent next to the man, back oozing blood and face planted in the gravel. Not a good way to go. But that was the road he chose.

He set his weapon on the ground and reached for a mask covering the hostile's head and neck. Same make and model from Sebastian's house.

He pulled it up then pulled down the man's collar.

Box tattoo.

"Figures," Gapinski said.

Yep. Figured. No surprise there.

But it did confirm what happened early yesterday morning wasn't a one off.

Another player had saddled up to the table.

And was playing for keeps.

THE BUZZ-SAW WARBLE OF THE SPEEDBOAT ENGINE HAD CUT OFF its angry announcement as soon as Torres and Celeste left the conference room, signaling their threat had officially arrived.

They left Grant behind with Lucas, Maggie, and Burt. Torres was confident he could hold his own, especially after the way he handled himself helping out SEPIO in Honduras. Never knew he was capable of putting a man down when they dated. Definitely not when they were engaged. But when the moment came, he didn't hesitate. So she knew her cousin was in good hands.

The two crept through a cavernous garage on the backside of the warehouse, the only light coming from a full moon and Miami's runoff through an open door at the far end and a lone emergency light hung at a far corner.

Torres felt like she was thrown back into the Israeli Defense Force again in the dead of night. Standing around with her unit at one of the border crossings at the West Bank or Gaza Strip just waiting for a suicidal truck to come barreling through the gate, or a bottle filled with kerosene and a rag all aflame to come crashing down on her head, or a rocket-propelled grenade to explode at her feet. The training taught her everything she needed for that moment creeping through a warehouse in Miami. But she didn't like it one bit. Had vowed never to return to such a life of violence and the unexpected and religious fanaticism.

Yet there she was, all three boxes checked in spades.

For all two years and four months, as required by Clause 16A of the Israeli Defense Service Law, she had fulfilled her duties to Mom's side of the bloodline, who was Israeli. Saw another side of the world that reminded her of home, with all of its hardscrabble, arid landscape punctuated by tropical beauty and rimmed by gorgeous beaches filled with Western tourists. The religious fervor was something different, though the constant threat of terroristic violence also reminded her of a home still riven by the cartels.

Given the experience of her own people—Mexicans from her father's side of the family tree—she couldn't help but feel for those on the other side. Those caged inside walls not of their making or choosing. Never once let her politics become known to her pureblood Israeli compatriots who already were a tough sell on not only her gender but also her ethnicity. Whoever heard of a Mexican-Israeli woman serving in the IDF? And a Catholic one at that? Had to be some sort of politically incorrect joke in there. One *tío* would have told in a heartbeat.

She chuckled to herself at the thought and smiled at the memory of the man who flooded her senses with every step through the cavernous garage. From the smell of oil and gasoline to the rattling of chains and lapping of the ocean through the open door at the end. From the sight of Lucas back at the conference room who had stolen her breath with the spitting image of his father to the burnt coffee from the break room made to *tío's* perfection.

Emotion caught in Torres's throat as she and Celeste padded forward, taut arms gripping weapons they were more than ready to put to good use as they scoped the place for Nous or the new religious whack job order or whoever was coming in on them hot and heavy.

Mantenga la calma, Naomi...

She wiped a bead of sweat with the back of her hand as they carefully, quietly moved through the dark garage, a cavernous space that held deep-dive equipment, a LiDAR electronic imaging contraption she and Grant had used a few years ago for a SEPIO mission in Honduras, and a smaller boat still saddled atop its trailer.

The waves continued coming in, their lapping rhythm and the distant city providing the only soundtrack as they passed the trailered boat. They approached the open door to the dock, its rough-hewn wood weathered from the decades glowing with moonlight from above. Not unusual for a door to stand open even that late at night, given Lucas and the crew were still—

Movement caught Torres's attention a pace away.

She stopped short and aimed for the floor, her finger curling around the trigger.

A rodent the size of a small cat scampered past, scurrying out the door to safety.

She heaved a breath and eased it out her nose.

"What is it?" Celeste whispered.

"Just a rat. Let's keep moving."

Torres had complained from here to high heaven to *tío* about the *regio ratas*, the Regal Rats as she called them, that seemed to have more say over the joint than her own uncle, scampering around like kings and queens, getting into this and that. It was an endless argument she wished she could still have.

They reached the door. A long red and black boat sat at the end of the dock, engine killed and body swaying gently in the nighttime current. A speeder for sure.

"I'll take point on the boat. Why don't you continue searching the garage," Torres instructed in a whisper.

"Split up?" Celeste said with surprise. "I don't reckon that's a good idea."

"Why not?"

"We haven't a clue who these blokes are! Or where they—"

"More reason to split and take on these *idiotas* one at a time!"

Torres felt a sudden urge to fight for her cousin and Maggie and Burt. To take on the bastards who had stormed her uncle's castle all on her own. Win or lose. For *Tío*.

But Celeste was in charge. And from the look of it, she wasn't used to being directed and challenged.

Celeste sighed, then nodded with resignation. "Fine. You take the boat, I'll scope the garage. But shout at the first sign of trouble."

"I understand."

Torres went to leave when a hand grabbed her arm.

"And be careful out there, alright? You don't have to fight this alone."

She offered a curt smile before heading off.

Problem was, that's exactly what she thought. Had she not gotten greedy and traded stolen artifacts on the black market, getting nailed by INTERPOL and nearly destroying her uncle's business reputation in the process, he wouldn't have been on the verge of bankruptcy. And without all that debt he wouldn't have drunk himself to death and wouldn't have had to expand his streams of income to include trinkets and papyri from the Middle East.

Leading to playing middleman for a relic at the heart of a religious conspiracy.

And leading to a boat of hostiles rolling up on his warehouse.

Torres tightened her grip as she padded slowly toward the boat, arm outstretched with the fish dead in her sights and resolve hardening.

Nothing to do but put every last one of them six feet under. Besides, as *Tio* always said, '*No hay que llorar sobre la leche derramada!*'

She neared the boat, a smile flashing across her face. No need to cry over spilled milk, indeed. Getting upset over something that has happened and cannot be changed was useless. Better to—

Noise caught her attention. Her breath seized in her chest.

A thudding, then a rustling.

So there was someone still on board...

Torres crouched, then side-stepped along the length of the boat, keeping it trained in her sight but seeing nothing and no one, the noise disappearing into the void of lapping waves.

She reached the stern, sweeping the entire length of the fish without any visual.

No entiendo...

She retraced her steps, weapon extended and heart pounding and breath heavy—

Thud, scrape, rustling.

And then she saw it.

A woman. Dressed in black with long blond hair, wrapped up into a bun but falling apart. Face bruised. Arms tied behind her back, mouth gagged.

And a wooden box toppled next to her, parchment falling out and scattered about.

Helen. The Coptic Muratorian Fragment.

And no one else on board.

So she'd been taken captive then. And with the pot of gold.

Torres reached for the edge to hoist herself aboard.

"Don't mind if I do, *chica*. And if you're lucky—"

A muffled *pop-pop-pop* echoed from the garage.

Then a shout.

And another set of *pop-pop-pops*. Different tone, different timbre.

Celeste!

CHAPTER 17

Torres's stomach sank to the dock as another round of *pop-pop-pops* rang out with livid intent from the maw of darkness at the other end that had served as a staging ground for her former life as a researcher and treasure seeker. It was followed by a round of shouting and tussling that obscured whether Celeste was the one in trouble or the troublemaker.

She couldn't help but feel a sense of desecration at what was transpiring inside the inner sanctum of all that she held dear. Not only because of the memories it held ogling and cataloging the latest haul of sunken treasure from the remnants of the *Flota de Indias* that had departed in two convoys from Seville. But more for what it represented: Tío Juan, and all that he had built and cherished until his last dying breath. All that she had *threatened* a few years back that nearly broke her uncle and nearly ended their relationship in a brazen act of greed and self-centeredness.

Thankfully, she was able to make amends before he passed. And she would be damned if she would let a bunch of two-bit terrorists destroy what *tío* had poured his blood, sweat, and tears into.

She shoved off from the weathered boards throbbing with memory, faltered a step in her pursuit, but recovered and darted for the garage at a full sprint, weapon extended and ready to—

Two men emerged. Both tall, both big, both clad in black.

With Celeste being dragged between them by her arms. Limp and unresponsive, feet dragging behind her.

"Hold it right there, *idiotas!*" Torres yelled, pulling up quick and aiming for the largest of the bunch on her left.

The men halted. Surprise written across their faces.

Which pleased Torres. Always enjoyed playing the part of the unexpected.

Numero Uno went to raise his gun.

Torres was quick on the trigger, firing a *one-two* warning shot. One sank into the dock just to the right of his feet. The other splintered the weathered wood and sent his feet jumping.

She smirked, tightening her grip and adjusting her aim.

"Lady, we've gotta go!" Numero Dos said.

"Like hell you do! Hand her over, or I'll toast your asses from here to Sunday."

Both men shifted on uneasy feet, looking at each other before throwing a worried glance behind their shoulders at the open door.

She shot at the dock again. Another *one-two* punch that reiterated her contempt. This time inches from Numero Dos, who didn't dance but widened his stance and tightened his grip on her partner.

Celeste stirred now at the sound of her second overture.

Then the men stiffened. They glanced at one another and nodded.

Numero Uno said, "Fine. You want her. Here you go—"

The men lunged toward Torres in a lumbering rush. Celeste dragging between them on her toes, head still downcast.

Torres froze. What should she do? No way she could risk

shooting the men with Celeste held between them. And she couldn't just let them get away. It all happened in slo-mo. Like some cheap Kindle bargain-bin thriller.

They hoisted Celeste up in the air with their powerful arms and threw her toward Torres.

The two women fell in a heaping tumble as the men continued running toward the boat. Apparently far more concerned with getting away than taking them prisoner.

The fall shook Celeste from her unconsciousness. Torres recovered and aimed for the men as the boat roared back to buzz-saw life. But she opted for checking on her friend instead, failing to make good on her promise to toast them. Too far away now anyway.

She helped Celeste up from the dock to sit. "You alright, Celeste? You shot or hurt?"

"Just knocked around a bit is all," Celeste moaned, rising to her knees as the speedboat roared to life.

"What happened—"

"Bomb..." she said, eyes suddenly snapping wide with remembrance before shuffling to her feet with an unsteady rise.

"Did you say bomb?" Torres asked, rising to her feet in a panic.

"Run!" Celeste screamed before an explosion catapulted her and Torres through the salted night time air pulsing with the reverberations of the blast, sending them splaying across the dock again.

The two faceplanted along the rough-hewn boards as the speedboat escaped into the night.

With their only lead.

A REVVING ENGINE CAUGHT SILAS'S ATTENTION. GROWLY AND echoey and sounding like it was making quick work of the water.

Damn. That means they're getting—

A sudden phantasmic blast of fire and fury bloomed from behind, the sound of the blast overshadowing the speedboat making its escape and light casting oranges and shadows across the lot.

He and Gapinski stood and spun around to find gouts of smoke billowing into the clear night sky, orange and red and yellow casting wicked illumination across their faces as flames roared to life from the back of the warehouse.

The first thing Silas thought of was Celeste, followed by Torres and the others.

Then the photocopies!

"No..."

He leaped over the dead hostile and rushed toward the warehouse entrance.

"Silas!" Gapinski called after him.

Silas reached for the door when a large hand fell on his shoulder, gripping it and pulling him back.

"What the hell are you doing?" he roared, yanking his shoulder free and darting for the door again.

"Silas!" Gapinski shouted, grabbing his arm.

"What?" Silas shouted back, yanking it with anger.

"If you're gonna run into a burning building potentially filled with terrorist whack jobs, at least bring cold, hard steel!"

Gapinski held out Silas's Beretta.

Silas ran a hand across his head. Must have forgotten to take it back from the gravel ground in the chaos.

He snatched it. "Thanks."

Gapinski nodded. With one hand he held his SIG Sauer, with the other he grabbed the doorknob. "On three."

"Screw three. Just open the damn door!"

He nodded and threw it open. Silas was ready with extended weapon.

Empty, but for the yellow light now obscured by a haze of smoke seeping through the warehouse's pores.

Silas didn't wait for his partner. He ran the length of the hallway, gripping his weapon and ready to put it to good use again.

No one came.

He coughed as he scrambled toward the conference room, the smoke growing thicker now in ribbons that meant nothing good.

What kept him going was the thought of Celeste trapped in a hellish maw at the other end. The blast looked like it had come from the back garage closest to the dock.

Just where he had left her and Torres.

Not even death itself would stop him from reaching her, rescuing her.

And along the way, retrieving the photocopies that held their only leads to this hellish mess.

The SEPIO pair rushed past the break room and then past the main office on their way toward the conference room.

When the door flew open and out stumbled Lucas and Grant, Maggie and Burt. Thick black smoke, billowing out from the top of the ceiling, chased them out. As did an orange glow that only grew worse by the second.

The group staggered toward them and fell to their knees, coughing and hacking as the hallway filled with smoke.

Silas did the same, followed by Gapinski, who echoed his own suffocation.

"Can't...breath," he complained.

"Get them the hell out of here!" Silas ordered on all fours, shoving Lucas toward his partner and waving Maggie and Burt to do the same. "You, too," he instructed Grant.

It was a sauna now, a mixture of heat and humidity as the tinderbox began to burn just past the thin sheets of drywall and fiberglass insulation and wood studs standing between them and the garage. The smoke was suffocating and blinding. They really did have to get the hell out of there.

"Where are you going?" Gapinski asked.

Silas said, "I gotta get the papers."

"No use, *amigo*," Lucas said, coughing. "The whole room is going up in flames!"

"I have to try!"

"What about the gals?" Gapinski yelled, voice hoarse now from the smoke.

Silas's stomach dropped to the floor looking into the room. It was worse than he imagined. A chapter straight out of Dante's Inferno.

Thick black smoke obscured most of the room now, but what he did see told him all he needed to know.

A wall of flames stood guard at the door leading into the garage, tendrils of fire reaching with hunger inside the room. A demonic sentry that was impenetrable.

No way was he getting through.

Panic gripped him like the jaws of a rabid dog, threatening to overtake him then and there. But he knew Celeste. She could handle way more than he ever could. Torres was a tough cookie herself. He would have to trust them to take care of themselves. And the Lord.

"I have to believe they're alright!"

They have to be alright.

Lord Jesus Christ, Son of God, they better be alright!

He waved Gapinski on and plunged into the conference room.

Heat slugged him in the face, the force of it nearly sending him backward. Tendrils of crimson and orange flames were flowing like reverse lava up the wall butting the garage toward the ceiling now, having chewed a hole inside. The smoke was a shroud of nothingness, blotting out all light and life inside except for the flames.

He shined a penlight into the void for a better viewing.

Strewn across the floor at the center of the room, a few yards away, he glimpsed precious signs of the photocopies. Must have scattered in the chaos of the terror and explosion.

Now or never...

Silas threw himself to the floor, pressing himself flat and jutting out his elbows. He knew he had a minute, two tops, to get what he needed. So he leveraged all that he had endured through basic training almost two decades ago. Might as well put Uncle Sam's earmarked dollars to good use after the fact.

He made quick work of the room, pulling himself forward until he reached his target. He could see several of the papers were already burning or completely consumed, but he pulled in what he could.

Holy cow was it hot as Hades! And growing worse by the second. Hands slick with sweat and running blind, he managed to slap together an armful of the photocopies, drawing them to his chest and elbowing back out of the room.

He was drenched by the time he reached the hallway. It felt a hundred degrees cooler and surprisingly the smoke had thinned.

"Make a run for it!" Gapinski shouted for him from the end, waving him outside.

Good idea.

A crash from behind startled him.

One end of the ceiling had collapsed, sending sparks and flames flying.

It's go time!

Holding his breath, Silas hugged what papers he could and sprinted down the hall, the sound of more collapsing spurring him on.

All the while praying to the good Lord above that his darling made it out alive without injury. And Torres and the others.

Gapinski and Grant met him at the door and pointed across the street at a vacant lot where the others were gathered, along with their idling Mercedes.

The two took off toward it.

Just as the back end of the warehouse collapsed in on itself, taking part of the other half with it.

Silas didn't look back. Instead, he ran into the arms of his love who was waiting for him next to Torres.

"Thank God you're alive!" Celeste cried.

He held her tight, then pulled back. "Are you alright? Are you hurt?"

"Just a bonk on the head from those bloody hostiles."

He pulled her against his chest again. "I thought I lost you..."

"Hey, what am I? Chopped liver?" Torres said.

Celeste giggled and pulled back. "If it weren't for her, I probably would have been. She saved my life. Dragged my bloomin' bum around the side of the warehouse to the lot out front before the inferno took over."

"Thank God!" Silas said.

"Did you get what you went back for, *amigo*?" Lucas asked.

Silas eyed the ground, looking for evidence of an answer to the man's question.

Scattered amidst the weeds and tall grass were wet, sooty photocopies of something. Looked like a handful of receipts and typed letters and other documents. But hardly any of the Coptic folio photocopies.

Silas's face fell. "Who knows what the heck we've got here."

"A whole lot of nothingburger?" Gapinski asked.

"Don't speak too soon," Torres said, kneeling to retrieve something from the weedy ground.

Silas turned to find her holding up the wooden box Helen had stolen from Hartwin, grinning proudly.

He sighed with relief and matched her grin. "Where the

heck did you find it? Don't tell me the knuckleheads had it with them on the boat."

"Oh, yeah. They did. And that wasn't all." She paused before adding, "Helen."

"So they got away with half their goods?" Gapinski asked. "Serves 'em right."

Torres shook her head. "Didn't have the heart to keep her all tied up. So I cut her bindings. The rest was up to her. Hope she took the get out of jail free card and jumped before they returned."

"Suppose us women have to stick together," Celeste said. "Even if she is our enemy."

"And my brother's lover," Silas added.

Wailing sirens in the distance caught his attention.

"Come on. We better split. The last thing we need is to get tied up with the authorities."

CHAPTER 18
SOMEWHERE OVER THE MEDITERRANEAN.

Sebastian paced the length of the Gulfstream cabin, his back hunched to accommodate his lanky legs and torso, his coifed blond hair brushing against the cloth ceiling with every step, his shoes clicking a Morse code of irritation and worry and barely contained rage across the ultra-thin granite veneers that ran the center aisle.

The imbecilic incompetence! The sheer stupidity! The Neanderthalic neglect!

He clenched his fists into his palms, not even noticing his well-manicured nails drawing thin lines of blood as they sank into his soft skin from the force of his fury.

A rumble of turbulence sent a shudder ricocheting through the jet. Sebastian braced himself against a creamy leather chair toward the rear of the aircraft before sinking down into it, finally allowing himself the luxury of rest after hearing his love had been kidnapped by the same people who had broken into his own home.

The box men.

They had come out of nowhere. A wraith, a phantom, a golem of an unknown sect spawned from the loins of some material entity imbued with an unknown intent that seemed to challenge his own.

Of course, there had been rumors of such men through the ages. Brutes and beasts biding their time to challenge Nous as the harbinger of a new enlightenment dawn. All unnamed, all masked, all hidden within the shadows—yet beaten back all the same.

Until now...

Sebastian clenched his fists again, a worry wrapped in the husk of anger worming its way through him. The brutes had broken out into the open under his watch. Had stolen into his very own home and stolen his very own lover, intercepting the next piece to the puzzle they needed to crush the Church and its central object of veneration. The Bible.

It was a challenge, an affront, a menace that threatened to not merely undo what Nous had been biding their time for two millennia to unleash upon the Church and offer the world in the wake of its death. But to unseat Nous as the rightful heir apparent for all that Christianity stood for.

Salvation. Resurrection. Ascension.

Except this kind of apotheosis of mankind that Nous promised would come neither from inner angsty guilt over behavior that fell short of some arbitrary mark set by some Spaghetti Monster and punishment of some fire-and-brimstone eternal existence. Nor would it come through some eternal church service in the sky, full of off-key grannies belting old hymns, and starched white shirts and ties, and really bad coffee that tasted of cardboard and kale.

No, no, no. *Enlightenment.* That is what Nous brought. What *he* was bringing to the masses. Pure, unadulterated empowerment to decide how to live and who to marry, to match one's internal clockwork with one's external bodywork, to plumb the depths of all that life has to offer in all of its multifaceted experiences and impulses and dalliances, free from the confines of bigotry and hypocrisy and finger-wagging zealotry.

The power to name and claim and deem what is good and evil in the coming Republic of Heaven—that is what Nous, what *Sebastian Grey*, was handing the world on a silver platter in their crusade to expose the Bible for what it was.

A man-made fairytale, bought and paid for by old, white men—the victors in a bruising, vicious battle to control the masses and gatekeep religious affection.

Pure and simple.

And all of his plans were being threatened. Starting with revelations that the bowl he had come to possess may not be what he thought it was—more performance art, a forgery even, than anything he could leverage to crush the Church. He nearly went public with the revelation himself had Hartwin not intervened with his own television stunt. Thank the gods he was spared that embarrassment—especially for the sake of his tenuous hold over Nous.

But that wasn't all.

Because an upstart mystery sect had risen from the trash heap of history to not only steal his thunder but steal his lover.

Oh, Helen...

Out of nowhere, he started invoking the gods and prophets of the Universe to come to her aid, to rescue her from the hands of the wicked men and stay the hand of Death itself.

Buddha. Krishna. Allah and Muhammad. Moses and Yahweh. Jes—

No, no, no. There would be no going there. No trembling at the feet of the man-god from Nazareth. Not now, not ever again.

That chapter in his sordid religious love affair was dead and gone. He would never utter and definitely would not invoke his name ever again. Never acknowledge his significance, especially in the wonder-working power type he was grasping for in his weakened state. Perhaps he might still entertain the notion that he was a wise teacher. Certainly not the lamb of God, come to take away the sins of the world, as that bloody fool John the Baptizer had announced. Definitely not the God of the Universe, in whom we live and move and have our being, who is capable of answering such pleas for mercy.

Sebastian sighed. Carrying on in this way, he felt pathetic and weak and—

Pain lanced up both arms, from stem to stern. He looked down to see himself clenching his fists with white-knuckling might.

He took a breath and let go, a pinkish hue returning from his death grip.

Rivulets of blood were pulsing with weak wonder from the eight punctures his nails had made. Sending his heart soaring with lustful delight, his mouth watering with rapacious desire.

And also conjuring a blessed memory from his sweetheart, the other wayward half to his soul.

It was the night the two of them were introduced a year ago down in the bowels of Castle Wewelsburg, in the very baptismal well where he himself had received his commissioning as Grand Master of Nous.

But this ceremony was of a different sort. Both primal and pagan, bathed in passion and sealed in blood.

Divina neuter.

Divine Feminine.

The yin to the masculine yang that so dominated the Order. And Helen was at the center of it all. So too was Sebastian, Borg officiating over a ceremony that made him pant just thinking about it while the Thirteen and Council of Five looked on at their union.

Paying no attention to whether anyone inside the cabin was watching, Sebastian brought one of his hands now slick with blood to his mouth, his lips curling over his palm and tongue licking it dry.

The heavenly taste of pennies sent his heart soaring, and the rest of him longing for the same taste of his love. His Helen, the one who had set him free.

Someone approached from down the aisle, head dipped and steps halting, as if he didn't know how to approach him.

Sebastian finished his shot of ecstasy and beckoned the man to his side.

"What is it?" he said, the other hand throbbing with the pleasure it bore.

"Helen, my Master."

Sebastian sucked in a lungful of air, his body tensed and bowels went weak at what the announcement might hold.

The aide offered a weak smile before responding, "She's alive."

He leaned toward the man, the ends of his mouth turning upward with a mixture of hesitation and hope.

"Alive?" Sebastian whispered. "Where?"

"Yes, sir. Miami. Our East Coast field office received a distress call an hour ago—"

"*An hour ago?!*" Sebastian exploded with interruption, standing with looming rage over the man who recoiled with surprise.

The mousy imbecile tripped over the arm of another seat and stumbled to the granite aisle, smacking his head against the floor.

"Yes, yes, sir..." he stammered, face draining of color and drawn with fear.

"*Why wasn't I informed until now?!*" Sebastian bent down over the man, face red and neck hot with rage at being kept out of the loop.

"We thought it best to wait until confirmation," the man said, sinking into the floor. "A cohort of Nousati picked her up just moments ago. I came straight away after I received confirmation of the rescue's success. I promise!"

Sebastian straightened, his mouth heaving hateful breaths and blood pulsing with equal hatred—all of it pent-up fury from his double losses, unleashed against this unsuspecting victim.

He took a step back and straightened his shirt, smoothing it before settling back in his chair.

"Good work. But next time, notify me the minute, the *minute* you receive information of import about any aspect and facet of the Order and Nous's missions—*anything at all! Do you understand?!*"

"Yes, yes, sir…"

"Good. Anything else?"

The man stood, body bent and will broken, his eyes not finding the courage to meet Sebastian's.

"Yes, yes, sir," he stammered, eyes fixed to the floor and hands wringing themselves to death.

"What is it?"

"The folio images. The decryption of Helen's communique is complete."

Two wins in one. Not bad.

Before Helen's disappearance, she had uploaded an encrypted, compressed file to a secure Nous server buried deep under the Wewelsburg operation center. It contained images she had hastily taken of the folio pages with her phone.

Always taking precautions and preparing contingency plans, she was. One of the many things he loved about her.

Sebastian's mouth widened into a grin. "Excellent. Where are they?"

"Waiting for you on a tablet device."

"And where is this tablet device?"

"It's…" the man trailed off and glanced behind him toward the front.

"Then why don't you be a good little dog and go fetch it for me!" he said through gritted teeth, mustering every ounce of energy not to strike out at the wretched creature again.

The lackey offered three mousy nods and trotted off to retrieve the device. Returning, Sebastian snatched it from the man and turned it on.

Displayed were an array of high-definition photos of the folios, their time-stained papyrus set against Helen's toned, black-clad legs.

Oh, how he longed to wrap himself around her again. To feel and touch and enjoy those legs, as well as the rest of her.

That would have to wait. Now it was time to translate.

He returned to the image, reaching in his jacket for a small journal and black pen. Then he set about his project, a sense of ironic satisfaction washing over him as he did what his twin had done for years. Something Silas never would have imagined him interested in, much less capable of doing.

That was the thing about Silas that Sebastian found so comical and yet enraging. He had underestimated him from the beginning of this new rivalry. All his life, really. Little did big brother know he had put his near-genius level mind to work learning Coptic. And why not?

He had already earned dual doctorates in physics and computer science. So the learning part wasn't the issue; that had always come naturally. It was a matter of dedication and perseverance. When he began taking on a larger role within Nous at the behest of Borg, the so-called Gnostic gospels unearthed in Egypt almost eighty years ago began calling to him, particularly in their original, pure form. The thought of immersing himself in the early Christian texts that those in power rejected as heretical called to him like the Sirens of Greek mythology—drawing him, wooing him, beckoning him to taste and see the enlightened goodness that the Church had rejected.

And taste he did.

It was as if he had been living a life stuck in a 50s-era black and white television show and then been suddenly thrust into a full-on high-definition existence. Like Dorothy falling from the heavens into Oz.

And this list makes clear they were valued for what they were...

A gateway into the secrets of the Universe. A knowledge so profound and enlightening that it would take a special conduit, a shaman even to transmit them to the world.

Him. Sebastian Grey.

When he was finished translating, he frowned. Aside from the interesting bit about the other Christian writings discovered in Egypt, not much to go on, and not much revealing. Other than the reference to the secondary source for the Gospels aside from the Book of Mark and the other Gnostic texts he had so grown to adore, there wasn't much to fuss over.

Sebastian returned to the tablet and noticed another entry at the end. From the thumbnail it looked blank, but he knew he should take a gander if Helen sent it along.

He tapped the image then scanned it, not understanding why Helen had included it in the batch.

Wait. There...

He furrowed his brow and squinted, noticing the faint impression of a notation at the top.

Leaning in, he took care to copy the thinly drawn characters of Coptic text onto his notebook. Leaning back, he studied what he wrote:

$\pi\alpha\chi o\mu\iota\upsilon\varsigma\ \pi\eta\gamma\dot{\eta}$

He understood what the letters spelled, what the two words translated into. But he wondered what it could mean.

Then he had it. Something he had learned during his study of those blessed Gnostic texts.

Brilliant...

Sebastian tore a page from his notebook then snapped his fingers, summoning the mousy man from earlier. He handed him the piece of paper and told him to instruct the pilot to turn the plane toward the location written on it. A speck of a city across the Mediterranean that had found fame, or infamy depending on your politics, in all things religious.

Hope rose as he thought about all the revelation it still held within its sands.

And all that it would mean for humanity. For Nous.

For him.

CHAPTER 19
MIAMI.

All Silas wanted was a hot shower, a terry-cloth robe, a generous bed with down pillows and matching duvet, light-blocking curtains, and a night with nothing but sheep and a day with nothing but possibilities.

Instead, he was crammed with the best and brightest of SEPIO inside a cheap hostel room dubbed "The most economical place in Miami," with two queen beds that smelled of cigarettes and mildew and bleach, walls shedding what was more likely than not lead-based mustard paint that would send them to an early grave after they paid their bill. While he complained about spending bank for their Mercedes ride, he now wondered about extending the same penny-pinching policy to their accommodations. They needed a quick, low-cost option that wouldn't attract attention to regroup before they split the city. But Silas was beginning to rethink the low-cost part of the deal.

Sheep and possibilities would have to wait. They had a long road ahead of them seeing through their mission to preserve the integrity of the Church's memory and teachings about the Bible. Beginning with the dive straight out of a Hitchcock movie.

Lucas, Maggie, and Burt insisted on staying put with the smoldering remains of their livelihood to deal with the firefighters and the police. Even at Torres's strong protests.

SEPIO warned them there could be further repercussions if the terrorists weren't convinced they had finished what they'd started. The crew weren't having anything of it, insisting on staying put and laying to rest their business—*Tio Juan's* business—and livelihood proper. No way they'd let a bunch of lily-livered, chicken-hearted hitmen win by scaring them off. Figured the danger passed anyway, since they'd have to assume the evidence had been cleaned up in the blast.

Silas finally relented, as did Torres, reluctantly leaving them behind after gathering what papers he had grabbed. Racing back up U.S. Route 1, they checked in with Zoe who was standing by for operational support before they retrieved contingency equipment from their Gulfstream. A few laptops and secure sat-phones and whatnot stowed away on board for such planning emergencies. Silas told her to stand by to help sort out the mess once they got set up at temporary accommodations.

It was still go time. And it had gotten both more tense and less all at once. Could do without the hostiles, but at least they had some leads.

He just prayed to the good Lord above they panned out.

"So, buddy, what's the plan?" Grant asked Silas as he finished setting up a laptop connection with SEPIO ops in DC.

"The plan, *buddy*, is to figure out what the heck is going on here before the next shoe drops."

"Oh, yeah?" Torres said. "And how do you figure we do that?"

Silas shrugged. "Like we always do."

"With a buck and a prayer?" Gapinski said slouched on one of the queen beds.

He threw a pillow at him from across the room.

"Hey!"

The laptop chimed with the arrival of the petite Italian with baby blue glasses standing by from DC.

The SEPIO crew waved and greeted her huddled around the laptop as Silas turned up the volume. Not the best way to go about planning the next stage of their operation, but it would have to do.

"How are you all fairing?" Zoe asked. "Sounds like you were put through the wringer over there."

"You're telling us," Silas said. "We're in one piece and no one was injured. At least too bad. So we can be thankful for that. Any further clarity on your end, Zoe, as to who these hostiles could be, the mystery box men?"

She cleared her throat. "Nada. It's like they spontaneously generated themselves a day ago. No references to any sort of markings or terrorists of these sorts in any of the world's databases. Not the FBI, not MI6, not INTERPOL, not the Vatican."

Silas frowned. "Copy that. Keep looking but don't spend too much time on it. These things have a way of revealing themselves."

"So where are we exactly with this whole sordid tale?"

He raked a hand across his close-cropped hair and sighed. "That's why we're camped out inside this cramped, crappy hostel."

"And why I insist on throwing the piggy bank to the wind when it comes to SEPIO accommodations," Gapinski complained.

"Here's what we know so far," Silas said, ignoring the man. "A year ago, a man by the name of Andrew Sterling brokered a deal between a mystery seller and Juan Torres to hire his company to sell a cache of Coptic papyri to Hartwin Braun."

"This is according to my cousin, Lucas," Torres added. "Apparently *tío* had been running large debts and was on the verge of bankruptcy. They saw the opportunity as a way to make some easy money. They were hired to verify the provenance and the authenticity of the papyri, and then brokered the final deal to Hartwin."

"And Sterling," Zoe asked, "he was the man you tussled with and ultimately killed at your brother's house, Silas? The one with connections to MI6?"

Silas nodded. "That's right. And apparently part of a mystery organization of seemingly sectarian whack jobs that brands itself with box men tattoos mirroring the Persian Gnostic sect Mandeans."

"Not to be confused with Nous," Gapinski added, "the other organization of seemingly sectarian whack jobs."

"So how does our archenemy factor into all of this?" Zoe asked.

"Hard to say," Celeste said. "But one of their operatives, Helen—"

"Sebastian Grey's lover, isn't that right," Zoe interrupted, "who, by the way, SEPIO has learned has just assumed the mantle of Grand Master of Nous."

A coldness rushed through Silas's veins at the news; his stomach sank with the realization his brother was indeed his chief rival now.

Celeste glanced at him, her eyes full of sympathy and solidarity. "We had not heard of that bit of news yet. But yes, that is correct. And it is she who stormed the conference room at Princeton, stealing the folios and running off until being intercepted by the mystery order and carted off. Showing a clear conflict between the two entities."

"And that's perhaps the plus side to the sordid tale," Silas said. "Thanks to Torres, who found both the box of folios and Helen stashed away on the hostile's boat, we now have the original mystery fragment referencing Gospel Zero that set off this whole wild goose chase into motion in the first place."

"What we presume to be the Muratorian Fragment?"

"The Coptic *version* of the Muratorian Fragment. But yes. As well as some papers we managed to retrieve from Torres's uncle's operation."

"What sort of papers?" Zoe asked.

Silas nodded for Celeste to answer, who had organized the crumpled, dirty, damp mess he managed to retrieve.

"Right. A good bit of booty actually," Celeste answered. "First off, there's a photocopy of a signed sales contract. It recorded the man we know to be Andrew Sterling's original purchase of thirteen Coptic papyri, in November 2011, from a one Ulrich Pauli. The contract said that Pauli himself had acquired the papyri in Frankfurt in the mid-1980s."

"Great. Another name to track down," Gapinski complained.

"And another German," Torres echoed.

"Seems to be the theme of the cinematic experience this go around."

"I'm just glad they're not an elite special-ops force from some pseudo-Christian religious sect like last time," Grant said.

"That we know of."

"Can we focus please?" Celeste said, holding up another crumpled photocopy. "Apparently Sterling also provided a scan of a photocopy—that is, a copy of a copy—of a 1982 letter to Pauli from an Egyptologist at Berlin's Free University."

"Wait a minute, Free University?" Silas asked.

"That's right."

"Hartwin said the man who handled the provenance for him was a graduate student on loan from Free University."

"The plot thickens..." Gapinski said.

"Sure does."

"And get this," Celeste went on, "a one Terrance Munson from the same university wrote that a colleague had looked at the papyri and thought one of them bore text from the Gospel of John, verifying its authenticity."

Silas tapped the box. "It was one of the others that had accompanied the Coptic Muratorian Fragment." He folded his arms and sat on the edge of the bed. "And those two pieces of evidence seem to give weight to their authenticity. Which doesn't bode well..."

"Ever the pessimist," Celeste said, flashing a wry grin. "Zoe, I'm sending you photos of the letters for your reading pleasure. Have a think on them and have a go at researching anything you can find about this man Pauli."

"Already on it," Zoe said, the clacking of a keyboard off screen confirming it. "In fact, already getting some interesting hits."

Silas stood again and started pacing. "By all means, fill us in."

On screen, the woman adjusted her baby blue glasses and took a breath. "I ran a search of public documents and found just one German city that had ever been home to Ulrich Pauli. In 1977, a German couple named Ulrich and Agnes Pauli established residency in Frankfurt. Judging from these public records, the couple never left. A few years ago, Ulrich incorporated Manda Art Limited."

"Wait a minute," Silas said. "Did you say *manda*?"

"That's right."

He looked at Celeste and nodded. "Aramaic word for knowledge. Like the bowl from Sebastian's house."

"And those box-men whack jobs," Gapinski said, sitting up with interest.

"A promising lead," Celeste said.

"Sounds like our guy," Torres agreed.

"Wait a sec..." Zoe said.

"What do you have?" Celeste asked.

"Seems too easy..."

"Tick tock, tick tock, Zoe," Silas said.

"Sorry, but I dropped Pauli's name and email address from

one of the invoices into Google and it flagged a site that tracks domain registrations."

"Domain registrations?"

"As in website domains. Get this, three weeks before Hartwin made his little announcement of his discovery to the world a few days ago, when only he and probably his inner circle knew of the goods and his name for it—Ulrich Pauli registered the domain name www.gospelzero.com."

Gapinski whistled. "Definitely sounds like our man."

Silas grinned. "And looks like our first piece of hard evidence linking a name to the cache of papyri. He still alive, Zoe?"

"Looks that way."

"Then it looks like we're going to Germany."

"Hold on," Grant said, eying one of the photographed pages on the other queen bed.

Silas walked over, arms crossed. "What do you got?"

"I'm looking at this letter, the one from the Egyptologist at Free University verifying the Gospel of John papyrus."

"From Terrance Munson," Celeste said, walking over as well.

"That's right."

"And?"

"And, well, look—" Grant pointed to a word, second line at the center of the page.

Silas and Celeste bent over for a closer look.

"I don't get it," Silas said.

"Neither do I," she agreed.

Grant shook his head. "Amateurs. That there word should be typed with the sharp *S*, a special German character."

"What of it?"

"Come on, man. It's the Eszett, literally meaning *s z*. And when the letter ain't available, it's almost always substituted by the double-*S* characters."

"Ahh, I see your point," Silas said, his German clicking into gear. "A sign the letter was typed on a non-German typewriter or after Germany's 1996 spelling reform, or both. Not in 1982."

Grant leaned back and grinned with satisfaction. "Exactly."

"Wait a minute," Silas said. "Celeste, didn't you say the sales contract was dated November 2011?"

Celeste nodded. "That's right."

He turned to Torres. "But your cousin said Sterling had only acquired the fragments a year before he sold them to your uncle last year. So two years ago Sterling was supposed to have bought them from Pauli, right?"

Torres nodded. "Sounds about right. Which means another major discrepancy."

"Bingo. And potential evidence of a major forgery."

Celeste seemed to consider this. "I hear what you're saying, but playing a bit of Devil's advocate here—do we really believe Hartwin would be duped by such a forgery? Not only because he and his brother have been avid collectors of artifacts, but also because the man is a renowned scholar in religious studies."

"The lady has a point," Grant offered. "It's pretty common for forgers try to unload their creations on the unwitting. Scholars like Hartwin are usually the last people they want eyeballing their handiwork."

"So what kind of forger might try to dupe one of the world's leading historians of early Christianity?"

"A pretty gutsy one," Silas said. "That man would have to have some serious cojones to even try to attempt such a feat. But also remember the grad assistant from Germany is the one who handled the provenance. Not Hartwin."

"Hold on a sec," Zoe said from the laptop.

Silas stepped over to the device. "What do you got, Zoe?"

"Have you inspected the papyri folios themselves?"

"Well, we translated them, so we had a look at them then."

"Yeah, but you were staring at the bark on the trees. What about the forest itself?"

She had a point. He gestured to Grant who had the box next to him on the bed and asked him to remove the folios. He did, and Silas helped him arrange them on the bed, each of the Coptic Muratorian Fragment folios one by one in three neat rows as well as the single Gospel of John fragment at the end.

They spent several minutes in silence, staring at the folios, searching for clues.

Silas took a piece of paper and hovered over one of them near the end. Then he brought out his phone and started typing.

"Whatcha looking for, partner?" Grant asked over his shoulder.

"I want to check on something that bothered me from the first time I translated these things...Ah, here it is!"

He put his phone next to the piece of paper, which bore two short sentences.

"Bingo!"

"Bingo, what?" Celeste asked.

"They're different!"

"What do you mean, different?" Grant asked.

"I brought up the English translation of the original Muratorian Fragment, then translated part of the corresponding end of the Coptic version. They don't match."

Everyone gathered around Silas, and he pointed to his phone. It read:

Of the writings of Arsinous, called also Valentinus, or of Miltiades, we receive nothing at all. Those are rejected too who wrote the new Book of Psalms for Marcion, together with Basilides and the founder of the Asian Cataphrygians.

"Now look at the Coptic version." He showed his rendering:

> *Of the writings of Arsinous, called also Valentinus, or of Miltiades, we receive them. Those too who wrote the new Book of Psalms for Marcion, together with Basilides and the founder of the Asian Cataphrygians.*

"See? The Coptic version changes *'nothing at all'* to *'them'* and then removes *'are rejected.'* And then it adds this weird paragraph and final sentence that doesn't at all appear in the original Latin Fragment."

"A pretty crucial set of revisions and omissions that changes the meaning entirely," Celeste said.

Grant scoffed. "That don't mean anything."

"Are you kidding me?" Silas said.

"For all we know, the original Muratorian Fragment changed the Coptic one we have! We've got two different versions. That's all."

Silas shook his head and shoved his phone in his pocket. The man was partly right. But it was also an important clue that couldn't be easily dismissed. Even for a skeptic like Grant, which surprised and frustrated him.

"Jolly good lead, love," Celeste said. "But let's keep going. I'm sure there's more to see in the forest of folios."

They all stepped back to the bed for another look.

"One thing I will say," Torres said, "the visual similarities between the two are striking."

They were. Both had the same oddly formed letters, made by what looked to be a blunt writing instrument. The ink was the same brownish pigment and tone and consistency as well.

"Do you think they were written by the same hand?"

Silas shook his head with confusion. "Looks that way. And all of it doesn't look right."

"What do you mean?" Celeste asked. "What's off about it?"

"Every ancient manuscript is really a collection of features, and we take all of them together when we evaluate these sorts of artifacts from the past."

"Such as?"

Torres answered, "Such as the writing instrument, how the script is stylized, the handwriting of the original scribe, the grammar and sentence structure, the syntax, the content itself —all of it is subject to analysis."

"And if any of these features has something that is off about them," Silas went on, "then we can consider the entire manuscript a fake."

"And in your judgment," Celeste asked, "from your collective years of scholarship and expertise, that is what we have here? A fake?"

Silas rubbed his chin and glanced at Torres, who didn't answer. He continued scanning the folios, focusing on the forest instead of the trees—the overall presentation of the artifacts instead of just the words.

Same blunt instrument used on both fragments, the Coptic Muratorian list and the Gospel of John. The ink pigmentation and stroking the same. Even the characters all corresponded, confirming they had to have been written by the same hand in the same Coptic script.

And then it hit him.

"Wait a minute. I want to check something."

Silas went to one of the other laptops and then brought up Google. He typed in a query, which led him to a website of a number of images of ancient manuscripts. He clicked on the first one and held it next to the fragment of the first chapter of John's Gospel.

A perfect match.

Every single word, in exactly the same order.

"Look," he said pointing with a giddiness that came from finding the exact-fit puzzle piece to a research mystery.

The SEPIO crew crowded around. Gapinski was the first to see it.

"Now that there is quite the coinkydink. What are the odds that every line on one side of the fragment corresponded exactly to every line on that their online image? Same amount of words per line, each line starting with the same word?"

"Exactly. But that's not all," Silas said. "Zoe, you suggested I evaluate the forest instead of the trees. And now I see a variety of problematic features."

"Like what?" Celeste asked.

"For starters, each of the folios seems to have been written with a reed pen, but the letters on this John fragment, blunt and thick, appear to have been made by a brush. Not only that, they weren't formed correctly. Like clenching a crayon instead of holding it naturally between the fingers."

"Which suggests what?"

"Which suggests a nonnative writer," Torres said.

Silas nodded. "Exactly."

"I don't know," Grant said, tilting his head. "Looks different enough to me."

"Are you kidding me? No way! And now that I'm reading this again—the whole forest versus trees thing—I'm spotting a handful of grammatical errors. Like if someone were to write *'he handed the book me'* in English."

"The kind of mistake that a nonnative speaker would make."

"Or a young child just learning the language. Hard to see how an adult native speaker would make such mistakes. And then there's this—"

Silas pointed at the laptop, then he folded his arms with satisfaction.

"What is this you've discovered?" Celeste asked.

"A Gospel of John manuscript written in Lycopolitan."

"Lico-whatchamacallit?" Gapinski asked.

Silas snapped a finger and grinned, revelation hitting him. "Of course! Why didn't I see it before?"

"See what, partner?" Grant asked.

"Both of these sets of fragments are written in a dialect of Coptic known as Lycopolitan, which died out during the 5th century."

"So, what of it?"

"So, Hartwin said the Coptic Muratorian Fragment dated to the early 6th century. Yet it is written in a dialect that died out decades before."

"Ahh, I'm picking up what you're putting down," Torres said, grinning herself now. "If authentic, it would be pretty bizarre to have the sole example of a text in Lycopolitan from the 6th century or later."

"And not just one, but two, given it seems pretty apparent that the Coptic Muratorian Fragment was written in the same hand."

"Yeah, but it is possible," Grant said, "that a scribe in the 6th century had simply copied an earlier Coptic text in the dead Coptic dialect."

"He has a point," Celeste said. "My British people still make copies of Chaucer without having spoken or written Middle English for centuries."

Silas said, "Yeah, but Coptic scribes didn't really do this."

Grant whistled. "And guess what other texts used the Lycopolitan variety?"

Silas squinted and shook his head.

"The Gnostic and Manichaean works from the Nag Hammadi library."

"That's right! Nice one, bro—"

Then another thing hit him. Something from Uncle Juan's warehouse just before the lights cut.

The notation on the backside of one of the folios!

He'd completely forgotten about the find during the mayhem.

Silas rushed to the first folio from the Coptic Muratorian Fragment. Top row, far left. He grabbed it and flipped it over.

"There you are..."

"There what is?" Celeste asked.

He held it up to the light, noted its location, and then pointed to a two-word notation scrawled in the same Coptic.

Silas read: *"Pachomius source."*

"Pachomius?" Gapinski asked. "Who the hell is that?"

"If I recall, a Coptic saint."

"Oops. My bad for cussing. But why does it matter?"

"Because the man was recognized as the founder of Christian cenobitic monasticism in Egypt," Silas answered. "And the Nag Hammadi codices were found in the region around his monasteries along the Nile near Luxor."

"Wait a minute," Grant said. "Torres's cousin said the provenance indicated Luxor was where the cache was discovered."

"That's right!"

"And *source*, the other word in the notation?" Celeste asked.

"What else?" Silas asked.

"Gospel Zero."

He frowned. "Or something connected to it. Why note the monastic saint and source on the underside of the folio, in the exact same spot on the underside of the fragment mentioning *'the one from Galilee prepared by the man from our Savior's homestead'* unless it was somehow connected?"

"No way that's a coincidence," Grant added. "You've got clear provenance documents pointing to Luxor and then a notation basically spelling out the same connection!"

"So, what, the monks got a copy holed up there or something?" Gapinski added.

Silas shrugged. "Only one way to find out."

"Right. Looks like we've got two leads now," Celeste said. "Germany and Egypt."

"Which means more frequent flyer miles," Gapinski said.

"How do you want to split the teams?"

"Given Grant's experience with some of this, how about us boys go south to Nag Hammadi and you gals head to Frankfurt to pay a visit to Urlich Pauli."

Celeste smirked. "Boys against the girls. I fancy that."

"Then game on."

CHAPTER 20
FRANKFURT, GERMANY.

Frankfurt was just as Torres had left it the last time she was in town. Cold and rainy, drab and dreadful. Smelled the same, too. Of beer and bratwursts, although the seemingly perpetual cloud of diesel fuel no longer hovered after much of the older polluting automobiles were banned. Ironically, she was back in town for the same reason that brought her there before.

Treasure hunting.

She had taken the nearly ten-hour flight last time around to broker a deal with the Spanish government for the final haul of treasure recovered from one of the ships from their famed treasure fleet that had sunk off the coast of Florida's Matecumbe Key, *Capitana*. Figured Germany's neutral ground was best for the negotiations. She and her uncle had heard rumors of the remains of the infamous ship still buried in the white sands of the Caribbean pockmarked with small patches of seagrass in nineteen feet of clear water. Torres led the charge that finally brought in the haul of last remaining gold and silver, and then brokered the deal that made her *tío* richer from that Spanish gold than he had been while trading in Venezuela's black gold.

That is, until he had to pay fines a few years later resulting from her trading in stolen artifacts on the black market.

It had started innocently enough. A few small pieces here and there from the collections she had discovered. The coins and figurines and pottery were worth hardly anything to anybody anyway. And with all the business she had been providing her uncle with her reputation and expertise in archaeology and Mesoamerican, pre-Columbian artifacts, she figured he owed her. But when she returned to another treasure ship, the *Urca de Lima*, and had taken some of the more elaborate gold pieces from the cache, that's when things went south.

After she had been caught by an INTERPOL investigation rooting out black-market dealers, the Cuban government leveled punishing fines against her *tío* and severed their relationship with him and his company—which rippled across his other business relationships. Thankfully, he had been able to maintain most of those contracts, but not before the damage had been done to his reputation.

And there she was, back in Frankfurt and back in the saddle of another treasure-hunting mystery. She just hoped she didn't screw it up. Hoped she could offer something to protect the Church that would continue her atonement for her thievery.

In her head, she knew such works paled in comparison to the ultimate sacrifice God himself made on her behalf on the cross, paying the price for her greed and lying and thieving in her place. But in her heart, after all she had put her dead uncle through...she still felt compelled to work to earn God's crazy-love favor and his gift of a renewed, rescued, eternal life. Especially after he had providentially provided a job with SEPIO after coming back to the faith. Seemed like the least she could do. Perhaps someday she would finally find release from the guilt that weighed her down.

Arriving at the largest city in the German state of Hesse and home to the European Central bank on a direct flight out of

Miami, she and Celeste retrieved their BMW rental car and drove to a SEPIO safe house in the heart of the city. The Order kept several such regrouping stations around the world. Simple two-room units with a bathroom and kitchenette to recharge, stocked with supplies they might need for the road ahead. Laptops, phones, food, weapons—you name it, they had it. The Order spared no expense when it came to preserving and defending the faith, as well as keeping their agents armed and ready to do it.

After gorging themselves on those bratwursts they had smelled earlier at a tavern on the ground level just below their flat, they showered and got to work, first checking in with Zoe back at DC operations.

"Hey, ladies," Zoe said from the laptop, face buried in a pile of papers she was shuffling about. "Meet any *gutaussehende männer*?"

Torres smirked. "Didn't know you spoke German."

"And no, we didn't meet any good-looking men," Celeste said. "Who do you take us for?"

Zoe shrugged, head down and continuing to sort her papers. "Time is ticking away, ladies. No time like the present to seize Cupid by the wings."

"But in Germany?" Torres said.

"Whatever it takes."

"Thanks, mate," Celeste said, "but I already have myself a *gutaussehende männer*, thank you very much."

"Yeah, but he's your boss."

She frowned and glanced at Torres, who shrugged her shoulders.

"Right, so what do you have for us?" Celeste said, getting down to business.

Zoe cleared her throat and pushed her baby blue glasses up the bridge of her nose. "A lot, actually."

"Break it down for us."

"Apparently, Pauli's art business is more of a side project. Or was, rather."

"What do you mean?"

"In the 90s, he and a friend went into business together. Some dude named Hans Müller. The company, UPHM Metallbearbeitung, or UPMA Metalworking based on their initials, won a lucrative contract to make precision engine components for Mercedes."

"Gapinski would be pleased with that," Torres quipped. "How lucrative?"

"Within a year it was drawing over two million in profit a year."

"Dang," Torres said. "I got into the wrong line of work."

"You and me both," Celeste said. "So what changed?"

"For one, Pauli's wife Agnes. She was diagnosed with lung cancer a few years ago. Then the company filed for bankruptcy a year after that."

"Let me guess. Right around the time our Brit Andrew Sterling brokered the deal between him and Torres's uncle, with the hopes of pawning off the man's cache of papyri to Hartwin Braun?"

"Bingo."

"Well, there's our motive," Torres said.

Celeste nodded.

"There's more," Zoe went on. "Looking over his company's public records, I spotted a peculiar detail."

"What sort of detail," Celeste said. "Four months after Pauli filed for bankruptcy, his auto parts company was sold to a company in Berlin."

"What company?"

"As far as I can tell some sort of shell corporation for a larger entity. Only known address is a postal box belonging to a parcel service in the city that's led nowhere. That's where the trail ends on that front."

"Too bad," Celeste mumbled. "But good work, just the same. Anything else?"

"Yes. I ran Ulrich Pauli and Egypt through some search engines and got a hit that seemed relevant. In 1991, someone with the same name had published an article in a prestigious German-language journal about using some newfangled techniques on the Nag Hammadi texts to aid in their translation."

"The Gnostic ones, where our new manuscript had scribbled a reference?"

"That would be the one. The journal listed his affiliation as the Egyptology institute at Berlin's Free University—the very place that had also employed Terrance Munson who had supposedly examined the man's papyri in 1982 and validated it as authentic."

"That seems weird," Torres said. "An auto parts metalworking executive connected with an article on the Gnostic gospels appearing in an academic journal, along with an academic background in Egyptology?"

Zoe nodded. "That's what I thought. I wondered whether they could possibly be the same man. I called several prominent Egyptologists and early Christian scholars, and they all told me that the article has remained influential. But none of them could recall who Ulrich Pauli was or what had become of him."

"The man just vanishes into thin air?" Celeste said.

"Something like that. I emailed one of our Egyptologist experts with the Order, asking whether he might have heard of Ulrich Pauli."

"Did he by chance know the man?"

"He did. Pauli had been a master's student from about 1988 until about the time the article was published. After some further digging at the university, apparently the man left without a final examination."

"Why?" Celeste said. "With all that work and prestige he was garnering?"

"That's the mystery."

She turned to Torres. "Why would a promising student, a young man who'd landed an article in a premier journal early in his studies, why would he suddenly drop out of his master's program?"

Torres shook her head, saying nothing.

"Good question, Celeste," Zoe said. "From all I can tell, Ulrich Pauli still lives in Frankfurt, and on paper he looks like an unremarkable local. A fifty-year-old widower, living in a flat on the top floor of a four-story apartment building just outside of the downtown area. Apparently quite the civic-minded fellow, writing eloquent letters to the editor of the local paper. And when the city commissioners gathered to hash out Frankfurt's annual budget, Pauli harassed the elected leaders about a proposed recession-year tax hike, getting quotes in the paper and a featured picture."

"Sounds like your run-of-the-mill *hombre*," Torres said. "If not a bit of an eccentric renaissance man."

"That he is."

"Can you send us that picture? Could help make a positive ID when we pay him a visit."

"Will do."

"Right. Good work, Zoe," Celeste said. "Text me the address so we can put to rest our questions surrounding the provenance of these manuscripts. As our beloved Order Master likes to say, it's go time."

The three women ended their conference. Ten minutes later, Torres was behind the wheel of their BMW navigating through streets lined by charcoal stone buildings sandwiched between newer modern iterations of gleaming glass and steel. Celeste was providing navigation through the punishing end-of-day traffic made worse by sheets of rain drenching the city.

Took some doing fighting both the rain and traffic, but soon they emerged from downtown onto a thoroughfare that led to the target, the rain rapping harder now and sounding like bullets pelting the roof, the sound of the rapidly swishing wiper blades adding to the intensity.

"What do you make of this forgery business?" Celeste finally said. "Seen anything like this in your line of work?"

"Not directly. Heard about a few cases of these things though. Stuff that would blow your mind."

"Like what?"

Torres made a turn. "In the mid-1980s, experts were duped by a master forger from Utah. This dude named Mark Hofmann claimed to have a stash of manuscripts that would turn the official history of the Mormon Church on its head. Almost got away with it too, he was that good. Used antique paper, made ink from historic recipes. He even artificially aged his manuscripts, using a gelatin concoction with some sort of chemical solution and a hair dryer."

"So this sort of thing is real, it's been done before? Manufacturing fake documents, like the Coptic folios?"

"Oh, yeah. Still happens, too. Crazy thing is, before Hoffman was exposed he scored a cool million or two selling his bogus manuscripts."

"Blimey! No joke?"

Torres chuckled. "No joke."

"But how did he get away with it? Seems like any scholar worth their salt would have smelled the fakes a kilometer away."

"You would think, but he targeted buyers who *wanted* the documents to be real, whether because of ideological or professional interest."

"How did he go about it?"

"Hoffman would express doubts about his finds, making the experts feel like they were discovering signs of authenticity in his documents that he'd somehow missed and overlooked. 'Do you really think it's genuine?' he'd say, and then just lean back quietly and let his victim delight in doing the authentication for him, proving what they already wanted to be true."

"Ballsy. Takes a right nutter to pull something like that off. And a man highly skilled in the arts of deception."

"Which means that anyone with skills good enough to fake a cache of ancient Coptic papyri would have no trouble manufacturing modern-day papers proving provenance. Receipts, certificates, and whatnot. Just like what we managed to retrieve from *tío's* warehouse."

"But I wonder if it's actually backwards," Celeste said.

Torres considered this. "What do you mean?"

"I was having a think about this on our flight over. Perhaps it's not the Coptic folios themselves that's hard to forge but the provenance. Anyone who could forge the latter could certainly forge the former."

"I don't follow."

"Think about it. A manuscript is something physical. To make a convincing fake, all you need are the right tools and materials to pull it off. Like the bloke who aged the antique paper with gelatin and a hair dryer. Provenance is something else entirely, isn't it? It isn't a physical object but a historical fact. It's made of dates and places, buyers and sellers. If you want to fake provenance, you need to rewrite history itself. Would take a lot of know-how to pull that off."

"And lots of money. I like the way you're thinking. And only one way to find out." Torres brought the car to a halt in front of a four-story apartment building still stuck in the Weimar Republic, most lights still on in the early evening.

Orange streetlights flickered on as time crept toward night. The structure of brown bricks stained black with age and weather bespoke the utilitarian nature of the accommodations. But a carpet of manicured grass and well-trimmed bushes with a thoughtful bench on the path leading to the entrance with blooming flowers offered signs of a modest middle-class life.

Still behind the wheel and gazing at the structure, Torres said, "Why would a man who profited from his nearly bankrupt business and the sale of a cache of papyri live in a dump like this?"

"Reminds me of home, actually," Celeste replied. "We lived in a similar flat in north London for a spell. But I do recall Zoe saying something about him and his wife living here their whole lives. Probably has sentimental value."

The two exited the rental car and made a run for the building through the pouring rain. A woman, hunched and haggard had just swiped her keycard at the entrance up ahead and it buzzed with loud annoyance before unlocking.

The pair trotted up to the door as she shuffled through.

Torres grabbed the door before it closed, startling the woman.

Celeste smiled and said something in German, presumably an excuse to allay her fears.

The woman nodded with a grin and took off down the hallway, taking a right at a juncture beyond a central stairwell and disappearing.

Celeste said, "Right. Up we go."

Pale fluorescent lighting four stories up shone down upon the pair as they ascended brick stairs, their footfalls loud and echoey in the vestibule.

"Where to now?" Torres asked when they reached the fourth floor.

Celeste checked her phone and hung a right, eyeing the numbers affixed to the doors. She spun around and headed left instead. "This away."

They walked through a poorly lit hallway under more pale lighting that flickered with nearly dead bulbs. Reaching the end, they found the unit.

"Here we are," Celeste announced before taking a breath and knocking.

They waited, glancing back down the empty hallway.

Torres felt uneasy knowing they were so exposed like this after having just been attacked and her cousin threatened with elimination.

The seconds ticked by. Still nothing.

"Perhaps we should solicit some neighbors for the cause?" Torres suggested.

Celeste walked to the door next to Pauli's and rapped it twice, then twice more.

Shuffling sounds could be heard on the other side, along with complaints in German.

The door eased open until a safety chain caught. Peering through was a short woman just over five feet tall, a mess of grey curls stuffed underneath a hot-pink hooded sweatshirt.

"*Hallo*. Do you speak English?" Celeste asked.

The woman eyed her with furrowed brow. "*Ja*. What is it you are wanting?"

Torres glanced down the hallway again, shifting on both feet and hands starting to sweat with anticipation.

"Right. Thank you, ma'am. We're looking for Urlich Pauli. We tried summoning him, but to no avail. Do you know where he might be?"

"You as well, ehh?" the woman replied.

Celeste frowned and glanced at Torres.

Torres replied, "What do you mean by that—you as well?"

"Another pair came rooting about here earlier. Two men, tall and muscular. Asking about Urlich and where he was. I asked if they were the *Polizei* and they said no. Just old friends come to pay a visit. But they looked far too young to be old pals. Say, you're not the *Polizei*, too, are you?"

Celeste went to answer when a man appeared at the top of the central stairwell.

Tall and lean with chiseled features and a mane of dark hair entering into its twilight years. Looking like an aged version of the picture Zoe had sent along earlier from the newspaper. He was holding bags of groceries in each arm and approaching.

"That looks like him..." Torres muttered.

The woman undid her chain and glanced down the hallway. "Ahh, lookie there. You are being in luck. There he is now." Then she slammed the door and mumbled something in German again.

The man raised his head with sudden interest. Then stopped cold in his tracks.

No one moved. Time seemed to stand as the two parties eyed one another with recognition.

"Ulrich Pauli?" Celeste said.

The man clenched his groceries tight against his body, then took a step back.

She raised her hands and did the same, conveying they were not a threat. Then she started speaking slowly and lowly in German, head bowed and eyes fixed on the man.

Torres didn't understand any of it, but looked on as Celeste negotiated with him, marveling at her instincts and skill.

Then the man sighed, almost with resignation at having been found out. He adjusted his bags before lumbering toward his door.

Celeste flashed her a hopeful smile as he opened it. The man shoved through and led them inside.

"What did you tell him?" Torres asked as they entered.

"The truth. That we're with the Vatican and have an inquiry about some recent manuscripts that have surfaced."

"Ahh, the Pope card. Works every time."

"And it's true. Sort of."

The cramped flat carried the same dim, dreary lighting as the rest of the apartment complex. A darkened hallway extended through the main area toward a bedroom in the back, door standing open. A brown cloth couch sat against the living room wall, a cream-colored crochet blanket resting across the back. On one side, it was flanked by a sliding door leading to a balcony, a modest wood table and chairs standing in front. On the other, a small kitchen with used dishes piled neatly in the sink. The place was hot and humid, smelling of grease and mothballs and body odor. Torres didn't know how long she could handle the space.

"Sit," Ulrich Pauli instructed in English. The women did as they were told, taking their place on the couch as he put away his groceries.

"*Bier*?" he grunted.

"Sure," Torres said, then mumbled to Celeste, "When in Germany, right?"

Celeste smiled at the man. "Thank you for seeing us, Ulrich. And sorry for giving you a fright."

Pauli said nothing, instead focusing on popping the top to three beer bottles. He sauntered over and handed two to the ladies, taking a seat at the table and promptly gulping down three swigs of his beer.

"I was wondering when you would be arriving," the man grunted. "What is it you are wanting to know?"

Celeste took the lead, first outlining all they had recovered and the picture they had already pieced together. Pauli's original receipts of purchase and subsequent sale to Sterling before Hartwin through Juan Torres. The letter from Munson authenticating the papyri. His time at Free University and the article on the Gnostic gospels. His former metalworking business and its subsequent bankruptcy before being bought out, right at the time of his sale. Even divulging the domain registration, at which the man chuckled and threw back more beer.

"Sounds like you have been doing your homework," Pauli said.

"The only problem is that it is all rubbish," Celeste said, folding her arms and settling back into the couch.

Pauli slammed his bottle down and leaned forward, pointing a finger. "It is not being rubbish!"

"For one, the letter from Munson is a fake, as it was typed using a device that rendered the German language using a version that post-dates the actual device. There is no way the typed letter is from 1982. The double *s* doesn't match."

"That is being a coincidence!"

"A coincidence? How about the fact the papyri folios themselves are written in a Coptic variety that died out decades before they were supposedly written? And that the gospel of John fragment matches exactly, and to a T mind you, one that is widely accessible on the internet."

At that the man flinched, his eyes widening slightly and darting to the left.

That definitely tripped him up. Torres had to hand it to her. Celeste was good. Could probably learn a few things from her to kick her own SEPIO career up a notch.

Celeste leaned forward. "Who bought your business, Ulrich? Because I have a hunch you are doing the buyer much more of a favor than he did you by taking your failing life's work off from your hands."

The man took another swig, then another. "I do not know for certain who this man was."

"But it was a man? A single individual? Because the sale was registered to a shell company in Berlin?"

"*Ja*. Both are being correct."

"And the man got you out of a bind, didn't he? Your whole life was about to end in a heap of debt and shame, just as your wife passed from her cancer. Did he ask you to broker the sale of a cache of papyri to Hartwin? Was that a condition of the sale?"

Pauli went to take in more beer when he saw that it was empty. He set the bottle down with a hollow thud.

"That is being correct."

Torres sat straighter, glancing at Celeste and trying not to grin at the find.

Celeste didn't look at her, instead concentrating on sealing the deal. "Do you have a name? Anything that could identify the man?"

Pauli paused, eyes darting as if considering his words. Then the man sighed, as if resigning himself to offering a confession.

He said, "It was being—"

The sliding door shattered with intensity, cutting off the man's answer and shattering part of the man's skull.

A bullet, from a shooter perched several yards away.

Ulrich Pauli's head snapped forward with gory explosion, his body slumping to the floor.

Celeste and Torres didn't have time to react. Neither to the imminent danger of a sniper perched God only knew where outside, nor to the macabre scene of blood and brain matter splattered across the wood table and slider door and carpeted floor.

Their only lead had just been assassinated.

And they could be next.

CHAPTER 21

Torres watched as the body toppled to the floor, Pauli's head partially blown to bits and the carpet starting to soak crimson from the wound. She threw her hands to her mouth, wanting to at once puke and scream at the sudden intrusion of violence.

The wall exploded just above her head, then again on the other side. Snapping her back to the moment, the body of their only lead still letting its blood across the floor in a heaping pile of contorted limbs.

Her head exploded with corresponding panic as chunks of mortar and splintered wood from a picture frame fell on her.

A corresponding double-boom echo of the violence was heard from outside the shattered window, the sound waves from the shooter's blast delayed even as the light waves from its destruction were more than seen.

Up close and personal.

"Get down!" Celeste screamed, shoving off from the brown couch and flattening on the carpet stained with crimson.

Didn't have to tell her twice.

Torres threw herself to the carpet as well, landing inches

from Pauli's shattered head, rain sheeting inside now and soaking her and the carpet.

Just as another bullet blast whistled past their backs and blasted in the kitchen, shattering the stack of dishes piled high in the sink and sending the women screaming and scrambling for cover.

"Don't they know they got the dude the first time?" Torres yelled, following Celeste crawling along the carpet toward the hallway leading to the rear bedroom.

Another blast shattered a vase of flowers resting on the countertop separating the kitchen from the living room. Sending shards of glass and water raining down and sending the pair lunging for the hallway.

"I don't think they're aiming for our friend Pauli anymore, mate," Celeste said as she dove for safety.

The corner where the living room met the hallway exploded with menacing violence.

As Torres rolled to safety just underneath the blast bite.

"Dang, that was close," she said, crouching against the wall along with Celeste and withdrawing a weapon from her back.

The two waited for more, precious seconds ticking by as the room settled into an eerie silence, even as voices rose with commotion and panic through the walls.

Nothing more came. No more blasts, no more shattered walls and vases and dishes. No more nothing.

Torres took in a stabilizing breath, trying to make sense of what had happened. "But if they weren't aiming for Pauli, that means they were aiming for us."

Celeste said nothing, her own weapon now clenched between both fists.

"Which means we don't have much time to get our asses out of Dodge. Who knows what might be coming."

Celeste nodded. "First things first."

"What's that?"

"We do a sweep of the apartment, looking for anything that might help our investigation."

"We've got a hot minute to get the hell out of here and you're saying we need to scope out the joint before we leave? Out in no-man's-land? With Lee Harvey Oswald getting his jollies on out there, waiting to pick us off? *Lo siento, hermano.* No way!"

"Not the living room. Bedroom at the back."

Torres pivoted toward Celeste. "Are you kidding me? Who knows who may be showing up here in the next few minutes. And that's not even saying anything about the German *Polizei* who are gonna be wondering why a Brit and a Latina Israeli were meeting with a German *hombre* missing a piece of his head!"

"Torres!" Celeste huffed. "Like you said, we've got a hot minute to complete our mission. Which, if you recall, is gaining actionable intelligence for SEPIO to figure out the plot meant to sully our understanding of the Bible and damage the credibility of the Christian faith. Now let's get to it!"

She stood without waiting for any more pleas of sanity from Torres, padding into a bathroom that sat between them and the bedroom.

Huffing and mumbling a curse under her breath, she ran a hand through her dark curls and stood, clenching her weapon tighter and following her boss inside.

The space was narrow and cramped, covered with a dated green-speckled tile that ran the length of the room. A shower stood to the right, empty. Celeste parted a curtain for a look outside, just enough for half her face.

"See anything," Torres said, heart ramping back up now with anticipation and head still swimming from the chaos.

Celeste said nothing, shaking her head and continuing her observation. A beat later she let the curtain fall and brushed past her.

"Let's check his bedroom. Has to be something in there that will set us on the right path to solving this whole bloody affair. Let's pray there is, at least. And that the psychopath has left his perch."

Torres crossed herself on instinct as she followed. Praying she was right on both counts.

She braced herself for more gunfire as they plunged back into the darkened hallway, the voices growing into a crescendoed muffle now on the other side of the thin apartment wall. She half expected a team of special-ops to come storming through the entrance. Surprised they hadn't by now.

No one came. And there was no more gunfire.

At least for now. Which meant they didn't have long.

A yellow security light anchored to the building outside showed faintly through the window, obscured by the lapping rain and partially drawn blinds. Celeste turned on her phone's flashlight. Torres did the same.

The room wasn't the sort of bachelor pad she was ever used to seeing. Grant had a helluva time picking up after himself when they lived together. It was always his socks. And half-eaten oatmeal left in the sink. Agnes must have trained the guy well before she passed.

The bedroom was neat and tidy. Everything had their place. The king bed was made, sheets crisply tucked at the edges and duvet smoothed to perfection. A lounger chair was free of clothes, another thing Grant failed miserably at. A book was resting face down on the seat. A desk sat at the window, gleaming with lemon polish under the outdoor light and clear of clutter, except for a penholder and a beige desk lamp. The closet was open, all the shirts and slacks neatly pressed and arranged. The room smelled faintly of the ocean. Probably a candle or fragrance oil. Used to savor the scent, but now it turned Torres's stomach. Reminded her of Miami and her uncle and all that had happened to the life he had built.

"Guy was a neat-freak, that's for sure," she said.

"Should make sweeping the place a right easy process," Celeste said, rifling through the closet with one hand, phone shining brightly with the other.

Torres walked to the desk when the chair caught her attention. The book lying face down.

She picked it up. Heavy, thick hardback. She pointed her phone's light toward it.

The Nag Hammadi Scriptures.

"*Eso es bueno...*"

"What's that you got there?" Celeste asked from the closet.

"A copy of the Gnostic gospels." Torres opened the cover. A note was scrawled on the cover page.

She gasped at who signed it.

Noland Rotberg.

"*Dios mío...*"

Celeste walked over. "What's that?"

Torres pointed at the note. "From one Gnostic to another," she read. "A note of dedication from Noland Rotberg!"

"The bloke whom Hartwin brought along to Princeton?"

"Exactly!"

"So the man who sold the papyri to your uncle who brokered the deal with Hartwin knew one of the men who was commissioned to authenticate it?"

"Wild, right?"

"And no bloody way that's a coincidence."

"Yeah, probably not."

"Good work, Naomi. Keep searching. There has to be more. I'll take the bed, you take the desk."

Torres nodded and tossed the book on the bed, then began working through the desk drawers, pulling them open and rifling through their content. Nothing but scraps of paper, old bills, a checkbook. Probably nothing. Then again, maybe something. Lots of somethings.

"Why don't you dump them out on the bed," Celeste said, pulling open a nightstand drawer. "We're running short on time."

"Didn't I say that before we jumped down the rabbit hole with a psycho on the loose…"

Torres complied, dumping out the contents at the center of the bed.

As she burgled with abandon, Celeste crouched below the bed, lifting off the duvet dropping over the side and shining her light underneath.

"Ahh-ha!" she exclaimed. "Gotcha, you little bugger…"

"What's that?" Torres asked, leaning toward her partner, body halfway under the bed.

Celeste scooted back out and grinned, holding up her prize.

A backpack.

"Score!" Torres said.

Celeste ripped open the zipper, fishing her arm inside. Her grin widened as she pulled out the trophy.

A laptop. Sort of thick and old-school, but a fabulous prize, nonetheless.

"Bet there's loads of intel on here. Emails, pictures, receipts," Celeste said before sliding it back inside. "Find anything useful in the desk?"

"Except for a thumb drive, nothing stands out."

"Let's grab what we can anyway." Celeste started stuffing the desk contents inside the bag. Torres joined until what was useful was packed.

Celeste went to the window and glanced outside, the sound of wailing sirens closing in now. Soon they'd be descending upon the complex. With them caught inside a flat with a body, head blown to kingdom come.

"Right. I don't know about you, but I'd say we overstayed our welcome."

"Agreed."

Celeste zipped up the backpack and slung it over her shoulders, then headed out into the hallway.

Torres took a parting glance at the room. She frowned. Not at all thrilled about the mess they made and the mess of prints they left behind. Between the dead body and the turned-over room—not good optics, as they say.

But as her *tío* used to say: '*Así es la vida.*'

Such is life, indeed. Especially with SEPIO.

Torres followed after Celeste, and the two padded quickly through the darkened hallway. No sign of any more snipers, no sign of life.

Celeste looked back at Torres, then nodded toward the door.

Drawing her weapon, her partner stepped out into the living room void and crouched, the wind whistling through the shattered window and a rumble of thunder echoing from the near distance.

Torres didn't have to think twice about it. She matched Celeste's crouch, bracing for a replay of sniper fire before shuffling to the exit.

None came.

Which meant the hostile had abandoned his pursuit. Or he —they?—were on their way, perhaps moments away to finishing the job.

She waited for Celeste, who was shuffling to the overturned body still lying prone on the floor.

"What the...Celeste!" Torres exclaimed in a whispered shout.

The woman ignored her pleas. She fished around the man, reaching a hand in one pocket before turning him over and doing the same in the other.

And pulling something out.

She smiled triumphantly, holding up a cell phone before crawling over.

"Show off," Torres said. "Now can we jet?"

"Sure thing, mate." Celeste stuffed the phone in her pocket and nodded, gripping her weapon. "Ready?"

Torres grabbed the doorknob and nodded herself.

Then she threw the door open, standing to follow her partner who darted into the hallway.

Coming up fast on a short woman sporting a pink hooded sweatshirt with her back to them. The neighbor.

The woman spun around and screamed, throwing her arms into the air and cowering against the wall as she spat frantic German at the two. Others up ahead shouted similar frantic cries of fright, ducking back inside their flats while a few approached the women with shaking fists.

Esto no está bien...

Celeste tried calming the woman, but it was no use. She glanced behind her and nodded toward the central stairwell.

"Come on!" she instructed, slinging a string of German at Pauli's neighbors now closing in.

The only word Torres recognized was *Polizei*. The neighbors got the hint.

They spread like the parting of the Red Sea as the two women padded down the hallway with extended weapons, doors slamming in their faces and voices quieting into muffled, frightful exasperation.

They came up fast to the stairwell. Heart hammering in her head, Torres followed Celeste's lead in whipping her weapon toward the lighted well. Hoping for the best but expecting the worst.

Nothing.

Without waiting, Celeste descended on quick feet. Didn't bother giving Torres a window to collect her breath and form a plan. Just plunged down into the void without a care for what might lay below.

Torres wanted to say something. Wanted to protest the

madness of all that had happened since leaving Princeton. Wanted to pull out and get back to her archaeological dig waiting for her in Libya that she was so rudely yanked from.

But she kept her mouth shut. Her head screamed at her to take control back, but her heart reassured her that trusting Celeste was the way to go.

Soon they reached the entrance door. Still locked tight, no one around, rain continuing its relentless assault. An ominous crack of thunder from above reverberated through the apartment building, threatening to finish what the hostile started.

Celeste pulled up to the door with a halt, clenching the door's handle with one hand and her weapon with the other.

They stood still as rain cascaded from the roof above in sheets a few feet past the entrance threshold, yellow security light casting it in ribbons of golden tinsel.

Torres could see their rental still parked on the road at the end of the path leading to the building, now sandwiched between two other cars. A ten second dash, tops. But one that a well-trained marksman could easily ruin with two kill shots named *Torres* and *Celeste*.

"What's the play?" she said on a shaky breath, glancing behind even as she feared Nous or the box men or whoever else was about to come storming through the front.

"Perfect. Our rental is right where we left," Celeste said.

"Anyone else?"

"No. Not that I can see."

"But they could be out there, right? A quartet of whack jobs lying in wait?"

"Perhaps. But I have to imagine they left once they saw their target fall."

"I thought we were the target."

Celeste smirked. "We were the consolation prize. This was as before in Miami. A clean-up job. And with those sirens now a minute from arrival...No I have to imagine they're on the run."

"Speaking of which. Maybe we should follow their lead."

Her partner tightened her grip on the SIG Sauer and turned the door handle. "Let's go."

The rain, cold and relentless, slapped their faces and soaked their clothes as the women dashed down the path toward their car, weapons held on taut arms but knowing they were helplessly exposed.

Shooter whack job is gonna whack with a bullet in their back if that's what he's after. Nothing they could do about that.

But nothing came. Only freezing bullets of rain until they reached the car and slid inside.

"Nice weather," Torres quipped as she fished for the keys, stomach aflutter with anticipation for a thwack of lead through the windows.

"For ducks, maybe," Celeste said, wiping her face with both hands.

Torres stuffed the key in the ignition and brought the BMW to life. "Let's get the heck out of—"

The back window exploded with shattering violence, the anticipated bullet thwacking into the dashboard and splintering the central ventilation.

The ladies yelled with surprise, bending for cover and peering out the car windows for the perpetrator.

In this case, it was plural.

Four men were spreading out from behind and coming in quick, their black gear slick with rain water shimmering in the yellow streetlights.

"So about that quartet of whack jobs lying in wait..." Torres said.

Another crack sounded, its bullet thudding uselessly into the trunk but too close for comfort before a succession of leaden thuds followed. Some catching their vehicle, others shattering the world around them.

"Go, go, go!" Celeste shouted.

"Don't have to tell me thrice," Torres mumbled.

Only problem was they were sandwiched between two aging, sagging buckets of bolts. Peugeots by the look of the lion logo she had glimpsed before climbing inside.

She threw the BMW into reverse and floored it, tires squealing on slick pavement before crunching the already destroyed back end into the car behind.

More bullets, more shattering from the surrounding cars.

Punching it to first gear, Torres peeled out, catching the left bumper on the car in front and threatening to leave them wedged as the hostiles neared.

But German engineering trumped the French in spades. She muscled past the car onto the road and angled for escape.

Just as her partner twisted behind to offer a *one-two-three-four* reply through the exposed rear window.

Her rejoinder was heard. Loud and clear.

As she cycled to the next gear and floored it, Torres glimpsed a man recoiling then crumpling to the road.

But not before a black Mercedes sedan came screaming after them. Hot on their heels and aiming for dead-center mass.

"Torres...Mate, get us out of here!"

"What do you think I'm doing?"

She was just glad her *tío* taught her how to drive a stick shift. Because getting them out of there meant using all her *coche* know-how.

The street was lined with cars, making it a frightening, fraught escape made all the more challenging by the relentless rain obscuring her vision and threatening their tires' purchase.

Gunfire sounded from behind again, going hide and wide and sparking off cars parked along the winding street.

Torres smirked. *Not so easy firing at a moving target, is it idiotas?*

She tightened her grip on the wheel and threw the car into third, cranking the accelerator and praying to *Dios en el cielo* they made it out alive.

"Celeste..." she said as the gunfire continued.

"On it." Celeste pivoted around and opened back up on the pursuing vehicle.

But her *one-two-three-four-five* bullets went equally high and wide, thudding uselessly somewhere beyond the threat at hand.

The hostiles behind braked to avoid the gunfire.

And Torres pushed the BMW faster through the congested streets of cars and buildings and—

A light up ahead changed to amber, threatening to change the dynamic of the chase real quick.

"Sonofa—"

"Torres..." Celeste said. "You've been hanging around Gapinski too long."

"Hold on!" she said, ignoring her and pushing the accelerator as the light turned red.

And traffic on both sides started moving.

She laid on the horn, not letting up as she made a split-second decision about what to do next.

'*Go big or go home*' her *tío* would always say, one of the many *gringo* phrases she heard him parrot as a teenager after he returned from business dealings in America.

She was about to put that maxim to the test.

Even as she laid on the horn, Torres also laid on the accelerator, pushing through the intersection and crossing herself for good measure.

Cars squealed and slid to a halt as she barreled on through.

She almost made it past the first lane, but not before the lead car kissed her rear door, driver's side.

Sending her pinballing at an angle into the next lane.

Where a flat-fronted delivery truck was waiting.

The BMW smacked it with force and cracked Celeste's window but kept right on going.

Unfortunately, the whack jobs hot on their heels had the same idea, riding her wake through the congestion and on to the other side.

Cars lumbered past them in the rain, headlights blinding Torres as she tried navigating them with the hostiles firing intermittently.

"I'd fire back," Celeste said, "but I worry how many bullets I have left. Not to mention the civilian casualties."

Torres continued pushing the BMW as fast as she dared in the urban streets, the buildings of stone and steel, dark and colorful, passing her in a wet blur.

They ducked into a dark underpass lit by faint orange light, relief from the relentless rain a godsend.

"This isn't working," Celeste said.

"Sorry, *amiga*. I'm doing the best I can with what I've got!"

"No, it's not you. It's—"

The hostiles smashed into their rental from behind with menacing force, jerking the car forward and sending the pair's heads along with it.

"Celeste..."

"On it!"

Celeste twisted around as Torres sped away, the overpass giving way soon.

The hostiles made a run for their rear a second time, speeding with singular kill-and-destroy focus.

This time, SEPIO was ready.

"Gotcha..." Celeste said right before she pulled the trigger.

A single bullet sped from her weapon and sailed out the shattered rear window.

Just as the hostile veered left, the bullet punching through their windshield and straight between the eyes of the passenger.

The man's head snapped back before he slumped forward.

"Nice shot, *amiga!*" Torres said.

"Bloody hell..." Celeste said as she twisted back inside. "Wrong bloke."

"Either way, you gotta teach me how to do that."

They sped out from the underpass into a boulevard divided by leafy trees, the rain having lessened. Soon, a bridge emerged. She recognized it from when they arrived at their SEPIO outpost, just across the Main River.

The Mercedes came up swift and sudden, having recovered from their injury and raring for a fight. Soon it was on their tail again.

"Give it a rest, *idiotas!*" Torres complained as the boulevard bent left through an intersection.

Thankfully green this time.

"Hold on!" She banked the car through eight lanes of idling traffic.

But she couldn't shake the hostiles. It smashed into their left rear corner.

Sending the SEPIO pair skidding through the intersection and smashing into a lamppost, sparks flying as it smacked into the windshield, leaving a spider web of cracked glass behind as it clanged to the road.

"Yeah, we ain't getting our deposit back on this bucket of bolts," Torres complained, throwing the car into fourth and flooring it.

A spray of bullets confirmed her complaint, more lead sinking into the trunk.

"What do I do?"

Celeste pointed ahead. "Make for the bridge."

"Then what?"

"Then we pray for a miracle," Celeste said as she twisted back to swat away the hostiles with her SIG Sauer.

Only to recoil into her seat from a spray of bullets from behind.

They breezed through another intersection just as it turned from amber to red, the SUV right behind.

The bridge lay up ahead. The pair were closing fast.

Torres gunned the BMW past its threshold, aiming for the other side without a plan.

Then the hostile's SUV did something curious.

It gunned around Torres and Celeste from behind, the Mercedes overtaking the BMW in no time.

Apparently, Gapinski was right: The Stuttgart automaker had more muscle than its Munich rival.

They were neck and neck now, barreling down the bridge toward destiny.

And then it was over.

The SUV smashed into BMW. Once then twice, sparks flaring between them.

Torres gripped the wheel, angling to keep the BMW on track. It was no use.

The Mercedes sent the car sailing through the flimsy metal guard rail.

Plunging into the watery depths below.

CHAPTER 22
LUXOR, EGYPT.

Silas yawned and rubbed his eyes in exhaustion. Another rough day, another rough flight. All twenty-one hours of it.

Just their luck, the Order Gulfstream jet parked in Miami had developed mechanical problems. Something about an indicator light that wasn't shutting off. So out of an abundance of caution, SEPIO operations routed the trio heading to Egypt onto a Turkish Airlines flight that went through Istanbul. Left around the same time that Celeste and Torres left for Frankfurt. At least it was first class, so no complaints from Silas there. As much as he hated flying, and as much as he hated flying commercial, he'd much rather suffer for a day getting pampered in the stratosphere than end up with a ticket to Davy Jones's locker because of a failed indicator light.

An Order-issued Gulfstream picked them up from Istanbul for the flight down to Luxor, Egypt. Figured it would give him and Gapinski and Grant a sort of airborne workspace to prep for the next leg of their mission seeking answers to questions that so far remained allusive.

The soft hum of the jet engines was interrupted by the *purr* of an incoming transmission from HQ. Since becoming Order

Master, Silas had taken the liberty of adding some much-needed technological upgrades to the full range of SEPIO operational support measures. In this case, retrofitting their jets with a pair of workstations complete with high-speed satellite-powered internet and a fifty-inch flat screen with teleconference capabilities.

As Victor Zarruq came online, Silas finished preparing himself a scotch in the minibar—one of the existing operational support measures he left alone.

"I see you've managed to navigate our newfangled comms equipment," Silas said, sitting in a leather recliner in front of the screen. Gapinski was roused from his sleep in the chair across the aisle. Grant was still passed out behind him.

The bishop chuckled. "Only thanks to Mr. Patel. Our friend from India is a masterful instructor in the art of technowizardry with an old luddite like myself."

Silas could see Abraham waving in the background, acknowledging the praise before getting back to work.

"Hey, have you heard from Celeste and Torres? How are they faring in Germany?"

"I wouldn't be too concerned with our gals," Gapinski said, sitting up with a yawn. "Doubt they had any issues. In fact, I'm sure they're sitting in some German spa while two blond hunks rub 'em down. Probably already solved the case and got mani-pedis to boot!"

"I don't know anything about any mani-pedis," Zarruq said, "as they have yet to report in from their adventures. But like Matthew said, I'm sure all is well. How are you boys faring yourself? Hope you were able to rest up on the flight over."

"For the most part. Then some more of us took an extra nap or ten down to Luxor," Silas said, smacking Grant's leg and rousing him with a startled snort.

"We there yet?" the man asked, throat thick with sleep.

"Almost. Captain announced an hour or so left a bit ago. And we've got work to do before we land."

"Coffee. Need coffee." Grant leaned forward and pointed at Silas's drink. "Or whatever you've got there."

"In the back."

The man sauntered off as Silas continued the debrief with Zarruq.

"What is the plan once you land, Master Grey?" Zarruq asked.

Silas's neck started to redden slightly, feeling like the man was questioning him with a skeptical eye. Then he shook it off and moved on. Zarruq only wanted to help, nothing more.

He leaned back and took a swig of his scotch. "The plan is to land and figure out the connection between Pachomius and the Gnostic gospels."

"You mean the unorthodox, unauthorized gospels?" Grant said, returning with a tumbler of amber liquid, no ice.

Gapinski put up a hand. "Can I ask just one knuckle-headed question before we get too far into this rodeo?"

"What's that?" Silas said.

"What are these Gnostic gospels you've been talking about anyway. And this Nag Hammadi nonsense? And why do you get all jumpy about 'em, Silas, whenever they're brought up, like they're porno or something?"

Silas almost choked on his drink at the suggestion.

"Was it something I said?"

Grant laughed. "That's quite the characterization, partner. The unorthodox gospels as Christian porn."

"Gnostic gospels," Silas corrected, throwing his friend a look. "And let's find another way to characterize them."

"Well what the hey-ho-day are they?" Gapinski asked again. "And why get so jumpy?"

Silas went to answer when he gestured to his friend. "Why don't you do the honors, Grant."

Grant took a swig and grinned. "Don't mind if I do." He settled back in his seat and explained, "The *Gnostic* gospels, as our good buddy Silas Grey classifies them, they're a collection of thirteen codices."

"Codi-whatchamacallits?"

Silas answered, "Codices. Basically, big books."

Grant nodded. "That's right. And for something like 1500 years, the mysterious Nag Hammadi books were just lying in wait, all buried-treasure like. Just sitting in a bunch of cliffs along the Nile River, forgotten in rural Egypt until a local farmer found them in 1945 near the Upper Egyptian town of Nag Hammadi. And boy was it the find of a century!"

Silas scoffed. "Find of the century my ass..."

"It was in the caves that these unorthodox Christian books were stashed?" Gapinski asked.

Grant took a swig and nodded again. "That's right. Fifty-two identifiable works written in Coptic, most of which no modern scholar had even known about. And they were chock full of new gospels, apocalypses, prayers, liturgical writings and acts of various apostles. And here's the important thingy for you Christian folks. Especially you Navy SEALS for Jesus type of Christian folks."

Gapinski smirked. "Navy SEALS for Jesus. Like we haven't heard that one before. But go on. What was the important thingy for us Christian folks?"

"The important thingy is that none of the aforementioned new gospels and apocalypses and prayers and—"

"Alright, just make your point, Grant," Silas complained.

"None of them were included in the Bible. They're *extra-biblical* texts, you might call them."

"No, *heretical*, you might call them."

"Tomato, tomahto. Anyway, their discovery provoked a massive rethinking on the early Christian movement in light of their, shall we say, less-than-orthodox revelations."

"In what way?" Gapinski asked.

"Well, the ideas found in the Nag Hammadi library don't often jib too well with the Bible, showing that a far greater diversity of ideas were floating around in the communities of people who considered themselves Christian than what anyone thought before."

Silas laughed. "Greater diversity of ideas floating—You've been reading Dan Brown again, haven't you? The thing about the Gnostic gospels is they actually contrast so starkly with *actual* Christianity that they showcase which beliefs were held and which weren't in the early Church."

"That's not what my latest research project is telling me..."

"Wait a minute." Silas turned toward his friend. "You've been doing research on the Gnostic gospels?

"Unorthodox gospels, but yes siree. The ones found at Nag Hammadi, in fact."

"I didn't know that. Why didn't you say something? And through which agency?"

Grant shrugged. "You didn't ask. It's been a freelance gig with some outfit in Berlin. Money was good, and they wanted some expertise with analyzing some other documents discovered in the region recently."

A worm of envy started twisting in Silas's belly. Here was one of his classmates from Harvard, doing cutting-edge research while he was stuck managing an unknown religious Order and fighting the Church's battles with new and old enemies. What he wouldn't give to be back out in the field, just him and old codices. Like Grant.

He shook away the feeling and returned his head to the game. Defending the Church from attacks leveled against its foundational beliefs in the Bible.

Silas asked, "So what is it you've been discovering in your research?"

"That there may have been a connection between the Nag Hammadi texts and Christian monks."

Silas sat forward. "What? Who?"

Grant did the same. "Saint Pachomius ring a bell?"

"Isn't he the reason we've spent almost a day flying the friendly skies?" Gapinski asked.

He grinned. "The one and only."

"Excuse me, sir?" Zarruq interrupted from the television, now joining the conversation and voice rising with indignation. "Are you suggesting that Pachomius the Great, the African founder of Christian cenobitic monasticism and celebrated by Coptic, Orthodox, and Catholic Christians as a great renewer of the Church—are you suggesting he had something to do with the heretical texts found at Nag Hammadi?"

The bishop's face was twisted with a mixture of revulsion and downright challenge, his bushy salt-and-pepper beard waving with the same. Silas grinned to himself. Go Bishop Victor!

Silas wasn't as familiar with the monastic tradition of the Church as he was its doctrines and teachings. But he imagined the African Bishop from Libya was, and was itching for a fight to defend his African homeland.

"I know, I know," Grant said, putting up a staying hand and clearing his throat. "Your type insists the texts could not have belonged to any sort of Christian sect, only to Gnostic heretics living in communities desiring access to secret knowledge revealed only to an elect few."

"Damn right!" Silas exclaimed, throwing his hands in the air. "No way they could have been read by orthodox Christians, like these monks you're suggesting."

"And especially not by the brothers and sisters of the Pachomian monastic community," added Zarruq. "Committed believers who were very much in line with the dominant Christian orthodoxy of the time."

"So what's your theory?" Gapinski asked Grant. "What were you finding in your research?"

Grant replied, "Some have contended codices were produced and read by Pachomian monks living and worshiping in the area where the codices were discovered."

"That's highly debatable," Silas said.

"What's debatable is the Gnostic category to begin with! Highly misleading. By my count, the discussion of the origin and use of the codices should move far, far away from being a study of that old canard 'Gnosticism.'"

"So where does this whole monkish aspect come into play?" Gapinski asked before Silas could intervene.

Grant replied, "Some of the scholars who first studied the manuscripts subscribed to the notion that they had belonged to Christian sects in the area, given that several monasteries sat close to the discovery site."

"Yeah, but I know the suggestion was also heavily criticized from other scholars," Silas said.

"And by the way," Zarruq added, "I'll have you know the Pachomian monks were the bastion of Christian orthodoxy!"

Silas nodded. "No way the Pachomian monks could have read such 'heretical' literature, much less safeguarded it!"

Grant turned to him and folded his arms. "Then what, pray tell, is your theory, oh Master Silas?"

Silas frowned. "My theory is like all the others who have regarded the philosophical and anti-biblical contents of the texts. Must have originated with a group of urban intellectuals educated in Greek philosophy."

"Greek urban intellectuals? No way!" Grant exclaimed, doubling over in laughter.

"You done now?"

"The kind of dude you're imagining would have simply read these texts in Greek, and not in Coptic, the language of the Nag Hammadi texts."

"Well then, what's *your* theory?"

"Rather than copied to be read by people just as skilled in Greek as in Coptic, the Nag Hammadi texts were translated into Coptic for the benefit of a monastic community which would have included a number of non-Greek readers."

"The Pachomian monks."

"The literary practices of Egyptian monks in the early centuries of Christianity do point to the fact they were reading more diverse literature than we might expect. This wasn't your run-of-the-mill churchy book. You know better than I do how often monks were criticized by those in Christian power for reading books on the naughty list. Non-canonical and apocryphal literature and whatnot. Yet there they were, stuffed in monastic libraries right between Fifty Shades of Black, White, and Grey."

Silas went to protest when Grant put up a hand. "And before you protest, let me add that you've got to deal with the archaeological evidence. Which my latest research was addressing."

Silas sighed. "Which was what?"

"The production techniques used in the making and writing of the Nag Hammadi codices and their relationship to other Christian books produced around the same period."

Grant scooted to the edge of his seat, becoming animated now. Silas's ears were burning; he wanted to throw something.

"Here's what I was discovering. The Nag Hammadi texts aren't unique. Their make-up and scribal practices closely resemble other books, including biblical manuscripts, which were likely to have come from the same monastic community as the Gnostic texts. Take P75, for instance."

"P75?" Gapinski asked.

Silas answered, "One of the most important New Testament manuscripts containing the Gospels of Luke and John."

Grant nodded. "Righto. They were discovered only a few

kilometers from where the Nag Hammadi texts were found, and there's a more-than-likely chance it came from one of the nearby Pachomian monasteries."

The man was right. Which was both irritating and concerning, for it meant he could be right about more than just P75.

Grant went on, "Then there's the cartonnage material used to stiffen the leather covers of the Nag Hammadi texts."

"Cartonnage? You're makin' my head hurt, man," Gapinski complained.

"Basically scraps of discarded papyrus. And in the case of the Nag Hammadi texts, these cartonnage papyri include a bunch of personal letters written back and forth between monks, suggesting that the codices themselves were produced by monks in the area."

Silas scoffed, shaking his head. "You know as well as I do that plenty of others have dismissed these fragments as completely irrelevant. The letters might have been simply collected from a local rubbish heap for all we know. No way they shed any light on the book makers."

"Or the documents were in fact the property of the people who made the codices and, as such, are valuable evidence for pinpointing the origin of these books. That the so-called Gnostic gospels aren't at all Gnostic, but Christian. Copied by monks and preserved for future generations when the dominant religious powers sought to squash them. In fact, one of the letters was addressed to a certain *'Father Pachomius.'* Which very well could have been the famous abbot Pachomius himself. If so, then it demonstrates a close connection between the makers of the codices and the nearby Pachomian monasteries."

Again, his friend was making an interesting point. And he wondered why the man was interested in making it in the first place. He was sure trying to sell them on his theory. And it annoyed the snot out of Silas.

Grant finished his scotch and leaned back. "If I were to put all my chips on the table, I'd say the Pachomian monastic collective, founded by Pachomius in the early 4th century and traditionally held to be the earliest Christian monastic organization, is the most likely community that owned and even copied the Nag Hammadi texts from their originals. That's what my research was concluding before my shoulder got tapped by Hartwin to come join his latest party."

He sat up and scooted to the edge of his seat. "You've got several Pachomian monasteries lying close to the place of discovery. Then there are the monks from these communities using the nearby cliffs where the Nag Hammadi texts were found for burials and kumbaya ascetic practices—all of it making it likely they would have manufactured and read these codices."

"But they're heresy! False texts teaching a false gospel!" Silas exclaimed.

"All the more reason why they were gathered together in a jar and buried in the caves. Amazingly, whoever performed such a task did so by creating a time-capsule of sorts to give us invaluable insight into the manuscript culture and reading habits of the early Christian monks."

The plane dipped and began to descend.

"So much for mission prep," Gapinski said. "This was enlightening, gents, as these sorts of things usually are, but what does any of this have to do with our current mission?"

"Here's what I'm thinking," Grant answered. "The Coptic Muratorian folios were copied by the same monks that copied the Nag Hammadi texts. Same script, same version of the language even. And you saw that notation, the reference to Pachomius as some sort of source."

"Even if I bought all the bull you were selling," Silas said. "And I don't, by the way."

"Thanks, pal," Grant huffed, settling back again.

"No problem," he said with a wink. "But let's just say for

kicks and giggles that I did agree. There aren't any remaining Pachomian monasteries left to explore."

"Now you tell us?" Gapinski said.

"Not necessarily..." Zarruq said, his face drawn and hand stroking his beard.

Silas turned to the man on the screen. "What do you mean? The three I can recall from the Nag Hammadi region all lay in ruin."

The bishop drew in a breath and leaned his head back, as if contemplating something he was hesitant to suggest.

"Victor, what do you know?"

The man startled, then answered, "There is another ancient monastic community still standing along the Nile several kilometers north of Nag Hammadi."

"How old?"

"From the 5th century."

"Yowzer, that's ancient old!" Gapinski said.

"It's known as the White Monastery," Zarruq went on, "arguably the most important ancient repository for Coptic texts and more generally for understanding early Christian monasticism. The community remained a literary powerhouse through at least the 12th century, gathering and transcribing and storing a wide range of various texts. In fact, there are documents from Byzantine Egypt mentioning people requesting manuscripts and even visiting this monastery's library to obtain copies of various documents."

The man paused, as if gathering his thoughts. He shook his head, almost disbelieving what he was about to suggest. He said, "It also contained the largest, earliest collection of texts documenting cenobitic monasticism."

"Pachomius's monastic movement, right?" Silas asked.

Zarruq nodded. "Exactly. There were letters, monastic rules, treatises and discourses from Shenoute, the abbot of the monastery, and at least his next two successors, comprising a library larger than that of any other 4th or 5th century monastery. Their discovery literally transformed the study of the Coptic language and broader Egyptian language family from the early eras."

"What is the connection with Pachomius?"

"While the evidence is sparse, enough of it survives to conclude a relationship between Shenoute's White Monastery and the Pachomian federation of monastic communities in the region. What is known, is that Shenoute inherited a monastery based on the Pachomian system."

Grant sat forward, showing interest in what the bishop had to say. "What's the story on that one, partner?"

"A link between Shenoute and Pachomius is deeply embedded in Coptic tradition and historiography, with Shenoute's monasticism even described as Pachomian monasticism. For Coptic monks and even Coptic believers, Shenoute was indeed a Pachomian monk. They contend that Shenoute and Pachomius were alike, in Christian practices and theological commitments."

"Which means," Silas said, "if the former monasteries of Pachomius in the surrounding Nag Hammadi region lay in ruin, whatever texts had been held there could have been transferred to the more established, enduring libraries of Shenoute at the White Monastery. Isn't that right?"

Zarruq nodded. "That is a possibility, yes."

"That has to be it, partner!" Grant exclaimed, standing with wide, excited eyes. "You saw it yourself. The Coptic Muratorian Fragment carried a notation pointing us back to good ol' Pachomius. And the only place connected to the man that's even remotely left standing after all these centuries is this White Monastery."

Silas took in a measured breath. It all seemed like wild speculation. But he had to admit, there was a ring of truth to it all.

The pilot came on the intercom to inform them they would be landing shortly.

Grant slapped Silas on the shoulder and sat down, reaching for his lap belt. "Looks like we've got ourselves a bona fide treasure hunt!"

"And finally we've got an X-marks-the-spot to check out," Gapinski said, buckling in for the landing.

Silas buckled in as well and nodded. Soon the plane touched down and they were climbing into an awaiting Mercedes SUV. And not a moment too soon.

His phone sent a pulsing vibration at his leg, announcing a call. He pulled it out. Then sighed.

Hartwin.

"I should take this. It's Hartwin."

"He's gonna be angrier than a goat on fire," Gapinski said, easing the car out from the private hangar.

Silas ignored him and swiped the phone to life. "Uhh, hey there Dr. Braun."

"Where on earth are you?" Hartwin shouted. "I expected you a day ago!"

He held the device away from his ear and winced. So much for pleasantries. "Yeah, about that...We made a little side trip. Then another, and now we're in Luxor."

"Egypt?"

"We were following a lead and—"

"And you didn't think to include us in on this lead? I must be saying, this is highly unprofessional. I can see why Princeton sacked you."

Low blow. But probably warranted after leaving the poor guy out of the loop.

Hartwin huffed. "Forgive my own unprofessionalism. And I am assuming your lead has bearing on the hunt for Gospel Zero?"

Silas hesitated. How much should he share? Technically, it

was the man's gig. But given the threat it posed to the Church, it was also SEPIO's gig. Which made it his gig.

He closed his eyes and made a decision. Hoping it was the right one.

"That's right. Too long a story to get into right now, but we think there's a connection with a Coptic monastery."

Hartwin hummed on the other end. "Interesting deduction. I suppose that could make sense. Mind if we join?"

"The more the merrier."

"Excellent! Bohls and I will leave shortly."

"What about Rotberg?"

"He made a side trip of his own, attending to some other business."

Silas didn't mind that at all. One less baby to sit. He told them where they were headed and ended the call.

"We've got company," he said.

"Hartwin?" Grant asked.

He nodded and stuffed the phone back in his pocket.

"Bet he was sufficiently pissed."

"You could say that. Luckily we've got the jump on them." He grinned and got comfortable for the drive.

Aside from the unexpected phone call, the day was appearing to be bright and sunny. All warm and happy and full of promise by Silas's estimation. He hoped the emerging day was a sign of good things to come. But he knew better, learning not to count his chickens before they hatched. Because inevitably a random meteor would come crashing through the henhouse and obliterate the goods. A vivid metaphor, yes, but proven far too true far too often.

Especially with SEPIO.

And yet touching down in Luxor was heaven. Not only because the gauntlet of flying was finally over, thank the Lord above. But also because it finally felt like they were making progress. That they were on to something that would prove useful. On the right course that would finally blow this whole Gospel Zero business wide open and lay to rest any speculation about what it might prove about the Bible.

That was the hope anyway.

Although, it might also have a whole lot to disprove about the Church's Good Book as well.

Which would be a whole other thing.

Either way, as Gapinski peeled out onto the main throughway toward destiny, he prayed to the good Lord above he'd throw them a bone.

Because they sure needed one!

CHAPTER 23

Silas pulled in a lungful of air through the cigarette between his lips, closing his eyes and reveling in the heat of the rising sun splashing across his face, the dry Egyptian air hovering in the mid-70s. The hills rolled along on either side of the narrow stretch of green snaking with the Nile between Nag Hammadi and Sohag, endless beige works of art that looked like some alien planet from *Dune*. Also reminded him of childhoods spent at Virginia Beach, and the endless mounds and castles he and Sebastian would build during summers with Dad. Those were the days.

He withdrew his cigarette and flopped his arm outside the open passenger side window, holding the nicotine-laced smoke a few beats before easing it out barely parted lips. His head swam with the tobacco's delight, however fake and fleeting it was. Figured he earned it after all that had happened the past few days since his last smoke outside his brother's home in DC. Man, that felt so long ago. Look at all that had happened since.

With him at the center of it. And probably his brother.

He took another pull on his cigarette and considered that angle. No way Sebastian wasn't in some way at the helm when the downfall of Christianity was concerned. Especially with

Helen showing up to steal Hartwin's folios. Nous was definitely on the hunt for anything that could bring down the Church and throw confusion on its central, foundational, basic belief.

And it doesn't get more basic than undermining the credibility of the books that were identified as genuine revelation from God about his story of salvation at the heart of the Christian message.

Yet the revelation of Gospel Zero was begging far more questions than Silas had answers to: What if all that people thought they knew about the Bible was a lie? What if all that the Church said about the Bible was a lie? How would people react and respond? What would it do to their faith—to *the* faith?

The world was about to find out...

"So what's your interest in all of this, cowboy?" Grant asked from the back.

"What do you mean?" Silas said.

"All of this running around and getting shot at and blowing things up—you're liable to get yourself killed! And for what? Just some book written by dead white guys?"

Silas scoffed. "It's not *just* some book, Grant. It's not even a book written by dead white guys, for Pete's sake!"

"Well then what is it, to you?"

He gazed out at the rolling, sandy hills. Good question. What did the Bible mean to him? Why was he fighting for it?

"When I was stationed in Iraq," Silas said, "I put all my chips on the table and gave my life to Jesus at a chapel service on our base."

"Got religion, huh? Fox-hole conversion?"

"It wasn't like that. Really it was a homecoming back to my faith after I abandoned it in college. One of the best days of my life, actually. You should try it."

"Yeah, yeah, yeah."

Silas turned around with a wry smile and winked. "Anyway,

the chaplain gave me this little red New Testament Bible. Read that thing from cover to cover so many times out there every chance I got. The thing nearly fell apart with all the passages I underlined and all the stories I re-read!"

"Why?"

"For one, I was fascinated with Jesus' story. The way he talked about turning from sin and asking God's forgiveness but also about the love of God—the perfect embodiment of grace and truth. His teachings about loving neighbor *and* enemy, the ones about putting it all on the line to follow him wholeheartedly. All he endured on the cross for all the boneheaded things I've done to God and others."

"I'll attest to that!" Grant quipped.

"Thanks, buddy. But it was also the promises it offered. That God would never leave me nor forsake me in all the crazy out there in the Middle East. That I could cast all of my anxieties and worries at his throne, because he cared about what I was going through. Even the fact that Jesus understands my life because he lived my life, opening the door to experience God's crazy love and mercy in times of need."

"The Good Book says all that?" the man asked.

Silas smiled. "Sure does. About the only thing that kept me sane and focused through the hell of war. Knowing my future was secure in Jesus and he was caring for me in the present. You should read it sometime. Might do you some good. Give you the same comfort."

Grant scoffed. "When hell freezes over..."

"Well, the Bible does say with God all things are possible, so I wouldn't count it out of the picture!"

The car fell into a silence as they continued snaking along the Nile toward destiny.

"Golly," Grant said looking out the window, "remind you of our grad school days as much as it does me, getting our hands dirty and breaking our backs working under Doc Pryce?"

Silas took a final drag and flicked the butt out the window, then smiled at the memory working together on the archaeological dig at the biblical city of Jericho.

He said, "Sure does. What a time that was, ehh?"

"Maximum freedom with minimum responsibility. Ahh, the life of a college student."

"Freedom? Speak for yourself. Pryce ran me into the ground."

"Yeah, you were his gofer, weren't you?"

"Whipping boy more like it. While you were his boy wonder."

Grant chuckled. "Whatever. Though I may have sucked up to him once or twice."

"Once or twice?"

"Either way, the sight of all that sand, holding unknown treasures, makes you wanna get your hands dirty again, don't it?"

Silas had to admit it. It did. His duties as Order Master, with all the paperwork and committee meetings and personnel headaches, had pinched out most minutes in the day for the sorts of deep-dive research that he reveled in as a professor. Not to mention any chance of joining in an archaeological project in the far-flung corners of the ancient Christian world. And now being engaged to Celeste anchoring him to DC aside from his role at the Order, it was even that much harder to follow his own personal whims and ambitions.

He envied the man behind him, with no commitments or responsibilities to anyone or anything but himself. Nothing other than the way the wind turned that day in his sail to guide him. It also made him wonder why he was on the project to begin with. He was never all that religious, preferring freelance spirituality to anything organized. And his research into the Gnostic gospels was a shocker.

Whatever. Silas rolled up his window. Like Grant said on

the flight over. Money. Had always been about the Benjamins with him. And boy had he raked it in, selling his academic background and personal ambition to the highest bidder—making bank along the way and building a reputation rivaling the piles of cash.

He did alright financially at Princeton, but the Order was a different story. Not vow-of-poverty level, but nothing to write home about. And certainly no glory in working for the Church in a world that was increasingly skeptical of organized religion generally and Christianity specifically. Most days he was fine with it all. But then he was reminded by people like Grant about all that he used to have in his former life before it all went to hell.

'My grace is sufficient for you, for my power is made perfect in weakness...'

Yeah, yeah, Lord. But it would sure be nice not to need that sufficient power in the first place. Can't we do without the weakness, insults, hardships, persecutions and calamities for just a year?

Soon the highway veered left, and Gapinski took them through rolling vegetable fields and groves of fruit trees before they rounded a town with another set of hills and cliffs straight ahead. It wasn't long before they exited and were passing an industrial park with large cylindrical vats, a water treatment plant perhaps.

Then they saw it. The White Monastery.

"No surprise where it gets its namesake," Grant said, scooting between the pair.

Not purely white, but a domed basilica built of limestone stood proudly behind a gated wall of the same sandstone hue. Colorful life-size images of the Madonna and Christ Child and another portrait of an unfamiliar saint or apostle flanked the entrance. A Coptic cross stood guard above the open gate as Gapinski slid the SUV inside toward the massive building four or five stories high. Looked like a pro-sports basketball arena, all big and boxy. Surprised it had lasted so long, across nearly sixteen centuries.

As they neared, Silas recalled some details he had read about it from the SEPIO database on the flight over. "Apparently, the monastery was considered one of the oldest Coptic monuments in Egypt," he said. "Even built on Pharaonic city ruins, using chunks of white stone from local Pharaonic temples to construct the compound."

Gapinski snorted a laugh. "Nothing like saying the old gods are dead by paving over their ruins with a monument to worshipping the King of kings and Lord of lords."

"Or in this case, the Pharaoh of Pharaohs."

Only a limestone church built in the shape of a basilica was left of what had served as a monastery for Coptic believers and other desert wanderers seeking a monastic life. Even then, most of it was a husk of its former self. Surprisingly, the wandering looked to be alive and well. A tour bus and several more cars were parked outside the massive walls of the original monastery.

Gapinski parked, and the men exited. A sign at the entrance instructed patrons to turn off their mobile devices to maintain the peace and tranquility of the spiritual experience.

Silas shrugged, switching off his mobile before shoving his Beretta at the back of his spine behind a jean jacket.

"Phones off?" Silas said to the other two. "And you got your Order-issued steel?"

Gapinski nodded. "Dead as a doornail. And packing for two." He held up two SIG Sauers before shoving them at his waist underneath a black coat.

"Good. Because the last thing we need is your Baby Shark ringtone to go blasting through the monastery."

Grant laughed. "Yeah, that'd kill the mood right quick, wouldn't it?"

Gapinski stopped, planting a hand on his hips and cocking his head. "What's your beef with Baby Shark?"

"No beef here, partner. You do you and all that jazz."

Silas ignored his partner and kept going through a dark passage leading into the interior, his heart quickening at what he saw on the other side.

Studded ends that had once served as pillars for the main nave of the church stood like broken teeth arrayed on either side of a vacant center within the compound. An entrance of dark wood stood open at one end, leading into the still-standing apse. Next to it, a tent of red canvas slung across wood beams sold icons of saints and tall prayer candles and other religious tchotchkes.

Silas nodded at an older woman seated behind a wood table, hunched and shrouded in a dirty white shawl. He understood why these things existed, that the proceeds often helped fund such Christian communities, and they supplied the faithful with keepsakes of the experience. Still turned his stomach how such sites of veneration often felt akin to an amusement park attraction rather than a site of religious affection.

He crossed himself before stepping through the door, marveling at what he found inside.

While the outside was a plain dirty-white facade, the interior of the basilica was pure eye candy. The columns supporting the apse were painted with intricate, interweaving patterns of golds and greens and whites; others held black and white waves reaching up the columns' length, interrupted by pink-and-white patterned rings edged with gilt. The walls and arches echoed this green, pink, and gold theme, stretching high toward the crown jewel of the basilica's visual feast: the Christ Pantocrator.

Above them hung a massive portrait of Christ the Giver of Life within one of the apse domes. The enlarged face of Christ stared down upon the faithful from up on high, one arm holding up two crossed fingers signifying the Greek letters of his name, the other clutching a closed book representing the Four Gospels.

How fitting...

Grant whistled. "It's enough to beckon even my wayward soul to the bosom of Christ."

Silas chuckled. "Well, there's still time. Even for a heathen like yourself."

"Fat chance."

"Come on, bro," Gapinski said, still staring up at Christ. "He's the friend of sinners. Even prostitutes!"

"Then I guess there's still hope for me after all," Grant said with a wry grin.

"Whatever. If he can take a guy like Matthew the tax collector and bring him into his inner circle, he's got room for you too."

"Matthew...Didn't he write one of your holy books?"

"Yeah, the Gospel of Matthew," Silas said.

"Speaking of which. Shouldn't we get to it?"

"Truly breathtaking, is it not?" an accented voice said from behind.

Silas spun around to find a petite man wearing a black habit and a silver cross around his neck on a heavy chain. His face looked young, and it was covered with a long black beard. Definitely one of the monks caretaking the joint.

Bingo...

CHAPTER 24

Silas smiled and looked back up at the fresco. "Yes, it is. And if you don't mind my saying so, are you one of the caretakers of the monastery?"

The man laughed. "What gave it away? The beard or the robe?"

"Well, both." They both shared a laugh.

"The heavy cross around your neck was a dead giveaway, too," Grant added.

"You got a library in this joint?" Gapinski asked, taking in the rest of the place.

The monk shook his head and frowned. "No, sorry."

Silas cleared his throat and threw his SEPIO agent a look before taking over.

"Forgive my friend, here. What he means to say is, we're with the Vatican on, shall we say, an exploratory mission."

"The Vatican?" the man exclaimed, eyes widening before growing narrow with suspicion.

It wasn't often he played that card. Though the Order was technically its own ecumenical entity, it still had ties to the Papal State and Catholic Church.

"That's right. And we were under the impression you may be holding books here. Ancient ones, from the early Church."

The man's frown deepened, and he darted his eyes around before settling back on Silas. "I am sorry, but there is no longer any library. It is true that this monastery's scriptorium and library were arguably the most influential in the region. It's also true that important copies of biblical books and monastic texts written or translated into Coptic have survived. However, our manuscripts were dispersed to libraries, museums, and private collections throughout Europe centuries ago. Only a handful remain in Egypt, with the largest collections in Naples, Vienna, Paris, and England."

"Is it true that the founder of the White Monastery, Shenoute, was one of the earliest Coptic authors who cited and quoted the Bible, showing how the Bible was used and interpreted in 4th and 5th century Egypt?"

The man brightened at this show of knowledge. He nodded. "That is correct. He and his fellow monks also documented the early beginnings of the monastic movement. Egypt was a hotbed for early Christian monasticism, particularly in the 4th century when men and women flocked to give themselves to Christ in this singular way. Anthony the Great was perhaps the most famous of these. Pachomius was another, launching cenobitic monasticism."

The trio stirred at the mention of his name.

Grant was the first to speak: "And there aren't any books left from this Pachomius character? No books or manuscripts or whatnot lying around from his shuttered monasteries?"

The frown returned. "No, no, there is not. There are no more books."

"Sure about that, partner?"

Silas threw Grant a look before chuckling. "You wouldn't happen to have a hidden compartment or secret chamber full of leftover ancient codices around here, would you?"

"A...a hidden compartment or secret chamber, you say?" The man grinned and chuckled nervously. "That is being super funny and ironic..." he muttered before trailing off and looking to the ground.

Silas furrowed his brow. "What's ironic?"

"Huh?" the man said, head snapping back up, eyes wide.

What's with this guy?

"I said, what's ironic about it? You said funny and ironic. Funny I get. Because the question is a little left field. I mean, why would you have a hidden compartment or secret chamber, right?"

The guide nodded. "You are being exactly right! Why indeed."

"But then you said ironic. As if someone else had asked you the question. Perhaps just that day, or just a while ago. As if my asking the question was connected to something else. But if that was the case, then the word you really wanted to use was *coincidental.*"

The man was looking even more panicked now. And completely caught off guard.

Exactly where Silas wanted him.

"Because irony," he went on, "means contrary to fact or expectation. Which is often confused with coincidence. The fact that I asked a question someone else has asked today, or that is connected to a similar event surrounding a hidden compartment or secret chamber, isn't contrary to fact at all. It's *coinciding* with fact, because my question happened at or near the same time of another. Which would make it coincidental."

The man fell silent, those eyes darting around before his face fell.

He looked like a proverbial deer in headlights.

What was that in the man's eyes? Boredom, irritation? A low-level panic he was trying to keep at bay?

Then the man's hands caught Silas's eye. Wringing to death,

round and round, like they could screw right off at any time and thud to the floor with a bounce.

And the man's feet were doing a little dance.

Definitely low-level panic he was trying to keep at bay.

Then the monk whispered. "There were...others earlier today."

Instinctively, Silas reached for his weapon. A fly-by pass to make sure it was where it was supposed to be. That it was ready, willing, and able to do what it was supposed to do.

Silas stepped closer to the man. "What others?"

That's when the man caught his breath before stiffening and taking a step back. Then another before hunching. As if making himself small.

Just as the barrel of a stout-nosed pistol shoved into Silas's kidneys.

And two more, into Grant's and Gapinski's spines.

"Sorry..." the guide muttered before being led away by another goon and disappearing into the crowd.

"Always something," Gapinski muttered. Grant said nothing, but his face said it all. Not happy.

"It would be most unpleasant if you were to make a scene," a voice said lowly in Silas's left ear, breath sour and laced with the trace of mint mouthwash that had its work cut out for it.

Silas clenched his jaw and took in a steadying breath. The box men. Or Nous.

His brother.

"Let's go," the voice returned. "Nice and easy and no one gets hurt."

"Gentle, gentle," Gapinski complained. "I'm breakable!"

"Come on man," Grant said. "Can't we work this out? I've got money if that's your thing. Or stocks and bonds. Even gold and diamonds. Whatever suits your fancy."

"Shut up!" one of the other goons growled before jabbing his weapon into his side.

The men led them down a small hallway toward a small chapel that had been roped off from the main. It was painted white, with the original ancient stone and brickwork showing through at spots. Six or seven carved walnut benches in two neat rows stood ready for use with red velvet kneeling pads making the veneration easier on the knees. Blue fans anchored to support columns blew stale air throughout the room and a small faded clock kept time for the worshipers.

Clangs and muffled voices drew Silas's attention toward the front. A wood wall matching the benches, ornately carved with squares and Coptic crosses, was erected before a small apse, the ancient stonework hidden behind with crumbling columns in parts and a fresco of some saint or apostle above fading with the passage of time. Fourteen small icons lined the top of the wall with a small replica of Da Vinci's *The Last Supper* at the center.

Cords of electrical wiring snaked out from under a purple curtain hanging from a narrow door at the center of the wood wall, the growl of excavation or some other power tools growing louder. Silas imagined them having blasted their way into the ancient stonework beyond, carried by the same ambitious hope that drew SEPIO to the monastery. Finding the source of the Church's sacred scriptures.

The thought sickened him. His stomach sank further at the thought of who would be waiting for him on the other side. Didn't know which was worse: his brother and Nous or an unknown headache rising to destroy the Christian faith.

Time to find out.

"In we go," the goon grunted.

Silas parted the curtain, his stomach dropping at the sight.

An altar of gold and ivory lay toppled on its side. A stone pitcher that held wine was shattered on the floor behind it, its contents soaking it crimson. Unleavened wafers were crushed and scattered about. Probably had been readied for a Coptic mass. What a desecration! But that wasn't all.

A hole had been chopped through the ancient floor. Large chunks of jagged stone, some ancient and some newer, were heaped in a pile at the wall and dust coated what was left of the floor. A set of stairs led down into a blackened void glowing dimly at the bottom.

A hidden compartment. A secret chamber.

Containing what, the fabled Gospel Zero? The idea was preposterous and bordered on insane. Yet sanity had been in short supply since his brother's house and the Hartwin announcement.

And someone down below thought it wasn't. The goons shoving them farther down the stone stairs sure thought the Q source was true enough to go through the trouble of traveling to a barely known monastery of a barely known monastic sect in the deserts of Egypt. To do who knows what to the monk above to extract the information they needed before smashing the floor to bits to uncover the passage they were now reaching.

Bearing something the good Lord above definitely only knew.

Silas dipped his head and started toward the end, even as Gapinski complained of the misery from behind. The passage was narrow and short but well-constructed of the same white stone above, smelling of earth and plaster but not of the dampness and mold you'd expect in such a chamber. Yellow tripods with lighting shone from the end of the crypt and voices echoed toward them now with excitement.

And two people were hunched over something.

One blond man, one blond woman.

They stood and turned.

"How nice of you to join us, big brother," Sebastian said. "And at just the perfect time!"

Power tools—cutters and saws and drills—were toppled

over on the floor and leaning against the passage wall. Three black duffle bags sat open at their feet. The yellow tripods were angled at the end of the passage toward something behind Sebastian and his lover.

"How the heck did you find this place, baby brother?" Silas growled as he inched forward, his bowels growing watery at the truth of the matter. "And what the heck are you doing here?"

"Now, now. No need to get snippy. I did what you did. Followed the clues. And with all the thanks and accolades due my dearest here for her quick thinking. I'm sure you remember Helen. In fact, she and I were just about to unveil the crown jewel of this lovely monastic establishment. You might as well join in the fun."

A coldness spread through Silas at the sight of his brother, made all the worse by a stone chest coming into view as Sebastian and Helen stepped aside.

Grant whistled from behind. "Now that there would make even good ol' Doc Jones drool with envy. Probably make a sweet Spielberg follow-up flick, too."

Silas took a cautious step toward the chest made of white limestone about the size of a bathtub suspended by two stout pillars anchored to the small chamber's floor. A wide set of three shallow stairs at the front led up to view the insides. His heart picked up pace with each step and breath grew shallow as he approached it.

Reaching the third stair, he chanced pressing his palms on the lid. It was cold and dry and seemed to pulse with an almost holy hum, though it was probably his imagination running wild at the possibilities of what lay inside. He let his hands slide across the lid, its surface rough with carved angelic beings. He eyed the chest, noticing that relief carvings of a man, a lion, an ox, and an eagle were etched onto each of the four sides, whorls of vines and flowers joining them to confirm what Silas dreaded.

"The tetramorph..." he whispered in amazement.

"The who?" Sebastian asked.

Silas cleared his throat. "The tetramorph. A symbolic arrangement of four differing elements into one unit. Derived from the Greek *tetra*, meaning four, and *morph*, meaning—"

"Thanks for the Reading Rainbow explanation, prof, but what the hell does it mean?"

"In Christianity, it's a composition of the Four Living Creatures from the Book of Ezekiel in the Hebrew Scriptures and applied to the Four Evangelists in the New Testament. Matthew the man, Mark the lion, Luke the ox, and John—"

"The eagle..." A drunken giggle escaped Sebastian's mouth. He moved closer to his brother, himself placing a hand on the chest lid.

Silas took a step back, folded his arms and nodded.

"So this is it then," Sebastian went on. "Gospel Zero! The source of the other Christian books."

He laughed. "I think we're getting ahead of ourselves here. Who knows what the heck this thing is."

"Only one way to find out," Grant said. Silas turned around and eyed the man, whose mouth was wide with delight and eyes wider with lust.

Sebastian matched his grin. "Only one way indeed..."

He motioned for Grant to help him lift the lid. Grant was eager to oblige. The two men stood at the third stair and grasped the lid with both hands.

"Ready?" Sebastian asked.

"Say the word, partner," Grant replied.

They heaved the lid, and it toppled off the back to the stone floor with an echoey crash.

Heart hammering in his head with anticipation, Silas joined the pair and peered over Sebastian's shoulder.

His breath caught in his chest at what he saw.

"My God..." Silas whispered. "Gospel Zero is real."

Stacked in five or six columns across and three rows deep were a collection of ring-bound books filling most of the chest. The rest was filled with a few crumbling scrolls, tablets, an incense bowl, and sealed jar.

He reached for the first of the books. Sebastian loudly cleared his throat.

Silas sighed. "May I?"

"An ask was all I wanted. Carry on."

He rolled his eyes and picked up one of the books.

It was heavy. Real heavy. Opening the leather cover revealed why. The pages were made of metal, their golden, coppery hue shimmering in the light. Probably some sort of metal alloy, lead or copper. Maybe even gold. Even more surprising was what was etched on their face. A generous ancient script, forming words and sentences and paragraphs.

All in Aramaic.

The language of Jesus...

He brought the codex over to the light and squinted, reaching deep into his academic language repository to read the first line, his heart an overwhelming beat now in the face of what he was certain to find:

John said to the crowds that came out to be baptized by him, 'You brood of vipers! Who warned you to flee from the wrath to come?'

Silas's arm dropped, and the book went with it, flopping to the floor with a dull clamor.

"Watch it, you sodden idiot!" Sebastian cursed. He scrambled for the book even as Silas's head swam with recognition.

The Gospel of Luke. Chapter three verse seven.

And the Gospel of Matthew. Same chapter, same verse.

A passage shared by neither the Gospel of Mark nor the Gospel of John.

The second source. The Q source.

Gospel Zero...

"Would you mind sharing with the rest of us, big brother, what the hell you just read?"

He went to answer when a scream split the subterranean air. Followed by shouting and the distinct spray of gunfire.

They had company.

Again.

CHAPTER 25
FRANKFURT.

A shiver ratcheted across Torres's shoulders, blanketing her skin with goose pimples, even under the thick, Order-issued terry-cloth robe wrapped around her body. Her nose felt tickly, and she sneezed into her arm.

She moaned and kept at her mission. It was going to be a long day. And without Airborne and Zicam.

Her body was holding fast to the chill that reached deep into her bones made worse by her still-soaked hair from the plunge into the icy depths of the Main. Irony of ironies, she was aiming a hair dryer blasting warm air toward the laptop they swiped from Pauli's flat, its underside exposed and battery lying next to her in a desperate attempt to revive the device that promised answers to their desperate mission. Zoe had recommended the little trick when they called in a panic that their only leads were lost to water. Torres was skeptical but kept at it, praying their jaunt through the seven circles of hell was worth it.

Another chill sent her skin crawling with a shudder. Irritated with her wet hair and longing for relief, she switched the dryer to *'Hot'* and aimed it at her wet head, tilting it and running her fingers through her long dark curls in a desperate attempt to keep from catching a cold.

"Torres, mate," Celeste said, armed with the same weapon and drying the contents they had swiped from Pauli's desk. She gestured toward the laptop. "No time to tarry when the fate of the Church is on the line."

She huffed, then resumed drying the device. "But I'm so cold! And I feel a cold creeping up on me after our near-death experience with Poseidon."

"Well then, here—" Celeste threw a coral hand towel at Torres's head. It unfurled and draped across her face.

"*Gracias, amiga,*" was her muffled reply. She pulled it off. "But after what we went through, I'm going to need a duvet to dry me off."

Torres tightened her bathrobe and tossed the towel to a table that sat next to a kitchenette. It landed next to three bags of rice resting next to their drying clothes. Inside were three cell phones submerged beneath the white grains. Another trick Zoe offered to resurrect their tech when they finally reached the safe house and phoned in their mission update.

Barely making it out alive.

After the BMW careened through the metal barrier, the car sank fast with its missing rear window thanks to those trigger-happy hostiles.

Somehow, by providential care or professional acumen, Torres's training with the IDF instantly kicked into gear. They trained for those sorts of possibilities, and once Torres realized the inevitable, something lodged back in her brain sprang into action. She drew in a lungful of air and braced for impact.

The thing sank fast, all two-and-a-half tons of the steel beast. It also hit the floor almost instantly, the airbags deploying on impact. On the plus side, it meant they wouldn't drown. On the negative, it meant they didn't have much between them and the hostiles.

The water was instantly chilling. So much so that Torres almost lost her breath from the shock. And it was pitch black. Couldn't even see the end of her own nose let alone Celeste. She reached for the woman, who clenched her hand before letting go. Time to escape.

And pronto!

Within seconds, Torres had unbuckled her belt and shoved through her door. She trusted her MI6-trained partner could take care of herself. She also trusted the woman had enough sense to grab the backpack filled with intel and also stay beneath the surface long enough to pop up out of range of the whack jobs who would surely be standing over the bridge ready to pick them off like fish in the proverbial barrel.

But where should she swim, which direction? It was still so cold and dark. She couldn't tell which way was which.

Eyes closed and lungs beginning to burn, she pulled herself beneath the surface and swam toward where she thought made sense.

A few agonizing minutes later, her fingers scrapped along the slimy, rough brick of one of the bridge columns. With burning lungs, she eased to the surface and panted for breath, even as she tried to stay quiet and hidden.

She moved along the wide, squat column to the center of the bridge, which happened to be the middle of the four supporting structures, heaving more desperate breaths and searching with rising panic for Celeste.

Honking cars and confused, concerned German voices echoed off the water from above now, sirens beginning to approach from the north.

They had to get out of there. And fast. Couldn't be caught up with the *Polizei*, and all the inevitable questions arising from an interrogation. Had no good answers why they had careened off the bridge, why they had been chased for miles by an SUV full of terrorist whack jobs slinging bullets left and right.

But then she heard it. The sudden surfacing of a body and the accompanying panicked inhalation. Other side of the column.

Torres inched around the opposite side of their grand entrance into the Main River. There she was. With the backpack.

Gracias Dios!

She wanted to rejoice at their cheating death—for the fourth time that evening. But Celeste, always the head-in-the-game type, directed them to the shore.

Shivering from the early spring water still chilled from winter and bone-weary from the chaotic hour, the two struggled to make it to shore, fighting the currents and fighting to maintain the waning adrenaline rush. But they did, climbing up from the river into a park that bore a set of stairs that brought them up to the city surface.

Given the late hour and the commotion at the other end, lights and sirens from emergency vehicles combined with the inevitable gawkers, they were able to make their escape and find their way back to the safe house.

Where long hours resuscitating water-logged electronics and documents awaited them.

Waving the hair dryer back and forth with one hand, Torres reached for the towel Celeste tossed at her with the other and put it to good use. She'd been at this for a while, her arm stiff now from the constant motion. As she dried her still-soaking hair, her mind replayed the past forty-eight hours—from Helen's entrance at Princeton to the terrorists who had rendered Celeste unconscious before annihilating her *tío's* business to what had just gone down in Frankfurt.

The sudden intrusion of such carnal violence reminded her of home. With the reports about such invasions and hostage takings and executions by the *sicarios* that terrorized many parts of Mexico. From Mexico City to Tijuana, Gutalajara to

Ciudad Juárez. Between the Juárez Cartel and the Sinaloans, La Familia Cartel and Los Zetas. The battles across her beloved country reached a fevered pitch during her childhood through the '80s and '90s when the Mexican government turned a blind eye to the implosion of her country. Even then, the violence had always been so distant, so otherworldly. Especially after her parents died and *Tío* whisked her to a life of privilege behind gated walls fueled by his oil money.

Now she was sitting in a safe house praying that the hostiles were long gone and wondering what the heck she'd gotten herself into by joining the Order!

A rumble of thunder interrupted the slapping of rain against the windows, their panes reverberating seconds later. It was still dark even though night was turning to morning, the sun shrouded by a thick canopy of clouds. She hoped the boys were faring better than them two. At least Silas and Gapinski. Grant she couldn't care less if the desert swallowed him whole.

Torres tossed the towel to the floor, now too wet to be of any use, and continued waving the hair dryer.

"Right. I think that should do." Celeste turned off her own hair dryer and tossed it to the bed. "What do you say we ring Zoe and have her take a crack at the laptop?"

"Let's hope our baptism didn't fry the thing."

"We shall pray toward that end."

Celeste fired up an Order-issued laptop and logged onto the proprietary app designed for SEPIO to call back to the mother ship where Zoe was waiting.

The petite Italian with those baby blue glasses appeared, head turned toward another monitor and fingers clacking away on her keyboard.

"Hey, ladies," she said. "Any progress with the tech you stole?"

Celeste said, "I prefer *swiped*, since the man was already dead. But, yes, we think we're there."

"If it helps you sleep better..." Zoe mumbled. "Did you fire them up, the laptop and phone?"

"Not yet. We were waiting for your instructions."

"Well, fire away."

Celeste nodded toward Torres, who then placed the battery back inside the laptop. The two held their breaths as she turned on the power.

A black screen greeted them and nothing else.

They flashed each other worried looks before the familiar Microsoft Windows XP logo and progress bar appeared, and the boot-up sequence started before the whimsical Windows XP chime sounded.

"Eww, how old is this laptop you stole?" Zoe moaned.

"*Swiped*," Celeste corrected. "Obviously it was around before you were born."

"Obviously."

"But you think you can hack into it?" Torres said. "And find what we need?"

"*Pssht*. You kidding me? I can hack into anything that breathes. Especially XP. What's the story with the phone?"

Torres reached for the bag of rice containing Pauli's mobile device. She fished it out. Definitely not as ancient as the laptop.

"Looks like a newer Android model. Moment of truth." She took a breath, then pressed the '*On*' button and waited.

No issue. Within seconds, it was asking for the passcode.

The ladies both breathed a collective sigh of relief and grinned with victory.

Celeste said, "The Android phone is ready."

"Perfect," Zoe said. "Grab a USB cable and hook it up to the SEPIO laptop."

She searched the desk and found one, then attached it to the phone before plugging it into the laptop.

Within seconds, the screen transformed into some sort of recovery mode, black with lines of white code starting to cycle.

Then the laptop, formerly stuck at the login screen, transformed as well. Same black screen, same lines of white code.

A minute later, another familiar chime sounded from the device, a throwback to Torres's tireless years at grad school slaving away over her own bulky Windows laptop writing papers and journal articles.

It was at the desktop screen. Ready to go.

Zoe pushed her glasses to her face and grinned. "Tada!"

"Golly, you're good," Celeste marveled.

"SEPIO doesn't pay me the big bucks for nothing."

"Big bucks?" Torres exclaimed. "I got into the wrong line of work."

"You and me both, mate." Celeste leaned over the laptop, hands at the keyboard already searching the C-Drive. "Thanks, Zoe. You're a charm."

"Don't thank me yet. I've still got to get into the phone."

"But you can, can't you?"

"*Pssht*. You kidding me? Just takes a little longer. It's why Page and Brin spanked Gates sideways in the device wars."

Torres raised a brow. "Page and Brin?"

Zoe raised one of her own. "For real? Like, the founders of Google."

"Hold on," Celeste interrupted. "There appears to be an encrypted folder on the C-Drive."

Zoe scoffed. "Encrypted? Windows? Let me at it."

An input window opened on the screen before transforming into a progress bar. Within seconds, the bar filled and the folder opened, spilling its contents on the screen.

A number of thumbnail images were arrayed across the window. Looked like people, and lots of them.

"Through the looking glass we go…" Celeste clicked on the first one.

The ladies recoiled with horror.

"Blimey!" she said, averting her eyes.

"Now we know our dead friend's extracurricular activities," Torres said, less nonplussed than her partner. "And the kind with kink."

"With a capital 'K'," Zoe said, face twisted with equal revulsion.

Celeste returned to the screen and kept scrolling through the images, and scrolling. And scrolling some more.

She mumbled, "We also know the bloke was into more than ancient Egyptian papyri."

"And auto parts," Torres added.

Her partner finally scrolled to the end. Nothing more than images.

Celeste huffed. "Well that got us nowhere. Can't imagine any reason to hide a gig worth of porno in an encrypted folder."

"Unless it was illegal."

"Maybe. But the first image looked legit. At least, what little I glimpsed."

Torres said, "Zoe, maybe you could see if there are any hidden folders."

"Good idea."

"On it," Zoe said.

Clacking was heard over the connection. Then the File Explorer window snapped to the top, where a grayed-out folder stood at the front of the line.

Named *Gospel Zero.*

Torres folded her arms. "How conveniently coined."

"The bloke did register the domain gospelzero.com, remember? Makes sense he'd hoard a stash of documents inside."

"Let's check it out."

Celeste opened the folder. Inside were several PDFs and saved emails.

"Might as well start at the top," she muttered before opening the first email.

It was from a new name in the mix, an Abram Kusnur.

"Who's Abram Kusnur?" Torres asked, arms folded and peering over her shoulder.

"Dunno. But it looks like he's the original source of the papyri." She pointed at the screen, it read:

Good morning, Herr Pauli,

It looks as though our mutual friend has found someone who can arrange the sale of the cache that we spoke about. How would you like to proceed?

Regards,

~Abram Kusnur

"The whole *'our mutual friend'* is interesting," Torres said. "Think he means Andrew Sterling, the broker who roped my *tío* into this mess?"

"Probably." Celeste sat back and folded her arms. "Zoe—"

"Already on it. Searching all known databases for named connections."

"And why use the honorific title?" Torres asked. "Herr Pauli seems fairly formal, don't you think?"

"You're right. Let's keep reading." Celeste brought up the next email.

Good morning, Herr Pauli,

All is in order. A buyer will contact you through our mutual friend, Andrew Sterling. His credentials are, well, sterling, and will be able to facilitate the sale. Remember your role. And remember all I have done for you.

Regards,

~Abram Kusnur

"There goes the Andrew Sterling theory," Celeste said.

"What about Noland Rotberg?" Torres asked.

"That's right. The book on the Gnostic gospels you discovered. Wasn't his name scrawled on the title page?"

Torres retrieved the book still wet from their swim through the Main River but less soaked. She opened the cover to the title page. Noland Rotberg's note was still there, though the ink had bled.

She tapped the name. "Could definitely be the 'mutual friend.' But then we'd need to make a connection between Rotberg and this new Kusner dude."

"Right. And who the bloomin' that bloke is is anyone's guess."

"Now here's something interesting," Zoe said.

"What's that, mate?"

"I found a hit on Abram Kusner."

"And?"

"Not much out there on him except for a business registered under his name. The same one listed on one of the receipts you found at Torres's uncles warehouse."

Celeste flashed a hopeful grin at Torres. "Nice job, Zoe."

"Not to burst your bubble," Torres said, "but wasn't the address listed as some dead-end postal box?"

Her partner frowned and leaned back. "That's right."

Feeling bad, she pointed at the laptop. "Maybe there's something else in the folder. Something more concrete. Have to imagine the hidden folder was some sort of failsafe should things go south."

"Right." Celeste scrolled past the emails and opened a PDF.

It was a wire transfer receipt linked to a bank in Zurich, in the amount of half a million dollars.

"Not enough to retire on," Torres said.

"But enough to pull someone out from bankruptcy. Which is what Pauli mentioned before...well, you know."

"And something that can definitely be traced."

"Send me the PDF and I'll see what I can do," Zoe said. "But I'm not promising anything. Hacking computers is one thing. Banks...that's a whole other thing."

Celeste snapped a picture of the PDF on screen and emailed it to her operations coordinator.

"BTW, the phone's ready," Zoe announced.

Torres picked it up. Sure enough, it was unlocked and ready at the home screen.

"Is there a Facebook app?" Celeste asked.

"No. But there is a WeShare app. Front and center."

"Check there first."

"Why?"

"Because unfortunately if you want to know the full measure of a twenty-first century man, or woman really, you go to their preferred social media app."

Torres smirked, opening up the app. "What, did MI6 teach you that?"

Celeste laughed. "WeShare wasn't yet a thing when I was serving Her Majesty, mate. Call it woman's intuition."

Torres scrolled through the man's newsfeed, filled with a bunch of posts in German from family and friends, adverts for books and men's hair products, news items that were surely shared by bots working for the Russian government.

But nothing noteworthy.

She clicked on the man's photos and began flipping through.

When something caught her eye.

Torres brought the phone closer, squinting for a look.

"No way..."

Celeste looked up from the laptop. "What did you find?"

Torres turned the phone and held it toward her. "Our man is sandwiched between two German dudes. Both look like Hartwin."

There he was. Ulrich Pauli, mouth widened into a joyous grin with a cigar sticking out between his teeth and arms draped around the two men's shoulders, each hand bearing a bottle of beer. One with blond hair, one brown. Both tall with chiseled faces. And both looking very much like Hartwin Braun.

Celeste gasped. "The twins…"

"A thousand pesos the blond there on the left is Hartwin and the other is his mega-bazillionaire brother what's-his-name."

"Markus."

"Which means Hartwin and Pauli definitely knew each other."

"A convenient fact left out before…well, the bloke met his untimely death."

"And a convenient fact left out by Hartwin. He never said anything about knowing the dude who originally owned the papyri folios. Yet there they are, smoking and drinking it up! Do you think Hartwin knew who had originally sold him the goods?"

Celeste scoffed. "Can't imagine why he wouldn't have! The whole thing was cooked up from the start. And you and Silas and Grant and those other two blokes were brought in to give cover to—whatever the bloody hell the man was cooking up."

"The biggest, fakest religious conspiracy of the century, that's what!"

"Right. Because we already suspect the supposed Coptic manuscripts were fakes."

"But why go through all the trouble, especially the notation on the back of the first folio."

"Which notation?"

"The one about Gospel Zero."

Celeste shook her head. Then her eyes went wide.

"It was all some sort of setup…"

"A setup?"

"A trap."

"Trap? I don't follow."

"Don't you see? The Coptic folios were the bait. The morsel to whet our appetite and lead us to the real prize."

"Which is?"

"Whatever the bloody hell is waiting for our boys at the end of the yellow brick road!"

"Then we should warn Silas and Gapinski."

Celeste turned to the computer. "Zoe, I need to get a message to the boys in Egypt. Can you ring me through?"

"Already on it. Just give me a sec—"

Zoe's face fell even as her words fell off. Then her eyes squinted before her mouth twisted upward.

"Talk to me, Zoe…" Celeste said with urgency.

"Sorry, but it appears their phones are down."

"Down?" she snapped. "What do you mean down?"

"I mean, down down. As in off."

"Shut off? But that isn't SEPIO operational protocol."

"Perhaps someone should tell that to our new Order Master," Torres said.

Celeste huffed before running a frustrated hand through her hair. "Blimey, Silas. What are you playing at?"

CHAPTER 26
LUXOR.

Silas spun toward the set of stairs at the end of the long, narrow passage, straining toward the intrusion, white light filtering down below promising an intrusive revelation.

Another spat of *rat-a-tat-tat* gunfire followed by another chorus of screams and shouts of protest confirmed the first round wasn't a mirage.

He walked straight to the closest Nousati goon and held out his hand.

"Give me back my piece," Silas demanded.

The man, all muscles and shoulders and no sense, shrugged him off, pulling out his own piece as the screams faded and gunfire picked back up.

"Sebastian!" he growled without turning around, staring the man down hard. "Give me back my Beretta."

The goon smirked and looked over his shoulder.

There was a silent exchange between the two, Silas oblivious to what wasn't being said as he continued facing forward to discern the threat, ready to engage once he was armed.

Then the grunt's face fell and brows furrowed before meeting Silas's eyes.

"Go on. Give it back," Sebastian echoed from behind.

One end of Silas's mouth curled upward with satisfaction. He held out his hand again. The goon slapped it with cold, hard steel.

"Thanks," he grunted before sliding out the magazine, inspecting it, and sliding it back in.

Ready, willing, and able.

He nodded toward Gapinski and Grant. "Theirs as well."

The goon went to protest when he was cut off by more screaming, more gunfire.

"We don't have time for this crap!" Silas said.

The pair held out their hands and Sebastian surprisingly obliged, commanding the other Nousati hostile to hand over their weapons.

Silas turned toward his brother as his partners were rearmed. The man was backed up against the stone chest with Helen, one arm braced against the object and the other shielding his lover. If he weren't mistaken, Silas caught the fleeting glimpse of fear before his face hardened.

"Go on then," Sebastian said. "Do your thing."

An odd feeling instantly surfaced. Something buried deep since Silas's teenage years in Falls Church, Virginia, when his father began his post at the Pentagon, and even deeper back in childhood globetrotting from bases in Europe to the South Pacific.

Something familial, something primal.

What was the word? He could hardly place it at first in the chaos, but it felt all at once familiar and foreign.

Then he had it.

Protection.

As strained as things had become between him and his brother, he wanted to protect him. Save him from whatever beasts up top were raising hell.

And hell they were raising. More *rat-a-tat-tat* gunfire and frightened cries for help and relief promised a wicked fight ahead.

Silas nodded and spun around back toward the stairs. "Stay put. Let us handle this."

He shoved through the two Nousati who looked more than willing to comply and guard their boss, trailed closely by Gapinski while Grant held back.

It was go time.

Silas came up fast to the stairs. One foot planted on the first, the other on the dusty stone floor, back against the wall of cut stone. Aiming straight toward the hole cut above.

Clear. For now.

Gapinski slid next to the side of the stairs and aimed into the void as another round of screams and shouts and spray of gunfire erupted.

"Any doubt who's coming in hot and heavy, chief?" he asked.

"Box men tattoo whack jobs."

"Roger that. So what's the plan?"

The chorus of chaos ceased. Giving them the window to act.

"Come at 'em as hot and heavy. Probably looking for the same stash of codices. And I doubt our helpful monk friend up top will hold back on the 411 if his life is on the line."

Gapinski chambered a round and nodded. "Then let's do this. Again."

Silas nodded and frowned, still seeing Grant back with the others. Whatever. He took the stairs by twos, weapon extended on taut arms, the opening above a void of white light and a big, fat question mark of what they'd find.

Within seconds he reached the surface, slowing and crouching, steadying his aim before finding it clear. Even the purple curtain was still closed. Not even a ripple of disturbance. It wouldn't stay that way for long.

He popped out, Gapinski close behind.

There was shouting beyond. Frustrated and frantic and full of searching purpose.

And vaguely familiar.

Followed by that also-familiar *rat-a-tat-tat* spray of gunfire, joined by a *pop-pop-pop* reply. Different tone, different timbre. Security, maybe. Or the Nous hostile who took the monk aside.

Silas stopped short at the curtain, the velvet's heaviness holding fast. "Won't be long before the hostiles come up on us."

Gapinski came up across from him. "On three?"

He took a breath and nodded, steeling himself for the fight ahead. "One. Two—"

On three, the SEPIO pair parted each side of the curtain with outstretched arms, guns at the ready. Weapon-first had always been a good rule of thumb that served Silas well on the field in the Middle East. Same with SEPIO.

They swept toward the small chapel, ready to engage, then stepped through the parted curtain.

The same wood benches, crowned by those crimson cushions and complementary kneeling pads were all that greeted them.

A shout, then a whimper echoed toward them—pitiful and pleading and petitionary in a foreign tongue. Through the chapel, down the hall, and back at the central apse at the entrance.

The SEPIO pair padded forward.

Just as a man popped through the chapel entrance. All shoulders and legs and muscles. Eyes widening with unexpected surprise and screeching to an awkward halt like a Mack truck.

Right before he began raising his weapon and taking a step backward.

Gapinski did the same. "Crapola..."

Silas beat him to the *one-two-three* punch, dropping the guy before he could pinch off his own shots.

"So much for the element of surprise."

Silas ignored him, padding down the aisle and pulling up to the entrance threshold, ready for the hostile's buddies to come back him up.

Gapinski pulled up on the other side, flexing his fingers around his weapon's grip and ready for anything that moved.

No back up came.

Silas took in a measured breath, waiting and glancing at the dead hostile slumped at his feet. A tattoo peeking above the man's collar at the base of his neck caught his attention.

"Box man brigade," Gapinski said lowly.

He nodded, then chanced a glance around the corner.

Four men, big and black-clad, were slowly advancing from the apse where they had met the monk earlier. All bearing menacing rifles, barrels black and long.

Silas glimpsed a spot they could use as cover to hold them off. Anything to keep them from finding and getting their hands on...whatever it was they found.

But they had seconds. If that.

"We gotta go. Follow me with covering fire," he said.

"Roger that."

Silas stepped out and popped off a *one-two-three-four* warning to the advancing hostiles. Gapinski joined with the same.

The hostiles faltered their advance, skipping backwards and scattering before raising with a *rat-a-tat-tat* reply.

Silas and Gapinski darted forward, weaving and pinching off more shots that felt useless in the face of so much firepower.

They dove inside an alcove that barely fit one man, let alone the SEPIO pair.

Then the gunfire opened up, round after round after round of relentless lead chewing at the ancient stone masonry in search of a kill.

Out of breath and out of options, the SEPIO agents

squeezed between two pillars etched into the stone, finding some measure of protection.

"I don't have to tell you how bad this is," Gapinski complained as the hostiles continued their assault.

No, you don't...

They were pinned. Had nowhere to run except back where they came. Even then, that was a dicey proposition with all the lead being thrown their way.

Silas chanced a glance back toward the chapel. And that's when he saw it.

Four figures darting out the entrance and down another wing of the monastery.

A blond man and woman, followed closely by two beastish men. Both carrying the black duffle bags he'd glimpsed down in the crypt.

Sebastian. Escaping with Gospel Zero.

"Are you kidding me?" he grunted.

Gapinski glanced back and saw the same. "Sonofa—"

Exploding stonework cut him off, sending him back against the wall.

"We can't let them get away!" Silas said, popping of a *one-two-three* response before a *click-click-click*. He slid the magazine to the ground. Empty.

The assault died down to a trickle. Seemed to do enough of a trick.

He stepped out of the way for Gapinski's own follow-up, sliding in a replacement.

"What do you propose, chief?" Gapinski asked, inching past Silas to face the box men hostiles. He aimed and popped off a few shots.

He chuckled. "Got one."

"You keep at it and lay down covering fire. I'm going after Sebastian."

"Without me? No fair! You can't leave me here hanging like this."

"You'll be fine. Besides, there are only like three left."

"Three against one ain't good Vegas odds."

Silas shrugged. "You've played with worse."

"True that."

"Ready?"

Gapinski took a breath and nodded, twisting back around and firing off *one-two-three* more rounds. "Score!"

Guess so.

Silas ran from the apse, leaping over one of the downed hostiles. The ancient wall to his right exploded from gunfire, the floor spat up puffs of splintered tiles from the same.

He kept going, hearing another *pop-pop-pop-pop* reply from Gapinski and another cheer of success. Had to be a hostile or two left by now.

Darting past the chapel entrance, he veered left and spotted his fleeing brother and Helen and the other two Nousati goons. They were fiddling with a locked door halfway down the hallway, oblivious to his presence.

He kept going, hiking his legs up and swinging his arms and heaving lungfuls of air to propel him forward. No way in hell was Sebastian going to get away with stealing such cultural artifacts. Much less putting the Church at risk with whatever they contained.

With a cry that arose from days of frustration and anger and resolve, he lunged for Sebastian's nearest goon bearing two black duffle bags slung around his shoulders.

Silas grasped the straps of both and threw his full weight against them, going down with the bags and bringing the Nousati along with him, his gun skittering across the floor in the fall.

The men toppled in a heaping pile, hitting the ancient

stone floor with a hard smack but hardly noticing the wincing pain.

Silas twisted to the side and went to his knees, wrenching one of the bags from the floor while the other remained pinned under the Nousati.

"Silas!" Sebastian called out, Helen giving a startled yelp and the other goon quickly coming to his partner's aid.

The second Nousati grabbed Silas by the back and threw him to the floor, the bag sliding off his arm and tumbling next to a large stone pedestal mounted with a cracked bust of some saint.

Silas twisted to his back.

And the Nous agent climbed on top, throwing a wicked punch into his temple, then another.

The light dimmed, and stars sparkled.

The hostile went to offer another punch when a massive arm came from behind and latched around the guys neck, yanking the man with one heave-ho.

Gapinski sucker-punched him in the gut, then again.

The man doubled over then recovered, lunging for Gapinski's face with his head. Once then twice.

His nose erupted in a geyser of blood before he staggered back.

Silas scrambled across the floor after his weapon. He reached it, grasping for its grip.

But a firm hand gripped his shoulder.

This time Silas was ready.

He pulled a leg back and horse-kicked the man, landing a foot against the Nousati's groin and sending him back to the floor.

Silas lunged for his Beretta and spun to his back.

Just as the Nousati recovered and took aim with his massive rifle.

Pop-pop-pop-pop.

The Nous hostile recoiled backward at the sudden jolt of lead sinking into his chest, blood blossoming and his rifle spraying the ceiling as he fell.

Silas secured the man's black bag.

A door suddenly heaved open on tired hinges, the light differential between the darkened hallway and brightness outside blinding Silas.

He shielded his eyes, catching a glimpse of Sebastian and Helen slipping into the courtyard. The other Nous agent darted after them, back bulky and oddly shaped.

The third duffle bag!

"No..."

Silas scrambled after them when the man turned around to open fire.

He saw the barrel raise then dove for the floor.

Bullets tore through the exit and skipped across the floor and walls with abandon. All high and wide and missing their marks by a mile. Which wasn't the point.

It was cover for Nous's escape. Which was complete when the heavy wood door thudded shut.

Silas checked himself, finding nothing but torn knees and stiff limbs.

Gapinski sauntered over, spitting blood to the floor and wiping more from his mouth. "At least we got one. That should count for something."

"You OK?" Silas asked.

"I'll live. Besides, they got the worst end of the stick."

"I'm not so sure about that. They got away with a bag." Silas reached down and held up the one he recovered from the dead Nousati. "At least we got this one and—"

"Not so fast..." a voice sounded from behind, buttery and bassy and familiar.

The men spun around.

Gapinski gasped. "What the..."

Silas clenched his jaw and tightened his grip around the bag.

Noland Rotberg.

Who was holding the monk from earlier around the neck with one arm, a gun to the poor man's temple with the other.

But that wasn't all.

Coming up behind him was a third man. Face drawn and head hanging slightly. As if acknowledging the awkwardness and betrayal and dumbfounded revelation of it all.

Silas's jaw literally dropped, his lungs gasping for a breath to explain it. His mind swam with confusion at who had joined the man who had become his enemy.

"What the heck?" was all he could manage before letting loose the bag to the floor.

His stomach going with it at with what it meant.

CHAPTER 27

Grant Chrysostom slid next to Rotberg, who grinned widely, those annoyingly ironic curled ends of his mustache wiggling with victorious delight.

"Grant?" Silas whispered, disbelieving his eyes and head growing faint with confusion.

The man offered a sheepish grin and rubbed the back of his neck. "Howdy, partner."

"Always something," growled Gapinski.

Silas shook his head, feeling like he was about to topple. "But...I don't understand. You've been working for this fool?" he exclaimed, gesturing toward Rotberg.

"Now, I say," Rotberg said with interruption. "I'm surprised a man of your stature didn't put two and two together earlier."

Silas narrowed his eyes and clenched his jaw and took a step forward.

"Whoa there, cowboy." He clenched his arm around the monk with a start and took a step back.

Gapinski grabbed Silas's arm to hold him back.

Silas yanked it back with irritation. "Let go of me. How could you, Grant? How could you betray me like this?"

Grant said nothing. He simply folded his arms and hung his head.

"Answer me!" he exclaimed, voice ricocheting off the ancient stone in livid echoes.

"Let's dispense with the histrionics, shall we?" Rotberg said. "And why don't you say we get on with the exchange."

"What exchange?"

"The man for the bag."

Silas said nothing. He stood feet apart. One hand clutching the bag, the other twitching to grab his Beretta shoved at the side of his jeans.

But he couldn't think straight enough to act on the impulse. And he didn't think he could act quick enough on the draw before Rotberg himself went into motion. Grant even. Who knew how far the man would take it given his involvement, whatever level it was.

And the look in Rotberg's eyes told him everything he needed to know about the wickedness that wouldn't think twice before blowing the monk's brains out the other side of his head. He knew he would eventually make the trade. Nothing was worth more than a man's life. Especially a fellow brother in Christ. Even at the expense of letting go of what could be Gospel Zero.

"So you're with the box men then?" Silas said, not willing to let the bag go quietly and also willing himself not to glance toward the pedestal that hid the other bag a few yards away. "Both of you?"

There was a slight hesitation and a look of confusion in Rotberg's eyes.

"Box men," he went on. "The tattoo we saw on your man I shot back at the chapel. One of many actually, starting with the one I took out at my brother's house."

"Look, man," Grant started. "I was just a hired hand. I don't know nothing about—"

"Shut up!" Rotberg said, then he smirked. "Appears to be the case. Though we have a slightly different name than box men."

"Care to enlighten the unenlightened?" Gapinski asked.

"Oh, I don't know. Seems like you're well on your way to solving the caper."

"Hartwin's in on it, then," Silas added. "You and he and Grant cooked up this heist. Whatever it is anyway. Because whatever is in this bag—" he shook it for good measure. "Whatever it is ain't what you think it is."

"And what do you think I think it is, Grey?"

"Gospel Zero. The fabled Q source. But see, we know the original treasure map, the Coptic version of the Muratorian Fragment, was a complete fabrication."

Again, the hesitation. And now Rotberg shifted on his feet, as if the news unnerved him. Whether at the revelation or at the discovery, it wasn't clear.

He glanced behind him at Grant before chuckling. "You just got it all figured out, don't you?"

Then he sank the gun further against the monk's temple with a rattle of his wrist. The man moaned in protest and began to whimper.

"But not all of it. And now it's time for me to go. Both of us. The bag for the man."

"And what if I say no," Silas replied on a breath that didn't seem all that convincing even to him.

Rotberg's eyes went wide, and he bared his teeth before shifting behind the monk, squeezing tight on the man's neck and aiming his weapon toward the floor.

"If you don't, in five seconds I'll blow his foot to bits. He'll live, and I'll continue with other appendages, his knees and shoulders, until you comply or we both die. Either way, your monk will be a goner."

The monk's face was twisted with horror as the stakes grew by the second.

"One," Rotberg announced.

Silas shifted on uncertain feet, gripping the bag with indecision and itching to pull out his Beretta and end this joker.

"Two!"

"Alright," Silas said with a sigh before throwing the bag at the man's feet. It thudded with a muffled clang.

Rotberg grinned, those wretched handlebars bouncing again with mocking glee. "Pick it up," he instructed Grant.

Grant stepped over and stooped to pick up the duffle bag. As he straightened, he caught Silas's eyes.

Silas wanted to puke, but he held his gaze, staring him down and not willing to give an inch.

Rotberg shoved the monk toward the SEPIO pair, training his weapon at the man's back.

"Don't move," he growled, stepping back with aimed weapon. "Let's go, Mr. Chrysostom."

Silas didn't move. No point with the weapon trained on the poor monk.

But he wanted to. Not at Rotberg. He wanted to rush the man he thought was his friend and rip his head off. Hadn't felt that betrayed since Sebastian. Was almost at the end of himself, but he couldn't let it distract him. Wouldn't let it bring him down.

Not with the Church's central belief in the Bible on the line.

The men continued backing up.

Gapinski himself looked like he wanted to pick up the baton and blow the man to kingdom come. He held firm when Silas put out a staying hand.

Soon the two men slipped past a wall, and their footfalls were heard across the stone floor before the heavy wooden door banged open and the men were running with one of the three Gospel Zero bags.

The poor monk ran in the opposite direction, past the pair and off to some other part of the monastery, a muffled whimper trailing him before a thudding door was heard.

When he was certain they were in the clear, Silas scurried over to the bag that had slid out of sight and out of mind in the melee.

"Well that blows," Gapinski complained. "Not only did your buddy turncoat on us, that whack job got off with the goods we've been after the past three days. Sorry, bro."

"It ain't over til it's over, pal."

"What do you mean?"

Silas reached the pedestal. He took a breath and crossed himself on instinct. Old childhood habit that was also an act of thanksgiving in praising the good Lord above for the show of protection.

He just prayed what he thought was left behind by his providence proved true.

He slid the bag out from its hiding spot, then set it down with a thud between him and Gapinski. It was heavy and loud, so that was a good sign.

"Would you look at that," Gapinski marveled. "The Order Master does know a thing or two about this gig."

Silas smirked before kneeling to the floor and unzipping the bag. Inside were half a dozen of the same lead books bound in leather covers they'd glimpsed earlier.

He allowed himself a relieved grin. "Bingo…"

"I guess one of three sacks isn't bad," Gapinski said.

Silas stood. "It's going to have to do."

"Should probably phone this in, eh?"

"Good idea. Hope the ladies fared better than us."

Silas pulled out his mobile device. He went to put in the passcode when he remembered he'd turned it off. Booting up the device, a string of texts and missed calls flooded the screen.

All from Celeste. And all warning him of a trap, with Hartwin and Rotberg potentially at the helm.

"Great..."

"What's up, doc?" Gapinski asked.

"You've been saving that for a while, haven't you?"

He shrugged. "What can I say. Love me some Bugs Bunny."

Silas punched Celeste's contact and put it on speaker. "The ladies have been trying to reach—"

"What is wrong with that bloomin' head of yours?" Celeste sounded through the tiny speaker.

Gapinski winced. "Bad day to be Silas Grey..."

Silas ran a hand across his head. "Uh, hey there, Celeste."

"Don't 'Hey there, Celeste' me! You broke protocol. We never turn off our mobile devices on mission. Didn't the last time that happened in Jerusalem teach you anything?"

"That was a bad battery. And I can explain!"

"I have half a mind to reach through the handset and wring your little neck after that stunt, switching off your bloomin' phone like that!"

"Now that would be some good TGIF television right there," Gapinski said.

"*Gapinski!*" the two said in unison.

He held up his hands and backed off.

Silas said, "Let me explain. We showed up at the White Monastery and were instructed to turn off our phones before entering. Bad call, I know, but it is what it is."

"Stuff and nonsense..." Celeste mumbled.

"Long story short, we found Gospel Zero. Or something like it."

"Really? So it's real?" Torres said.

"Not sure exactly. Got a duffle bag full of codices, but we were intercepted by our box men friends before we could verify."

"And this is why we don't shut off our bloomin' mobiles!" Celeste said.

Silas took a breath. "Duly noted. Anyway, Sebastian ran off with one of the bags filled with—"

"Sebastian?"

"That's right. He was here with his lover and a few of his Nous henchmen. They escaped with another bag of these lead codices that seem to bear the fabled Q source."

"That's wild," Torres said.

"You're telling us. But that's not all. Guess who else showed up, running off with the final bag of the Gospel Zero codices?"

"A bloke by the name of Noland Rotberg?" Celeste said.

Silas twisted up his face in surprise. "Yeah, how did you know?"

"Because that's why I've been trying to reach you. To warn your bloomin' bum!" She huffed, then sighed. "Sorry. We've been having it out over here ourselves."

"Box men tattoo dudes?" Gapinski said.

"Who else? They took out our man Ulrich Pauli. Nearly took us out as well."

"My God..." Silas said. "Are you alright? You didn't get hit or hurt or anything, did you?"

"We're fine. Soaked as cats, but we did manage to gain some critical intel that's painting a clearer picture of what's transpiring here. Pauli knew Rotberg."

"And also Hartwin," Torres added.

"Always something," Gapinski growled.

The two women explained all they had learned from Zoe and from what they had recovered at Pauli's flat.

"Hartwin, that little weasel..." Silas said, shaking his head. "They must have planned this—whatever it is, from the start."

"But that's not all," Gapinski said, nodding toward Silas.

His face fell. He rubbed it with his free hand, then said, "No, it's not."

"What are you playing at?" Celeste asked.

"Well..." Silas looked at his partner, still disbelieving the turn. The man nodded. "Grant is also involved."

"Grant?" Torres said before launching into a string of Spanish.

"But how, he's your mate?" Celeste said.

"Not sure," Silas said. "Far as I can tell, he was a hired hand. But who knows how far he's involved."

"Then what the heck do we have here?" Gapinski asked, kicking the duffle bag. "Is it real? Is it a conspiracy?"

Silas ran a hand across his close-cropped hair again. "I don't know. But Hartwin is on his way. Should be touching down soon."

"So are we," Celeste said. "Chartered a jet from Frankfurt to Luxor. Have to imagine only an hour or two out by now."

"Good. We'll meet you at the airport, then rendezvous with Hartwin."

"Sounds like a sound plan. Because that German has a lot to explain."

"You bet he does."

THE DRIVE FROM THE WHITE MONASTERY BACK DOWN TO LUXOR was a long, silent one. Silas was grateful Gapinski left him to himself, to his thoughts about Grant and what it all meant. Had zero interest in talking about it. All that mattered now was figuring out what was in the duffle bag and bringing this blasted mission to a close.

Before it was too late.

Silas pulled a long drag on another cigarette, holding the nicotine-laced smoke before easing it out his nose in a wispy haze taken away by the rush of wind past the open car window. He chuckled to himself, realizing the only reason he picked the bad habit back up from his Ranger days was after his bitter betrayal by his brother. And there he was, puffing away on his third one after a friend from another lifetime yanked the rug out from under him.

Whatever. And no surprise. Life was one big betrayal anyhow. All starting when his mother died during their childbirth. His brother certainly understood the depths of life's betrayals after that priest used him for his own wicked ends. And then the death of Dad at the Pentagon and the death of his career at Princeton and—

He took a final drag and flicked the butt out the window.

Knock it off, Grey. Just knock it off...

He huffed the smoke out the open window, closing his eyes in the face of the sun slipping toward the horizon, hoping its fiery light and warmth would recenter him.

Deep down he knew that it was bull, that life was nothing but a box full of betrayals passed out like Halloween candy. God was better than that. The Holy Scriptures, the very book he was fighting for, reminded him of that countless times. The Book of Hebrews, chapter thirteen came to mind. Quoting the Hebrew Scriptures, the author wrote: "*'I will never leave you or forsake you.' So we can say with confidence, 'The Lord is my helper; I will not be afraid. What can anyone do to me?'*"

The Bible was filled with promises like that, and it was right. Celeste was proof. As was his new family with the Order, and his new life as Order Master. Didn't make Grant's move any easier. Not in the slightest. And there'd be plenty more where that came from in the years ahead, as hard to take and hard to understand as it might be.

At the end of the day, it didn't matter what Grant did or what didn't make sense in life. God was still God, and still good.

Silas also had a job to do. A mission to complete. And he needed his head on straight.

Two hours later, they pulled into Luxor International Airport, heading straight back to the private hangar where they had left their Order Gulfstream. Another one was parked next to it.

With Celeste and Torres waiting for them at the bottom of the stairs.

Gapinski pulled to a stop. Silas got out and rushed to Celeste. The two embraced.

"Thank the Lord you're alright," he said, holding her, breathing her in.

"Same with you, love," Celeste said. She pulled back and playfully hit him on the arm. "You gave me quite the fright you know, not being able to reach you, knowing you had launched yourself into no uncertain doom and were on the ropes."

"No uncertain doom? And on the ropes? I wouldn't say that. I mean—"

She gave him a look then pointed a finger at him.

He laughed and held up his hands in surrender. "I'll shut up. Point taken."

"Good lad."

Silas looked over her shoulder and around the hangar. "Where's Hartwin? Has he touched down yet? Did you make contact?"

Celeste nodded toward the Gulfstream. "Arrived before we did. Flew commercial out of Jerusalem."

Torres walked over with Gapinski. "We took the liberty of rendezvousing with the good professor and setting him up inside. Played it cool, like we were old pals by now and offered to give him a bit of R&R in our cool, luxurious jet. Bohls ran off to video the attractions in the city. Figured you wouldn't care, and figured it would give you a chance to get down to business without a YouTuber on hand."

"WeTuber," Gapinski corrected. "Not Google, WeNet."

"Whatever. Same difference. Anyway, he's all yours."

Silas narrowed his eyes and nodded. Time to get some answers.

He ran to the airstairs hanging out from the jet's entrance and took them by twos. Reaching the top, he stepped inside and spotted the man sleeping in a seat.

His seat.

Silas took a breath and started for the man with a shout. "Hartwin!"

The professor snorted awake. He sat up and blinked. "Ahh, Professor Grey. Good to see—"

"You've got a lot of explaining to do!" Silas grabbed the man by his collar and yanked him from the chair.

The man gave a startled shout and slung a string of German at him without deterring Silas from getting down to business.

Starting with a show of interrogatory force.

He threw Hartwin against a closet, the thin paneling shuddering under his weight.

"Oy, Silas, love," Celeste said. She put a calming, if not forceful, hand on his shoulder. He ignored it.

"We know you've been playing us!" Silas shouted, his arm pressed against Hartwin's throat.

The man's eyes went large, and he darted them to Celeste with a panicked plea.

"Come on, Silas, let the man go," she said, pulling his shoulder back.

He held the man a beat longer, then let go in a huff. "We're not leaving until you answer every one of our questions, so you better make yourself comfortable."

"What is this that you are talking about?" Hartwin said with exasperation. "Why is it that you are interrogating me?"

"Because Noland Rotberg just showed up with a platoon of terrorists at a monastery that, by the looks of it, was guarding Gospel Zero—taking part of it with him in a black duffle bag!"

Hartwin gasped and sank into his seat. "What? Rotberg, you say? But, but, but—I don't understand..."

Gapinski and Torres filed past him in the aisle. Celeste came up to Silas's side.

Stepping toward the man, Silas folded his arms and widened his stance. Ready for the kill.

He said, "You're going to answer every one of our questions until we're satisfied. Understand?"

The man nodded. "You must understand, I had no idea! None whatsoever where Rotberg went off to, let alone that he was being capable of such madness."

"We'll get to what you knew. Let's start with why the heck you invited me to your little meeting of the minds at Princeton in the first place. Was it to give you cover and play the Church for a fool, knowing that a verification from a prominent Order Master would do the trick?"

"No, nothing of the sort!"

"Then why did you bring me on board, the man who once sat in your office chair?"

"It was Grant Chrysostom! He said you were being the man to verify the Coptic folios and solve the riddle of Gospel Zero's location. You and Naomi Torres."

Silas's pulse faltered at the name. Figured as much, but the confirmation was unnerving. At least now they got the first piece, how the Order got roped into the mess.

"And the cache of papyri? Where did they come from?"

He studied Hartwin's eyes, looking for a flinch, a widening of the eyes, a tell of surprise. There was nothing. Eyes weren't darting about and face wasn't shiny with sweat, which you'd expect if he were lying. Breathing was a little erratic, which you would expect under the circumstances.

Hartwin swallowed. "A man in Miami. As I said before."

Silas glanced at Torres and nodded. She said, "Juan Torres. That his name?"

He nodded. "That is being correct."

"And what do you know about him?"

Gospel Zero | 323

"Nothing. Only that he was approaching me with the early Christian papyri, bearing all of the necessary documentation and being most patient while I and my team analyzed and verified the fragments before finalizing the sale."

"What about Andrew Sterling," Silas added. "Name mean anything?"

He shook his head, saying nothing.

Same steady eyes and unflinching face and erratic breathing. Seemed to be telling the truth.

"What about Ulrich Pauli?"

There it was. The tells he was looking for. Eyes going wide before blinking rapidly and face falling with slightly opened mouth and head dipping toward the floor and a hand scratching his nose before it covered his mouth and fell to his lap.

Then Hartwin cleared his throat and sat up straight and shook his head slightly. "Ulrich Pauli, you say?"

"That's right," Torres said. "We got a nice little mugshot of the guy sandwiched between you and your *hermano*."

Celeste said, "And the bloke got a nice rifle shot clear through his head from several yards away in his flat in Frankfurt."

"What?" the man exclaimed, eyes wide and that hand reaching for his mouth again. "He's...dead?"

"I'm not sure how else I would describe a rifle shot clear through the head, but yes. He clearly knew something and was killed for it."

"So you knew him?" Silas asked.

Hartwin nodded.

"How?"

"Old family friend."

"And you're claiming here and now that you had no contact with the man?"

"No, I did not!"

Celeste added, "But he claimed he was the original custodian of the papyri."

"What? But that is being impossible!"

"A cache that just so happened to end up in your lap," Silas said, "claiming to prove the existence of a secret source for the Christian Gospels. So how do you explain that?"

"And how do you explain the picture?" Celeste asked.

He went to offer a response but groaned instead, hanging his head and putting a worried hand to his forehead. "Oh, Markus. What have you done…"

Silas glanced at Celeste, a glimmer of hope rising. "Markus? Your brother is involved in this mess?"

Hartwin raised his head and frowned. "I may know what this is about."

CHAPTER 28

"Explain," Silas growled.

He sat across from Hartwin and leaned forward with eager interest. He had calmed somewhat since his initial outburst, realizing that all may not be as he once thought.

Originally, it seemed the signs pointed to Hartwin orchestrating a massive religious conspiracy to throw shade on the Holy Scriptures and undermine the Church. With his liberal academic leanings and interpretation of the Bible, it sort of made sense. A stretch, but Silas could see a motive, especially with Noland Rotberg on board, and then the fruitcake Trevor Bohls. Then when the pieces began to fall into place exposing the Coptic folios and the chain of custody documents for the frauds they were, it all made sense to finger Hartwin.

Now...not so much.

Hartwin had probably been hoodwinked by his brother as much as they all thought he was hoodwinking them.

Grant was a wild card, but knowing he was always open to the highest bidder, and given his extensive contacts and expertise in the fields of archaeology and Semitic languages—

looking back it made sense for him to be tapped to help orchestrate the conspiracy. Just how he fit wasn't yet clear either.

Silas knew he would have to proceed with caution, eyes and ears fully engaged with Hartwin. Had zero margin for error now that Nous and the mystery sect had copies of this purported Gospel Zero. Using them who knew how to undermine the Bible and the Church and the faith.

Time was not on their side. It was go time. On the double.

Hartwin said nothing, head bowed and eyes slitted. He looked miserable, like he wasn't so much waking up from a nightmare as he was waking up into one, spinning wildly in a vortex of ghoulish figures and hellish plots with no way out and nowhere to run.

Silas put a hand on his knee. The man startled and looked at him.

"Professor Braun..." he said, gentle yet prodding, "Please, in your own words. What's going on?"

Hartwin licked his lips and swallowed. "Before I am telling you, I am needing you to explain why you are believing Pauli is being involved."

Silas folded his arms and leaned back. "Well, for starters, the Coptic papyri you bought from Juan Torres was actually brokered by a one Andrew Sterling."

"Yes, I remember the man. Not his name, but he was being very thorough along with the fellow out of Miami. I showed you his documentation!"

"Sterling bought the cache of folios from Pauli."

"Dear me..."

"We'll get to that so-called documentation, but Sterling was an operative with an unidentified terrorist group. The same ones who assaulted the woman who barged into the conference room at Princeton and stole your box of folios, taking her hostage and confiscating the goods."

"Dear me..."

"Thankfully, we recovered the papyri and were able to use it to lead us to the White Monastery. We also recovered copies of the original bill of sale documenting the purchasing agreement of the originating cache, listing Pauli who we then traced to something called Manda Art."

"Did you say Manda?" Hartwin said, biting his lip before putting a hand up to his mouth again.

"Right. Pauli's side project when his metalworking business shuttered."

The man's head dipped again. "I see..."

"Those same mystery terrorists assassinated him at his apartment in Frankfurt," Silas went on, "and nearly took out my agents, Celeste and Torres here."

Hartwin turned to the women. "Your agents? You are being with him, Naomi?"

She nodded. "Sorry we were less than forthright about our connection. But we wanted to maintain a sense of control over what was going on with your Gospel Zero revelations. So we preserved my cover as a former treasure hunter."

He turned away and nodded.

"One thing you should know, professor," Silas said, "is the two gals recovered a translation of the Nag Hammadi Gnostic gospels from Pauli's apartment. On the inside flap was a personal note written to Pauli from Rotberg."

"Noland?" Hartwin startled.

Silas nodded.

"Showing a clear personal connection between the two men."

"That's right."

He sighed. "I was being totally unaware of such a connection."

"Well, for a number of reasons we are pretty well convinced that all the supporting documentation you were given is fraudulent. Pauli was about to confirm it, too, before he was taken out. We are also convinced both the Coptic version of the Muratorian Fragment and the Gospel of John fragment are fakes."

Hartwin frowned. "Why? All the tests were checking out perfectly! The science doesn't lie, Grey."

"The *science* isn't the problem. The history is. Both of the pieces were written in a style of Coptic that died out decades before they were supposedly written. They were also pretty clearly written by the same person, with the same blunt instrument. And the Gospel of John fragment is an exact replica of the only remaining Coptic Gospel of John fragment, found at the beginning of the 20th century, which is totally available online for anyone to view—and copy. That's not even touching on the fact the Coptic version clearly altered the Latin Muratorian Fragment."

The man's frown deepened. "I knew something about it all seemed suspect. Seemed too easy…"

"Why is that, professor?" Celeste asked.

The man chuckled. "Very rarely does anything like this come along and present itself. But Sterling was so convincing!" He pounded his plush leather arm rest and huffed, easing his balled fist open and muttering something under his breath in German. "I suppose the American saying is being correct. If it is being too good to be true, it probably is being false."

"Then why did you take the bait?" Silas asked. "Surely you know of other such stories about lost papyri claiming to hold new evidence of Christianity. The Gospel of Jesus' Wife, for instance, is the latest such nonsense to come to mind."

Hartwin shrugged and grinned. "I suppose I was wanting my name in lights. Wanting to publish my *magnum opus* opening up New Testament studies in a way that would leave a lasting mark. Being remembered for generations and being talked about in lecture halls across the world. Like those who had discovered the Dead Sea Scrolls or the Nag Hammadi texts."

Silas could understand the sentiment. Who wouldn't want to be known among the greats? Their name and reputation chiseled in the annals of history?

"And, if I can be so transparent," the man went on, "I expected it to confirm what I myself had believed about the faith to begin with across the last decade. That Christianity did indeed arise within a matrix of power plays between competing factions, suppressing some Christian gospels and letters while endorsing others that bolstered the prevailing views about Jesus' person and work, his divinity and resurrection. I suppose I was allowing my biases to carry me away..."

"I think we all can appreciate your honesty and humility, professor," Celeste said, glancing at Silas.

Silas nodded. "Agree. I imagine we all let our biases color our interpretations on a whole number of things, faith included. At any rate, we've made the connection between Rotberg and Pauli, the originator of the cache. Apparently, there was a connection between Rotberg and Grant we didn't know about either. We've made the connection between Pauli and your brother, and you I suppose. But I do believe you when you say that you didn't know he was involved. So what's the missing piece to this? What do you know about why Markus might be involved? Why would a mega-billionaire start-up founder of an up-and-coming social media platform give one rat's bottom about some obscure academic theory of the Christian Gospels—about Q or Gospel Zero?"

Hartwin shifted in his seat before folding his arms and staring at the ceiling, as if gathering his thoughts to unearth something long dead.

He said, "You are being right there was a connection between the Paulis and the Brauns. Going back generations. Our parents were godparents to each other's children."

"Are you kidding me?" Silas exclaimed. "You didn't connect the dots when you saw the papers documenting the provenance with Pauli's name on it?"

Hartwin shrugged. "If I am being honest, I wasn't looking that closely. And as I said before, a graduate assistant I had helping was being responsible for verifying the provenance."

"You mean the one from Berlin, who had connections to Pauli's alma mater? That one?"

"*Ja...*" was all he said.

Silas said nothing more, clenching his jaw with anger and giving Celeste a sideways glance.

"But you've got it wrong about Pauli's side project," the professor went on.

"You mean about Manda Art?" Celeste asked.

"*Ja.* Manda Art was Markus's company."

"Your brother's? What did he want with ancient religious relics? What reason did he have to busy himself with such things?"

"Every reason! And it isn't what he wanted with them as much as what he wanted to do with them."

"You've lost me," Silas said.

"Me too," Celeste added.

"You're probably being aware of some of my archaeological exploits. Particularly the ones in Germany, my homeland."

Silas took a breath, praying away the envy that always threatened to overtake him in moments like that when reminded of other people's accomplishments. Surprisingly, nothing came. He was fine. A small victory in his every-present struggle against his fatal flaw.

He nodded. "I am. And I've been impressed by your work." He had been, and he was able to genuinely express it. Even to the man who took his former job.

Hartwin smiled and dipped his head. "*Danke schön Professor.* But...and I am not believing I am admitting this, but it was much more my brother's work than it was being my own."

An interesting admission. "How so?"

"Markus had always been a spiritually interested young man. Much more than I, in fact. Whereas he had dutifully served as an altar boy, I was goofing off and playing sports and chasing girls."

The man laughed and allowed himself a wide grin before his face fell back into serious contemplation.

Silas chuckled to himself. Sounded like a mirror image of him and Sebastian.

Hartwin continued, "But that curiosity got the better of him once the internet opened the doors to other people groups and ideas and spiritualities. It was like Alice through the looking glass—going down, down, down into an unknown world he had been shielded from by our parents and religious upbringing."

"So then it was the exposure to non-Christian religions that changed him?" Celeste asked.

"Not only that. Our parents were not having anything of his questions or his interests outside the Church. Could not tolerate him questioning Christian dogma, even resorting to beating him with a belt and locking him in his room as punishment for his religious insolence." The man's face twisted at the memory, and an emotion shuddered through him that Silas couldn't place. Rage at what had happened to his brother? Regret at not being able to stop it?

Silas frowned. What a way to live. And the surest way to snuff out one's faith. Especially the faith of a curious, spiritually interested child.

"Yet he was undeterred," the man went on. "The more he interacted with people outside the Church through message boards and chat rooms on the internet, the more he grew to question Christianity as the sole bearer of spiritual enlightenment. Especially the Bible, that was being a biggie for him. And the way some Christians were living was not helping. Including *Mutter und Vater*."

He paused, sighing and slumping in his seat, as if the memory of his brother's transformation weighed him down. "Then our parents died."

"I'm sorry to hear," Silas offered. "I didn't know..."

Hartwin waved a dismissive hand. "Nobody is knowing as we are not talking much about it. It was an armed burglary gone bad during the night. Markus found them shot dead in their bedrooms the next morning. Father in the back of the head, mother in the face. It was being a gruesome way to die. And the two of us had slept straight through it all."

"My God...I can't even imagine."

"Worst of all, Markus had left the door unlocked after coming in late that night from a party. Blamed himself for their deaths. Still does. As fraught and mildly abusive of a relationship they had, he still dearly loved *Mutter und Vater*. Always trying to please them, he was." He sighed and shook his head. "Their death was the final proverbial nail in the coffin of his faith. Not understanding why a good God could allow such wickedness to overcome his parents, especially ones so devoted to him. To Markus it was seeming so random, so senseless. And he wanted nothing to do with it."

The man sniffed and wiped away the emotion from his eyes. The jet was silent, the SEPIO crew not knowing how to respond.

Hartwin broke the silence, saying, "Alongside his spiritual interest was an insatiable appetite for technology and all the progressive potential it meant and opportunities it could bring to healing and uniting the world across nations and peoples and languages. He learned to code before his thirteenth birthday and authored several games all on his own. Our parents' deaths seemed to spark in him an urgency to bring all he was learning to bear on a world rent by evil and wickedness."

"You're talking about WeNet?" Silas said.

"*Ja.* When we went to university in America, Markus studied computer science and ran himself ragged during the nights and weekends creating his little utopia on the internet."

Gapinski chuckled. "Not so little anymore."

Hartwin grinned. "No. It is not."

Silas sat back, folding his arms and glancing up at Celeste. She looked as concerned as he was about the revelation.

A man burned by his Christian parents whose lives were then snuffed out by pure evil, who then abandoned his faith in search of an alternative to Christianity. And with gobs of money to do so, even perhaps feeling like he should exact his revenge on the faith that burned him so. With all the tools at his disposal to spread his revelations across the globe. He feared whatever was going down was just the beginning. Especially if Markus was somehow part of this new mystery box men sect.

He said, "So what you're saying is, there might be a deeply personal element to his interest in seeing the Church fall. His loss of faith. The way his parents bludgeoned him over the head with it. The way they themselves were literally bludgeoned to death, and his unresolved questions about their death."

Hartwin nodded. "But there was a darker side, as well. An interest in the spiritualities that had been rooted in our land. The Germanic and Nordic *völkisch religion.*"

"The folk spiritualities and religions of German."

"*Ja.* Particularly the Ario-Germanic ideology that sought to pull German Catholics loose from Rome during the days of Nazi Germany."

"So the architect of WeNet is a goose stepper?" Gapinski asked.

"No! Not in the slightest. He is not a fascist. He is a humanitarian, through and through. A dreamer who longs to unite the world and enable all the people to live in peace and love and harmonious oneness!"

"OK, John Lennon..."

Hartwin went on, "His interest in the religious faith that followed those who sought a more authentically German, more nationalistic, religion led down a path that repudiated Christianity entirely. But his repudiation wasn't the post-Weimer Republic variety of Hitler and his cronies. He sought enlightenment from the best that spiritualities around the world had to offer. Traveling and buying up obscure religious relics and codices that would inform his spirituality."

"Which I imagine his billions from WeNet funded," Silas said.

"Not only that," Celeste added, "he was in a position to do something on a grander scale. Orchestrating the grandest hoax in the history of the Church in order to shred it to pieces!"

Hartwin waved a finger. "Now that is going too far! We are not knowing for certain that it is being a hoax."

"Except we can verify that both the Coptic Muratorian Fragment and its accompanying chain-of-custody documentation are indeed frauds."

Hartwin stood. "But not Gospel Zero! We have proof. It is being right there in that bag that you recovered. And until it's proven otherwise, I will not believe it has all been a farce." He took a breath and slumped back into his chair, muttering, "I cannot believe it has been a farce..."

Silas felt for the guy. The pinnacle moment of his career, when he went on national television and put it all on the line, his reputation and career, all for something that would probably turn out to be a lie. And one concocted by his brother, no less.

But another part of him didn't. The man said it himself. The only reason he went for Sterling's bait in the first place was because it confirmed his bias—the same one that's been behind the latest and greatest conspiracy thrillers topping the bestseller charts.

And yet, there was truth to what the man was saying about Gospel Zero.

He stood and walked over to the black duffle bag resting on a seat. "He's right. We don't have proof that Gospel Zero is fake news. Yet. And Nous and Rotberg and now probably Markus each have copies of...whatever it is we recovered in the crypt of the White Monastery. Which means they're sure as hell going to get down to business analyzing what it is. And exploiting it to bring down the Church—even if it turns out to be fake news, which could still be spread far and wide across all WeNet platforms."

Gapinski snorted a laugh. "Yeah, WeShare will have a field day with this. And it don't even need Russian bots to do Markus's dirty work."

Silas nodded.

"Sounds like a job for SEPIO."

"Right. I'd say it's time we get cracking," Celeste added.

"Been a while since I've gotten my hands dirty with recovered treasure. Even the Christian kind," Torres said.

Silas grinned. "That's what I'm talking about! So how about it, Hartwin? How about we get down to business and finish what you started, alright?"

The professor said, "As long as you are being honest about where the academic inquiry leads, I am being game."

"I wouldn't have it any other way. But first things first. I know—"

A static interruption sounded through the Gulfstream's speaker. "Uhh, is anyone there?"

"Zoe?" Celeste said, clutching her chest. "You scared me half to death."

"Nice to hear from you, too, Celeste."

"What are you playing at? What's wrong?"

"Silas with you?"

"Yeah, I'm here," he said. "We're all here. But why didn't you call my mobile?"

"I tried, but it's turned off."

Celeste raised an I-told-you-so brow.

He threw her a wry grin. "Uhh, sorry about that. Hope everything's alright."

"Hardly. I take it you haven't seen what has been streaming on WeShare?"

Now he threw her a worried look. Markus Braun.

"Always something," Gapinski said, shaking his head at his cell phone.

"What is it?"

"It's trending again, #GospelZero. And now there's a video announcement flying around the interwebs of some dude with a wicked-cool handlebar mustache saying there'll be an unveiling of epic religious proportions tomorrow at noon, Berlin time."

Noland Rotberg. And now probably Markus Braun. Maybe even Grant.

Gapinski shoved the phone into his pocket and shook his head. "Why are these things always revealed at noon? Why not mid-morning or late afternoon? Although I suppose noon German time would put it..." he trailed off, figuring out the math on his hands.

Silas ignored him, running a worried hand across his head.

"What are we going to do, Silas?" Celeste asked.

He looked at her, trying not to show the fear that was worming its way through him and screeching at him to run and let someone else lead the charge into the maw of hell.

Then he recovered, taking a breath and setting his jaw.

"We're going to fight, dammit."

"Oh, yeah, with what?" Torres asked.

He grinned. "The only two things we need. Science and history."

Silas hustled to the awaiting pilot reading a magazine at the front of the plane. He instructed him to fly to the nearest SEPIO outpost, which was fittingly enough in Jerusalem. And to do so pronto.

The end was finally in reach to bring this whole blasted mission to an end.

Yet...what the heck they would find was anyone's guess. And now with Rotberg and Grant back in play, and possibly Nous, and with a ticking clock on the line—his stomach churned with dread, wondering if he was opening Pandora's Box. Unleashing something that would destroy the Church.

Time would tell soon enough.

CHAPTER 29

Silas raked another frustrated hand across his close-cropped hair. It was a seven-hour flight to Ben Gurion International Airport, which would only give them a few hours once they arrived at the Jerusalem SEPIO outpost to put the lead codices through any sort of rigorous analysis.

Not at all ideal.

And with the added ticking clock into the mix until #GospelZero blew up the internet—it was all too much.

Get it together, Grey!

No time for whining about it. Play the hand you're dealt and get on with it, as Celeste would say.

He threw back a swig of the scotch he'd just prepared himself from the minibar, the steady, quiet hum of the Gulfstream joining the amber alcohol to soothe him into activation.

Then and there.

"Alright, Hartwin. It's go time."

The man snorted awake from his seat. "What? Here? I thought you wanted to wait until more ideal conditions."

"No time. Besides, might as well use the time to see if we can translate any of what's on these so-called Gospel Zero lead folios."

Silas raised a table next to his seat he often used for research during transatlantic flights. He brought the bag down with a thud and took another swig.

Go time, indeed.

Hartwin came over as Silas unzipped the bag. "I was hoping we could take a crack at the codices. I am being most eager to have a look."

"You and me both, pal."

He spread open the bag, a jolt of adrenaline raising the corners of his mouth at the sight of ten or twelve thick books. They were bound in the familiar faded, rough leather with six leather straps holding the pages together through holes punched at even intervals, the edges of its lead pages shimmering in the cabin light.

A drunken giggle escaped through a hand raised at Hartwin's mouth. "Marvelous. Simply marvelous…"

Silas picked up a codex, taking care of the leather bindings and stiff cover. He opened it, mouth curling upward again at the sight.

Hartwin gasped. "Aramaic? I wouldn't have had any idea…"

"What's the deal with the Aramaic?" Torres asked, craning over Silas's shoulder.

"Aramaic was the language spoken during Jesus' day," he explained.

"So why is it surprising to see them written in Aramaic?"

"Because, my dear," Hartwin jumped in. "All the available codices of New Testament books we have are written in Greek. Koine Greek, to be precise. A sort of common-folk version of the classical Greek of the day. Used for business receipts, correspondence, shopping lists. Most scholars assume the original copies of the New Testament books were written down in this language, even though the common spoken language of the day was Aramaic."

Silas added, "But there are some who challenge Greek

primacy, suggesting the New Testament books were originally written instead in Aramaic and then translated into Koine Greek before being passed around throughout the early Church. In fact, one version of the Bible is the Syriac Peshitta."

"And now Gospel Zero..." Hartwin whispered, mouth agape with lust.

Silas returned to the codex. He imagined whatever cache of books they had were out of order from the original groupings they discovered in the stone chest in the crypt, mismatched and jostled around in the escape. He remembered the first one began with Jesus' baptism at the start of his ministry. So he brought a finger up to the first line to translate.

What he read made him smile. Brought tears to his eyes, in fact.

"Are you kidding me..."

"What is it?" Celeste asked, followed by Torres and Gapinski with the same question.

Silas showed the lead folio to Hartwin, who matched his grin.

"The Sermon on the Mount," the professor said.

He nodded. It was one of his favorite parts of Jesus' teachings, from the Gospel of Matthew. It appears in Luke's Gospel as well, but at a slightly different part in the narrative. He translated what many have known as the Beatitudes:

"Blessed are you who are poor, for yours is the kingdom of God.

"Blessed are you who are hungry now, for you will be filled.

"Blessed are you who weep now, for you will laugh.

"Blessed are you when people hate you, and when they exclude you, revile you, and defame you on account of the Son of Man. Rejoice in that day and leap for joy, for surely your

reward is great in heaven; for that is what their ancestors did to the prophets."

The next part was an interesting interruption. In Luke, a series of woes for the rich followed the blessings and a teaching on enemy love. But part of what he saw in front of him was found later in Matthew after the Sermon on the Mount, while the other was later in Matthew's Sermon. Still interesting. It read:

Jesus said, "Love your brother as your own soul. Protect them like the pupil of your eye."

Jesus said, "You see the speck that's in your brother's eye, but you don't see the beam in your own eye. When you get the beam out of your own eye, then you'll be able to see clearly to get the speck out of your brother's eye."

He furrowed his brow at the misplacement but figured it was part of the arrangement of—he couldn't believe he was saying it—of Gospel Zero.

Silas shook his head and turned the lead folio, taking care of the ancient lead pages and watching that he didn't snap the leather bindings.

There it was. The teaching on love for enemies he had expected before:

"But I say to you that listen, Love your enemies, do good to those who hate you, bless those who curse you, pray for those who abuse you. If anyone strikes you on the cheek, offer the other also; and from anyone who takes away your coat do not

withhold even your shirt. Give to everyone who begs from you; and if anyone takes away your goods, do not ask for them again. Do to others as you would have them do to you.

"If you love those who love you, what credit is that to you? For even sinners love those who love them. If you do good to those who do good to you, what credit is that to you? For even sinners do the same. If you lend to those from whom you hope to receive, what credit is that to you? Even sinners lend to sinners, to receive as much again. But love your enemies, do good, and lend, expecting nothing in return. Your reward will be great, and you will be children of the Most High; for he is kind to the ungrateful and the wicked. Be merciful, just as your Father is merciful."

This was wild, seeing such teachings etched in the original language of Jesus on clearly ancient metal pages. He turned the folio again with care, then translated:

Jesus said, "Come to me, because my yoke is easy and my requirements are light. You'll be refreshed."

"Don't give what's holy to the dogs, or else it might be thrown on the manure pile. Don't throw pearls to the pigs, or else they might make it into mud."

Jesus said, "Whoever looks will find, and whoever knocks, it will be opened for them."

Another curious interruption from what he recalled, expecting Jesus' teaching on the quality of fruit borne by trees, a sort of metaphor for the good works that people themselves bear. He turned the folio. Alright, there it was:

> "No good tree bears bad fruit, nor again does a bad tree bear good fruit; for each tree is known by its own fruit. Figs are not gathered from thorns, nor are grapes picked from a bramble bush. The good person out of the good treasure of the heart produces good, and the evil person out of evil treasure produces evil; for it is out of the abundance of the heart that the mouth speaks.
>
> "Why do you call me 'Lord, Lord,' and do not do what I tell you? I will show you what someone is like who comes to me, hears my words, and acts on them. That one is like a man building a house, who dug deeply and laid the foundation on rock; when a flood arose, the river burst against that house but could not shake it, because it had been well built. But the one who hears and does not act is like a man who built a house on the ground without a foundation. When the river burst against it, immediately it fell, and great was the ruin of that house."

"This is marvelous!" Hartwin exclaimed, clapping his hands before leaning back over Silas's shoulder.

Silas nodded and smiled. Yes, it was.

He turned another folio page. A laugh slipping through in awe at what he read.

The Lord's Prayer.

He cleared his throat and translated aloud:

> *He said to them, "When you pray, say:*
> *Father, hallowed be your name.*
> *Your kingdom come.*
> *Give us each day our daily bread.*
> *And forgive us our sins,*

> *for we ourselves forgive everyone indebted to us.*
> *And do not bring us to the time of trial.*
>
> *"So I say to you, Ask, and it will be given you; search, and you will find; knock, and the door will be opened for you. For everyone who asks receives, and everyone who searches finds, and for everyone who knocks, the door will be opened. Is there anyone among you who, if your child asks for a fish, will give a snake instead of a fish. Or if the child asks for an egg, will give a scorpion? If you then, who are evil, know how to give good gifts to your children, how much more will the heavenly Father give the Holy Spirit to those who ask him!"*

It went on like this. Next was the Parable of the Sower, both found in Matthew's and Luke's Gospels.

"Hmm," Hartwin muttered. "The Parable of the Sower..."

Silas spun around. "What are you thinking?"

He shrugged. "I was thinking it was being interesting that this teaching is also in Mark's Gospel. I had always assumed that Q, or rather Gospel Zero, didn't overlap in content with Mark.

"I guess that was the theory. But maybe not."

"Although..."

"What is it?"

Hartwin smiled. "It is being nothing."

Silas shrugged and turned the page. It went into another familiar parable. Again, also in Mark's Gospel as it was in Matthew and Luke:

> *The disciples asked Jesus, "Tell us, what can the kingdom of heaven be compared to?"*
>
> *He said to them, "It can be compared to a mustard seed. Though it's the smallest of all the seeds, when it falls on tilled*

soil it makes a plant so large that it shelters the birds of heaven."

"Curious..." Silas muttered. The rest of the folio was illegible. He turned to another folio page.

And nearly dropped the codex.

"What the heck?" he exclaimed.

"What is it?" Hartwin asked, craning over his shoulder. Then he gasped. "*Mein Gott! Das Evangelium von Thomas.*"

Celeste asked, "What's he going on about, love?"

Silas swallowed hard, his mouth going dry from disbelief.

It didn't make sense. Why would this text be sitting here next to what was recognizably the Christian Gospels? Didn't make sense in the slightest. What manner of wickedness is—

"Silas?" she said again, touching his shoulder.

He startled, then took a breath. "Sorry. Professor Hartwin said..."

Silas trailed off, checking the folio again. Heart hammering in his head, bowels going watery at the revelation.

"As Radcliffe used to say," Gapinski said, "we're not getting any younger over here, bro."

"The Gospel of Thomas," he said with a rush, as if spitting the words out would make them less real.

"The what?"

"A Gnostic gospel?" Celeste said.

Silas nodded, saying nothing.

"But that's impossible. If I rightly understand it, they weren't even written until well after the original Gospels, the ones recognized by the Church."

Hartwin chuckled. "I am sorry, my dear, but you are certainly not rightly understanding the matter. It is thought that many of the Gnostic gospels were written at or around the same time as the Church-sanctioned ones."

Celeste offered a muffled huff, not accustomed to being shot down so directly. "Well then, why would the Gospel of Thomas, or portions of it, be sitting alongside passages recognizably orthodox, from the Four Gospels?"

"It makes perfect sense, actually!"

"Do tell..."

Silas cleared his throat. Time to play interference. "Interestingly, there are passages from the Gospel of Thomas that appear in Matthew's and Luke's Gospels. Like the Parable of the Sower and some of the other smaller passages I read. I noticed them as I was translating. Wondered why they appeared where they did. Now I know. They were from the Gospel of Thomas."

"As well as Gospel Zero!" Hartwin exclaimed. "It is thought that almost one-third of the Gospel of Thomas is shared with Q, meaning they are found in the New Testament Gospels. Making Gospel Zero a distinct, autonomous type of early Christian theological work that bridges the Gnostic gospels to the orthodox ones!"

"Now that's a stretch, Hartwin. We don't even know what the rest of it says!"

"Go on then! Stop dilly dallying."

Silas took a breath before he said something he regretted. Then he went back to the codex and translated what had stopped him in his tracks. He read it aloud:

These are the hidden sayings that the living Jesus spoke and Didymos Judas Thomas wrote down.

And he said, "Whoever discovers the meaning of these sayings won't taste death."

Jesus said, "Whoever seeks shouldn't stop until they find. When they find, they'll be disturbed. When they're disturbed, they'll be amazed, and reign over the All."

Jesus said, "If your leaders tell you, 'Look, the kingdom

> is in heaven,' then the birds of heaven will precede you. If they tell you, 'It's in the sea,' then the fish will precede you. Rather, the kingdom is within you and outside of you.
>
> "When you know yourselves, then you'll be known, and you'll realize that you're the children of the living Father. But if you don't know yourselves, then you live in poverty, and you are the poverty."

"There, that wasn't so bad," Hartwin said, clearly jubilant at the connection between the received Gospels and the Gospel of Thomas. "It's also being rather instructive, isn't it?

Silas turned toward the man. "Instructive? In what way?"

"Christianity has always prided itself on being a revealed religion, having received revelation from God that was transmitted into a well-ordered book. The Bible. But there are those of us who know better. Are knowing that it was far messier than that—with all the debates and power plays that went into cobbling together the book."

Silas shook his head. "Whatever." He continued translating, reading aloud the next folio:

> *Jesus said to his disciples, "If you were to compare me to someone, who would you say I'm like?"*
>
> *Simon Peter said to him, "You're like a just angel."*
>
> *Matthew said to him, "You're like a wise philosopher."*
>
> *Thomas said to him, "Teacher, I'm completely unable to say whom you're like."*
>
> *Jesus said, "I'm not your teacher. Because you've drunk, you've become intoxicated by the bubbling spring I've measured out."*
>
> *He took him aside and told him three things. When*

Thomas returned to his companions, they asked, "What did Jesus say to you?"

Thomas said to them, "If I tell you one of the things he said to me, you'll pick up stones and cast them at me, and fire will come out of the stones and burn you up."

"Ahh! There you have it!" Hartwin exclaimed.

"Have what?" Celeste asked.

"Disagreement amongst Jesus' followers on who he is! One of the primary reasons the minority gospels and texts were being suppressed by the Church in the first place. Those in power wanted to maintain a certain aura about the person of Jesus. That he was the Son of God. That he was divine."

"But he was, dammit!" Silas said. Then he caught himself and took a breath. "Sorry. What I meant to say was that from the beginning of the Jesus movement, his followers believed him to be not just divine but God himself. This wasn't something written into the Bible and voted by committee hundreds of years later."

Hartwin went to respond, but Silas plowed forward. "Jesus himself taught this, equating himself with Yahweh, the I AM God of the Hebrew Scriptures, saying in John's Gospel: *'Very truly, I tell you, before Abraham was, I AM.'* The Apostle Paul did the same, teaching that Jesus *'is the image of the invisible God, the firstborn of all creation; for in him all things in heaven and on earth were created...For in him all the fullness of God was pleased to dwell.'* And then the writer of the Book of Hebrews echoes this core teaching of early Christ followers, writing that Jesus *'is the reflection of God's glory and the exact imprint of God's very being, and he sustains all things by his powerful word.'* Clearly, from the beginning the oral transmission of Jesus' story and the letters circulating about him were unified in their understanding of Jesus' person."

The professor smirked. "We shall see about that." He took the codex from Silas and cleared his throat. He read:

Jesus said, "Where there are three deities, they're divine. Where there are two or one, I'm with them."

Jesus said, "I'm the light that's over all. I am the All. The All has come from me and unfolds toward me. Split a log; I'm there. Lift the stone, and you'll find me there."

"Ahh! And there *you* have it!" Silas exclaimed.

"There we have what?" Gapinski asked.

"One of the reasons why the Gospel of Thomas was rejected as heresy. As well as all the other so-called gospels and Christian texts discovered in the Nag Hammadi cache. A clear polytheism, with the reference to three deities. And also clear pantheism."

Gapinski snickered. "Panty-what?"

Silas frowned. "Not pantyism. *Pantheism*. Equating God or the divine with the whole of the universe. The All, as the case may be in the passage."

"Like Star Wars. May the force be with you, and all that jazz."

"Bingo."

He grabbed the codex from Hartwin, who didn't protest. He turned the folio and read:

Jesus said, "How miserable is the body that depends on a body, and how miserable is the soul that depends on both."

Jesus said, "How awful for the flesh that depends on the soul. How awful for the soul that depends on the flesh."

Silas smirked and gave the codex back to Hartwin. "There you have it again. Another main reason many of the so-called Gnostic gospels were rejected as Gnostic."

"And why is that?" Celeste asked.

"Gnostics were rejecting the physical and exalting the spiritual," Hartwin acknowledged.

Silas nodded. "The Church, historic Christian orthodoxy, has never denigrated the body or the flesh or the physical like the Gnostics did."

The professor scoffed. "Oh, come now, professor. Never? You are being too generous, methinks. And biased."

"You're right that there have been times when Christians haven't respected the physical world." He chuckled. "My Catholic ancestors would roll over in their graves at the clear Gnostic lyrics of Protestant hymns that talk about flying away when this life is over to some heaven in outer space. As if God was going to just junk this planet, and the afterlife was just one perpetual church choir, eating casseroles and drinking really bad coffee for eternity."

"It isn't?" Gapinski asked.

"No!"

"Thank the Lord! It always gave me the heebie jeebies when Grandpappy belted the harmonies on *I'll Fly Away*."

"When God created this world, he declared it very good," Silas said. "Now, it may be broken and busted, but the New Testament makes it clear he still intends to put it back together again. We're earthlings; we were made for earth, *this* earth. Jesus intends to bring us back to this world at the new creation and make all things new again, right here."

"Not according to Gospel Zero," Hartwin said.

"Yeah, well, the Gospel of Thomas was rejected along with the others for denying this central message of the Church. That's not even touching on the fact the book was written a century after the original Gospels, which means it copied elements of the originals that combined nicely with Gnostic ideology, yet contradicts historic Christian orthodoxy. No matter what some lead pages claim. The Gnostic texts are also incredibly anti-Jewish, whether outright denying the Hebrew Scriptures or simply not rooting their narrative and teachings in the Jewish covenantal narrative. Which, by the way, the New Testament books without equivocation do—rooting the teachings of the Church in the one, single story that God has been telling from the very beginning through the Old Testament."

Hartwin folded his arms in a huff. "Are you finished, Professor Grey?"

"Doc, I'm just getting started! Another thing—"

"Always something..." Gapinski muttered, shaking his head and face alight with the soft glow of his mobile device.

"Now what's happened." Celeste asked.

"Another player has decided to join the #GospelZero hashtag bandwagon."

Silas and Celeste crowded around Gapinski's mobile device, just as the Gulfstream began dipping and banking. Ben Gurion Airport must be just around the corner.

But the sight on the screen blew up his relief.

There was an image of a table in some nondescript room of gray concrete, maybe cut stone. No, wait—a live-stream video image of some room with flames flapping behind a table stacked with vintage books, covered in leather and pages gleaming beneath the light.

Looking like the same pile of codices sitting in the black duffle bag on their table.

Silas let a curse slip under his breath.

"Gospel Zero?" Celeste said, folding her arms.

"Is there any doubt?" Silas replied. "Rotberg must be getting ready, offering a taste of what's to come."

Celeste bent toward the screen for a closer look. "But this isn't on WeShare, is it?"

Gapinski shook his head. "Facebook."

"But the original post we had seen from Rotberg was on Markus's platform. Which we assume is because the man was behind the conspiracy to begin with."

"What are you getting at?" Silas asked.

"What I'm getting at, love, is that this may not be Rotberg."

He furrowed his brow, then relaxed it with realization.

"Nous," they both said in unison.

"What's this gibberish scrolling at the bottom?" Torres said, pointing over Gapinski's arm.

Scrolling across the screen was a revolving maxim: *'For nothing hidden will not become manifest, and nothing covered will remain without being uncovered.'*

"That would be the Gospel of Thomas," Hartwin said. "A mantra of Gnostic secret knowledge."

"It also mirrors what Jesus said in the Gospel of Luke," Silas said. *"'For there is nothing hidden that will not be disclosed,'* he said, *'and nothing concealed that will not be known or brought out into the open.'"*

"Which means it is also being from Gospel Zero," Hartwin added with a wink.

Silas frowned. "They must have pulled it from one of the codices missing from the bag."

"Which means they also translated the other codices," Celeste said, "and are ready to release them into the wild."

"Along with the box men tattoo dudes," Gapinski said. "Or dudettes, as the case may be."

The captain announced they would soon arrive at Ben Gurion Airport and requested they buckle in for the landing.

Silas sat down and buckled in. Celeste joined him.

"What are we going to do, Silas?" she said.

He shook his head and sighed. "I don't know."

His stomach churned with dread at the possible revelation of an alternative set of books that would undermine the Bible going viral across the internet—from not one but two sources, Nous and the Rotberg-Markus partnership.

What he did know was that he was also buckling up for the fight of his life.

And the Church's.

CHAPTER 30

"What the hell am I going to do?" Silas mumbled to himself as he paced SEPIO's Jerusalem field office a few kilometers away from the Temple Mount.

He stopped pacing and sighed, his inner Radcliffe scolding him for his unnecessary potty mouth. Under the circumstances, it seemed warranted.

Fine. What the heck am I going to do?

Either way, he was screwed.

In T-minus fifteen minutes he was going live on the internet. Torres and Celeste had hatched the plan behind his back with a little technowizardry from Zoe. Some sort of live-stream, simulcast chat with the world through Facebook and WeShare and any other social media platform SEPIO thought would help mitigate the fallout from the viral posts teasing the discovery of Gospel Zero.

He'd prefer going in Beretta blasting to destroy the Church's enemies trying to undermine one of the foundational elements of the faith. The Bible, God's Word, the Creator's self-revelation of himself and his story of rescue to the world.

That's how Uncle Sam did it, anyway.

It was also how SEPIO did it sometimes. But only when they were defending themselves from hostile forces.

This was different.

Required a softer touch, wielding ones and zeros instead of pistols and assault rifles to make the point that the Bible we have contains God's Word; that there was plenty of historical and archaeological evidence to suggest it cradled God's revelation to humanity about his story of rescue and re-creation; that the books included in the final canon had been widely understood throughout the Church during the early centuries to be authoritative and genuine revelation of God; that there was no powerful plot, no sinister conspiracy of suppression, but instead the books of the Bible included in several lists from Church leaders and widely circulated among church communities were the ones God himself wanted us to have.

The pen is mightier than the sword, they say. In this case, Silas was hoping it was his tongue combined with the viral power of social media to pull one helluva jiu jitsu move on Nous and the box men tattoo mystery sect.

He resumed his pacing through the cavernous conference room as he waited for Zoe to finish writing the code to open up a secure socket on the internet that would send out his message across the social media platforms—something about bots that reminded him of Russian election meddling and Tom Clancy technothrillers.

All the while worrying about how the next hour would go down as they tried to expose Gospel Zero for what it was—a complete hoax, a forgery cooked up by Markus Braun and his cronies, Sebastian and Nous even, to cast doubt on the Bible. Influencing believers and non-believers alike.

Because if people couldn't trust the Bible, the very Word of God, then why believe anything the Christian faith had to offer? If what the Church had said about the Bible for two millennia was a lie, then why believe anything it said?

Including Jesus' sacrifice on the cross as the singular payment for our rebellion against God and his resurrection of the dead, paving the way for our own hopeful resurrection.

Silas felt himself on the edge of a panic attack when the door swung open. In walked Celeste. The burden was suddenly lighter, and he felt more capable with her at his side. Like he could conquer anything, climbing the summit of Mount Everest with plenty left over to go conquer Mount Kilimanjaro.

She threw her arms around his neck and gave him a peck on the cheek. "You've got this, love."

He closed his eyes, and for one brief moment he let himself believe she was right. That he did have it. Had full control over a situation that had spun wildly out of his control and threatened the Bible, the Church, and the spiritual walks of Christians across the world.

He took a deep breath, the scent of lavender and vanilla a balm to his synapses firing on all cylinders every which way.

Reality was, he wasn't so sure he had any control over what happened. Didn't believe in the slightest that he could pull off what needed to be done in order to secure people's continued belief in the Bible.

'My grace is sufficient for you, for my power is made perfect in weakness...'

Silas took another deep breath, thankful for the reassurance of both Celeste and the Holy Spirit to carry him through the next hour.

But he had to face the facts: It was David versus Goliath all the way. And his sling was feeling mighty empty, void of anything to swing at the forces threatening the Church.

#GospelZero and #ChristianityCanceled had been trending across Facebook and WeShare with viral posts for the better part of the past day. Two social media accounts had been teasing revelations that would shock the world and expose the Church for what it was: a religious community built on a book crafted by men in power to secure their powerful ends. Which is why Silas had been preparing for the lecture of his lifetime.

For the past few hours, he and Hartwin had been poring over the codices in another room to arm himself with all the knowledge he needed to prove they were fakes. His Princeton replacement had even come around to the idea after the two compared notes. Which Silas considered no small victory. They had focused on the forest instead of the trees—as with the Coptic Muratorian Fragment—and discovered a few crucial facts about the folios. He just hoped he could use their findings to convince the world they were fakes and why the Bible in its modern form was right and true and still believable.

The door thudded open again. In walked Zoe and Abraham, each with faces buried in laptops balanced on their palms. Gapinski joined them, huffing and puffing as he hefted several bags bearing boxes of who knew what.

"Over there." Zoe pointed to a long metal table at the center of the space with her free hand. He obliged, hefting his load on top.

"What is all this stuff?" Silas asked.

"Gear," she said, face a furrowed mess of concentration.

"Alright then. Say, where's Torres?" he asked, craning toward the door. "Haven't seen her since we arrived."

"Tracking down a lead she hopes will help right the ship," Celeste said.

"What lead?"

She shook her head. "She's been mum about it since we landed. And radio-silence, too. Which has me a bit worried as I myself haven't seen or heard from her since."

Silas nodded, not allowing himself to join her in that worry. Too much on his own mind.

"BTW," Zoe said, settling into a chair, "I got the results of that trace on the bank transfer I ran."

"The half million dollar transfer into Pauli's account?" Celeste asked.

"That'd be the one."

"Please tell me it was from Markus Braun."

"Sure was." Zoe continued clattering away at her laptop. "The guy used his personal account, too. What a rookie."

"Way to go, mate. That confirms it, then."

"Confirms what?" Silas asked.

"Markus paid off Pauli's bankruptcy debt."

"And paid for his involvement in his conspiracy, too."

Celeste nodded. "A definitive link between Markus and Pauli. We found it."

And not a moment too soon.

Arrayed around the perimeter of the dim room lit by white recessed lighting were several workstations. A massive television display took up one side of the wall, with another one bought from a local electronics store standing next to it. Both were showing news feeds on Facebook and WeShare of the trending hashtags and the shot from each account of the countdown to the Gospel Zero revelation. Off to the side was a chair, a backdrop, a video camera, and a pair of lights. All of it arranged for Silas's internet appearance defending the Bible and exposing the conspiracy.

A jolt of nervousness ratcheted up his spine, spreading goose pimples across his skin at the thought.

'My grace is sufficient for you, for my power is made perfect in weakness...'

He thanked the Lord above for the continued reassurance. Then prayed he came through.

Abraham and Gapinski were unboxing the equipment he brought in. Several laptops, maybe twelve or fifteen. Lots of computing power concentrated in that room now. Zoe was seated at the table clacking away.

Silas leaned over her shoulder. "So what's all this about? The equipment, what you're clacking away?"

"One word. Bots."

"Bots?"

"Yeah, the autonomous programs scattered across the internet that can interact with computer systems and users."

"And, what, you've deployed them to change people's minds about the Bible?"

Zoe shrugged. "Hey, if the Russians could meddle in an election, my bots can surely influence a social media campaign to discredit the Bible and bring down the Church."

"And this will work?"

"Hello? Russian election meddling?"

Silas stood straight and ran a hand across his head. He was itching for his Beretta now. Itching for a good ol' fashioned fight at the OK-Corral, not one built on a buck and a prayer and some Russian-inspired bots. Although Gapinski was right that pretty much every SEPIO mission was built on a buck and a prayer. And the Lord had certainly come through before.

He flashed a worried look at Celeste. She picked up on it and asked, "Why don't you break it down for us, Zoe. What's your plan for these...these bots of yours."

Zoe spun around and pushed her baby blue glasses up the bridge of her nose.

"The plan is to send out my little AI army across the internet to infiltrate the social media platforms and boost our messaging about the Bible."

"AI army?" Gapinski exclaimed. "Sounds like Terminator 8!"

She laughed. "Not exactly. The bots will replicate themselves across the internet, creating fake profiles that drive traffic to your social media posts exposing Gospel Zero for what it is—a conspiracy and hoax and forgery. Then, they'll boost the likes and shares and social proof to send your defense of the Bible into the stratosphere, influencing hearts and minds to counteract the social media war of Nous and box men tat dudes."

"Like the Russian election meddling?" Silas asked.

"Bingo."

Silas went to respond when something caught his attention at the back of the room. The large display brought in for the mission. It was sparking to life. The one with the table full of codices, framed by a backdrop that looked straight out of Transylvania.

And someone was taking a seat. Tall and blond and echoing the profile of the man readying himself to give a defense of the Bible on the internet of all places.

Sebastian Grey.

Silas's heart sank at the truth of it. Another head-to-head match with his brother.

"Looks like it's about to get real, folks," Gapinski said.

"Those bots of yours ready to work their magic?" Silas asked.

"Already deployed, and ready when you are."

"Good. Because it's go time."

Again.

With Sebastian first up to bat.

CHAPTER 31

Sebastian Grey had been waiting for this moment his whole life. The chance to let the world in on a little secret he'd long suspected since those horrid years under the weight of that priest. Literally, the man pressing against him in his office under the cover of darkness and secrecy.

And now he had the goods to expose the Church for what it was.

A lie. A complete and utter fabrication filled with hypocrites and imbeciles believing in fairytales spawned from the loins of a book cobbled together by men and for men.

And yet...the revelation didn't come together quite like he had imagined. His translator finished more of the bowl that had hinted at a Secret Book he had thought was the glorious Gospel Zero. On the bright side, there was a juicy nugget referring to an imperial seal that held a potentially explosive secret. He had already dispatched Nousati on the hunt, but they would see.

Then there was the not-so-good side. Turns out the original reference to a lost book was for something else entirely, a known Gnostic text. Which could have been not only embarrassing had he jumped too soon, but devastating for his rise to Grand Master. François would surely have had a field day with his misstep. Thank the Universe for the duffle bag of lead codices that fell in his lap!

His vocational near-death experience had given him pause, however. To see himself jump at anything so quickly that might expose the Bible as a lie, to destroy the Christian faith…it was a rather remarkable moment of self-reflection. Given his brushes with wickedness in that backroom parish office, perhaps he could be forgiven for latching onto anything that would bring the Church to its knees.

Although if he was honest with himself, it was probably because the bowl confirmed what he wanted to be true in the first place. That there was no such thing as divine revelation because there was no such thing as the Divine. Again, probably a deep-seated reaction to all he had endured at the hand of that priest, a Vicar of the Spaghetti Monster in the sky who was supposed to care for and protect his soul. Not fondle it!

But deep down he knew it was more than that. He wanted neither to be true. Wanted no Spaghetti Monster in the sky telling us what to do—telling *him* what to do. Certainly didn't want a divine screed to measure his life by, with any sort of accountability or responsibility to God that such a screed would demand. *'Do what thou wilt shall be the whole of the Law!'* someone had wisely inveighed. Damn right. And yet his bias had surfaced as a weakness, clouding his judgment and nearly costing Nous—costing *him*…

A worry suddenly surfaced, spreading a cold dread through his veins. He glanced at the lead codices arrayed before him. What if he had seriously misjudged them as well? What if he had been so blinded by his hatred of God and the Church that he was mistaken here, too—that he would believe a similar lie about the Bible? Even a forgery that promised to offer a secret book, a truth and story above the one claimed by the Church?

No matter. Even if the whole Gospel Zero affair did turn out to be the fakest of fake news, his performance would fly around the internet and serve its purpose well before it was debunked anyway. That was the beauty of social media. Every post and tweet amplified misinformation and disinformation at lightning speed, subverting our ability to discern truth from untruth, rewarding such lies even, and calcifying what people believed despite contrary evidence. Oh, yes, the damage would be done regardless.

He giggled at the thought. Time to get to work.

He stood in the chamber where he had been christened Grand Master earlier in the week, the books recovered from the White Monastery spread out before him, an orange glow from flickering candles offering enough light to expose the Good Book for what it was.

Destroying Christianity along the way.

He tingled with a nervous excitement. So much so that he worried he would stumble his way through the announcement. Blessedly, Helen was standing across from him next to the camera, flashing a smile that infused his veins with all he needed to carry on.

A large display stood across from him, keeping track of the social media platforms and social proof of his live-stream announcement. It was all humming along to perfection, just as he had planned.

It was also time.

The cameraman pointed to him and offered a thumbs up, a green indicator light telling him it was his moment.

He grabbed it with both hands without delay.

"Greetings. I come to you as a messenger of light, bearing a message of enlightenment that shall be for all people. My name is Sebastian Grey, and I bear tidings of the coming Republic of Heaven that is even now active in our midst. But first things first..."

Sebastian spread his hands before him. "Several months ago, seventy metal books were discovered in a crypt in Egypt. I am here today to share that these are the earliest Christian documents by far and central ones to Christianity that have remained hidden for almost two millennia."

He leaned forward, grinning widely before adding: "Until now. They have been dated to mere decades after Jesus' death. Each book or codex is composed of lead folio pages, arguably the most important discovery in—"

Suddenly, the feed was cut across WeShare. Facebook wasn't faring any better, suffering some sort of glitch.

He narrowed his eyes with barely contained rage. "Silas..."

"What happened?" Silas asked, turning to Zoe.

"Was it one of your bot thingys?" Gapinski asked.

"Wasn't me. Judging by the looks of it, the guy's feed was completely cut off."

"Cut off? How?"

"By someone with the keys to the internet and social media."

"You think Markus Braun had something to do with this?" Silas asked.

"I'm not sure who else with this sort of techno power."

Silas shuffled toward the chair and camera, readying himself for action. "Then it's go time. Turn on the camera, release your bots, and hook me up to WeShare and Facebook and any other social media platforms. Because we may not have long."

Abraham continued working as Zoe joined Silas at the recording station. Celeste and Gapinski walked over as well, mostly for moral support.

"I believe in you, Silas," Celeste said as Zoe finished attaching a mic to Silas's shirt.

He flashed a grin. "I know."

His palms were growing moist now, and he could feel his pulse racing, his head feeling faint from the adrenaline spike. He'd been preparing for hours—for his whole life, really. Most of what he wanted to share he had taught through previous lectures. But still...

He closed his eyes and took a breath, praying the good Lord above would carry him through.

For the Church's sake.

"You ready, cowboy?" Zoe asked.

He nodded.

"Then go for it. You're on."

Silas swallowed, then began with an introduction.

"Hi there, my name is Silas Grey. I'm a former professor from Princeton University specializing in ancient Christian artifacts who is now the Master of a Christian order dedicated to exploring the faith. I was part of a team of people who analyzed recent discoveries relating to the Bible. You probably know of it as Gospel Zero. While there were only hints of the discovery earlier in the week, I am here to tell you today that Gospel Zero is real."

Silas took a breath, Celeste smiling and nodding him along next to the camera.

"I am also here to tell you Gospel Zero is a fake. The codices you saw earlier in your news feed by a one Sebastian Grey, who just happens to be my brother, they are real. They are what we discovered. However, on closer examination, I and the lead archaeologist, Hartwin Braun, realized the codices were forgeries. Here is why."

Mouth running dry, he took a sip from a water bottle at his feet. Probably looked like a fool and complete amateur, especially to the likes of Trevor Bohls. Whatever.

He swallowed and set the bottle down. "Upon examining the codex pages, all written in Aramaic, we noticed there were a lot of Old Aramaic forms that were at least 2,500 years old. But they were mixed in with other forms that were younger, so we took a closer look and pulled out all the distinct forms that we could find. I have never seen this kind of mix before of Aramaic characters. The youngest Aramaic scripts are dated from the 2nd and 3rd centuries. Which proves these lead books could not possibly have been written during the first century of Christianity as previously claimed. Then there is the matter of the oldest scripts, clearly written by some forger who couldn't tell the difference between a *kaph* and a *resh!*"

Silas wiped his forehead beading with sweat now, worried it was sounding like one big information dump. But he pressed forward.

"How were they different you may ask? I understand the use of the word *forger* is pretty strong. But there were major inconsistencies in how the forger did the stroke order for the letters engraved on the lead folios, which you would never have seen back in the day. Scribes had a very specific process for writing things down, and several characters were flipped. Which tells me this was the work of someone hastily copying down from some other source, rather than an original."

He took a breath and girded himself for what came next.

"What I am saying is that this is absolutely, positively, scientifically *not* some sort of Gospel Zero. Not even close. Of course the media bit the Gospel Zero announcement hook, line, and sinker. And the way these things work in the age of social media, it went zipping across Facebook and WeShare and all the other WeNet platforms without any serious investigation. Add to that the fact it is the Lenten season, the period in the Christian calendar of spiritual reflection leading up to Holy Week when Christ died and rose again, and you've got yourself a bone fide made-for-streaming religious conspiracy special. Maybe Ron Howard will join to direct the WeWatch episodes!"

He chuckled at this quip, then drew serious again.

Silas continued, "All this to say, Gospel Zero is a fraud. We can trust the Bible we have, the real one gifted to us by God himself and the Church. Not only because God crafted it, empowering the writers to communicate everything he wanted to communicate to us about himself and his story of rescue. But also because he preserved it, the actual one we have that the Church has recognized for millennia."

He sat forward, getting ready for the kill. "There is a remarkable harmony and unity of the Bible across the sixty-six recognized book—and even the seventy-three ones of the Catholic tradition. All of it written over 1,500 years, by forty people, in three different languages! Yet there is a remarkable harmony and unity in the story it is telling about our rebellion against God and his plan to forgive us, rescue us, and put us and our world back together again. But don't just take my word for it! The evidence is remarkable to support this claim.

"Take the New Testament alone. Nearly 25,000 ancient manuscripts of the Christian text have been discovered in several different languages showing remarkable harmony and unity and *consistency* of the religious text. The oldest copy we have dates back to AD 150. That means we have copies of Jesus' story being written down and the Church's story being recorded, within nearly one hundred years of the original events!

"Now compare this with the writings of Aristotle, for instance, the ancient Greek philosopher. There are only forty-nine ancient manuscripts—the oldest one copied 1100 years after his death! The only other manuscript we have that compares to the Bible's wealth of manuscripts is Homer's *Iliad*, coming in at six hundred. This doesn't even cover the wealth of archaeological discoveries confirming the events of the Bible. By the middle of the 20th century, something like 25,000 biblical sites had been confirmed through rigorous archaeological excavation. No discoveries have proven the Bible false."

Silas leaned back and took a breath. Enough of the evidence review. Time to go to the heart of the matter.

"The Bible is the foundation on which the Church stands. It is authoritative, it is trustworthy—and not only because of the wealth of literary and archaeological evidence. Billions of people have found inspiration and truth in its pages for so many things. For forgiveness: *'If we confess our sins, he who is faithful and just will forgive us our sins and cleanse us from all unrighteousness'*—1 John chapter one. For salvation: *'If you confess with your lips that Jesus is Lord and believe in your heart that God raised him from the dead, you will be saved'*—Romans chapter ten. For hope in the face of death: *'Since we believe that Jesus died and rose again, even so, through Jesus, God will bring with him those who have died'*—1 Thessalonians chapter four. And perhaps the greatest of all, God's love for the world: *'For God so loved the world that he gave his only Son, so that everyone who believes in him may not perish but may have eternal life'*—the Gospel of John chapter three."

He took another drink and shifted in his seat.

"Then there are the practical promises found in the Bible. God says we have no reason to fear, for Deuteronomy chapter thirty-one reminds us: *'it is the Lord your God who goes with you; he will not fail you or forsake you.'* God says we can bring him all of our worries to handle: *'Do not worry about anything, but in everything by prayer and supplication with thanksgiving let your requests be made known to God.'* And perhaps the greatest words ever uttered, by Jesus himself in Matthew's Gospel chapter eleven, *'Come to me, all you that are weary and are carrying heavy burdens, and I will give you rest. Take my yoke upon you, and learn from me; for I am gentle and humble in heart, and you will find rest for your souls. For my yoke is easy, and my burden is light.'*"

He offered a nervous chuckle, wondering how all this was playing across the internet. "But you don't want a sermon. Instead—"

"Ahh, crap," Zoe said.

Silas used the interruption to catch his breath. Then he noticed the live-stream post fritzing out. Just as it had before with Sebastian.

He went to ask what was wrong when another post appeared on the WeShare news feed. A blank white set with a wood stool. Plain and simple. Definitely not Nous's setup from before.

Which meant it had to be the box men sect.

A man soon stepped into view. Silas was bracing for Noland Rotberg.

Except he was wrong. Because the man who he expected to take his place wasn't the one who sat down on the other social media profile live-streaming the destruction of the Church.

It was the new enemy of the Church. And his rival.

Which he was not expecting in the slightest.

CHAPTER 32

Sitting on the stool was a man about Silas's height. And Hartwin's. Same build and angular face as the German professor Silas had sparred with the past few days, with that equine nose and long forehead.

But it wasn't Hartwin.

It was his twin.

Markus Braun.

"Zoe? What the heck is going on?" Silas asked, shuffling over to her side at the conference table.

"Damn he's good..." Zoe whispered. She caught herself and blushed. "Oops. Sorry for cussing."

"Don't worry about it. Just talk to me."

"Right. Looks like Markus cut the cord. Or at least people working for him."

"What?"

"I'll spare you the techno details, but the guy with the keys to the social media kingdom just kicked you and your brother to the curb."

"Always something," Gapinski complained.

"Can we recover?" Silas asked in a panicked rush. "Can we get back online? Are the bots doing their viral thing? Are—"

"Silas, I've got this!" Zoe said, putting up one hand while the other kept typing. "I had already put into place a redundancy capture of the feed, replicating it on multiple servers and saddling our little bots army with the goods before dispersing it across the globe. On top of that, the AI algorithm was spreading the post, sharing it and liking it and—"

"While I respect and appreciate the technowizardry, Zoe, spare us the techno details."

She huffed and pushed her glasses back up her nose. "The lame-man's version is that I saved your video feed, created multiple versions of it, posted it on several fake profiles across the socials landscape, and have been spiking it with likes and shares."

Silas sighed with relief.

"We're not out of the woods yet, but at least—"

"Shh, he's starting..." Celeste said, pointing to the large display of WeShare.

Markus smiled into the camera, his trademark jeans and black t-shirt showcasing his SoCal-cool reputation, with some ambient music filtering in the background. Very Zen and New Age and techno utopian.

The man clasped his hands together and bowed. "Namaste, my fellow Earthlings. My name is Markus Braun. Welcome to a very intimate, if not unusual little chitchat. As you know, I'm a humanitarian as much as a techie, having funded programs combating climate change across the globe, alleviating hunger and providing clean water in Africa, funding literacy and education programs for girls in Haiti. What you may not know is that I have also had a little side project financing more spiritual endeavors. Yes, I know, this may come as a surprise, but I am quite a spiritual person. And the latest fruits of my endeavors surfaced what my brother hinted at earlier in the week at his press conference."

He paused, scooting to the edge of his seat, as if signaling that his news was that significant of a revelation.

Silas rolled his eyes. "Get on with it..."

The man did. The live-stream shot panned out to reveal a stack of books resting next to him. They were arranged in a pyramid, their metal pages glinting in the soft light. Markus grabbed one from the top and brought it to his lap.

"For the past week, Gospel Zero has been trending—partly coined by my brother but also made viral by you lovely people." He smiled and extended his hands toward the camera.

"And goosed by you, no doubt," Silas muttered.

"My side project," Markus went on, "has unearthed several very, very old books that contain precious insight into the faith we've all come to know as Christianity. You can see them displayed here. It's what my brother promised, and what I aim to unveil to you today. Never has there been a discovery of this magnitude, with either Christian manuscript evidence or Church relics on this scale from the earliest years of the Christian movement."

He opened the book carefully and held it up.

"As you can see, each page is the size of a greeting card and cast in lead, bound with stiff leather covers and bound together by leather rings. Etched upon each page is Aramaic writing, the language Jesus spoke during his day, which was completely set aside by the other so-called Gospels and Christian books in favor of the horrid Greek. Yet here we have the original purity of that language, written down and revealed for the world." He tapped the book and grinned earnestly, as if he, among all the peoples of the world, had a secret to share. Markus continued, "And I want you to hear them this day."

Clearing his throat, he read:

> *The disciples asked Jesus, "Tell us, what can the kingdom of heaven be compared to?"*
>
> *He said to them, "It can be compared to a mustard seed. Though it's the smallest of all the seeds, when it falls on tilled soil it makes a plant so large that it shelters the birds of heaven."*
>
> *Jesus said, "The kingdom can be compared to someone who had a treasure hidden in their field. They didn't know about it. After they died, they left it to their son. The son didn't know it either. He took the field and sold it.*
>
> *"The buyer plowed the field, found the treasure, and began to loan money at interest to whomever they wanted."*

"This passage from Gospel Zero is also from the Christian books known as the Gospel of Matthew and the Gospel of Luke. It's also in another book. A rejected—no, *suppressed* book. A book denied its voice, its truth from the believing community."

Again, the man paused, leaning forward and leaving the viewer in continued suspense.

"The Gospel of Thomas."

Silas frowned. No surprise there. But it did pose a significant problem without a proper rebuttal. One he was now itching to make.

"What does Gospel Zero do to the equation—this revelation of another gospel that was hidden from the world, containing insights into spirituality and truth? What it does is bring into sharp focus the questions about who chose which Gospels to include in the final product!"

The man set down the book and leaned back in his chair, crossing a leg and folding his hands in his lap. "It's time for us to have ourselves a little chat about the Christian Bible. Because it isn't at all what you've been told."

THIS WAS NOT GOOD.

Markus kept at his presentation, making a meticulous effort at walking through all the details of the codices and folio pages. Offering close ups and talking in slow, hushed words. Almost as if he were unveiling a new smartphone or wearable device. Looked like Steve Jobs when he was at his best.

Just when Silas didn't think he could take any more of the blathering idiot trending on Facebook and WeShare, the door to the field office opened.

Silas turned around, his face scrunching with a mixture of disbelief and rage.

It was Torres. With Grant at her side.

The room stood in awkward stillness at the turn.

"What the heck are you doing here?" Silas growled, walking toward the man with every intention of landing a blow across his face. Instead, he opted for a finger pointed into his chest.

Grant sighed, took a step back, and put up his hands in surrender. "Look, I understand my being here is awkward."

"*Awkward?* That characterization is so far out of orbit it's not even in the same universe!"

"Alright, boys," Celeste said, stepping between the pair. "Let's put away the swords, shall we? We're running an active mission, here. Torres, what's this about? I assume this is where you ran off to the past half day."

She nodded. "Yeah. Long story to get into now, but Silas, you'll want to hear what he has to say."

Silas laughed. "Why the heck would I want to do that?"

"Because he's got a story to tell. And he wants to tell it."

He clenched his jaw and glared at his friend. "Talk."

Grant took a breath and stepped forward. "You have to

believe me. I had no idea what all was going down between them two."

"Between them two? What about us two?" Silas exclaimed. "Hartwin said you recommended me."

"That's right. I did! You're the best there is in the business of all things religious relics."

Silas went to bite back a reply, but was touched by his words. He shook his head. "Then what the heck was this all about? How did you get wrapped up in this conspiracy of Markus Braun?"

"It's like I said before. I was in it for the money. Pure and simple."

"That I know. So what's the story you said you wanted to tell?"

Grant took a breath and glanced at Torres. She nodded for him to continue.

He said, "Several months ago, some recruiter tapped me on the shoulder and connected me with Manda Arts Limited. Didn't know at the time, but it was your dead bloke Andrew Sterling."

"Sterling? And you didn't think to tell us about that connection?"

"I didn't know what to do when I found out about it. I freaked, OK? So sue me!"

Silas swallowed back another outburst. "What happened next?"

"Like I said, I was recruited by Sterling for Manda. Asked to...well, help with a cache of religious texts. So I hopped on a flight to Berlin—"

"Berlin?" Celeste said. "Are these the same texts that were purported as the Coptic Muratorian Fragment?"

Grant swallowed and nodded.

"So you saw them before we did at Princeton?" Silas asked.

He scratched the back of his neck. "You could say that..."

"Are you kidding me?"

"All I needed was for you to verify the folios and make sure you put together the connection with Pachomius. Then Helen showed up and the—what do you call them, box men tattoo fellas...and, well, the whole plan went to hell."

"And what plan was that?"

Grant hesitated, then answered, "To get you to the White Monastery where a cache of lead codices that had been cobbled together were stashed in some dead dude's crypt."

Silas's eyes widened, and they met Celeste's.

She said, "Cobbled together. As in, manufactured?"

Grant nodded.

"By whom, pray tell?"

He looked at Torres, saying nothing. She said it for him. "By a team Grant put together to forge the Coptic Muratorian Fragment and provenance and Gospel Zero. Then Markus put together another crackpot team to broker the Fragment and get the codices hidden away in the White Monastery. Not sure how, as even Grant wasn't in on that part of the deal. But the dude didn't plan on your *hermanito* stumbling across them, that's for sure. Sebastian's one smart cookie and pretty well screwed up Markus's plans. But man, what a few million can buy..."

The news hit the room like a neutron bomb, the fallout sucking all life and light from the room and silencing it to a tuning-fork ting.

Silas gawped for words, but none came.

Torres continued, "I remembered a scheme Grant went on about from when we were engaged. Had to do with manufacturing documents to bolster an ancient cache of codices. Even wrote about it on some internet academic sites as a way to warn the professional guilds about the possibility. Had it all worked out, didn't you, dear?"

Grant offered an awkward grin but said nothing.

"Markus must have caught wind of the scheme," she went

on. "Hired him to create all the provenance and history, the actual artifacts himself. Everything needed to pull off the perfect conspiracy."

"But then what role did my brother play in all of this?"

"Sebastian?" Grant shrugged. "Beats me. I'd wagger he was as hoodwinked as Hartwin was."

Silas nodded. Had probably heard the same announcement he had, then rushed to cash in for Nous. Getting played like the rest. Including him, the Order, and the Church.

"I didn't know what it was for," Grant said. "I swear, had no idea. Thought it was part of some elaborate joke on the Church."

"You expect me to believe that?" Silas said lowly.

"Look at me, Silas. Look at me!"

He did, staring down the man who stared back with unblinking eyes.

Silas was the first to blink, his face falling and brow furrowing. He did believe him. The guy could be clueless. A genius, but a clueless genius whose one constant moral principle was money.

"I do, Grant...I do." Then it hit him: "That's why you were all Johnny-on-the-spot about the German *s*, back in Miami."

He nodded. "Tried to derail the scheme subtle like once I saw what was going down."

"But you didn't actually blow it up," Silas said, arms crossed. "You even encouraged it, giving us this lame-ass spiel about Pachomius and the Gnostic gospels to make us connect the dots!"

Grant said nothing.

Silas sighed. "Why didn't you bring me into it once you saw what was going down?"

Grant shrugged. "I was paid. Fair and square. Signed the whole non-disclosure agreement and everything. And..." He trailed off, hanging his head in shame.

"And?"

"And...I got myself into a bit of trouble in Vegas."

Silas frowned. "Gambling? This was about gambling debt?"

Grant said nothing. But said all he needed to say.

He shook his head. "Friendship should be thicker than a damn sack of Benjamins, Grant. Even those paying off gambling debt."

"How much were you paid, if I may ask?" Celeste said.

Grant hesitated, eyes averting and head dropping to the floor.

Silas asked, "Grant, how much were you paid?"

"A million five," Torres said.

Silas had no words. Far more money than he'd probably make the rest of his life.

"But there's more to the story than bad debt. Isn't that right, Grant? Go on. Tell him."

"Tell me what?"

"About his sister."

"Mary?"

Grant bowed his head, then took a breath. "She's dying. A rare form of cancer."

"Oh, buddy," Silas said, putting a hand on his shoulder. He knew Mary pretty well during their time at Harvard. She was in the undergraduate program, Pre-Med if he remembered. He went on, "I asked about her at Princeton, and you seemed evasive about it."

"She didn't have any medical insurance," Torres explained. "Needed costly treatments. That's where most of the debt came from. And the trouble that followed it, trying to pay it back before things got *muy loco* with his lenders."

"And the gig seemed like the best way out. For us both..." Grant offered.

Silas felt horrible. Made total sense. What wouldn't any of us do to help a family member on the brink. Even with how bad things were with Sebastian, there's a part of him that would still move heaven and earth to help him.

He said, "Again, sorry about your sister. And I can totally understand your motivation. As much as it put us in a bind—the Order and the Church."

Grant managed a weak smile. "Thanks, partner. And I really am sorry for the mess I created."

"I know. But we need you to tell your story. To verify that Gospel Zero is a total fabrication—the whole shebang."

Grant hesitated, then slowly nodded. "Again, sorry, dude."

"Don't want your sorry. I want to know you're ready."

He took a breath and offered another nod.

"All I have to say is, you better deliver."

"I will, partner. You can count on me. And, Silas...I really am sorry."

Silas offered a weak grin. "I know. And I'm thankful you stepped up now. But if you don't deliver, I'm kicking your ass from here to Timbuktu!"

Grant laughed. "Permission granted."

"Oh, I don't need permission. You know I can put the hurt on you."

"Uhh, guys," Zoe said, interrupting their banter. She was pointing at the WeShare display.

"What is it?" Silas asked.

"Our boy Markus is stepping up his attack on the Bible."

IN THE MEANTIME, AFTER UNVEILING THE GOSPEL ZERO CODICES, Markus had been styling himself as the latest expert on Christianity.

"The Bible was not sent from heaven by email or text or a WeShare post!" The man chuckled, face widening into a toothy bro grin. "The Bible is entirely the product of man, just like every other revered religious text. The Koran. The Bhagavad

Gita. Man, not God. The Bible did not fall magically from the sky. It was created by tribal scribes as a historical record and frankly it has evolved through endless translations from Greek to Latin to German to English, countless additions with some books added and others not, and several revisions. So many that one could scarcely recognize our modern iterations from the supposed original sources. History has never had a definitive version, neither do we."

Markus smiled again and brought his hands together at the center of his chest. He continued, "The fundamental irony about Christianity, is that the Bible as we know it, and especially the Gospels that were included in the final product, was put together by the pagan Roman emperor Constantine the Great—who only became a Christian on his deathbed! Constantine was a keen political entrepreneur who could see that Christianity was rising fast. So he backed the winning hand to bring political stability, which also meant backing the factions that held the power within the Church against the minority voices. Voices that put pen to paper in order to express their own truth regarding the things of God and good news of Jesus."

He was getting animated now. And clearly just getting started.

"The Church calls them the Gospels. Gospel literally means *'good news,'* yes. And anyone who sided with those other voices, those other forbidden gospels in the Bible over Constantine's literary version was deemed a heretic. That word is a relic of that period of history during his reign, which is literally Latin for 'choice.' *Haereticus*. Those who 'chose' their own truth regarding the Christ of history were the world's first heretics."

The man paused, taking a sip of water that had been sitting off screen.

He continued, "Fortunately for us, testaments to those minority voices Constantine and the Church tried to suffocate managed to survive. The Dead Sea Scrolls represent some of those voices, which was found quite by accident hidden away in a cave near Qumran in the Judean desert around the 1950s. Then there are the Coptic texts from 1945 at the Egyptian city of Nag Hammadi. These documents speak of Christ's ministry in very human terms. Not the divine ones the Church manufactured! He was all about alleviating poverty and helping the least of these and raising up peacemakers.

"Of course, in keeping with their tradition of suppression and rigid dogmatism, the Church tried very hard to keep these unknown gospels from seeing the light of day. Of course, it makes sense. Since the scrolls highlight glaring historical discrepancies and fabrications, clearly confirming that the modern Bible was compiled and edited by men who possessed a political agenda — to harden into dogmatic belief the divinity of the man Jesus and use his powerful, inspiring teaching influence to gain and maintain their own power base.

"Now, of course, there have been well-meaning people, clergy and pastors and theologians and what not, who have sincerely held beliefs that require their opposition to these documents as false gospels. Heretics, if you will. Again, understandable. The Bible Constantine cobbled together has been their truth for seventeen centuries."

He stood, grabbing for the fake Gospel Zero codex and taking a step toward the camera. He grinned, pausing for dramatic effect. "This book isn't all there is either. There is another revelation. The emperor code that promises to reveal all. Which I promise to unveil next time we meet again for another lovely community chat. Namaste, and remember: All is One, and One is All."

"This has got to end," Silas said, dragging Grant back to the camera setup. Literally, by the arm.

"What's he playing at—this emperor code business?" Celeste asked.

"I don't know, and we don't have time. Are we back up and running, Zoe?"

"Umm, give me a minute."

Silas huffed, and directed Grant to the stool. "When we're back up, I need you to spill the beans on Markus's conspiracy."

Grant hesitated, taking a breath and folding his arms. "I'm not sure about this, Silas..."

"Grant...Come on, we don't have time for this!"

"But—"

"Don't *'But'* me! You're the only one who can stop this now. The only one who can make this right."

"But the money. My debts, what happens to them?"

"Well, did you get the money?"

"Yeah."

"Did you pay off your debts?"

"Well, yeah."

"Then what's the big deal?"

"He might have some SoCal social media mafia come after me, that's what! Canceling my ass from here to high heaven."

"The price to pay for betraying a friend. And for trying to bring down the Church."

"I told you, that was an accident!"

"And sometimes accidents have consequences, pal." Silas turned to grab the mic he had used earlier.

Grant grabbed his arm. "But why me?"

Silas smiled, grabbing the mic and affixing it to Grant's shirt. "You know, I've been asking myself that the past week. Sometimes we're chosen without our knowing and without our permission for such a time as this. In this case, you were plucked for this reason. Personal reasons aside. God chose you for this, I just know it."

"But you know I don't believe in any of that hocus-pocus bull."

"I know. But I do. So do it for me. For what we once had as friends."

Grant took a breath, not breaking eye contact. Then he offered a smile and nodded.

Silas slapped both hands on his shoulders. "Thanks, pal. Just tell your story." He turned to Zoe, who was manning the camera again. "We ready?"

Zoe nodded. "I hope so."

"Hope?"

"I mean, yeah. I'm pretty sure. I've recruited more bots and reactivated the redundancy—"

"Zoe..."

"Right. Lame-man's version. Don't worry about it. Abraham and I got the social media platforms back under our thumbs. Ready?"

Grant was white now, his face beginning to shine with sweat. But he nodded. Within seconds, the camera was streaming again, and he was telling his story. All of it, just the way he told it to Silas earlier without missing any of the sordid details.

Silas looked over Zoe's shoulder, seeing the likes and shares of the live-stream post increase exponentially.

Then the post vanished. Same as before.

"Zoe..."

"On it!"

Silas turned to Grant, who had stopped the story at the news. "Keep going, buddy. You're doing great. Let Zoe work her magic."

"You can work your magic, right?" he mumbled at his techie.

"We're back," Abraham shouted from across the room.

"Threw up another redundancy post and now adding more from multiple profiles for good measure."

"Way to go and good thinking, Abe," Zoe said.

It went this way for several rounds. Grant telling his story, the social media gods trying to suppress his voice, and Zoe and Abraham playing interference. Soon, Facebook and WeShare and Insta and Twitter were all deluged with an army of SEPIO bots—Navy SEALS for Jesus, as Grant would say—all sharing and spreading the news that Grant had been hired by Braun to concoct the largest conspiracy to have rocked the Church.

Then just like that, it was over.

"And...we're out," Zoe announced.

"How are we looking? Did it work?"

She hesitated, staring at the laptop. "Hard to say. With all of Markus's likes and shares, and how viral his own post went. Conspiracies tend to have a life of their own on social media. You saw what happened with that post about the U.S. presidential candidate running a child-enslavement ring out of an ice cream shop. Some crazy person shot up the place trying to free them!"

Silas sighed, hope dimming and feeling like Markus Braun had won.

"But...It looks like your boy did the trick."

"Really?" he said, craning over her shoulder.

"Yeah, look." She pointed to a new hashtag trending across social media: #GospelNero, a nod to the Roman emperor who launched a massive wave of Christian persecution to cancel the Church in the 1st century—just as Markus tried to in the 21st. Even other social influencers were now mocking the whole thing as a gigantic scam, wondering if Russia was in on it, trying to bring down Christianity and divide America and the American Church.

Nope, just a German with a chip on his shoulder.

Silas sat back with a sigh, letting his arms flop to his side.

Completely exhausted, completely spent—from all of it. From the initial attack at Sebastian's place to the original news about Gospel Zero, from the showdown with this new mystery sect to Grant's betrayal and then holding court on the internet debunking the fraud.

He was about ready for that hot shower and terry-cloth bathrobe now. And nearly ready for that sailboat repair shop—with the Golden Retriever and Celeste on each arm, and that bucket of Coronas.

Definitely the bucket of Coronas!

Celeste came up behind and rubbed his shoulders. "Your boy came through."

He closed his eyes and grunted with pleasure from the massage. "He sure did."

The Church was safe. So was the Bible.

At least for now.

But the nod to something else developing was unsettling. Some coded message left behind by an emperor? Sounded more like the latest thriller trending on Kindle than anything to take seriously.

And yet Silas knew better.

They may have won the battle—and just barely. But the war was still raging. And now on two fronts.

Where it would lead next, God only knew.

No doubt with his brother and now it appeared Braun at the center.

Along with SEPIO and him out front in the lead—fighting for, preserving, caretaking, and defending Christ's Church.

CHAPTER 33
WASHINGTON, DC. THE NEXT DAY.

A steady hum permeated the dimly lit modest chapel of Indiana limestone, filling the sacred space with a sense of holy significance. Little flames danced on four long candles near the solid white limestone altar in front of an intricate limestone facade of miniature statues of the four Gospel writers—Matthew, Mark, Luke, and John—standing guard behind oak altar rails with kneeling cushions patterned in red and gold. Beautiful stained glass windows depicting biblical scenes in crimson red and leafy green, gold yellow and indigo blue hung void of their awe-inspiring light, the sun having set several hours ago.

Silas continued meditating, eyes closed, legs outstretched and arms folded, sitting on a polished oak pew in the third row of the restored Bethlehem Chapel a floor beneath the nave of the Washington National Cathedral. It was Rowen Radcliffe's happy place before terrorists blew it all to hell a year ago. Crews had worked hard to restore it to its original modest grandeur during the past year. Silas had taken up residence inside almost an hour ago to, as Celeste would have said, have a think on all that had transpired the past several days.

He was meditating on Grant's betrayal, and how it simply fit the pattern of his life of late. But his return and all the aid he brought to bring to light the conspiracy that threatened the authenticity of the Bible was a reversal he didn't see coming—reminding him there were still people in his life who did the right thing, even on the other side of betrayal. Perhaps he could yet hold out hope for his brother.

Silas leaned back at the thought, disbelieving there was any hope for such a reconciliation, let alone such a reversal. But, as the Good Book reminded him, *'for God all things are possible.'*

Then there was the bullet SEPIO helped the Church dodge by warding off yet another fake new story seeking to undermine the credibility of the Christian faith and the Bible. He prayed to the good Lord above about his own future contending for the faith, about his leading SEPIO in all of this fighting-for-the-faith business.

He shook his head and took a breath, letting out a long sigh before ending in a disbelieving chuckle. Because fighting for the faith had never really been his thing. Never cared much about it until that military-base chapel service brought him back to the faith he'd let wither during adolescence and into college. Actually, the whole idea made him sick to his stomach.

He had seen up close and personal what happens when religious zealots are incited to fight for their faith. It was one of the reasons he had sworn off anything that smacked of the military for a life of tweed jackets and tenured teaching. He had one aim: inspire a new generation that Christianity still made sense in a world with super colliders and semiconductors, the human genome and human suffering. He thought recovering the sense of wonder imbued in relics was the way to go, as well as offering tidbits along the way of the story God told in the Bible about his grand plan to fix our broken, busted world.

Yet he recalled what he saw in his former students at Princeton. The skeptical looks on their faces and all their questions about faith and doubt. He tried to give them the proof they needed that the Christian faith was still relevant, still reliable, but he was never really convinced he was all that convincing.

Fighting for the faith. What a gig.

Fighting for people's souls, more like it. And the soul of the Church.

Because he knew as well as anyone with what he had witnessed up close and personal that there were those who were actively trying to dismantle and destroy the Church with a ferocity Jesus himself predicted.

Like Nous and the new mystery box-men sect. His own brother, for that matter. And that wasn't even touching on those inside the Church who were actively trying to reimagine the faith for a new day, radically transforming it from all it had been for two millennia.

Yet Silas knew that if the Church had survived the persecutions of Nero and Diocletian; the heresies of Valentinus and Arius, Marcion and Pelagius; the alternative anti-Christian worldviews of the Enlightenment and communism, it would certainly survive whatever else the twenty-first-century world could throw at it.

Including whatever Sebastian or Braun or any other whack job could cook up.

And yet...he wondered whether he was up for it all. Up for contending for and preserving the faith, in fighting for and defending what the Church had always believed.

Especially whether he was up for leading the charge.

A moment suddenly sprang from memory. It was from that very spot, when Silas had been meditating on much of the same concerns after a similar mission to save the story of Jesus from confusing corruption—another conspiracy with his brother at the helm. Rowen Radcliffe had popped down to convince him to join the Order's cause defending and protecting the Christian faith by becoming a SEPIO agent.

Said he could discern in Silas the rare qualities of academic acumen and physical pluck that would do the Church a world of good.

He grinned at the memory, as well as the confidence the former Order Master had placed in him. Seemed so long ago, so much had happened. He longed to hear those words again, encouraging him and reassuring him. And wishing Radcliffe was still alive as Order Master so that he didn't have to bear the mantle and responsibility himself.

'My grace is sufficient for you, for my power is made perfect in weakness....'

There was that voice again. Silas had to give it credit, too. Because the good Lord above certainly had come through. Not only this past week but the past few years, and even more through the ups and downs at Princeton, through grad school, and definitely through his tours of duty through hell. Through the emotional turmoil of losing Dad during 9/11 and across the expanse of his childhood and even up to his birth.

God was there with Silas through the entirety of his life; he was not silent through all the crazy. And his power had been more than enough for him to see him through it all. A smile sprung to Silas's face.

Lord Jesus Christ, Son of God, thank you for your presence, for your power, for your protection, and for helping me persevere.

The whisper of someone entering the chapel caught his attention. He glanced behind to find Bishop Zarruq was walking down the aisle, his cassock swishing slightly with each step.

"Mind if I join you?" he asked.

"Please," Silas said, moving down the row to give him room to sit.

Zarruq sat silently, a slight smile hanging on his face as he stared forward. Silas joined him in that silence, wondering what he was thinking. They remained that way for several minutes, the HVAC hum providing the only soundtrack for their quiet contemplation.

"I was told I might find you here," the bishop finally said.

Silas said nothing, the Four Evangelists capturing his attention.

Zarruq shifted around in his seat to face Silas. "I wanted to express how deeply thankful I am for your leadership the past week, jumping into the fray of it all and commanding an impressive counterattack that unraveled the conspiracy threatening the Church."

"Well, I really had little to do with it all," Silas demurred. "Celeste and Torres were the ones who put together the major connections, and then Torres was the one who brought back Grant to expose it all."

"Nonetheless, I'm thankful it was you that Radcliffe chose as his replacement."

"You are?" Silas sat up straighter, turning toward the man with relief.

"Absolutely! Your academic acumen, with all of your biblical and theological knowledge and understanding, combined with your physical pluck from your years in the American military have shaped you to be the man of God the Order needs for such a time as this, methinks. Let alone the Church."

Silas chuckled, reddening at the compliment. "That's pretty much what Radcliffe said, word for word, after an early mission for SEPIO."

"There you go! And all the Lord is asking from you in your role as Order Master, Master Grey, is to be faithful and available."

Silas considered this. Faithful and available. Putting it like that didn't sound so bad.

"I like that," he said. "Sort of relieves the pressure from getting it a hundred percent right."

"It's all the Lord is asking from any of us. Availability to him and his calling on our lives, and faithfulness to that calling. However unique or mundane it may be."

Silas nodded and fell into a contemplative silence.

Zarruq shifted again and cleared his throat. "In other news, I'm afraid there is no rest for the weary where the Order is concerned."

He cocked his head. "What do you mean? Has something happened?"

"Unfortunately, yes. At our archaeological dig in Libya."

Silas's stomach sank. "No...The one Torres was heading?"

The bishop nodded.

"What happened? Was there a cave in, or illness, or—"

He couldn't bring himself to say it. But he did: "Please don't tell me there has been an attack."

"None of the above. Yet."

"What do you mean?"

"Apparently, one of our operatives has picked up chatter of an impending—something. Targeted at Western activity in the region."

"An attack? Against the Order?"

"We're not entirely certain."

"Is anyone identifiable? A band of local radical Muslims, ISIS perhaps? I know they've made a resurgence there and have been threatening local churches. I guess Nous would surely want to hinder any archaeological digs that favored the Church. And probably our new mystery sect."

Zarruq waved a hand. "There is little known yet. We're not even sure we are the targets. However, references to a basilica and an excavation have us worried. Which is why the trustees would like you to go oversee the last of the excavation work, along with the rest of SEPIO, should anything arise."

Silas sighed, closing his eyes and rubbing his face with his hands. "I swear it's like whac-a-mole," he complained. "You stamp down one threat to the faith only for another to come rising up to take its place."

"I understand, Master Grey. It's all rather suspicious. Especially with the timing of Braun's announcement yesterday."

"Braun? Why him?"

"Something the man said has concerned me. A reference to a so-called emperor code."

Silas shrugged and stretched out his legs. "Sounded like some lame attempt at thriller fiction to me more than anything."

"Regardless, you leave tomorrow. Along with the rest."

"Tomorrow?" Silas exclaimed, sitting up.

Now Zarruq shrugged. "The demands of the Order, my friend. And saving the Church from no uncertain doom."

He mumbled. "No rest for the weary, is right…"

"Not when you're Order Master. Besides, remember what Christ himself told the apostle Paul: *'My grace is sufficient for you, for my power is made perfect in weakness…'*"

Silas smiled. "I've been hearing that a lot lately."

"Then perhaps it's a word the Lord himself has for you, Master Grey. For these fraught times."

The bishop stood, joined by Silas. They moved to the center and embraced before the man sauntered down the aisle.

Silas watched him leave, a prayer springing to his mind.

You know what, Lord? I believe you. I believe your Word. That you're with me, you're empowering me, and you chose me for such a time as this. Thanks for preserving the Bible's truth. For me and for the world.

The man left through the open door and passed from view, his cassock and shoes echoing with a whisper down the hall.

One more thing Lord: Thanks for the help. Because I've got no chance of making it without another Radcliffe at my side.

"No chance indeed…"

Silas left the chapel and ambled down a hallway still

smelling of fresh plaster and paint, the repairs not yet finished after terrorists had brought it to its knees a year ago. Down for the count, but not out. It had been that way for the Church since the beginning.

Down a hundred times over. But not out.

Not yet.

And not under his watch.

Silas reached his study and went to press his hand against the keypad security device when he hesitated.

But only for a second.

Because those sweet words of comfort and courage that had guarded his heart and mind the past week had finally infused his veins with exactly what he needed. Strength for today, bright hope for tomorrow, and a peace that surpassed all understanding—especially considering all he had endured, all he was called to do.

The good Lord's crazy love was sufficient. For his power was made more than evident in the midst of weakness.

Silas knew it. He had witnessed it, he had felt it.

He believed it.

He was the Master of the Order of Thaddeus. Its mission was to protect, instruct, fight for, watch over, heed the once-for-all faith entrusted to God's holy people.

And it was time to act on it.

Time to lead.

Silas slapped his hand against the device with purpose, then shoved through the door after the keypad flashed green.

Ready to jump back into the saddle protecting the Church and preserving the faith.

With the Lord and SEPIO at his side.

ENJOY GOSPEL ZERO?

A big thanks for joining Silas Grey and the rest of SEPIO on their adventure saving the Church! **Enjoy the story? Here's what you can do next:**

If you're ready for another adventure, you can get a full-length novel in the series for free! All you have to do is join the insider's group to be notified of specials and new releases by going to this link: www.jabouma.com/free

You might also like my apocalyptic sci-fi thriller series, *Ichthus Chronicles*. Set 100 years in the future, the last remnant of Christianity is threatened from forces inside and outside the Church, written in the vein of the *Left Behind* series. Start the adventure today: www.jabouma.com/books/apostasy-rising-1

If you loved the book and have a moment to spare, **a short review is much appreciated.** Nothing fancy, just your honest take. Spreading the word is probably the #1 way you can help independent authors like me and help others enjoy the story.

AUTHOR'S NOTE
THE HISTORY BEHIND THE STORY

To say we live in interesting times is an understatement—especially given what the world walked into at the start of the second decade of the 21st century.

As I finish this book, the World Health Organization just declared a global pandemic, the stock market wiped out three years of growth in a few weeks, and my community is facing the greatest instability since 9/11 and the Great Recession.

What do you do when life goes so wrong?

Turn to the anchor of our soul: the Word of God, gifted to humanity to remind us who he is, who we are, and what we have in him.

That's why I wanted to write this book on fighting for the Bible. Literally, in this case, when its authenticity was threatened by going on a mission to prove the conspiracy fake news and blow some things up along the way. But also figuratively, because both inside and outside the Church there are those who would want to twist the history and nature of the Bible to be something it is not: merely a manufactured, man-made book cobbled together by dead, white European men to suppress minority Christian voices and push a dogmatic agenda while angling for power.

Couldn't be further from the truth! Though there is certainly an element of faith involved in the Bible—trusting that the Good Book's words are God's Words, an act of divine self-disclosure to humanity preserved through the ages—there is also good historical reason to believe the Bible we have is exactly the book God wanted us to have.

As with all of my books, I like to add a note at the end with some thoughts and research that went into the story. I am to definitely craft an entertainment-first tale, a story that's mostly about giving you a thrilling ride. But I also like to add a bit of insight and inspiration for faith. So, if you care to learn more about the foundation of this episode in the Order of Thaddeus, here is some of what I discovered that made its way into SEPIO's latest adventure.

Q Source and Gospel Zero

When I started writing this series a few years ago, one of the "what ifs" I had written down for future story ideas was this: What if Q was discovered? And what if what was discovered was different from the Bible we have? Eventually, this is the story that came from those what ifs.

Everything mentioned about the theories surrounding Q source, or Gospel Zero as I called it, in chapters 7 and 8 are accurate. It is true that for centuries, scholars of the New Testament and origins of early Christianity have theorized a secondary or even third and fourth set of sources behind the Gospels. It is also true that the scholarly consensus is that both Matthew and Luke used Mark's account of Jesus as a basis for their own accounts. Some of their material came from their own sources, the ones Matthew and Luke used for their accounts, whether oral or written. Then there was Mark, which scholars of all ranks and persuasions acknowledge as a sort of Markan priority. Then around 230 verses are shared between the Gospels of Matthew and Luke that aren't in Mark. Hence 'Q Gospel' or 'Q document' was coined from the German *Quelle* for 'source' to account for this mystery document.

However, it is equally true this isn't a big deal! Victor Zarruq's explanation in chapter 8 about the Bible, particularly the Gospels, is an important one. The genre of the Gospels isn't like modern historiography or biography. Matthew, Mark, Luke, and John, were all taking actual events and teachings preserved in the oral tradition and memory of the believing community and shaping them into a narrative that told very specific aspects of the Jesus story in order to proclaim the good news of God's crazy love in his life, death, resurrection, and exaltation. The form is *bioi*, which mirrors how other ancient writers talked about the lives of important ancient figures. Which means the fact that Matthew and Luke relied on others when they wrote their Gospel isn't unusual or an anomaly.

Another story angle is an interesting fact: The Gospel of Thomas shares some elements of Jesus' teachings found in Matthew, Mark, and Luke. Of course, I leveraged this in chapters 23 and 28 for the forged lead codices at the heart of the conspiracy—which were also based on a fascinating real-life forgery of seventy metal books allegedly discovered in a cave in Jordan purporting to be early Christian documents. However, the Gospel of Thomas was written a century after the original Gospels, leading one to conclude it copied elements of the originals that combined nicely with Gnostic ideology, yet contradicts historic Christian orthodoxy. The reasons in chapter 28 are good ones for why the Church rejected the Gospel of Thomas and other Gnostic texts as non-Christian—and why they have no place in the Bible.

The Bible We Have Is the Bible God Wanted Us to Have

One of the main story themes is that the Bible we have is the one God wanted us to have. And what we have—the historical books, poems, Gospels, and letters—all of it was received by the Church early on, within the first few decades of the Jesus movement. Everything outlined in chapter 12 about how the Church decided on the canon of books is accurate—and important. Although certain people (I'm looking at you Dan Brown!) would want us to believe a bunch of dead white guys chose only certain books and threw away other ones—and that early Christian leaders conspired with the Roman emperor Constantine to create the Bible in order to suppress minority voices that didn't help their version of Christian events—this is just not historically accurate.

It is true that by the mid-2nd century, there were already lists of books widely used throughout the church. Irenaeus regarded the twenty books that later appeared in Eusebius' "acknowledged" category as canonical books, most of what we understand to be the New Testament. Silas quoted from this list in chapter 12 during his argument with Rotberg, as well as the other important list, Athanasius' *Festal Letter 39*. Then there is the Muratorian Fragment, a major plot point covered in chapter 10 that explores the historical and other details of this fascinating evidence of the canon of Scripture. It is indeed perhaps the oldest known list of the New Testament, listing twenty-two of the twenty-seven books. The translation that appears in the prologue and much of it in chapter 12—except for the forged portions uncovered in chapter 19—reflect the document's actual translation.

What's important to realize is that both Irenaeus' list and the Muratorian Fragment date to the end of the 2nd century. Which means that the majority of the books we've come to know as the New Testament were already being widely acknowledged as authoritative for faith and life in the Church —within one hundred years of them being written! Eventually, these books were inducted into what we call the canon of Scripture by the Council of Carthage, which really only affirmed that those were the ones that were already being widely used as authoritative books within the Church for faith and life. There was three criteria given by the early Church for a book to be included in the canon, which I covered in chapter 12: orthodoxy, apostolicity, and catholicity. The Church used these strict measurements to discern whether a book should be included in the Bible, or not as was the case with others.

The Bible was formed through a deliberate process, involving both God and people. The books included in the canon had to meet certain criteria and were already being widely used and thought of as authoritative for faith and life by the time they were considered Scripture. It's also worth noting that the people involved were not white Europeans! There is a compelling tradition that Mark was from North Africa, and of course the other authors were ethnically Jewish. Further, the North African Church was largely involved in canonical discussions in addition to their Middle Eastern neighbors.

Alternative Gospels, Christian Forgeries

Another story theme is the so-called Gnostic gospels, the ones the Church deemed foreign to the Story of God. I dealt with some of this theme in *The Thirteenth Apostle*, where a similar threat to the Story of Jesus surfaced. However, in this book I wanted to broadly address the Gnostic texts because of the misinformation regarding these alternative books.

The Gnostic gospels are a collection of fifty-two works written in Coptic that were discovered in rural Egypt by a local farmer in 1945 near the town of Nag Hammadi. Although some believe the Coptic monasteries of Egypt, such as Pachomius and his monks, were responsible for their replication and publication, others roundly disregard such fantasy. I merely used Grant's suggestions in chapter 22 and the cryptic notation referencing the monk in chapter 19 as a plot device, rather than advocating that view. Keep in mind, that none of these new so-called gospels and texts written in the name of apostles were included in the Bible—for good reason. New Testament scholar Michael Bird explains why:

> The decision not to include their writings was not born out of realpolitik. The canon of the Orthodox Church was not designed principally for oppression and promulgation out of a quest for ecclesiastical power. Rather, it was driven by a desire to be faithful to the apostolic faith and to define the consensus of the worldwide church on the writings that make up its register of sacred books. (Bird, *The Gospel of the Lord*, 291)

He goes on to say these other gospels "failed to capture the hearts, minds, and imaginations of Christians in the worldwide church...they simply failed to convince the majority of their antiquity and authenticity as stories of Jesus" (294). In fact, these other books were never really ever serious contenders for the final canon in the first place, as the lists attest.

Now through the years, other so-called Gospels have tried to contend for a coveted spot in the Christian canon—the most recent was the Gospel of Jesus' Wife that sent the media into a frenzied state of glee nearly a decade ago. Except that turned out to be a forgery, in the same way the Coptic Muratorian Fragment was in chapters 19, 20, and 24. Several articles listed below outline this magnificent attempt at subverting the faith. I loosely followed this contemporary account as a guide for my own story, taking some of the main players and making composites, such as Urlich Pauli, and taking creative license with some of the story details.

Here is what is true about the Bible, compared to these subversive non-Christian texts: There is a remarkable harmony and unity across the sixty-six recognized book—and even the seventy-three ones of the Catholic tradition—in the story it tells about our rebellion against God and his plan to forgive us, rescue us, and put us and our world back together again. The evidence is remarkable to support this claim, from manuscripts to archaeological sites, which Silas mentions in chapter 29.

God's Revelation to Humanity

A Swiss church leader from the mid-20th century by the name of Karl Barth once said, "God encounters man in such a way that man can know him. He encounters him in such a way that in this encounter he still remains God, but also raises man up to be a real, genuine knower of himself."

The Church begins with the assumption that God has spoken for the specific purpose of rescuing and putting us and our broken world back together. God has chosen to make himself known so that we can understand him, so that we can really know him. We can say things about God because he has told us things about himself. Deuteronomy 29:29 speaks about this very thing:

> *"The secret things belong to the Lord our God, but the revealed things belong to us and to our children forever..."*

God revealed, therefore we can know! One of the primary ways we know him and encounter him is through a book filled with letters and poems, histories and laws. A little thing we call the Bible. For millennia, the Church has believed that God himself is speaking to humanity through this book so that we can be a real, genuine knower of God and the life he intends for us. Because the Bible's words are God's words, we also believe that everything in it is trustworthy, authoritative for issues of faith and life, true, and without error in all that it affirms.

God himself is the author of this mysterious book. All Scripture is God-breathed; it isn't human-breathed conversation about God. This book, this Story has been breathed by God using regular people in their time and place to speak to us in our time and place. This book has authority because God has authority. And he influenced the writers in such a way that they wrote everything that God wanted to tell us about his Story and our own story.

I was reminded the other day how amazing this book is, that God has spoken plainly to us using words and sentences and paragraphs and books that we can read and understand. One of the more interesting things to realize about the Bible is that God used the universal common language of the day to speak to us. This is especially clear when it comes to the language of the New Testament, which is called Koine Greek.

This wasn't classical Greek, the kind that was used by the educated elite, by philosophers who wrote complicated books and speculated answers to complicated questions. No, this kind of Greek was the language of farmers and fishermen, housewives and carpenters. The language of ordinary people. Which means God has not hidden himself away behind tricky codes and pie-in-the-sky philosophies, behind secret sayings and knowledge that belongs only to the educated elite. No, he has spoken to us in a common language that belongs to common people—like you and me. God's Story belongs to all people! And in it, God has spoken loudly and clearly.

"All Scripture is God-breathed," Paul wrote in 2 Timothy. From beginning to end, from the Old Testament to the New

Testament, the entire Bible contains God's revolutionary Story of Rescue that anyone can read and understand.

Silas's final, impassioned defense of the Bible was right: The Bible is the foundation on which the Church stands. It is authoritative; it is trustworthy—and not only because of the wealth of literary and archaeological evidence. But because billions of people have found inspiration and truth in its pages for so many things. Consider some of what it promises, what it reveals about the heart of God:

- *'For God so loved the world that he gave his only Son, so that everyone who believes in him may not perish but may have eternal life' (John 3:16)*
- *'Come to me, all you that are weary and are carrying heavy burdens, and I will give you rest. Take my yoke upon you, and learn from me; for I am gentle and humble in heart, and you will find rest for your souls. For my yoke is easy, and my burden is light.' (Matthew 11:28–30)*
- *'Be strong and bold; have no fear or dread of them, because it is the Lord your God who goes with you; he will not fail you or forsake you.' (Deuteronomy 31:6)*
- *'Do not worry about anything, but in everything by prayer and supplication with thanksgiving let your requests be made known to God.' (Philippians 4:6)*

Amazing promises from an amazing book that offer the hope of God's forgiveness, the gift of new life, and the comfort of care when life goes bad. A book that really can be trusted to be exactly what God wanted to reveal to us about himself and his heart for the world!

Research is an important part of my process for creating compelling stories that entertain, inform, and inspire. Here are a few resources I used to research the history behind Q source, the Muratorian Fragment, the Gnostic texts, and Christian forgeries:

- Bade, Joel and Candida Moss. "The Curious Case of Jesus's Wife." The Atlantic, December 2014. www.bouma.us/gospel1
- Saber, Ariel. "The Unbelievable Tale of Jesus' Wife." The Atlantic, July/August 2016. www.bouma.us/gospel2
- Turner, Ryan. "Does the Gospel of Thomas Belong in the New Testament?" CARM, 3/20/10. www.bouma.us/gospel3
- Wright, N.T. and Michael Bird. *The New Testament in It's World*. Zondervan, 2019. www.bouma.us/gospel4

GET YOUR FREE THRILLER

Building a relationship with my readers is one of my all-time favorite joys of writing! Once in a while I like to send out a newsletter with giveaways, free stories, pre-release content, updates on new books, and other bits on my stories.

Join my insider's group for updates, giveaways, and your free novel—a full-length action-adventure story in my *Order of Thaddeus* thriller series. Just tell me where to send it.

Follow this link to subscribe:
www.jabouma.com/free

ALSO BY J. A. BOUMA

Nobody should have to read bad religious fiction—whether it's cheesy plots with pat answers or misrepresentations of the Christian faith and the Bible. So J. A. Bouma tells compelling, propulsive stories that thrill as much as inspire, offering a dose of insight along the way.

Order of Thaddeus Action-Adventure Thriller Series

Holy Shroud • Book 1

The Thirteenth Apostle • Book 2

Hidden Covenant • Book 3

American God • Book 4

Grail of Power • Book 5

Templars Rising • Book 6

Rite of Darkness • Book 7

Gospel Zero • Book 8

The Emperor's Code • Book 9

Deadly Hope • Book 10

Fallen Ones • Book 11

The Eden Legacy • Book 12

Silas Grey Collection 1 (Books 1-3)

Silas Grey Collection 2 (Books 4-6)

Silas Grey Collection 3 (Books 7-9)

Backstories: Short Story Collection 1

Martyrs Bones: Short Story Collection 2

Group X Cases **Supernatural Suspense Series**

Not of This World • Book 1

The Darkest Valley • Book 2

Against These Powers • Book 3

Luck Be the Ladies • Novelette

End Times Chronicles **Sci-Fi Apocalyptic Series**

Apostasy Rising / Season 1, Episode 1

Apostasy Rising / Season 1, Episode 2

Apostasy Rising / Season 1, Episode 3

Apostasy Rising / Season 1, Episode 4

Apostasy Rising / Full Season 1 (Episodes 1 to 4)

Apocalypse Rising / Season 2, Episode 1

Apocalypse Rising / Season 2, Episode 2

Apocalypse Rising / Season 2, Episode 3

Apocalypse Rising / Season 2, Episode 4

Apocalypse Rising / Full Season 2 (Episodes 1 to 4)

Faith Reimagined **Spiritual Coming-of-Age Series**

A Reimagined Faith • Book 1

A Rediscovered Faith • Book 2

Mill Creek Junction **Short Story Series**

The New Normal • Collection 1

My Name's Johnny Pope • Collection 2

Joy to the Junction! • Collection 3

The Ties that Bind Us • Collection 4

A Matter of Justice • Collection 5

Get all the latest short stories at: www.millcreekjunction.com

Find all of my latest book releases at: www.jabouma.com

ABOUT THE AUTHOR

J. A. Bouma believes nobody should have to read bad religious fiction—whether it's cheesy plots with pat answers or misrepresentations of the Christian faith and the Bible. So he tells compelling, propulsive stories that thrill as much as inspire, while offering a dose of insight along the way.

As a former congressional staffer and pastor, and award-nominated bestselling author of over forty religious fiction and nonfiction books, he blends a love for ideas and adventure, exploration and discovery, thrill and thought. With graduate degrees in Christian thought and the Bible, and armed with a voracious appetite for most mainstream genres, he tells stories you'll read with abandon and recommend with pride—exploring the tension of faith and doubt, spirituality and culture, belief and practice, and the gritty drama that is our collective pilgrim story.

When not putting fingers to keyboard, he loves vintage jazz vinyl, a glass of Malbec, and an epic read—preferably together. He lives in Grand Rapids with his wife, two kiddos, and rambunctious boxer-pug-terrier.

www.jabouma.com • jeremy@jabouma.com

facebook.com/jaboumabooks
twitter.com/bouma
amazon.com/author/jabouma

Made in the USA
Columbia, SC
26 May 2025